1638
THE SOVEREIGN
STATES

THE RING OF FIRE SERIES

**To purchase any of these titles in e-book form,
please go to www.baen.com.**

1638
THE SOVEREIGN STATES

ERIC FLINT
GORG HUFF
PAULA GOODLETT

A Baen Books Original

Baen Publishing Enterprises
P.O. Box 1403
Riverdale, NY 10471
www.baen.com

ISBN: 978-1-9821-9287-7

Cover art by Tom Kidd

First printing, September 2023

Distributed by Simon & Schuster
1230 Avenue of the Americas
New York, NY 10020

Library of Congress Cataloging-in-Publication Data

Names: Flint, Eric, author. | Huff, Gorg, author. | Goodlett, Paula, author.
Title: 1638: the Sovereign States / Eric Flint, Gorg Huff, Paula Goodlett.
Other titles: Sovereign States
Identifiers: LCCN 2023020377 (print) | LCCN 2023020378 (ebook) | ISBN 9781982192877 (hardcover) | ISBN 9781625799302 (ebook)
Subjects: LCSH: Russia—History—17th century—Fiction. | LCGFT: Alternative histories (Fiction) | Science fiction. | Novels.
Classification: LCC PS3556.L548 A618696 2023 (print) | LCC PS3556.L548 (ebook) | DDC 813/.54—dc23/eng/20230608
LC record available at https://lccn.loc.gov/2023020377
LC ebook record available at https://lccn.loc.gov/2023020378

Printed in the United States of America

10 9 8 7 6 5 4 3 2 1

Contents

To Eric
who gave Paula and I,
and hundreds of others,
our starts in the literary world.

In spite of your wishes, my friend, I hope you are somewhere arguing politics with Robert Heinlein and others. While free to create characters, worlds and universes, and to tell stories.

Free as well, to eat, drink and be merry,
with no concern for consequences.

—Gorg

CHAPTER 1

Industrial Accident

Ruzukov foundry, Ufa, Russia
July 18, 1637

Izabella Utkin looked up from the desk in her office and grinned. "Welcome, congresswoman. Hey, everyone. It's the congresswoman from District Two of the state of Ufa."

"Appointed, not elected," Vera Ruzukov pointed out as she looked around the office and at the smaller, younger woman. Izabella was five foot three with blue eyes, golden blonde hair and a curvaceous figure. An attractive young woman who'd settled down a lot since she'd married Alexander Volkov. The office was a smallish room off the main foundry floor where the noises of factory work could be heard in the background. There was a drafting table against one wall and Izabella was seated at a rolltop desk. A couple of clerks sat at smaller desks.

"Well, we can't hold a proper election until we get some sort of count on the number of people in the district," Izabella said.

District Two of the state of Ufa was the northern district, which included the part of the state north of the city of Ufa and east of the border with the state of Kazan, and the possible state of Perm. (That hadn't been settled yet.) The borders had been drawn in the constitutional convention and were tentative and would only last until a state's government accepted or rejected the constitution.

Which Vera knew was a pretty darn big stick. If, for instance, Perm failed to ratify, there was nothing to stop Kazan—or Ufa, for that matter—from annexing the territory that was now on

1

the map as Perm. They would have to get the permission of the federal government, but still, it rather intensified the stakes with regard to whether or not to join.

In the meantime, in need of a congress and with a lack of means to elect one, Czar Mikhail had decided to appoint the governor of Ufa. Alexander Nikolayevich Volkov, Izabella's husband, had gotten the nod, and had appointed Vera Sergeevna Ruzukov to be the first congresswoman from District Two. Which appointment, Vera suspected, Izabella resented a little.

"Anyway, I'm not here about that. I'm here to see my husband. Where is Stefan?"

"He's over at Efrem Stroganov's new copper factory, helping to install the steam boiler for their generator system."

Ufa still didn't have, and wasn't likely to get in the near future, any sort of central power grid. What it had instead was something over a hundred small steam-electric generation plants, each owned by an individual business, and most selling their excess electricity to nearby buildings. Localized brownouts were daily occurrences. Efrem Stroganov was just in from Moscow, the second son of one of the great families, and was using his bank account to get into the large-scale manufacturing of copper wire. For which he needed heat, acids, electricity and drawing equipment to purify, melt, and draw the wire.

The New Ruzuka Foundry had gotten the contract to make the actual steam engines that would power the whole thing. The New Ruzuka Foundry was owned by Stefan, Vera, Izabela, and about half the villagers in New Ruzuka. It was a big contract and a lot of money, but also a new industry for them. Since the foundry had been built, it had been making guns or parts of guns.

There was a boom. A big boom, like a large gunpowder charge going off. Vera and Izabella ran out of the foundry building, onto Irina Way, and saw a mushroom cloud. An actual mushroom cloud. And it was in the direction of Efrem Stroganov's new copper foundry.

Vera started to run and got less than a step before Izabella grabbed her arm. Vera almost slugged her, but Izabella shouted, "Get the men! We're going to need their help!" Then, rather than going back into the building, Izabella ran across the street to get the factory there to send men to help.

✦   ✦   ✦

Stefan thought he was dead again. The blast hadn't come from Efrem Stroganov's new foundry, but from a building next door, where they did something with chemicals. He thought it was making cleansers or fertilizers. However, the blast was enough to knock down the building they were standing in. Not knowing what was going on, but knowing that the firebox was made of crucible steel and weighed over three tons, Stefan—a big man by any measure— grabbed Efrem Stroganov and his foundry manager, and dragged them with him to the ground next to the boiler. It was an almost instinctive reaction. Not to combat, but to industrial accidents.

Having done so, Stefan lay there while the world fell down on all of them. They ended up in a little tent, with the firebox holding up a chunk of the collapsed ceiling and one of the rafters lying across the three of them, not quite crushing them because the newly installed firebox was holding up one end.

The fire from the explosion started to produce smoke and there was no way out. They were well and truly trapped in a mostly wooden building that was apparently on fire. Stefan looked around their little hidey-hole and saw a foot attached to a leg under rubble.

Then, Efrem Stroganov shouted, "Get off me, you great peasant oaf!"

Stefan tried. There wasn't much room and one of his feet was trapped in an even more confined space and was at least sprained, possibly broken, when a bit of wall or roof had landed on it. But pushing up with his back, he managed to lift the roof of their tent a little, and free his foot. He got to his knees and then crawled over Efrem to get to the other foot he could see.

"I said—"

"I heard you," Stefan interrupted. "But there is a man down over there. Check on your foundry manager." In the excitement, Stefan had forgotten the man's name.

"Don't give me—" Efrem Stroganov stopped and Stefan grinned. By now the fact that Stefan had killed a man with a single blow of his fist was well known from Shavgar to Moscow. And apparently Stroganov had just remembered it.

Realizing that his reputation for violence might have its advantages, Stefan shifted around and grunted as the movement exacerbated the pain in his right foot. But he got his back against the boiler and, using his left foot, tried to push up a heavy timber that was pressing against the leg of the unknown man.

Then, quietly, from behind him, he heard Efrem Stroganov say, "Thank you, Stefan Ruzukov." It was said quietly, but with intensity. Stefan looked over and saw where Efrem was looking and realized that if they'd still been standing where they had been when the roof came down, they'd be dead for sure.

Not knowing what to say, Stefan said, "Reflex. Help me with this wood."

Efrem looked over at Stefan and laughed. "Good reflexes, man. Good reflexes." Then he rolled around so that he could add his leg muscles to Stefan's. They got the beam lifted, but the man was dead.

"We need to get into the firebox," Stefan said.

"Why?"

"It's designed to keep fire in. So it ought to do a decent job of keeping it out. Don't you smell the smoke?"

Efrem sniffed. "Yes, but I hadn't realized. Ufa always stinks of smoke and fire."

That was true enough. With all the factories in the city now, the place always stank. But Stefan was used to that stink. This was wood burning, not coal or oil. By now Ufa was getting regular shiploads of oil from the Safavid Empire, and the city was using every drop to provide power to run machines that were making people, including Stefan, rich. In fact, Stefan was now worth more than his old lord, Colonel Ivan Nikolayevich Utkin, had ever been. He laughed. Assuming that they survived to enjoy that wealth—which didn't seem likely at the moment.

Stefan found the door of the firebox. The firebox was huge, designed to produce a lot of steam fast. It was double walled with an air gap and would have been surrounded in firebrick if the installation were completed. It had a yard-tall door on one side, to allow people to get into the thing to clean the oil jets, shovel in coal or remove ash as needed. It would be cramped, but they could all squeeze in.

Meanwhile, Efrem was checking on the foundry manager. "Iosif, wake up."

"Iosif." That was it. Iosif Ivanovich Putinov was the foundry manager's name. "Bring him over here." Stefan grunted as he tried to shift more fallen second floor out of the way to get the firebox door open.

❖   ❖   ❖

By the time Vera, Izabella, and the people they could gather got there, at least four buildings were in flames. They were all around a big hole in the ground where a brand-new chemical plant had been earlier that morning. And all four buildings were completely engulfed in flames.

Izabella took one look and said, "Oh, Vera. I'm so sorry."

"Forget that. Stefan's already died on me once, and I told him not to do it again. I won't believe he's dead until I see the body."

She said it strongly and with conviction, but Izabella didn't believe her. Then there was no more time to talk. Only to bring water and throw it on the fire. There were fire engines in Ufa now. This wasn't the first fire, not by two dozen or more.

It was, Vera thought, the worst yet.

But there was a pump wagon that was based on a design that Brandy Bates Gorchakov had seen in a movie. And it was in use, with six big men seesawing the handles to produce a steady stream of water from the river.

Between the wagon and the bucket brigades, they were containing the fire, but not putting it out.

Izabella looked over at Vera. The woman was taller than her, with her dark hair in a tight style with a ponytail down the back. Her greenish-brown eyes were wet with unshed tears. The stocky woman's face was set in hard lines, something that Izabella rarely saw, for Vera was as gentle and caring a woman as Izabella had ever known. She almost always had an easy and open smile. Right now, though, her face was frozen and her hands moved with mechanical rhythm as she moved bucket after bucket along the line to the fire.

Inside the firebox it was pitch black and getting decidedly hot. Hot enough and stuffy enough so that Stefan was starting to wonder if that was going to prove a better death than the flames. They at least would have been quick. What made it worse was, Stefan knew the design of the firebox. It was specifically designed so that a worker could come in with soap and water and move around to clean and dry the thing. It had plenty of room for one man, was cramped for two, and uncomfortably close for three. It was double walled for insulation, but also for reverse flow. A pipe entered at the top of the furnace, then opened into the space between the inner and outer wall. The air flowed down between the walls and into the firebox. What terrified Stefan was that that intake was high enough so that the smoke would be sucked into it and they would all die of smoke inhalation while they slowly cooked. He needed something to take his mind off it.

"Do you think that Perm will join?" he asked Stroganov.

"What? Right now, I don't care! How are we going to get out of here?" There was more than a bit of panic in Efrem Stroganov's voice.

"We don't!" Stefan said harshly. "We stay here till the fire's out or we die here." He took a breath. "If we're lucky, they will get the fire under control before we bake. If not, I'm sure our funerals will be elegant. I would rather think of something else. So, *do you think that Perm will join the United Sovereign States of Russia*?" He enunciated each word. By this time most people referred to the United Sovereign States of Russia simply as "the Sovereign States," but Stefan used the whole name.

Efrem stared at Stefan in confusion for about five beats. Then he laughed. It was a short bark of a laugh, but it was a laugh. "They'll either join us or join the Muscovites," Efrem said. "The way the constitution worked out doesn't give them a lot of choice. If they try to sit on the fence like Shein is doing up around Tobolsk, either we or the Muscovites are going to eat them whole.

"In fact, that's what that moron, Birkin, should have done last winter. He should have turned east at Kruglaya Mountain and made for the Kama River."

"General Tim would have seen that play a mile away," Stefan insisted, and Efrem snorted another laugh.

"You guys put a lot of faith in your boy general." He waved away Stefan's protest. "I'm not disagreeing, not really. But he is young and, well, I don't think anyone is as good as you folks think Boris Timofeyevich Lebedev is. I think there's too much chance in war. And it's more about being lucky than good."

"Are you CRAZY!" Iosif Ivanovich shouted. "We have to get out of here! And you idiots are sitting around talking politics!"

Stefan felt him move as he tried to get to the door of the firebox. Stefan reached out an arm and slammed the man back against the inner wall, hard enough to rattle his teeth and maybe crack his skull if his head hit the wall.

"If that door opens, we DIE!" Stefan shouted the last word into the man's face. Or at least where he thought the man's face was. You couldn't see a thing in this oven. And it was an oven. The inner wall of the firebox was hot. Not yet burning hot, but hot. And Stefan was covered in sweat.

He turned his head the other direction, and said to Efrem, "So, which way do you think they'll jump? I know your family owns quite a lot of land up that way."

"That's why I'm building a copper foundry. There are extensive copper deposits in Perm. My cousin in Moscow will be pushing for Perm to join the Muscovites, just as I've been pushing Uncle Anatoly to join the Sovereign States. The problem is, my uncle is more afraid of Ivan Vasilevich Birkin than of your General Tim."

"Well, that's stupid," Stefan said. "We have a river route right up to Perm. Birkin will have to go overland."

"That probably won't make any difference if I die here today," Efrem said, not frightened so much as thoughtful. "With me dead, Uncle Ivan will probably go with the Muscovites."

"Well, then it will be better for everyone if we don't die," Stefan agreed, and they continued to talk, with Iosif Ivanovich sobbing quietly next to them.

Vera looked around. The rescuers were making progress. Several of the fires were out, and the rest were struggling as the fire wagon continued to pump water onto the fuel that the fire needed to continue.

They were starting to collect the bodies. There were a lot of them, but none from the chemical plant. Apparently, the blast in the chemical plant was extreme enough to leave no bodies, at least not large enough pieces of bodies to be identified, but a lot of people in the surrounding buildings had died of smoke inhalation or been burned to death.

Vera was starting to lose hope in spite of herself. Several bodies had been recovered from the still burning ruins of the copper foundry. None of them were the size to be Stefan, but if he'd gotten out, he'd have been fighting the fire with the rest of them. "Where are you, you great fool?" she muttered. "You'd better not be dead." She wiped the tears from her eyes, and went back to moving buckets of water from the river to the fire.

Stefan heard the sound of water hitting hot metal and flashing to steam. It was a distinctive sound. Stefan wished he'd been wearing his tool belt. He hadn't worn it because Izabella insisted that as a member of the service nobility, he shouldn't wander around with the tools of a blacksmith. By now the inner wall of the firebox was hot enough so that they all had cloth between their bodies and the hot steel wall. Stefan still wasn't ready to risk the door of the firebox not knowing what was outside of it, but he wanted to let the people out there know that there were people alive in here. So he asked Efrem, "Do you have anything metal on you?"

"My pistol."

Stefan slapped his head. He had his pistol too. It was a status symbol to wear one of the new caplock revolvers and Stefan owned a factory that made metal parts. By now, most of the workers in his factory owned caplock revolvers.

He pulled his pistol and pounded it against the inner wall of the firebox. The whole firebox rang like a bell.

Vera didn't hear the firebox ring. The sound was muffled by the outer wall of the firebox, but that didn't make it silent, and one of the people looking for bodies heard it. The firebox was only about a quarter exposed. Three quarters of it were still covered in charred wood. But the hose was pointed at that area and soon enough it was thoroughly soaked.

Inside the firebox, the water pounding on the outer shell was deafening, but the temperature started dropping almost immediately. A half turn of the crank and the door was unlatched. Stefan tried to push it open and managed to get a crack of perhaps a quarter of an inch. During the fire, wood had fallen against the hatch and blocked it, but it was enough for water to spray in and they all welcomed that.

It was only minutes later that they were released, and discovered that they were the only survivors of those in the building. Efrem was ready to murder the chemical factory owners and workers, but they were all dead too. Over fifty people had died and if they had gone wrong with the firefighting, it could have been much worse.

Ufa was a boomtown and a war base and the center of government, all at once. People stood on the docks as the steamboats came, holding up signs and shouting that they had work. If a man or a woman in good health reached Ufa and didn't have a job by the end of the day, it was because they didn't want one.

There were women working in foundries and factories and canning plants. And sitting on rafters, hammering roofing tiles into place, or painting roofs with tar shipped up the Volga from the Caspian Sea.

When you live like that, grabbing people off the boat and putting tools in their hands with little regard for their skill, two things happened. One was you got a hell of a lot done in a very short time. The other was that accidents happened. Some of them were messy accidents that killed lots and lots of people.

Everyone in Ufa knew that, or at least they should have known that. On the other hand, Vera had almost lost Stefan twice now, in the Kazakh attack and now in this disaster, whatever had caused it, which they would probably never know in any detail. Some sort of safety measures needed to be put in place, even if it did decrease production.

For one thing, stuff that blew up making big holes in the ground and mushroom clouds needed to be off on their own, away from other businesses and her husband, *dammit*!

Congress, Ufa Kremlin
July 19, 1637

Vera's speech was moving and her proposal for a congressional investigation into the cause of the accident wasn't unreasonable, but... The plan to put a moratorium on new chemical works until the cause was determined was shouted down. The demand that if they weren't going to shut them down, they at least had to move them away from other factories and people's homes passed in the House and the Senate, and was approved by both consuls.

But it ran into Olga Petrovichna Polzin, the effective mayor of Ufa (though her husband still held the official title) who insisted that such regulations were a matter for the city government of Ufa, not the federal government, and not even the state government. Olga didn't object to the regulation nearly as much as she objected to the precedent that the federal government could impose regulations on the city without even consulting her. She brought suit, and within a week the case landed in Czar Mikhail's in-basket.

It happened that fast because both Olga and Vera knew all three members of the Sovereign States Supreme Court and their wives. Which meant that none of the judges wanted to be on the record as ruling against either of those two formidable women.

Office of the czar, Ufa Kremlin
July 26, 1637

"Have a seat, ladies," Czar Mikhail said, "and let's work this out."

The office was a large room. The walls were stained wood to a height of three feet, then white painted plaster above the wood. There was a large stove for heat in one corner. Not in use at present, except for a small fire to make tea. There was a couch that he gestured the women to, and four chairs before the large desk.

Vera and Olga took their seats. Czarina Evdokia and Princess Brandy Gorchakov were already seated. With Vera and Olga involved, Czar Mikhail wisely wanted support. Brandy's son, Mikey, was just over a year old and in the care of one of the czarina's ladies in waiting, along with the youngest of the czar's children. After the trip from Grantville, Brandy was less insistent that baby Mikey go with them everywhere.

"Olga, you first," Mikhail said, looking at the thin woman with graying hair and frown lines around her mouth.

"I don't want the congress making laws and regulations for the city of Ufa," Olga said. "You know what will happen. Someone will bribe a congressman and all of a sudden Ufa cloth merchants will have to wear purple robes or some such silly thing, because it will give the cloth merchants of Kazan an advantage. Or, for that matter, the cloth merchant that has cornered the purple cloth market. Most of the congress won't care, because it doesn't affect their cities."

"Vera."

"So instead we have anarchy, where every city decides for itself, and no one is safe because the local mayor got a bribe to let them dump their waste in the drinking water. Or, as is the case here, put a bomb next door to where other people are working. And don't tell me that a local mayor can't be bribed." Vera's voice was tense.

"Maybe they can," Olga said. "But at least they'll be living in the same city they made dangerous. You congress people are only visiting. Well, most of you are. Even you, Vera. Your official residence is in New Ruzuka, and you spend a lot of your time there. So you guys won't face the consequences of whatever stupid, unthought-out rule you put in place because you're upset about something."

"Brandy, what do you think?" Czar Mikhail looked at the up-timer woman. She was tall and thin, with clear blue eyes and smooth skin, and the amazingly straight teeth that most up-timers had.

"As loath as I am to suggest this," Brandy said, "I think we need another bureau."

"No!" Czarina Evdokia said, holding her hands up to hide her eyes. "Not that." Then she laughed. "Why do you think we need another bureau, Brandy?"

"Because it helped prevent mine accidents in West Virginia and kept the mine owners from forcing miners to risk their lives unnecessarily." Brandy had grown up in a mining town with miners who remembered the company goons and the all too often fatal working conditions. While not a fan of intrusive government in general, in some cases she figured it was necessary. The truth was that she'd been seriously concerned about the corners that had been being cut from the moment she'd arrived in Ufa. Actually, she'd been concerned about the corners cut since the Ring of Fire happened. Because it wasn't just Ufa. Those same corners were being cut in Magdeburg, Amsterdam, Venice, and Vienna. The new tech of the up-timers were, on balance, making the world safer than it had been, but people were still putting other people's lives at risk to make a buck, or in this case, a ruble. "What we need are professionals who have a real understanding of the risks involved and can make educated decisions based on risk and cost. And when they put regs in place, those regulations need to be applied all over the Sovereign States, not just in one city."

That didn't end the argument, but it set in place a foundation for a new approach. Meanwhile, Czar Mikhail found for Olga on the basis that while congress did have the authority to make laws governing all of the Sovereign States, it didn't have the authority to make laws that applied only to Ufa, and not Kazan, Shavgar or other places. That killed the bill in congress because the representatives of other cities weren't going to impose such restrictions on *their* home towns.

✧　　✧　　✧

In the meantime, in consultation with the Dacha, Olga and the city council of Ufa put in place a set of regulations about the placement of buildings and what sort of industry could be placed where. Which, among other things, necessitated that the New Rezuka Foundry move to new quarters that were too far from the Kremlin to walk easily. On the other hand, they set up a steam trolley that went for an eight-mile route and was within reasonable walking distance of most of the town.

East of the Southern Ural Mountains
August 2, 1637

Ivan Yurisovich looked at his maps, then he looked around. He was in forested hills, rocks breaking up the grass as much as the trees did. There were birds in the trees and the grass was starting to turn to straw. There were nuts in the trees. It was a pleasant place even in August. Ivan was a large man with a thick brown beard. His clothing and boots were machine made, but designed for rough work. He was southwest of the Berezovsky gold mine. He wasn't sure how far southwest because no one knew exactly where the Berezovsky gold mine was. The information from Grantville on this was maddeningly incomplete. It, for instance, didn't mention at all the gold mine found in Kazakh, but there were quartz deposits here and the other indicators were good, so he pulled out his metal detector.

It had two wheels and weighed sixty pounds, what with the batteries and other components, but it worked. The copper coil produced a magnetic field and resonated with metal deposits in the ground.

For the next day and a half, Ivan Yurisovich got gradually more and more excited as he moved his metal detector over the dry stream bed and found more and more gold. Most of it was powder, but as he went upstream, the bits got bigger.

Then, on August fifth, he found the main vein. It wasn't the Berezovsky gold deposit, not nearly. But it was big. Making careful notes on his maps, he collected up his gold, his equipment, and his mules, and headed back to Ufa.

Czar's palace, Ufa, Russia
August 8, 1637

Mikhail woke in a cold sweat. He suffered nightmares. He had since he was sixteen and they'd only gotten worse for most of his reign as czar of Russia. They'd gotten worse until Bernie Zeppi showed up and Mikhail was introduced to the concept of democracy and, especially, representative democracy.

Evdokia stirred beside him. She rolled over to face him and said, "Again?"

Mikhail laid back into the pillows. "Yes! I truly hate royalty. I despise the whole concept."

"Yes, Your Majesty," Evdokia said. "You've mentioned that before."

"And I hate being the czar most of all."

"I know, Mikhail," Evdokia agreed again, softer this time. Mikhail, like Claudius of Rome, didn't want the crown, but had never found a way to put it down. And for much the same reason, the fear of anarchy. "Was it the Time of Troubles again?" she asked. Mikhail's nightmares often repeated themes. The "Time of Troubles" nightmare had seen the family die or Mikhail abdicate, then all of Russia collapsing into anarchy, famine, and war. The mothers of slain sons condemning him before God for failing to do his duty. They would point at the bodies of their dead children and scream that he should have stopped it.

"Yes. This time the Kazakhs were condemning me too."

"Put it aside, Mikhail. Stick to the plan." She reached over and turned a switch and an actual lightbulb came on. There were a few even here in Ufa and, of course, the czar's bed chamber had one. Two. One on her side of the bed and one on his. She looked at her husband. Mikhail was a chubby man, not at all the sort of man anyone would imagine leading armies or leading a country. But, gradually, over their marriage, Evdokia had learned that appearances lied. In spite of his appearance and what he thought about himself, she had come to realize that Mikhail was the strongest man she'd ever met.

"Yes, of course," Mikhail snarled. "First, send my boy general out to fight the best, most experienced, commanders in Russia to a standstill. Then, of course, convince Shein and the governments of all the states to follow Salqam-Jangir Khan's example, and actually join the United Sovereign States. And, having done that, protect them from anyone who has a grudge to settle against them or just wants what they have." Mikhail rolled over to face her and pounded his pillow. "And while I'm at it, I'll stick one of Vlad's internal combustion engines up my bum and fly us all to the moon."

"You've been talking to Bernie too much," Evdokia said.

"That one came from Brandy." Mikhail grinned at her. "Your buddy can be exceedingly crude, you know."

"Well, you can skip the moon part," Evdokia said. Then she reached out and touched his cheek. "I hate royalty too, you know. I was almost poisoned too." Mikhail's first wife had only lasted four months and it was almost certain that his mother had poisoned her.

"So we learn how to make representative democracy work. And we *can* learn new things, my husband. We've proved that. And we will find ways of keeping in contact with the rest of the world. Ports on the east, a land route, maybe south around Poland, but some way of staying in contact with the USE so we don't fall behind the West again. And then, if we're very lucky, Alexi will be able to reign instead of rule, and no one will try to murder him for the crown." She patted his cheek again. "Then those mothers will be blessing your name. At least some of them. Now, go to sleep because, for now at least, you still have to make decisions and those decisions will, if we're lucky, keep us all alive and even most of our people."

Mikhail looked at his wife. She was a chubby woman with brown hair and brown eyes. And he loved her with all his heart. He, in turn, reached out and touched her cheek.

She leaned in and kissed him. "Now go to sleep. There will be more meetings tomorrow."

CHAPTER 2

Airplane Troubles

War room, Ufa Kremlin
August 10, 1637

The war room wasn't quite an auditorium, but it was large. It was also unfinished. Ufa and the Ufa Kremlin were under construction, and it showed here. The walls were half plastered and the map table that was planned wasn't installed yet. On the unfinished north wall was a map of the United Sovereign States of Russia that Czar Mikhail was fully aware was at least half fantasy. None of the Volga states except Kazan were actually states. They'd all sent representatives to the convention, but none of them had yet ratified the constitution. Ufa was a state but not all—or even most—of the Yaik Cossacks had agreed, and there was a good chance that at least some of them wouldn't.

Also, Perm, Solikamsk, and the northern states mostly hadn't ratified and, of course, neither had General Shein in Tobolsk or the settlement at Mangazenya. The Don Cossacks hadn't signed on yet, but they were making noises like they wanted to.

Muscovite Russia controlled access to the Baltic and what was left of Arkhangelsk. They controlled the Volga down past Nizhny Novgorod, all the way to just the other side of Kruglaya Mountain. They were also lobbying the various Cossack tribes to join Muscovite Russia, or at least not to join the Sovereign States.

Muscovite Russia was the term that had come into use to describe that part of Russia that was still under the control of the Boyar Duma and claimed to be the legitimate government of Russia. Much of Russia's manufacturing capability was concentrated in Muscovite Russia, and a lot of the army had stayed with the Boyar Duma. But defections from Muscovite Russia to the Sovereign States were becoming more common.

He looked over at Tim, still amazed at the youth of his general. Tim now had a beard, a quite respectable, if short and well-trimmed, black beard. But he still looked young.

Tim looked back and said, "The Muscovites are held at Kruglaya Mountain and I honestly don't need most of the army to hold Kazan. We've been improving the fortifications all spring, and with the shipments of Portland cement we've been getting, we now have concrete bastions. I am fully confident that the city of Kazan is secure. The state of Kazan, at least the part of it that's upriver of Kruglaya Mountain, is still occupied by the Muscovite army and they have been forting up too. If you want, I can take the army out of Kazan and circle around them, try to cut them off and starve them out. That won't be easy, but it's certainly possible."

Mikhail shook his head. "No. We have another use for the army. Salqam-Jangir Khan is suffering more raids from the Zunghars. Apparently Erdeni Batur wants to prove his military acumen. From what our agents in the area are telling us, he wants to recreate Genghis Khan's Mongol empire. Reconquering the other Mongol tribes, which includes the Kazakhs, is the first step toward that goal. I wouldn't approve of that even if Kazakh wasn't a state in the Sovereign States, considering that Russia didn't fare all that well under the Mongols the first time. We need to start putting together a force to assist Salqam-Jangir Khan's defense of Kazakh. And it can't be you that goes."

"Why not? It's not like I'm really needed in Kazan."

"Politics, Tim. According to the constitution, national forces supersede state forces. If I send you as the senior commander of the United Sovereign States of Russia forces, you would be in overall command of all the forces. Not independent of, *in command of*, and that might start a revolt of Salqam-Jangir Khan's sultans, which is the last thing we want."

"I could—"

"No, you couldn't, because we also can't have the precedent that the national army is subject to state control. I'll grant that they're sovereign states, but they don't order my army about."

Tim looked at Czar Mikhail for a moment, then nodded in

agreement. "In that case, Czar Mikhail, I would like to recommend that we brevet Ivan Maslov to brigadier general, and put him in charge of an independent, but cooperating force. That will consist of most of our forces. Meanwhile, I'll stay here and we'll see about making sure that General Ivan Vasilevich Birkin can't do us any lasting harm."

The meeting went on and they discussed fortifications and technological changes in warfare and fighting, the *golay golrod*, or walking walls, and how they might be combined with steam trains. The walking walls were a Russian tool of war that went back centuries, but steam and steam trains were new, and Russia, especially Czar Mikhail's Russia, wasn't just dealing with the increasing effects of the tech of the Ring of Fire. It was doing so in a pressure cooker of political, military, and economic necessity.

Moscow Kremlin
August 10, 1637

Ivan Nikitich Romanov wasn't a particularly honorable man, nor overly brave. Neither was he an idiot. In the shakeup after Sheremetev's disappearance, he'd ended up in charge of a fractious Duma of boyars. And Muscovite Russia was leaking ability like a sieve, as more and more people headed east to join Mikhail's Sovereign States. He needed a victory, needed one desperately, both to secure his position as the Director-General of Russia and to keep Muscovite Russia from dissolving into warring factions that Mikhail or the Poles would gobble up at their leisure. Hell, perhaps even the Swedes would grab a bit more near the Baltic.

So almost since the day Director-General Sheremetev had disappeared, he'd been looking for a way to get around Kruglaya Mountain and Kazan. And he thought he'd found it. The village of Yagoshikha, which the Sovereign States constitutional convention had renamed Perm and made into the capital city of the state of Perm, was the key. Yagoshikha and the Kama River, which actually bigger than the Volga before it joined it. And the Kama joined the Volga below Kazan. Take Yagoshikha, and all the fortifications on Kruglaya Mountain and around Kazan were meaningless.

At least, that's what he told himself and the Duma.

New orders were cut, and Ivan Nikitich, not trusting the security of the radio network, had them sent by courier.

Hunt, state of Kazakh
August 10, 1637

Alla Lyapunov was riding a horse and considering how she'd gotten here, riding among the sons and daughters of the Kazakh upper nobility, with an Ufa-made AK4.7 carbine in her saddle holster. The AK4.7 carbine was better and more expensive than anyone else in the group had. The 4.7 was the model number, not caliber or year. AK3s were flint and wheel locks. AK4s were caplocks, and the AK4.7 was a caplock with a clip of chambers that could be fired one after another. It was a very expensive rifle and one not normally available. Hers was the only one in the group of young Kazakh nobles that she was hunting with. The group was about an equal mix of male and female with some adults along to act as chaperones, to make sure that teenage hormones were kept in check.

That was fine with Alla. She wasn't ready for that sort of thing yet, though boys were starting to get interesting. She also didn't speak the Kazakh language, so she was missing most of the talk, except when someone translated for her.

It gave her time to think about how she'd ended up here. She'd never have believed that crazy cousin Vasilii would become important. And now he was a person of import in the Sovereign States, and so was his doxy, Miroslava Holmes. Well, they were engaged now and would be getting married soon. But Miroslava Holmes had been a whore in Nizhny Novgorod and in Ufa, before she met cousin Vasilii. And according to Alla's family, "once a whore, always a whore." Besides, Miroslava was just plain strange.

Alla giggled and got a curious look from the Kazakh girl riding beside her. "I was just thinking that it would have to be a strange girl for my weird cousin, Vasilii," she said in Russian. The Kazakh girl nodded understanding in spite of the fact that Alla was speaking Russian. Oddly, Alla didn't like the Kazakh girl agreeing. He was crazy cousin Vasilii, and his fiancée was a former whore who was probably "autistic," according to Tami Simmons, whatever autistic meant. But it wasn't all right for other people not in the family to think so.

"Yes, it's well known that she is a witch, but he's a witch too. Did he really make a flying machine?"

"He designed the steam engine system for the plane they are working on in Ufa, and he was involved in designing the steam system for the dirigibles all the way back to the test bed." Of that part, she could be proud, even if it was strange.

"What's it like to live with a witch who can read your mind?" the Kazakh girl, Raushan, asked.

"She can't read minds."

"Ha! I was there when she killed Bey Nazar. She knew what he was going to do before he did it. And she knew about the gold. She knows too much, your mother to be."

That was another thing. Vasilii had adopted Alla. She was his daughter and heir, even if Miroslava had a baby. So the family lands would stay in the family. Assuming Czar Mikhail won the war.

Someone shouted and the dogs started barking, and they were off. They were riding through hilly grasslands, full of mostly dry creek beds dotted with trees of varying sizes. For the next few minutes, they rode in a mad dash after a fox that was doing its best to escape. The Kazakh adults hunted with eagles. Teens, though, hunted with dogs and bows. And, in Alla's case, with her new AK4.7 carbine.

So they were riding over rough country on the small Kazakh horses, which were only slightly larger than ponies, but hardy. The ground was covered in brown grass that rippled as they rode, until a hound got the fox. The fox fur would be used for Kazakh outerwear, but this hunt was a way for her to become known to the daughters of the Kazakh nobility.

That was another strange thing. How had Czar Mikhail managed to bring the Kazakhs into Russia? Papa, her real father, had always said that Mikhail was a weak man. Good and kind, but weak. Too weak to rule Russia. He'd said that right up to the day Sheremetev had sent the dog boys to kill him and the rest of Alla's family.

Yet here she was. With the wild Kazakhs who were now part of Russia. The Kazakhs were a steppe people and, in the minds of Russians, were a wild and barbarous people. They weren't actually proving to be nearly as wild as the stories her grandmother told would suggest. At least the Kazakhs were part of the Sovereign States, because Mikhail employed up-timer witches. And it was Czar Mikhail who had given Miroslava the family name of Holmes after a fictional detective. Because Miroslava was a detective, the only licensed private detective in all of Russia. And she didn't solve crimes by reading minds. She did it by seeing and noticing things that other people didn't notice. Alla had seen it.

She rode up next to Raushan and said, "She doesn't read minds. She notices things."

"What?" Raushan looked blank. She'd been watching the lad whose dog had the fox as he took it from the dog and held it up.

"Miroslava. She doesn't read minds. She notices things and assembles scenarios. That's what Cousin Vasilii says."

"Oh!" Raushan said. "What does she notice?"

That was harder to explain. The example that stood out in Alla's mind was the bent-over nail in the killer's boot. But the truth was that Alla had noticed that. And that was only the last case, the one after she got here. She knew that Miroslava had solved several cases while Alla was still hiding back in Moscow. Then she remembered Cousin Vasilii describing the way he and Miroslava had met.

"I'd been asked by Vera to look into a murder because I read up-timer mysteries," Cousin Vasilii said. "And I was examining the wall where the bullet should have landed when Miroslava told me that I was looking in the wrong place."

"You were," Miroslava said.

"Yes, dear. I know. But I hadn't seen the actual murder. So I didn't know how the victim was standing when she was shot," Cousin Vasilii said to Miroslava. Then he turned back to Alla and continued. "That's part of Miroslava's talent. She'd been there, knew how the woman was standing when the shot was fired, and could tell from that and the location of the entry and exit wound where the bullet came from and where it went after it went through the woman's body."

Alla explained to Raushan, "Things like the way someone is facing when they get shot, and how that tells you where they were shot from."

"That still sounds like magic to me," Raushan said.

"Sort of. But I'm starting to understand what's happening. And, anyway, she can't read minds, so your thoughts are safe." Then she grinned. "Well, sort of safe. She also watches people's faces, and can make a pretty good guess when they're lying."

Alla spent another ten days among the Kazakhs before she, Vasilii, and Miroslava were called back to Ufa. They spent part of each day moving south in their *khibitkha* with all the other wagons and horses of the moving city, then around noon they would stop to rest the horses, feed the stock, set up camp, and cook the meals which were often stews and smoked meats. The country was mostly flattish, because they were still mapping out the rail line that would eventually lead from Ufa to the Aral Sea.

The *khibitkha* was a huge wagon with a yurt on it pulled by a bunch of oxen. The wheels on the *khibitkha* were as tall as a tall man and two feet wide, three at the axle. It took three strong men to lift one, and ropes and pulleys to put one on the axle. But their *khibitkha* was pulled by a steam tractor. And every day after they reached the new campsite the tractor would be taken loose from the *khibitkha* and put to other uses, often grading the prospective rail route.

Ufa Kremlin
August 18, 1637

Another day, another meeting, Mikhail thought. The Volga states were still being obstreperous. And by now Mikhail was wondering how he was going to get them to see reason past the visions of tolls and tariffs dancing in their heads. Mikhail couldn't afford to pay them the tariffs they wanted, and the economy of Russia couldn't afford the tariffs that they would charge the steamboats that plied the Volga from Kazan to the Caspian Sea.

"I think we need a bit of gunboat diplomacy," Bernie said.

"What exactly is gunboat diplomacy?" Mikhail asked.

"Someone used to send gunboats down the coast of South America to get the countries there to respect the rights of American businesses. I don't remember who."

"It was Teddy Roosevelt," said Brandy. "Gee, Bernie, didn't you pay any attention at all in high school? I was no college prep girl, and even I know it was the big stick guy."

"One, your discussions of American history are a lot more recent than mine. They were last year, not in another century. And two, no, of course not. I was too busy with football and girls to pay attention to history."

"Dumb jock," Brandy said.

"You leave him alone," Natasha said. "I like my dumb jock just the way he is."

"Gee, thanks," Bernie said.

"Settle down," Mikhail said. "Bernie, what did you have in mind in terms of gunboat diplomacy?"

"Well, it's the tolls that are keeping them from joining."

"Not entirely," Brandy corrected. "They are also considering how much more power they will have as the leaders of independent nations than as the leaders of states within the United States of Russia."

"United Sovereign States, Brandy," Mikhail said.

Brandy rolled her eyes. "You know that is going to bite us on the backside at some point, Czar Mikhail. In spite of clause 17b, someone in eighty years or so is going to decide that sovereign means that they can leave if they want to."

17b was the clause that said that a state in the United Sovereign States of Russia had to get permission from the congress and the czar before it could leave. That clause was there because of the American Civil War back in that other history.

Suddenly there was a siren going off and all political discussion stopped.

In the air, near Ufa
August 18, 1637, two minutes earlier

Vladimir pushed the throttle for the right outboard engine forward, because it felt like that prop wasn't spinning quite as fast as the others. He wished the props had an rpm meter. He looked around out of the windows. The sky was blue with a few puffy white clouds. They were at about eight-hundred-feet height above ground, and out from Ufa, the terrain was mostly forest. The cockpit was large, with room to look around and handle the controls. He liked the *Nastas'ya Nikulichna*. For a fixed-wing aircraft in the seventeenth century, she was big and strong. He turned the stick and brought her to a fifteen-degree angle. As she shifted into a slow turn, he felt a creak and a pop. He looked around and couldn't see the problem, but the steam was dropping. Meanwhile, he was way too low and over forest, not plain.

"We're losing steam," Vadim Ivanovich said. "What happened?"

Vladimir barely heard him.

They were too low. The air cushion landing gear would let them land on all sorts of terrain, but not in the middle of a forest canopy. He pushed more steam to the turbines to try for more lift and tightened his turn. The right wing dropped farther and the nose dropped.

He turned the stick back the other way, trying to level her out, and she started to respond. But they were still losing altitude way too fast.

Vadim Ivanovich was yelling something, but Vladimir didn't catch it and was too busy to care.

He pulled the stick back and it was sluggish. The *Nastas'ya Nikulichna* had a power assist for the controls, but as the steam pressure dropped, so did the power assist. He could still control the flaps and rudder, but it took a lot more muscle. He got her nose up, but he was still turning to the right and now he was down among the treetops.

He missed two and just as he was about to reach the plain around Ufa, he clipped a treetop with his right wing. That ripped off about five feet of wing and jerked the plane a quarter turn to the right, which sent him over the Ufa River. He struggled to straighten her out, and he fed power to the fans that inflated the bags for the ACLG. The bags were barely starting to inflate when he hit the river.

An air cushion landing system without power is essentially a flat-bottomed boat. That kept the crash landing from being an absolute disaster, but Vladimir had bruises on his shoulders from where the safety belt jerked him when the *Nastas'ya Nikulichna* hit the water and went from fifty miles an hour to a dead stop in what seemed like only half a second.

Vadim Ivanovich was sitting at the engineer's seat and just staring into space. As the *Nastas'ya Nikulichna* floated on the Ufa River, Vladimir noticed a smell. He looked down and saw that Vadim Ivanovich had wet himself.

The guards on the Kremlin tower saw his landing, and the air horn started blasting.

He got Vadim Ivanovich up, and they went to the door of the plane. "Can you swim?"

Vadim Ivanovich jerked and blinked, then said, "Yes."

"Good. Take the rope and swim over to the shore."

Vadim Ivanovich looked down and blushed. Then nodded and took the rope.

Moving city of the Kazakh state
August 18, 1637

Alla was reading in the yurt on wheels that Miroslava and Cousin Vasilii used. The rail line was mapped out most of the way to the Aral Sea, but the moving city was still less than a third of the way there. But the convention was finished. Most of the sultans had signed the documents, but there were three holdouts, in spite of the clear majority in favor of it. All three of the holdouts had their territories to the south and east of Kazakh and that was worrying.

Meanwhile Togym had his herders out putting in rail along the mapped route of the rail line to the Aral Sea, and every mile of rail cut the time the trip back to Ufa would take by a lot.

The radio started to clatter. It wasn't dot dash. They were using a standard four-bit byte for each letter and an aqualator to convert the code to feed into a teletype machine that typed out a message. The clatter was the little paper tape being typed on.

Alla had seen a disassembled aqualator back in Ufa. It was a set of tiny tubes that did calculations as the liquid flowed through the tubes. Vasilii said that they duplicated the effect of a computer, but that, compared to a computer, they were slow. Alla didn't believe that part. Nothing could do calculations faster than an aqualator. She got up and crossed to where the paper tape was coming out of the opening in the side of the unit. She pulled the tape out of the opening and read it.

THE NASTAS'YA NIKULICHNA CRASHED.
GET BACK HERE.

Alla took the tape to Vasilii.

Vasilii Lyapunov took the radio telegraph to Salqam-Jangir Khan and started talking about arrangements to leave.

"Not yet," Salqam-Jangir Khan said. He was a stocky man with pale skin and slightly Asiatic features, black hair, black eyes, and a thin black mustache. "First, you will be married here." He pointed at the floor of the yurt. "With us. Before all my sultans and beys." He gave Vasilii one of his ready smiles.

"Salqam—" Vasilii started.

"It won't take long," Salqam-Jangir Khan insisted. "And I want it done here first. You can have another after you get back to Ufa. But you're *my* nobles as well as Mikhail's, and this will be done properly by Kazakh custom."

Vasilii looked at the young khan's grinning face, and knew it was a lost cause.

There were compromises that had to be made, and they were.

In a normal Kazakh wedding, the bride is presented to the groom's family in a ceremony called a *betashar*. She shows proper deference, then her veil is lifted and the mother-in-law kisses her cheek, welcoming her into the family, and puts a white scarf on her head to proclaim her a married woman.

But Vasilii only had his cousin, now his adopted daughter. So Alla was the one who kissed Miroslava's cheek, welcoming her into the family. This was followed by several hours of feasting, in this case with a fair chunk of the upper nobility of the state of Kazakh.

They rushed through it as fast as they could because by now Vasilii was desperate to get back to Ufa and see what Vladimir had done to his airplane.

Outside Ufa
August 20, 1637

The *Nastas'ya Nikulichna* was pulled up onshore, under a tent and under guard, and in another tent Vladimir was going over what had happened again. Vladimir was the one insisting on the interviews, and that was based on movies from up-time, like *Airplane*, as much as anything. He knew that in the movies they investigated any plane crash meticulously. So he was the one insisting that every bit of the plane be photographed in place, then examined in detail. He was the one who interviewed everyone on the plane. In this case, just himself and Vadim Ivanovich, the flight engineer.

And neither one could tell him much. He'd been so busy that he didn't know what he'd done in any detail. And Vadim Ivanovich had determined that he would never set foot in another airplane for any reason, but that was about all.

So he was here in this tent by the Ufa River, wishing it wasn't quite so hot and looking at so many pictures that he didn't have a clue what they meant.

Meanwhile, there were those who wanted to scrap the steam power system and he was close to being one of them. The problem was the Muscovites and Shein. Between the two, Ufa had a very difficult pipeline to get the internal combustion engines that were now in production in Amsterdam, Magdeburg, and Grantville. Mostly Amsterdam and Magdeburg, now that the R&D was mostly done. They were still steel block engines, but they were lightweight and air-cooled and it had cost a medium-sized fortune to smuggle a set of four of the things from the Swedish-held Baltic coast, then through Muscovite Russia to Ufa.

So if they were to go with internal combustion they were limited to one airplane. Or they had to put everything off until they took one of the engines apart and reverse-engineered it, then built the factories to make each of the parts needed to make their own engines. The blocks were easy enough, but the spark plugs were going to be a big hairy bitch to produce.

And Vladimir, even after looking at all the pictures until his eyes crossed, still didn't know what had gone wrong.

Outside Ufa
August 25, 1637

The train reached the graded road with the single thick wooden rail almost forty miles south of Ufa, and only a little over an hour later they were pulling up to the city. On their way back, they'd run into five stretches of rail, from a couple of miles to this longest stretch right next to Ufa, and on all those stretches once they hit the rail, they lowered the drive wheels and sped up to ridiculous speeds. And in this last stretch, where there was tarmac road to go with the rail, it was a ride as smooth as it was fast. Alla was frankly amazed at the progress that was being made.

As they pulled into the station, there was a delegation waiting for them. And that delegation included Czar Mikhail himself. He shook Cousin Vasilii's hand, then took Miroslava's hands, just as if she were a princess or a boyar's wife. Then he said, "I'm sorry that we have to rush you right back to work, but Brandy tells me that a plane crash investigation is much like any detective work. We need to know what went wrong. And why."

After that, Alla was sent off to Vasilii and Miroslava's rooms in the Dacha, while Miroslava and Vasilii went to look at the crashed airplane.

In the small tent next to the plane, Miroslava looked at the map that showed the distribution of pieces. It wasn't like one of the crashes Vladimir and Brandy talked about. Only the tip of one wing and most of the air cushion's skirt had ripped loose. The bit of wing over three hundred yards from the place where the plane hit the water, and skirts from the air cushion all within a couple of feet of where they should be.

The photos made it clear that the plane had hit a tree, and there were some people insisting that all that had happened was that Vladimir had done something wrong and lost altitude too fast. That was a possibility. Miroslava looked at Vladimir's description of the events, then she put the typed sheets back on the table and went to the airplane and sat in the pilot's chair to read them. Having looked at them, they were in Miroslava's head, so she didn't need the actual pages anymore. She read the images in her mind.

In this case, that was especially convenient, because she could go through Vladimir's description and copy his moves. In that way, she found several inconsistencies.

That didn't make Miroslava think that Vladimir was hiding something. Having a consistent story meant you were Miroslava, or that you were lying. Normal people never remembered things accurately.

So she went through the whole thing and copied every move, and saw where pieces were missing or repeated, then she called Vladimir and had him go through it all again, this time sitting in the pilot's seat.

Then she did the same thing with Vadim Ivanovich's statement and followed his moves. There weren't as many of those. The engineer handled the engines, and while he did have a job while the plane was in flight, eighty to ninety percent of his work was done on the ground before and after flight. Most of what he did in flight was control how much fuel was used by the boiler and control the airflow over the condenser. In the process of this part of the investigation, she learned that Vadim Ivanovich had soiled himself. Something that wasn't in either of the reports. And she learned that he'd been yelling at Vladimir to cut power to the engines one at a time. Something he'd forgotten about in the panic of the landing.

Vadim Ivanovich wasn't a coward, but he wasn't comfortable with heights. The combination of the fact that he was way up in the air and that he could see trees coming at him through the windows of the cockpit had caused his mind to go blank and he'd lost some of his memory of the events leading to the crash. Or maybe he'd hit his head. He wasn't sure, but there were blanks in his memory.

After her interview with Vadim Ivanovich, Miroslava knew that one, it was pilot error at least in part, and two, it wasn't the pilot error that everyone thought it was.

She looked around to see Vasilii talking to Vadim. Comforting him. Miroslava didn't know how to comfort people. So, in spite of the need for a quick answer to what went wrong, she waited until Vasilii was done. Then she said, "Vasilii, I need to see every place where the steam goes, especially on the right wing."

It took almost fifteen minutes to find it, even though she was pretty sure what she was looking for. And it wasn't in the joint itself. There were three joints that had pulled loose in the crash, probably from the tree that ripped off the tip of the right wing. But there was only one place where the escaping steam had melted the doping on the skin of the wing.

Private office of Czar Mikhail, Ufa Kremlin
August 26, 1637

"It was pilot error, but only in how he responded to the problem. The original problem was the failure of a faulty linkage between the feeder tube and the turbine for the right outboard engine. When that happened, they lost power and Prince Vladimir did the natural thing. He fed more steam to the engine. But that was the wrong thing to do. What he should have done is feathered that engine, and fed more steam to the right inboard engine."

"But how could I know that?" Vladimir asked.

"You couldn't," Miroslava said.

Then Vasilii spoke. "The mistake, if you can call it that, was inevitable and represents the greatest single weakness in the steam power system. It's centralized. On an ordinary four-engine airplane you have four engines. If one fails, you have three left.

But while the steam turbines are simpler devices operating at lower temperatures, they have one flaw. They are all powered by a single steam boiler."

"Are you saying we should abandon the steam planes and go to internal combustion?" Czar Mikhail asked.

"No, Your Majesty, at least not for the Hero-class airplanes. The single steam boiler and condenser shouldn't be a problem, but in the rush to get the Heroes into production, we skimped on gauges. Vadim knew they were losing steam pressure, but he didn't know where they were losing it. Nor did he have the means of stopping the feed to that turbine. Miroslava and I have gone over the events that led to the crash, and I think that even if Prince Vladimir had had the gauges there wouldn't have been time for him to read them and respond correctly. What is needed is an aircraft engineer who can keep track of the feeds, has the gauges to tell where a problem is, and the ability to cut off the steam to that turbine or system so that a steam leak in one turbine doesn't bleed the steam from the whole system."

Vladimir spoke. "The other problem was also pilot error. The test flight should have been done at greater altitude. And that was my bad decision. Altitude gives you more time to counter problems and if I had been five hundred feet higher when we had the problem, I could have landed even with all the engines out. There would have been time to respond and find a place to land. The only time a plane should be that low is when they are taking off or landing. Ferrell Smith in Amsterdam told me that several times."

"So what we need is to give Vadim the gauges and cutoff controls to keep that sort of failure from bleeding the whole plane dry?" Mikhail asked.

"Not Vadim," Vladimir said. "I doubt we could get him up in an airplane again, even with a gun at his back. He wasn't comfortable flying even before this. After almost dying..." Vladimir shook his head. "But, yes, the next engineer should have those controls."

CHAPTER 3

Zunghar Attack

Ufa docks
August 27, 1637

Ivan Maslov walked down the gangplank and saluted General Boris Timofeyevich Lebedev. Ivan was a thin young man with hair and beard the color of a ripe carrot. He had piercing blue eyes that you normally didn't notice because his face was dark with freckles.

"Welcome to Ufa, Ivan," Tim said. "You won't be staying long."

"Why not?" Ivan asked, looking at his friend and noting Tim's expression. Tim was black haired with olive skin and dark eyes. He'd recently grown a Vandyke-style beard that was as black as his hair. And right now his frown was worried.

Tim held out a radio telegraph message.

ZUNGHARS HAVE TAKEN ALMALIQ. STOP.
WILL SOON THREATEN ALMATY.

Ivan read it, then said, "What are we supposed to do about it? It's going to take us months to get there and the Zunghars will have taken Almaty before an army could get there. And I'm talking about cavalry here, of which the Kazakhs have more and better than we do."

"That's what you and I are going to figure out. The maps are in the Kremlin." He pointed.

Fifteen minutes later, they were in the war room of the Ufa kremlin, examining a map of the state of Kazakh. Most of the

30

work on the room was finished now. The walls were painted white, but the map table wasn't set up yet. So they stood and drew with their fingers on the map hanging on the wall. It was built of information provided in the various atlases that had come back in time with the Ring of Fire, and information provided by scouts, explorers, and the Kazakhs.

It was detailed, but not all the details could be trusted. It showed Lake Balkhash, a huge body of water that snaked through the area between Kazakh and China. The Zunghars had their greatest strength in the area of the Tarbagatai Mountains east of Lake Balkhash.

"The Zunghars have invaded Kazakh lands south of the lake," Tim said, pointing. "They've already sacked the city of Almaliq and we think they will soon be threatening the city of Almaty. At this point, we don't know a lot more than that. Intelligence from Salqam-Jangir Khan's troops are unreliable in terms of the strength of their forces, and the fact that the khan is close to a thousand miles away isn't helping command and control. Or, for that matter, intel gathering.

"We need someone on the scene as soon as we can possibly get them there."

"What about the *Princess Anna*?" Ivan asked.

"Down for repairs." The *Princess Anna* was the smaller dirigible, built in a hidden valley out of spare parts. There had been two large dirigibles, but both had crashed. One right in Ufa, shot down by rocket fire. The other lost to bad weather in Germany. There was supposed to be a third under construction in Bor, but it was the better part of a year away from completion.

The *Princess Anna* was a boxy little thing. Little for a dirigible, that is. Even so, it dwarfed the Hero-class aircraft, but it didn't have quite as much carrying capacity as they did. Aside from a couple of trips to the Baltic, it had mostly just shipped supplies to Hidden Valley. It was subject to serious hydrogen leaks and structural problems, but it did have a working radio with a big antenna. That and the height it could achieve made it a useful temporary link into the radio system anywhere in Russia. "We may use it to provide a radio link to the Aral Sea once it's up again, but we certainly don't want it anywhere near combat."

"Are you sure? It's huge and it's in the sky. Whatever this

wannabe Genghis Khan says, it's still going to impress the hell out of the Zunghars."

"I'll talk to the czar about it," Tim agreed.

New Ruzuka Foundry, Ufa
August 28, 1637

Vasilii came into the New Ruzuka Foundry carrying a satchel full of contracts. He saw Izabella talking with Stefan. They were five feet from an induction furnace where a worker was heating a rod of iron to white hot.

Vasilii went up to Izabella. "Hello, Izabella. I have—"

"Stop right there, Vasilii Lyapunov." Izabella held up her hand. "That had better not be another contract."

Then there was a bang as the drop forge slammed into the white-hot rod and turned it into an iron trough.

Vasilii stopped. This wasn't the response he was expecting. "What's going on? Do you object to making money now?"

"We're having to move." Izabella waved around at the shop floor. "And besides, we have the clip contracts. We have contracts for revolvers. We have the steam turbines for your airplane, and we can't find another skilled machinist for love or money. Just how do you expect us to fulfill another top-priority government contract?"

Vasilii wasn't sure what to do. The engine was just outside in a large wooden crate on a wagon. It was one of the four aircraft engines that they'd managed to smuggle in from Amsterdam, and he wanted Stefan to take the thing apart and reproduce all the metal parts, because they were going to need internal combustion engines for the smaller aircraft. Because the smaller the aircraft, the less wiggle room there was to stick in extra bits like a boiler and a condenser.

Vasilii looked at Stefan pleadingly. Stefan sighed and said, "Okay. Come into the office."

They went into the office and Izabella went to her desk and sat in her padded swivel chair. Stefan went to the stool next to the drafting table and waved for Vasilii to explain.

Vasilii told him what he wanted.

Stefan and Izabella said it was going to take a while. The iron mines in Muscovite Russia were producing a lot and the ones in the Ural Mountains were starting to produce as well. But they had to smuggle in the Muscovite iron and the Ural iron was just starting up. Also, the copper mines, which were mostly in the Urals, were producing well. That part was fine, but converting that ore into copper and steel was taking time, and even more time was being taken up by machining that steel into parts.

There was a shortage of labor from Poland to Tobolsk, and from the Arctic to the Black Sea. It was worse in Muscovite Russia than in the Sovereign States, but it was bad enough in the Sovereign States. A skilled machinist could write his own ticket. Stefan, by now, had twenty of the expensive fellows and each and every one of them was building himself a house in Ufa, and they were going to own those houses. Inflation was creeping in, but only creeping because those skilled machinists with the machines that Stefan had were putting out twelve to twenty times as much as a blacksmith would.

And it wasn't just the New Ruzuka Foundry. There were several foundries in Ufa, but they were all working at, or more often beyond, capacity. In Vasilii's opinion, Stefan's foundry was the best, or at least the most innovative. Not only was Stefan creative in the way he looked at things, he'd gathered other creative people around him. That was why Vasilii had brought him a project that in some ways more properly belonged to the Dacha. Because if the various plants in Ufa were overworked, the Dacha was even worse.

Still, by begging and pleading, he got them to take on the job.

Ufa Dacha
August 28, 1637

Vadim Ivanovich would never fly again, but that didn't stop him from being a hardworking man who wanted to make sure that those who flew would have the best equipment. He made notes then adjusted a magnet in a small sheath of copper coil, then read the output on a voltmeter and made another note.

The aqualator computer blocks were developed in Grantville after the Ring of Fire. They had hard limits on their utility and they were much heavier than the integrated circuits that they used up-time, but they could be made with down-time tools and they would work for basic digital processing of signals. The trick was converting the aqualator's mechanical output into electrical signals.

And the Hero-class airplanes were going to need aqualators to help run their systems. They would need to take the input from the steam gauges and make them into readable numbers and at least semiautomatic responses. Also to make sure that the radio on the plane worked, that the batteries were charged but not overcharged, and a hundred other tasks.

There was, by now, a standardized machine code for the aqualators, and Vadim was building the connectors that would tie the Ufa-made aqualators into the electrical system of the Hero-class airplanes. The planes wouldn't have computer screens or a keyboard. Instead, they would have a set of switches and numeric readouts with electromagnetic actuators controlled by the aqualator's output.

Vadim moved another actuator and marked down another reading. The Heroes wouldn't be fly-by-wire aircraft, but they would have automated systems to make flying easier and safer. This was a retrofit into an already built system, which made some things easier and others harder, but generally limited their options, which was speeding things up because they weren't going back and forth between fifty answers for each question. Vadim snorted to himself. *Just four or five answers.*

Ufa docks
August 28, 1637

The *Ilya Muromets* was made in Murom and named after that city's most famous hero. It was sixty feet long and twenty wide, with a steam engine and four cannon, two on the port side and two on the starboard. And Ivan Nikitich Romanov was going to be really pissed when he found out that his brand-new purpose-built steamship had dumped the captain and the dog boys over the side as soon as they passed Nizhny Novgorod on their way to the front.

Bernie Zeppi looked over at the former chief engineer—and now captain—of the *Ilya Muromets* and said, "Sorry, Captain, but we're going to have to change the name. After much debate, mostly between the two eldest of Czar Mikhail's children, the new class of large aircraft are going to be called *Bogatyr* or *Polianitsa*, which I translate into hero and heroine. Which means that one of them is going to end up named *Ilya Muromets*."

"That seems most unfair, *Okolnichy* Zeppi," the captain complained, but he was smiling when he said it. "After all, we named ours first and, besides, it was built in Murom, the original Ilya Muromets' hometown." Then he sighed. "I'm more concerned about what you're calling me. I'm not a captain. I'm an engineer."

In fact, Gennady Bobrov was of *streltzi* rank and had worked at the Dacha from 1632 to 1634, then been sent to the Gorchakov family property in Murom to build steam systems for steamboats. He'd been there when Bernie and Natasha used Murom as the base for rescuing Czar Mikhail from the hunting lodge where he was being held.

At the time, Gennady had been unwilling to risk his new family on a fool's errand that had no chance of working and every chance of getting him and his new wife and child killed.

It wasn't until months later that he realized he'd backed the wrong horse. Then it took more months to smuggle his wife and daughter out of Murom, during which time he'd been tapped as the engineer for this war boat. Aside from the four breech-loading cannon, it had black-powder rockets and heavy oak armor above the waterline.

"I feel the same way," Bernie assured him. "*Okolnichy* isn't a rank that I ever aspired to."

"I'm serious, sir," Gennady said. "I'm a good steam guy and I know this ship's systems but, frankly, I would prefer to be in a factory in Kazan or Ufa, building steam engines to power riverboats. I know how to do that. I very much *don't* know how to command a ship in battle."

Bernie looked at the man and nodded. "Very well, Gennady. I'll speak to Czar Mikhail about it, and we'll see what we can do."

It was fifteen minutes later when Czar Mikhail's secretary waved Bernie into the czar's office. Czar Mikhail was doing paperwork and a servant was at the teapot. Czar Mikhail looked up as Bernie came in. "So is Gennady the new captain?"

"Gennady doesn't want it, Mikhail," Bernie said as Mikhail waved him to the couch. "He got his wife to Kazan, and they're happy there. Happy enough, anyway. He didn't want to come here in the first place. He can't go back to Murom, so when he was told to bring it the rest of the way here, he did so. But he has no desire to live on a steamboat with his wife and family back home in Kazan."

"It seems a perfectly reasonable attitude," Mikhail agreed. "And it's convenient anyway. I have a number of *deti boyars* who would love such a post, in command of a powerful military unit and still sleeping in a bed every night and having hot meals prepared."

"Just don't give me any fire eaters, please. This is supposed to be a diplomatic mission. We want to show our teeth, not go around biting people to prove we can." Bernie accepted a cup of Turkish coffee that had arrived by way of the Caspian Sea and the Volga River system. "How are the other balls you're juggling doing? What's going on with Tim and Ivan?"

"I just got another radio telegram from Salqam-Jangir Khan," Czar Mikhail said. "Asking me to expedite."

"Hmm," Bernie said. "Ivan Maslov is bright enough, but he's really not a steam guy. I don't think he'll be that much direct help in putting together the expedition. How about if we send him to Salqam-Jangir Khan on the Scout?"

The body of the first of the *Razvedchik*, or Scout planes, was finished. Its airframe had been finished for months, waiting on the engines to arrive. It had one 110 hp engine and a chain drive that went from the engine to an ACLG system. It was a pusher design that Vladimir had bought from the M&S aircraft design firm.

"And you want to risk him in a brand-new plane with a brand-new pilot?" Mikhail asked.

"Well, we're not sending him Tim, so having Ivan show up in an airplane strikes me as a good idea."

"Certainly. I'm just not sure how good an idea it will be to have Ivan Maslov die in a plane crash on the way there."

"That's a good point." While by now the Sovereign States had a good number of dirigible pilots, it didn't have any airplane pilots except Vladimir and Brandy Bates Gorchakov.

And while Vladimir had more experience on the larger multiengine planes, Brandy had some experience on small planes. Not a lot, but in this very unsafe world, enough.

"Okay. As soon as they get the wingtip fixed on the *Nastas'ya Nikulichna*, we'll send him to Shavgar.

"Let me have a talk with Ivan Borisovich Petrov," Mikhail said, and Bernie lifted an eyebrow. Ivan Borisovich Petrov was the son of

Boris Petrov, who had been in Grantville with Vladimir when he'd recruited Bernie back in 1631. Boris was now the Grantville desk in the Embassy Bureau in Muscovite Russia, while Ivan Borisovich was the Grantville desk for the Embassy Bureau in the Sovereign States.

"I know he's young and I know he's in the Grantville desk in the Embassy Bureau, but he's sharp and he's trustworthy."

Bernie nodded. The lofted eyebrow wasn't about Ivan Borisovich's competence. It was the political consequences of going around the head of the Embassy Bureau. The Russian legally enforced nepotism was still there in the United Sovereign States, and it sometimes forced Mikhail to install people he didn't fully trust in positions of authority in the Embassy Bureau. Simeon Budanov was thirty-five and might well be working undercover for the Muscovite government. Or he might just be an incompetent. In either case, he was jealous of his prerogatives and didn't like Ivan Borisovich's access to the czar one bit.

"Why don't you let me talk with Ivan Borisovich?" Bernie asked. "That won't be quite as blatantly going around Budanov."

"I don't care about..." Mikhail stopped, and waved Bernie to go ahead. The issue wasn't what Budanov would do to Mikhail. It was what he would do to Ivan Borisovich.

Bernie invited Ivan Borisovich Petrov to dinner, and he and Natasha discussed who to see. Who to see turned out to be the new head of the China desk at the Embassy Bureau, Kirill Blinov. Bernie knew Kirill. He was half Chinese, half Russian, and had been doing the real work of the China desk even before he got the job.

"I know Kirill a little. You think we can trust him?"

"As much as anyone in the Embassy Bureau," Ivan Borisovich said with a grimace. "But yes. He's making a bit on the side, but in his case that makes him more trustworthy, not less."

"Get him aside and have him find us some native guides who aren't afraid of the notion of flying in an airplane."

Ufa river docks
August 30, 1637

Brandy Bates Gorchakov strapped Yury Arsenyev into the front seat of the still-unnamed Scout plane. The plane was sitting on the bank of the Ufa River, just upstream of where the Ufa River merged into the Belaya River. The wooden pier stuck out about twenty feet into the Ufa. It was a warm, clear day. The cockpit of the plane was a bit cramped with the two of them.

Arsenyev was a Cossack trapper and they were about to learn if he could hack flying. She got him belted in, then climbed into the back seat. She set her switches, and the ground crew chiefs pulled the prop to start the engine. It started right up.

She engaged the fan and as the air was forced into the air cushion, the plane began to move. It slid out over the water and gained speed rapidly. She pulled back on the stick, and up they went. As soon as they were off the water, she cut power to the fan for the ACLG and pulled the lever that tightened the straps and pulled the skirt up tight against the flat bottom. The engine was only a hundred and ten horsepower, but the plane was very light for its wing surface, so they gained height rapidly.

Once they had a thousand feet, she winged over into a tight turn, the sort of maneuver that moved the direction of gravity away from down, or at least moved down over to the side a bit. That, combined with the open cockpit in the observer's seat was enough to turn anyone with a fear of flying into a gibbering wreck.

Yury Arsenyev was yelling all right, but it was in excited joy. Brandy was convinced, but she stayed up for a quarter hour to give him his money's worth. Then she brought the Scout around for a landing on the Ufa River and skimmed up onto the shore, cutting power to the engine.

Ariq Ogedei wasn't as thrilled by the flight, but he wasn't overly bothered, either. A Khoshut, one of the four main tribes of the Oirat Confederation, Ariq had been a refugee since his clan lost one of the more or less constant clan feuds. He was Yury's brother-in-law and partner for years. The sister that connected them had died in childbirth a few years back. They made their living as trappers, but supplemented it by providing the Embassy Bureau with mapping and intelligence information.

They would be acting as guides on the trip to Shavgar, and also as political advisors. Since they were both able to handle flying, the project could move forward.

Residence of Bernie and Natasha
August 30, 1637

The town house that Bernie and Natasha lived in was right next door to the Ufa Dacha, and not far from the Kremlin. It was relatively small, but exceedingly modern, with electric lights and indoor plumbing. While they now had tubes and were working very hard at making them themselves, they didn't have enough or the right type for microwaves, so the kitchen used an oil stove that used oil shipped up from the Caspian Sea. That, and the lack of other modern conveniences meant that Bernie and Natasha needed servants.

That wasn't a problem for Natasha. She'd grown up in a house full of servants, and many of the servants she had now were people she'd known since early childhood.

Bernie was less comfortable, partly because he was generally less at ease with servants, but partly because a fair percentage of the servants didn't approve of Bernie being married to Natasha. Up-timer or not, he wasn't a prince, and "their" Natasha deserved a prince. So most of them saw him as an interloper. But they had since he'd arrived, so Bernie was used to it by now and they were used to him. In fact, their resentment had mellowed somewhat.

Mags, one of those servants, placed Bernie's eggs before him with the barest of disapproving sniffs, and then went for coffee. Coffee was more available than orange juice in Ufa. It came up from the Ottoman Empire via the Black Sea, up the Don River, over a short stretch of land to the Volga, and up to Ufa, making the inclusion of the Don Cossacks in the Sovereign States important to its economic welfare. The Turks had oranges too, but oranges were perishable, and the trip from the North African orange groves to Ufa was long and mostly slow. By now there were steamships on the Don River as well as the Volga, because they'd been bought by riverboat owners who worked the Don River. Mostly they were Russian built, but some of them were Ottoman built. Technology was spreading, and by now it wasn't spreading from just one place. The old Dacha near Moscow, the new Dacha in Ufa, and several Ottoman cities on the Black Sea had become centers from which the technology spread.

Coffee arrived, and with it fresh-baked rolls with butter. The

butter was from Kazakh cows herded up from the state of Kazakh
to Ufa in a cattle drive. There was a complex of slaughterhouses
just downriver from Ufa now, complete with steam-powered ice
houses to load refrigerated beef and mutton onto refrigerated
steamboats to take that meat from Ufa to the Caspian Sea and
to Nizhny Novgorod, Perm, and Solikamsk.

People were getting rich. And among those people were Bernie and Natasha. They owned over a dozen steamboats now, as
well as interests in over a hundred businesses here in Ufa and
in Kazan. That didn't include the wealth that by Sovereign States
law was theirs, which was at the moment divided up among the
boyars of Muscovite Russia.

The issue was getting that money from here to Grantville,
where Ron Stone and several members of the Barbie Consortium
were holding what was now approaching a hundred million dollars
of United Sovereign States of Russia debt. That, with the defla-
tion that the USE dollar had experienced over the last five years,
was in dollars that were closer to 1960 dollars than 2000 dollars.

In any case, it was a lot of money. And they needed some
way of getting that money to Grantville. Bernie thought he might
just have a way of doing it.

But that way was dependent on the Don Cossacks biting the
bullet and joining the Sovereign States. He wanted to smuggle
money and some gold through the Black Sea to the Bosporus,
the Sea of Marmara, and into the Med, where it would travel to
Venice and take a plane to Grantville. It was risky, and to make
it happen they needed to open a regular smuggler route with
Sovereign States–owned ships that could make the trip with as
few cargo transfers as possible.

Which led right back to the Don Cossacks joining the Sovereign
States, and owning the Don River right down to Taganrog Bay.

It was about then that Natasha came in, gave him a kiss, and
joined him for the last little bit of breakfast.

"We need a rail line between the Volga and the Don. Probably between Tsaritsyn and Kalach," he greeted her with a hug
and a smile.

"Yes, dear, I know," Natasha said. "The Don Cossacks have
been demanding such a rail line since the beginning of the convention. The wagoneers of Tsaritsyn have been insisting that it will

destroy their business for as long as the idea has been around. And it's a syndicate of the wagoneers of Tsaritsyn that controls the government of Tsaritsyn, which is why Tsaritsyn is refusing to join the Sovereign States until the Sovereign States government promises that no such rail line, no canal, no nothing, will be put in place. Besides, what we actually need is a canal, not a rail line—and a big canal. Big enough for ships on the Caspian to transfer to the Sea of Azov."

"Yes, but that's a project that's going to take at least a decade. In the meantime, we need a sixty-five-mile railroad to move goods from the Volga system to the Don system and back."

"Which brings us back to the politics, and why Mikhail is getting ready to send us down the Volga in gunboats to make sure the oligarchs of Samara, Saratov, Tsaritsyn and Astrakhan realize that Czar Mikhail's patience isn't unlimited. Eat your sausage."

"Yes, dear."

CHAPTER 4

The Volga States

Conference room, Ufa Kremlin
September 1, 1637

Czarina Evdokia smiled as the two scouts were shown in. The room was two doors down from the war room, but this room was finished. It had a long table with chairs on rollers and a hardwood floor polished to a high gloss. There was a tea service against one wall and electric lights in sconces along the walls. "How did you like your first flight, Yury? And you, Ariq?" She waved them to chairs.

Yury smiled at the memory, and both men relaxed. Which Mikhail knew was what his wife intended. Men like Ariq Ogedei and Yury Arsenyev weren't comfortable in the presence of royalty, and that either made them too diffident or it made them bluster. Evdokia was getting very good at putting people at their ease.

"They both did fine, and the *Nicky*'s repairs are complete," Brandy said.

"Good," Mikhail said. "Now, Yury, tell me about the Zunghars and Erdeni Batur, this new leader of theirs?"

"I think the first thing to note is he is a new leader, and his ancestry isn't from Genghis Khan, so his hold on the tribes is weak. Not that he's weak. He's a hard man and driven, but there are several factions that think that if the four tribes are to be joined, they ought to be joined by a descendant of Genghis Khan. They don't like him restricting them, and the only reason he's been able to keep power is because they hate each other more than they hate him." He shrugged. "Well, they also know that

42

if they break apart, all the old blood feuds will resurface." Yury stopped and considered a minute. "Finally, they're afraid of him. He's proven that he's willing to use torture and to kill whole families. You must understand. The difference between fear and respect in a barbarian is thinner than a single hair." Another pause. "I know. Ariq here is a barbarian."

Ariq started to make a rude gesture, then looked at the women in the room and restrained himself.

"It's not unique to barbarians. A number of people get the two confused," Evdokia said. "All too many see kindness as weakness."

"It's because they are cruel by nature and are only kind when they are afraid not to be," Ariq said. "But not all men"—he blushed—"not all *people* are made that way." He gave the czar and czarina a seated bow.

Ufa river bank
September 3, 1637

By this time, the *Nastas'ya Nikulichna* was repaired and the new valves were installed. The new skirt for the air cushion was attached and the steam was up. The steam system of the Hero class wasn't fast. It took up to fifteen minutes to get the steam up to workable levels, and this time it had taken longer because Vasilii was checking all the controls twice. He turned on the steam to each engine individually, and had Vladimir bring up that engine to full power, then turned off the steam and saw how long it took for the line's pressure to drop. Not long, as it turned out. Finally, they were ready and Vasilii gave Vladimir the thumbs-up.

Vlad fed enough power into the fans to inflate the skirt to about half full. That reduced the friction on the air cushion landing gear a little, but not much. Just enough so that you could feel the balance of the engines as you brought them up. At this pressure on land, even all the engines on full would barely move the *Nicky*. He brought up and balanced the engines. In theory, they should be perfectly balanced. But, in fact, that never happened. That was part of the reason why each engine had its own throttle.

Vlad spent a few seconds feeling the way the plane shifted under the force of the engines. Then, once everything was as balanced as he could make it, he fed more steam to the fans feeding the air cushion, and the plane began to move for real. More power, and it was like they were on flat ice. Then, like they were already in the air. The speed came up fast, and as soon as it hit sixty miles per hour, he pulled back on the stick and they were flying. He brought the stick back to neutral, which left them at a twenty percent up-angle and they gained altitude fast. He cut the steam to the ACLG and turned on the motor that tightened the straps, pulling the air cushion up tight against the body. Then he opened the rear release and gave a bit of steam to the fans so that there would be a continuous airflow over the condenser.

He kept them at 20 degrees until they had reached a thousand feet, then pushed the stick forward a little so that they slowly dropped to 10 degrees up-angle and their airspeed picked up.

"You ready?" Vasilii asked Vlad.

"Not yet. Let me get us up another couple of thousand feet. And I want to be heading back toward the river before you screw things up."

"Okay."

Vlad took them through a rising turn until they were at four thousand feet above the ground and facing back toward the city of Ufa. Then he said, "Go ahead."

Vasilii pushed a lever, and cut off steam to the right outboard engine. What Vlad noticed was that the other three engines picked up a little. He feathered the right outboard even though it was already effectively feathered by Vasilii and fed more power to the right inboard. Cruising speed was sixty-five to seventy-percent power to the props. With one prop down, he was up at ninety-plus-percent power to the right inboard, and he was still in a slow right turn, and his right wing was dropping. He used the pedals to shift his rudders to the left to counter the drift, and that stopped the dropping of the right wing. But he had to use the wheel to move the plane back to even bubble. Even a small plane is slow to react compared to an automobile, and while a plane like this one was faster to react than an airship, it was slower than most planes. Flying a plane was about thought, not reflexes. Vladimir realized that that was the real pilot error when the *Nicky* had crashed. He'd panicked and let reflexes take over from thought. That was deadly in the air.

They repeated the process with all the engines, each individually, and even two engines at a time, both right and both left. With two engines off, especially two of them on the same wing, they were going down, but not necessarily crashing. By putting the rudder all the way over and lifting the dead wing, he was able to turn the spiral into a curve wide enough so that they could decide where they were going to come down. He could also control the other system so it was a safe bet everyone would walk away from the plane. It was even likely that once the two dead engines were fixed, they would be ready to fly again.

They were back down on the side of the Ufa River. Czar Mikhail looked to Vasilii and said, "Well?"

Vasilii grimaced, then said, "I'd like more time, but I saw the latest radio messages. Salqam-Jangir Khan is riding hell-for-leather east, along with about half the state legislature, and he needs us there now."

The czar looked at Vladimir. "Load it up then. I've made a couple of changes. Brandy is going to fly one of the Scouts in formation with you, and I've sent the *Princess Anna* ahead to the Aral Sea with a load of fuel. Gasoline for the Scout, mostly."

While the steam planes could use heating oil as their fuel, the radial engines of the Scouts weren't so flexible. They needed gasoline with enough alcohol in it to have a high octane number, or else the spark plugs fouled or burned out.

Meanwhile, Miroslava, Ariq, and Ivan Maslov came aboard, followed by a bunch of gear that was stowed. Yury would be going with Brandy and getting flying lessons.

There was a set of replacement panels for the skirt. Since the skirt was designed to leak air anyway, it was made in pieces about a foot long that had holes in them so that they could be easily sewn into gaps where a piece had torn. They had enough to replace the whole skirt, but since the skirt could be expected to wear out first in the back, what would actually happen would be that they would have enough replacement skirt segments to replace the trailing edge about three times. After that, they would have to have new skirt segments made locally.

They were also taking a deaerator with them to deaerate lake or river water because any dissolved gasses in the water would, over time, damage the boiler, engines, and condenser.

A plane designed to carry sixteen people including crew would be carrying five and still be the next thing to overloaded because of all the gear they were taking.

✧   ✧   ✧

With the steam still up, they topped up the fuel tanks. And they were off. The Scout's max cruising speed was about seventy miles per hour, so the *Nicky* was cruising at less than her best speed. To maintain formation, they brought the angle of attack up a little, and decreased the steam to the engines. They made it about two hundred fifty miles down the Yaik River.

At this time, the location that Vladimir thought was marked as Orsk in a world atlas from Grantville was occupied by a fishing village of the Yaik Cossacks. They landed on the river, which was a job because the river had trees on both sides. It was also not navigable by a riverboat, and probably would have killed them if they'd had pontoon landing gear, because there were clumps of grass and land that stuck out of the river here and there, but the ACLG flowed right over them. They pulled up to the bank and then Brandy landed the Scout and, using gas cans, they refueled.

While they were refueling, a small delegation from the village arrived and asked them if they were from Ufa. They spoke a local patois that was a mix of Russian and Kazakh, but they were surprisingly well informed about what was going on in the wider world. They had fish to sell and everyone had lunch together. They also asked about what the plane would need in the way of landing facilities. The rail line was supposed to pass about forty miles west, where the land was flatter and less forested, which the local village leader felt was an unfortunate choice.

"You t'ink can arrange radio here?" the headman asked. The man was clearly bright, but the village was isolated and the language had shifted a lot.

"I will ask," Vladimir said, and he would. But he didn't think it likely that there would be a radio in the next few years. There were too many other places that had priority, and tubes were still in short supply.

After lunch and getting the steam back up, they took off again. From Orsk to Alty-Kuduk was three hundred and fifty miles, which the *Nicky* could manage, but the Scout plane couldn't, so when Brandy started getting low on fuel, they found a bit of savanna and landed so they could refuel the Scout's tanks.

The last leg was short, just over a hundred miles, and they landed at Alty-Kuduk while the sun was still up.

Alty-Kuduk
September 3, 1637

The bay had made an excellent landing field for the *Nicky* and the Scout. The *Princess Anna* was already there, and had unloaded gasoline, which the Scout required. The *Nicky* could drink gasoline, but it preferred fuel oil.

The next morning, having been unloaded, the *Nicky* flew back to Ufa for another load of fuel. It was a stopgap. A large load of fuel was on its way to Alty-Kuduk by wagon, and General Tim was organizing a steam train carrying two tanker wagons full of gasoline and fuel oil. The train would also bring a steam engine and boiler to go into one of the riverboats that would take the fuel oil up the Syr Darya River to Shavgar.

Their problem was they were trying to drive to the east end of Kazakh without a road or a gas station. So the whole thing was improvisation.

Because of that, over the next five days, both the *Nicky* and the *Princess Anna* flew back and forth to Ufa, ferrying fuel to Alty-Kuduk, with the *Nicky* making stops at the village on the Yaik River to set up a fuel depot, which, if they maintained it properly, might get the village a radio after all.

Ufa docks
September 3, 1637

There was a brisk morning breeze as Bernie and Natasha walked up the ramp from the dock to the steamboat *Ilya Muromets* and were saluted by the new captain, Leonid Belyaed. "Welcome aboard, ma'am, sir. Your room is ready."

He was in a blue coat with brass buttons and epaulets. That was partly because he was of the service nobility, and partly because there were now two cloth factories in Ufa and three in Kazan, and the cost of cloth was about a third of what it had been in 1632. He was also wearing a billed hat, which was apparently copied from the one the ladies of Kazan had had made for General Tim's uniform.

Leonid hadn't gone overboard with the embroidery, though. Just a bit around the front edge. Bernie neither smiled nor commented while they were turned over to a fresh-faced ensign to be shown to their room.

In their room, with the door closed, Bernie pointed at his head and laughed.

Natasha hit him in the shoulder. "It's not his fault."

"It's not Tim's, either. It's Ivan's, and it's going to bite him on the backside too. Tim has seen to it. Along with his brevet comes a new uniform and Tim has had special headgear designed for it."

The *Ilya Muromets* had a generator and batteries to power the radio, and since it had the electricity anyway, it was wired for an intercom and an in-ship phone system. The phone rang and Bernie looked around and saw the headset. He picked it up. "Yes?"

"We're ready to cast off, sir," said a voice Bernie didn't recognize.

Bernie wasn't at all sure why he was getting a call. "Very well," he said, not knowing what else to say.

"Thank you, sir," said the voice and hung up. Less than a minute later they felt the riverboat pulling away from the dock. They were on the way.

Ufa was located on a spit of land between two rivers. One side had the Ufa River, the other the Belaya River. The Ufa flowed into the Belaya, which flowed into the Kama, a couple of hundred miles downriver. The Kama flowed another couple of hundred miles to the Volga, and flowed into it about fifty miles downriver of Kazan. It wouldn't be until they were going down the Volga toward the Caspian Sea that their real mission would start.

That would have made this a really long trip if they were going by horse and wagon. For that matter, it would be a really long trip even if they were going by unpowered river barge. But they were on a steam-powered gunboat with a cruising speed of ten knots. Also, the whole trip was downriver, so that added the current of the rivers to their speed. The Volga was big, but not particularly fast flowing, so their average speed downriver was going to be around fifteen knots per hour, but they would be traveling all day, every day, with only occasional stops to refuel and re-water. The steamboats didn't bother with condensers. They filtered the river water and deaerated sometimes. That probably cut the fuel efficiency of their boilers and engines by half, but it was a great deal cheaper in initial cost.

For the next two days, including around ten hours docked and refueling, Bernie and Natasha had a mini-vacation, mostly undisturbed except for phone calls from the bridge, where the captain seemed intent that they be informed of every action the riverboat took.

Then they arrived at Samara.

Samara docks
September 5, 1637

The town of Samara was booming. It was one day from Kazan by riverboat and the escaping serfs that were less trusting of Czar Mikhail had run here. Not all of them, but enough to double the town's size in less than a year. There was construction everywhere.

They were met by Timofey Ivanovich Razin, the newly elected mayor of Samara. Timofey was around thirty-five and had brought his family east. He was a Cossack with a captured Turkish wife, and a man on the make. Samara had no radio, and it was far enough from the network so that to be tied in they would either need more radio stations or Samara would need a tubed radio. Bernie managed, barely, to keep from slapping his forehead. *Why don't we have a broadcast station in Ufa?* Bernie went through the rest of the greetings and first discussions in something not quite a daze. Samara *generally* liked the new constitution, but . . .

They wanted assurance that the supreme court wouldn't find that they were required to return escaped slaves. And they also wanted exceptions to the interstate trade clause. States couldn't "impede" trade with other states. And the court in Ufa had already, in almost its first decision, determined that "impede" meant "tax." The court's opinion had been occasioned by a cattle drive up from Kazakh. As a test, Togym had demanded a ten-percent tax on the sale price of the beef. The court, with Czar Mikhail sitting in, had determined that Kazakh couldn't tax goods sent to the rest of the Sovereign States, and Ufa and the rest of the Sovereign States couldn't tax goods sent to Kazakh.

Timofey Ivanovich Razin thought that was fine for Kazakh, but not for Samara, whose major value was as a transshipment port. They needed the income from those boats. The right to tax goods moving through their state was folded in with the unwillingness to return escaped slaves as giving too much power to the federal government.

✧   ✧   ✧

Once they got back to their cabin on the *Ilya Muromets*, Bernie told Natasha about his realization.

"Bernie, we've been working on a broadcast station since Vladimir got here with the tubes. It's not that easy. For one thing, the tubes my idiot brother brought weren't the right tubes, and the alternator design used by the Catholic station proved much more difficult than we thought it was going to be. We abandoned that approach back in the first Dacha."

"I remember, but we're making our own tubes now!"

"Barely. And, as I just said, the tubes for a broadcast station are harder to do. They need a harder vacuum." Natasha shook her head, then continued. "But we're very close. Close enough so that we've set up a factory in Kazan to mass-produce tunable crystal sets."

Bernie had to be satisfied with that.

Kazan
September 5, 1637

General Tim was back in Kazan and at a party, being buttonholed by a very odd committee of two: Father Kiril and a mullah. They were willing to accept freedom of religion when it came to established faiths of the book, Christianity, Islam, Judaism. They could even choke down Buddhism, because it had been around a very long time and if you squinted hard you could allow that it had "a book" of sorts.

But when it came to this new cult of "God's Ring," something had to be done. The Ringers were a group of people, some of whom had been to the Ring of Fire in person and, having found an actual unquestionable act of God, decided that Judaism, and therefore all the rest of the religions of the book, were nonsense. That if God wanted to make a point, he or she wouldn't need to send one guy to Palestine or even part the Red Sea temporarily. He would do a Ring of Fire, something that couldn't be argued with and left visible and obvious traces. Not even "traces" but cliffs hundreds of feet high!

They then proceeded to insist that they had figured out what God meant by the Ring of Fire. Which wasn't all that different from what the people of the book said, except they wanted the saved to give their money to them, not the Christians, Muslims, or Jews. And certainly not the Buddhists, who didn't have a clue about anything.

There were dozens of Ring of Fire sects by now. The one that

Father Kiril and his unlikely ally were incensed about had come to Russia by way of Poland, and, while not violent, took the view that freedom of religion only made sense on the premise that all the religions before theirs were false and therefore it didn't matter which one you wasted your time on. But all religions were now superseded by the Ring of Fire, which was clearly God's true message—His *own* message, literally carved in stone—so the doctrine of freedom of religion was seriously in doubt.

"Gentlemen, I don't disagree," Tim told the clerics. "But, when it comes to freedom of religion, the court has decided it does include the out-and-out pagans of the steppes, so presumably it includes the Ringers as well. And that means if a mob incensed by an injudicious sermon attacks them, I'm going to have to react. That could include bloodshed, which none of us want, I'm sure."

Every time Tim turned around, he was having to play politics. The Muscovites were suppressing the Ringers with a vengeance. So were the Ottomans and the Safavids. The Poles weren't, though; being, as always, slackers when it came to faith. And while the Ringers existed in the USE, they were less common because there were a lot of actual up-timers in the USE, including priests and pastors who were happy to debunk the Ringers with the comment, "I was there. I was the one God moved." And some variant of "I don't know what it means" and "It doesn't mean what that lying creep says." But the farther you got from the Ring of Fire, the more people were starting new religions based on it.

Kazan was pretty far from the Ring of Fire.

"Can't you at least talk to Bernie Zeppi, Brandy Bates, or Tami Simmons? Get them to—" the mullah started.

"Not Bernie Zeppi," Kiril said. "He's as likely to disrespect our faiths as the Ringers."

"In all honesty, I don't know what Princess Brandy or Tami Simmons believe. But Father Kiril is correct. Bernie will almost certainly say 'Let them go to hell or heaven in their own way. It's none of your business.'"

"The saving of souls *is* my business," Father Kiril insisted. The mullah nodded in firm agreement.

Thankfully then, an aide came up and interrupted. "I'm sorry, gentlemen. Duty calls."

"Thank you for rescuing me, Goram. But you could have done it ten minutes ago," Tim said.

"We have a message from double oh three, sir," Goram said quietly.

Tim didn't jerk, but he almost hissed, "Not here." 003 was one of a few military agents that Tim had in Birkin's camp. It was an in-joke and a cover at the same time. Their names were never mentioned. 003 was on Birkin's staff and mostly trusted, but a great deal of what Birkin did these days was compartmentalized. For one thing, Birkin was suffering regular defections, as things in Muscovite Russia got less stable.

Both sides were being forced to learn about operational security.

Not all the defectors were real.

In another room, Tim asked, "What does Three have to say?"

"Birkin has new orders from Moscow. He is to leave a blocking force here and move the army overland."

"Overland where?"

"That's the part that no one knows. One rumor is that he's to take Solikamsk as the first step in taking the Babinov Road and hitting Shein in Tobolsk."

Tim snorted. "I almost wish it was that."

Goram didn't say anything, but his expression was questioning.

"It would pull them out of position," Tim explained. "And convince those jackasses in Solikamsk that they need to join the Sovereign States if the Muscovites aren't going to eat them." Tim called up in his mind a map of the Sovereign States that included Muscovite Russia. "We could use armored riverboats to bypass them and take the Volga all the way to Bor before the winter freeze. We might even get lucky and take Nizhny Novgorod. That would quite possibly end the war."

"But you don't think they actually would."

"If Birkin were in charge, not a chance," Tim said. "He's good. They both are." Tim was talking about General Ivan Birkin and his cousin and second-in-command, Iakov Birkin. They'd had some expensive lessons last winter, but they'd both learned from them. Learned altogether too well. "But, of course, they aren't in charge. Who are the orders from?"

"Deputy Director-General Ivan Romanov."

It would be nice to say that Ivan Romanov was the epitome of the flaws in the Russian rank-by-family system that was so much the bane of the Russian army, but it wasn't really true. What he was was ambitious, and completely untrustworthy. He would—and had—betrayed the nation and family in search of his own profit and aggrandizement. It was apparent that Ivan Romanov thought he should have been czar, not his nephew. But he'd never been in a position to seize the crown. There had always been someone in the way.

Not anymore, apparently. With Sheremetev missing, Ivan was in effective control of Muscovite Russia. And apparently doing a good job of holding the boyars in check.

So there were Romanovs in charge in both parts of Russia now, and it could be that Russia was setting up for its own version of the War of the Roses. None of which told Tim what Ivan Romanov was planning.

Moscow Kremlin
September 5, 1637

Ivan Romanov thought he was probably going to be crowned czar of Russia sometime in the next few months, and that prospect was bringing him less joy than he had expected. His son Nikita was on the family estates and his idiot nephew was proving that he was less idiot and more cowardly than Ivan had realized. He was afraid of power, Mikhail was. And the damned up-timers had shown him a way to abandon the power of the czardom without having his head removed, so he'd jumped at it.

But Russia wasn't the sort of nation that could survive democracy. The Russian character was too strong. It needed a strong man to rein it in, or it would run wild. Democracy might work in Germany or that mythical America, but never in Russia. Ivan knew that and so had Sheremetev, but Sheremetev lacked something. Something essential to being a czar. He lacked legitimacy. That was why Ivan Romanov was probably going to be forced to take the crown by an increasingly desperate Boyar Duma.

Meanwhile, smuggling between Russia and the Sovereign States was constant. Copper, silver, and gold, as well as furs and, increasingly, beef and mutton were flowing into Russia from the Sovereign States, and iron, steam engine boilers, chemicals, generators, and all the things that were now being manufactured in Russia were flowing out east to the Sovereign States.

Which was actually *helping* the Russian economy. His minister of finance had shown him the numbers. Almost, Ivan would have been willing to let Mikhail have the Sovereign States for a few years until it collapsed from its inconsistencies and internal conflicts. Almost. But that couldn't happen. Every day the United Sovereign States of Russia existed, Russia got weaker. Politically, if not economically. Serfs and slaves were still running east, especially southeast, and the Cossacks were leaning more and more in Mikhail's direction. Without the Cossacks, Russia had much less protection against the Turks and Tatars.

He went to the cabinet and pulled out the map. The very secret map of the next campaign. It would go into effect as soon as the rivers froze solidly enough to take the steamboats out of service. The army investing Kazan would leave a blocking force, march north and east to Perm and take the city, then, using the Kama River as their road, they would march to Ufa and end this stupid war.

Tobolsk Kremlin
September 5, 1637

In a large log cabin pretending to be a castle, there was a room with log walls and a ceramic wood stove big enough to sleep on. The room had a table and kerosene lamps. In that room, Mikhail Borisovich Shein was looking at a map not dissimilar to the one Ivan Romanov was examining. It showed Perm and Solikamsk, Verkhoturye and Tobolsk, and Ufa. Little Ufa, which was now probably the second-largest city in Russia. It was bigger than Tobolsk by a wide margin, and Tobolsk was growing every day.

Ufa was the danger. Ufa and the United Sovereign States of Russia, not Muscovite Russia.

How did he do it? Shein wondered. He almost believed the nonsense about the up-timers enchanting Mikhail. Now, with the up-timer maps, there were more routes through the Ural Mountains than were known without them. Also, Ufa was sitting pretty much right on one of them, right on the Silk Road, which meant that just blocking the Babinov Road wouldn't keep the Sovereign States' army out of Siberia. Shein started the process of shifting more of his army south, away from the Babinov Road, to guard his southern border.

It was fall and the armies of Russia—all the Russias—were shifting in preparation for the winter campaign season.

CHAPTER 5

Kazakh

Ufa Kremlin
September 10, 1637

The war room in the Ufa Kremlin had electric lights and phones, but Bernie insisted it was still like something out of an old movie. It had a series of maps on pull-down rods so that they could go in moments from a map of all of Russia from Poland to northern China to a map of the entrenchments around Kazan. The map table was completed but at the moment didn't have a map on it. And everything was moving in advance of the October rains. Farmers and armies both needed to get things done now before the land turned into freezing mud.

After five days of carrying fuel to Alty-Kuduk, the *Princess Anna* was back on its main mission, which was to fly around high enough to be out of range of anything on the ground and take pictures. Pictures of troop movements, pictures of the Volga and the Kama rivers and the boats on them, pictures of the fortifications around Bor and Nizhny Novgorod.

Tim was back here in Ufa for the moment, with twenty thousand men, most of them *streltzi* or peasant volunteers designated Second Army. This was the relieving force for the state of Kazakh. They were forming up and marching out as soon as Tim got them organized to be trained on the march. Not that they were entirely untrained. There were a lot of *streltzi* and quite a few *deti boyar* officers. Many had served with him over the winter in Kazan.

And every man jack of the army had an AK4.7 with at least ten chambers, and a new pair of boots. In fact, each man had a complete outfit in green and tan camouflage patterns. The

55

green and tan was a compromise and the staff had almost gone with white. Had, for the great coats that each soldier had to go with their uniforms. The idea was that the green and tan would provide some concealment in summer, and in winter they'd be wearing the great coats anyway.

The factories of Kazan had been busy last winter and this summer, and not just the factories of Kazan. Murom was still turning out steam engines and plows and all sorts of things, and after the riots following Natasha's freeing of the serfs, they had rebuilt. Not that the Sovereign States got most of its output. Most of its output went to making the Sheremetev clan wealthier, but after a few months of Sheremetev administration, the city's loyalty had shifted back to the Gorchakov family and quite a lot of its production found its way to Kazan and Ufa. That wasn't only true of Murom. There were mica capacitors in most of the radios in their radio network and pretty much all of them came from the mica mines in northwest Russia. There was a great deal of wealth flowing into the Sovereign States from Muscovite Russia and a lot of the soldiers in the Second Army, who had never owned a new outfit in their lives before they joined the army, were now well clothed. Even more of them had never owned the good canvas boots that the army issued.

Morale, according to Tim, was at dangerously high levels.

Mikhail's morale wasn't nearly so high. With the news from Kazan about Birkin's secret orders and word from the radio network that Shein was shifting troops south away from Verkhoturye, it was starting to look like Uncle Ivan was planning a northern strategy and Shein was playing right into it. If Ivan Romanov could take Shein's Siberian state while the United Sovereign States of Russia was busy fighting the Zunghars in east Kazakh, then he might well be Czar Ivan Romanov of Northern Russia by spring of next year. Yet Mikhail had to defend Kazakh.

Mikhail walked over to the map of Kazakh and touched a spot on the map. Vladimir should be just about there.

In the air, over the Syr Darya River
September 10, 1637

The radio crackled. "Scout One to Big Mama."

Vlad grinned. "Cut it out, Brandy."

The radio in the Scout plane was loosely modeled on up-time

ham rigs, but only loosely. In spite of the need for it to fly, they'd focused on sturdy over lightweight. The darn thing weighed thirty pounds when you included the battery, which also powered some other instruments. The radio on the *Nicky* was even heavier, but it was also tunable and could be used to direction-find if there were two known radio sources on the ground. Which there weren't, this far from "civilization." They'd been flying by a combination of compass and landmarks for about three hours.

The Scout's airspeed was seventy-two MPH and they'd picked up a southwest head wind of about fifteen MPH. What that meant was the two planes weren't going exactly the way they were pointed at their proper cruising speed. In this case, to travel at 123 degrees southeast, they were actually on a heading of 112 degrees southeast and their ground speed was closer to sixty-eight MPH.

"The Scout's getting a bit hungry. We need to set down so Big Mama can feed her."

At this point, and pretty much all the way from the Aral Sea, the Syr Darya had been a broad winding river with plenty of room for the two planes to land.

Ariq Ogedei pointed to the southeast, a fairly straight section. And Vlad nodded. "Okay, hon. Follow us down and we'll feed the baby bird."

Ariq Ogedei was acting as navigator because he knew the terrain. Well, knew it from the ground. From the air was a whole different story. But they were using the complex workaround that had been worked out by the designers of the Jupiter series back in Amsterdam. And, by now, after several trips back and forth from Ufa to Alty-Kuduk and back to ferry fuel, Ariq had the routine down, and was doing a decent job of mapping their route. There were lists of landmarks and distances to tell future pilots where they were, as long as they were in the area where the *Nicky* had flown.

"Bringing engine speed down," Vlad announced before he decreased the thrust on the props gradually. That was to warn Vasilii of what was going on so that Vasilii could shift steam pressure to other systems as it was pulled from the steam turbines that were the *Nicky*'s four main engines. Right now, he fed the excess steam into the generator.

"Deploying skirt," Vlad continued and flipped the toggle that loosened the straps that pulled the air cushion skirt up tight against the *Nicky*'s short, broad lower wings. Then he started the fans that would force air into the skirts to expand them. Unlike an inflated tire, the *Nicky*'s skirts didn't have to actually hold pressure. They were designed to leak and were more about directing the airflow than containing it.

"Flaps at fifteen," Vlad continued as they neared the river. No one really needed to know that but him, but Vlad had been drilled and announced his actions on landing, takeoff, or maneuvers as a matter of course. He was also teaching Vasilii, Miroslava, and Ariq how to fly, which made stating his actions a part of teaching them what to do.

Vasilii was okay as a pilot, and Ariq was quite good, but Miroslava simply couldn't relax. Vlad liked the woman, but sometimes her condition made him uncomfortable. The thing about flying is there were times you had to be *on*—takeoff, landing, in-flight emergency—but most of the time it was just dull. Much duller than, say, driving a car. Especially in this time, when there generally were no other planes in the sky, or as now, just one that was flying with you. Miroslava was in emergency mode from sitting in the seat to exiting it and you couldn't fly that way, not for any extended period of time. You needed to be able to turn it down to a state of relaxed readiness and Miroslava wasn't relaxed at all.

They got down and switched Ariq and Yury to give Ariq stick time and Yury practice on the *Nicky* navigating. Ivan Maslov took the navigator's seat for the next leg.

Thirty minutes later, the Scout fueled and crews having had a break, they were back in the air. And five minutes after that they got a radio message that wasn't from Brandy. They had caught the khan.

"Salqam-Jangir Khan to aircraft. Come in. Over."

"That's Salqam-Jangir Khan's voice," Vasilii said.

"I recognized it," Vlad said.

"This is the *Nastas'ya Nikulichna* en route to Shavgar. Over."

"Can you land?" A short pause. "Over."

"Where are you?" Vladimir asked. "Or where are we relative to you, direction and distance? Over." Though the radios used different frequencies to transmit and receive, if both were transmitting at once you could get a feedback loop that would blow your ears off. So best practice was the old "over and out" system.

"You are south-southeast of us, and I'm not sure how far out. At least miles." Another pause. Vlad clicked the transmit button to remind the khan, then, "Over."

"Wait one. Will be talking with the Scout accompanying us and will call you back. Out."

"Brandy, you get all that? Over."

"I copied, Vlad. Slow left turn till we're pointing their direction. Over." And without waiting for Vlad to agree, the Scout banked into a left turn until it was pointing north-northwest. Vlad followed suit and they saw the troop of horsemen in the distance. The troop of horsemen didn't, at this distance, look all that different from a herd of horses. Or, for that matter, a herd of cattle. And the flight had flown over any number of those on their trip.

Just minutes later, they landed on a wide plain filled with scrub grass. The Scout scared the horses. Its engine was louder than all the props of the *Nicky*. It took a few minutes for the horses to be settled. Then Salqam-Jangir Khan examined the *Nicky*.

After inspecting the plane, Salqam-Jangir Khan wanted them to take him and twenty of his troops with them to Shavgar. "I know it will be crowded, but the men can stand."

"It's not the room. It's the weight, Salqam-Jangir Khan," Vasilii said before Vladimir had to, and Vladimir was reminded that Vasilii and Miroslava were both nobles of the state of Kazakh and knew Salqam-Jangir Khan better than Vlad did.

"Well, how many can you carry?"

"Considering the fuel and equipment we're taking, you and two others." That would make a total of seven on a plane that was designed for sixteen, including twelve passengers and four crew. But the *Nicky* was loaded down with extra fuel and a deaeration unit, so that they could deaerate river water to top up their water tanks as needed. The steam system leaked. Not a tremendous amount, but more than the design had allowed for. Enough so that they needed to add water after every flight.

"Very well. Togym, you and Aidar Karimov will come with me. On Vasilii's mythical airplane." The khan grinned at the older sultan. Aidar had proclaimed that there were no such thing as airplanes the last time he and Vasilii had spoken about it.

"Why is the bottom wing shaped like that?" Sultan Karimov asked in quite good, if accented, Russian. "I sort of understand the shape of the upper wing. It's a bit like a soaring eagle drawn by a child, but the lower wing is strange."

"This is copied from the design of the Model Five Jupiter," Vladimir told him. "The lower wing is essentially a flarecraft wing."

Which produced nothing but a look of incomprehension on the face of both sultans and the khan.

"I'm not an aircraft designer and Vasilii could probably explain it better, or at least more accurately. But, in effect, the upper wing is for flying and the lower wing is for landing." Vlad looked at Vasilii's expression and laughed. Because it was clear that Vasilii found his explanation lacking. "There was, up-time in the future that my wife came from, a kind of aircraft called a flarecraft, because it operated on something called the flare effect, which happens when a plane gets close to the ground. The flare effect allows a plane to use less energy to fly if it's very close to the ground." Vasilii was still looking at him like he was the slowest kid in math class, but Vladimir didn't care. "The flare effect lets a plane get more lift out of shorter wings and, in this case, that's expanded to give the air cushion more area."

"And why is it important that the air cushion have more area?"

"The more area, the less pressure you need. So the slower you can be going when you take off and land."

"Don't let him fool you, Salqam-Jangir Khan," Brandy said. "Vladimir is a technical semi-literate." She shrugged. "So am I, truth be told. But we're decent pilots, and Vladimir is quite a good spy."

"You admit he's here to spy on us?" Sultan Karimov demanded.

"No. As it happens, I'm mostly here to spy *for* you," Vladimir said. "And to help with that, we have with us Yury Arsenyev and Ariq Ogedei. For military advice, we have Brigadier General Ivan Maslov." He waved at the young redheaded man with the short red goatee. "Between us and the planes, we will be trying to locate the Zunghar forces for you and help you get in position to mousetrap them." Then Vlad had to explain mousetraps, which Salqam-Jangir Khan agreed might be of great use in cities.

Finally, they got the khan and the two sultans onto the plane and up in the air. At which point Sultan Karimov discovered that he loved to fly. Togym agreed that it was an interesting view out the windows and certainly faster than the fastest horse, but was otherwise not that impressed. The khan, too, could take it or leave it.

For most of the rest of the flight, Togym, Ivan, and the khan were discussing the military situation and the use of maps with movable tokens on them in keeping track of military situations. Now all they had to do was land safely.

Shavgar, outside the walls
September 10, 1637

As the *Nicky* and the Scout circled the city before landing, Brandy saw that it was walled and about the size of Magdeburg's Altstadt and Neustadt combined, i.e., quite a bit smaller than Greater Magdeburg. And on either side of it up- and downriver there were large rich green and brown fields.

After a circle around the city, Vlad radioed and told her to follow him down. Then he landed on the river and taxied up onto the bank of the Syr Darya, just downriver of the city wall. Brandy waited until the *Nicky* was down, then followed and pulled up next to the larger plane.

As she cut her engines, Salqam-Jangir Khan was stepping out onto the lower wing of the *Nicky* and waving at the crowd that had gathered. He called some names, and men in dress that was more Arabic than Kazakh came forward. Their clothing was more cotton than wool, with little fur.

But they came equipped with swords and armor. With a few quick phrases, Salqam-Jangir Khan put guards around the two planes. They had outrun their fuel. It was still on the river, though it had left before they had. They weren't empty, but they didn't have enough gasoline to send the Scout home. Brandy and Yury climbed from the Scout and went over to the *Nicky*, where they were blocked by the city guards until Salqam-Jangir Khan spoke again, at which point they were let through.

Then, in a combination of Kazakh and Arabic, Salqam-Jangir Khan made a speech. He talked about the constitutional convention, his agreement for Kazakh to become a state in the United Sovereign States of Russia, the rights of citizens, even slaves, to vote and be equal before the law. And especially he talked about Brandy Bates, now Brandy Bates Gorchakov, who was an actual up-timer, a woman who along with her fellows in the town of Grantville had been moved from the future and the other side of the world to central Germany. Final incontestable proof that the Ring of Fire had happened.

The response was subdued. Brandy was getting many less than friendly looks from parts of the crowd. The crowd was mostly, but not entirely, male. The western Kazakhs that she'd met before now were different than this crowd. The women among the herders were out and about with the men, but this was a city, and a Muslim city. While there were some women in the crowd, it was mostly men. And a number of them didn't much care for Brandy Bates up-timer, that was for sure.

Erzhan watched the people come out of the plane and he was furious. Erzhan was not a fool to believe in djinn or fabled folk from the future, and he'd said so, and continued to say so even as the evidence of strange things in the west mounted. Yes, he had his doubts as word of the so-called up-timer Bernie Zeppi and his miracles in Moscow grew. He was sure that at least most of the tales had to be spread by charlatans using the legends to sell snake oil to the unwary.

They had to be.

There was no Ring of Fire, so there couldn't be up-timers and people couldn't fly. The stories of flying whales and the like, were nothing but tales told by the gullible, repeating and expanding on what others told them. He'd been telling people that for years.

And now, right out there in the field next to the town, were two airplanes. They weren't the flying whales that the legend talked about, but they had flown in, landed on the river, and then moved onto the field.

That had brought the whole town out to see. Then the khan had gotten out, and, standing on the platform that was part of the plane, he made a speech harping on this woman who was supposedly an actual up-timer.

"No one can doubt now."

Erzhan snorted. He could doubt now. Erzhan wasn't a rural bumpkin herding his cattle between grazing lands. He was a wealthy landowner who grew cotton, wheat, and rye. And his enterprises used quite a lot of slaves. Unlike others, he wasn't one to run off to the hinterlands because the boy khan believed

Russian liars about a new kind of musket. And now here was the boy khan stepping out of a flying machine before the whole city and insisting that this proved that the Ring of Fire happened.

Well, it didn't.

It was just a trick that someone had come up with in the west. They probably stole it from China. That was where the west got most of its innovations. Gunpowder, clocks, who knows what. In fact, now that he thought about it, there had been some Chinese scholar who had made himself some wings and jumped off a building. He died, but a bit of practice, and who knows? But it was just a trick, not proof that Allah had actually transported a town full of Christian heretics from the future.

If Allah were to do such a thing, it would be a Muslim town, not Christian.

After the speech, they were taken into the town and given rooms in the khan's palace. Brandy and Miroslava, but not Vlad and Vasilii, were introduced to the khan's wives, Damira, Evnika, and Lunara, and son Bahadur. Bahadur was a cute two-year-old. Damira was senior and about five years older than the khan. Evnika was insistent that she learn to fly, and Lunara wanted to know how paper money worked and how it could be introduced into Kazakh.

The harem wasn't a cage. At least, Damira, Evnika, and Lunara didn't see it as such. They saw it as a protection against the dangers of the outside world. And Brandy had to acknowledge that those dangers did exist. But the price was too high. She preferred the option of facing those dangers on her own.

Shavgar market
September 11, 1637

The capital of the state of Kazakh was a city. Brandy had noticed it yesterday, flying over the place. It was even more evident now, as she, Damira, and a small army of guards wandered the market stalls. This was a new thing for Damira. Based on what he'd seen in Ufa and on the practices of the herder Kazakhs, Salqam-Jangir Khan was leading by example, and with appropriate guards was allowing his wives to leave the harem. Damira had, as senior wife, insisted that she be first.

"Timur the Lame," Damira explained, "rebuilt Shavgar as one of his northern outposts of 'civilization.'"

They were on a paved plaza with a stone-lined pool in the center. The pool was kept filled by slaves with buckets and, in turn, emptied by other slaves with buckets who took the water to homes and stalls, and used it for washing or making tea. Alcohol wasn't completely unavailable in Shavgar, but it wasn't as common here as it was among the more tribal Kazakhs to the north and west. The new state of Kazakh was large and diverse. Much more diverse than Brandy had imagined.

Damira pointed out the ornate tomb of an Islamic scholar from a century ago and some madrasas, and Brandy noted that much of the construction of the city was stone, including a fair amount of marble.

From the flight in yesterday, Brandy knew that the city was surrounded not by open plains holding cattle herds, but by farmland growing rice and wheat and an amount of cotton, as well as other crops. And this city had slavery, out-and-out slavery, and a lot of it.

Kazakh was huge. And it wasn't all one sort of place. Yes, it had the herders who traveled with herds from grazing land to grazing land, where the women were often riding the herds right along with the men, but it also had this place and the surrounding farms which were, when it came right down to it, plantations not that different from the ones in the antebellum south. And Brandy realized that the same thing was almost certainly true back up-time in places like Texas and California, part one thing and part something else. She snorted a laugh, realizing that the same thing was true in Virginia at the time of the Civil War, or there wouldn't be a West Virginia.

The market square they were visiting was full of shops and the shops full of craftsmen and women.

That morning early, the muezzin had called the faithful to prayer. And it was clear from the looks she was getting that the arrival of the *Nicky* and the Scout had hit the town like an earthquake.

"In spite of the innovations that had seeped through to us," Damira explained, "and in spite of the Jahangir making the deal with your Czar Mikhail, about two thirds of the people of Shavgar don't believe the Ring of Fire actually happened. At least they didn't before yesterday. Before yesterday, I was one of the ones that didn't believe.

"It was a legend, a tale of far-off lands to fool the gullible. 'Allah wouldn't do such a thing, and he certainly wouldn't do it in Christian lands' is the opinion of most of the scholars and religious leaders in Shavgar."

"They don't seem happy to see us," Brandy noted as someone made a warding gesture at her. Word that Brandy was an actual up-timer was out and in spite of the airplanes, a fair percentage of the mullahs were insisting that the Ring of Fire was a lie, and Brandy was a fraud.

"They're embarrassed," Damira said. "And they're too stubborn to admit they're wrong. Some never will and will insist that you are a liar until their last breath."

"Will they believe our reports on the placement of enemy forces?" Brandy asked.

"Jangir will, and that's what matters," Damira reassured her. Damira liked the khan in a sort of big-sisterly way. She was older than him and remembered his early fumbling, but was very proud of what he had accomplished. Especially now. Jangir's son was her child, and would be khan after him, not replaced by the son of one of his other wives when they had them. That took a lot of the pressure off her, and made her position a lot safer.

There were silks from China in the marketplace. Shavgar was actually a stop on the Silk Road, and the road hadn't closed when Henry the Navigator had passed the Cape of Good Hope. It was still operational, even if by now it had shrunk to a back road of commerce.

"Tell me about the railroad," Damira demanded.

Brandy tried. They talked about the route and the use of the river and the steam-powered riverboats. And while they talked, the guards and people listened. And the notion that Shavgar might again be a stop on the restored Silk Road flowed out from their conversation to the town.

While Brandy and Damira were spreading the word about the economic boom that was about to happen, Jangir, Vladimir and Ivan Maslov were discussing the military disaster that had already started.

"Grantville didn't have a complete history. The Zunghar weren't even mentioned, not in the 1911 Britannica or any of the others. At least, I didn't find them. Who are they?" Vladimir asked.

"They are four tribes who have joined together under Khara Khula, who died three years ago. His son, Erdeni Batur, took over, but at first his rulership was weak. He wasn't his father. Like me, he's young. He needs victories to prove to the other tribal leaders that he can lead them to greatness. We are all descendants of the Mongol Horde of Genghis Khan, and several of the Zunghar tribes are led by literal descendants of Genghis Khan." Salqam-Jangir Khan laughed. "Martial tradition doesn't cover it. Half the tribal leaders believe that they are the natural heirs to Genghis Khan, and Erdeni Batur isn't an heir to Genghis Khan, at least not on the right side of the blanket. But that doesn't make him weaker, not exactly. It makes his rule more fragile, but what will shatter it is a lack of victories more than defeat. Even Genghis Khan lost battles."

"I know he lost the Battle of Samara Bend to our Bulgarian ancestors," Ivan Maslov agreed. "But he still took Bulgaria and Russia. That's something he had in common with Tim. He understood that a battle is just a battle, not the war."

"I thought your General Tim never lost." Togym grinned.

"Most of Russia thought Tim had 'lost' while Birkin had Kazan invested last year," Ivan said. "But we all saw how that turned out."

"So Erdeni Batur can afford tactical losses, but what he can't afford is to be seen as too cautious," Vladimir said. "Do you think that's why he hit Almaliq?"

"No. He hit Almaliq because it's a rich prize with a lot of loot and it puts him in place to take Almaty, which is a stop on the Silk Road, and which the railroad would make much more valuable than it is right now. I don't think Erdeni Batur knows what he'd have if he took and held Almaty, but he'd learn about it."

The khan, using his finger, drew a line on a map that went from central China to the Aral Sea. It passed through Almaliq and Shavgar. "The amount of wealth that will fall off the steamboats on that route will be phenomenal. Not soon, but we could, with the trains, steamboats, and airplanes, compete with the trade around the Cape of Good Hope.

"We have to protect Almaliq," the khan finished, looking at Ivan. "Have to!"

CHAPTER 6

Getting Steam Up

Ufa Kremlin
September 14, 1637

It was midafternoon, but you couldn't tell that from where they were. They were in the war room where the lights were artificial and constant. The map table depicted the state of Kazakh and the territory northward to Ufa. It bore little markers showing the estimated positions of riverboats, trains, and military units. A clerk came in and handed Czar Mikhail a radio message.

> AIRCRAFT AT SHAVGAR WITH SALQAM-JANGIR KHAN.

"He must have made excellent time," Czar Mikhail said, speaking of the khan, and not realizing that he'd been picked up by the plane en route. He passed the note to General Boris Timofeyevich Lebedev, who nodded and handed the note to a clerk. The clerk took a small wooden square with a crown on it and moved it to the Kazakh capital. The little squares representing the two aircraft were already there, but reversed to indicate an unconfirmed estimate. They were flipped right side up.

General Tim said, "Well, they've got Ivan there with them. I just hope they listen."

"You have a lot of faith in General Maslov." Czar Mikhail's voice made it almost a question.

"Ivan has his weaknesses, but he's the best tactical thinker I know, and the second-best strategic thinker."

"Who's the best? Strategic thinker, I mean."

"You are, Your Majesty."

Czar Mikhail looked at him for a shocked moment. That was the sort of thing he was used to hearing from toadies, not from Boris Timofeyevich Lebedev. For a moment, he was furious that Tim would turn toady on him, but then slowly, he realized that Tim actually meant it. He changed the subject. "You think the planes are still there?"

"Probably. They will have to wait for the fuel. And the fuel will have to wait for the steam engine to be installed." There were already riverboats on the Shar Dia River, but the steam engines were made in Ufa, Kazan, and parts in Muscovite Russia. They'd been shipped by train, but even though they were now at the Aral Sea, they hadn't, at last report, been installed on the riverboat.

Mikhail looked at the map table and considered. That was probably happening right about now.

Alty-Kuduk
September 14, 1637

Fedot Vitsin pulled the pipe wrench, and the nut tightened. Fedot was a big, well-muscled man and working down here in the engine compartment of the *Aya*, he wasn't wearing a shirt, displaying the fact that he would rival your average bear for fur. His hair was matted and soaking at the moment, because the nut he was tightening was on the main steam feed pipe and until he got it tightened, steam was leaking into the dark, hot hell that was the engine room of a steamboat.

Fedot grunted with satisfaction and crawled out from under the boiler. "Okay, Aybek. Tell them we're going to test them again."

Aybek grinned, stuck his head out the hatch and yelled, "Engine test!"

Fedot shoved the lever and the cylinder rods started to move. He engaged the prop and slowly, carefully, moved his hand over the pipe fitting where the nut had been loose. If there was a leak under stress, he'd feel it.

Nothing.

And the steamboat was pulling against the dock like it was trying to pull it down.

Aybek called down. "Skipper wants to take us out around the bay. Disengage the prop so they can unmoor."

Fedot pulled the lever back to neutral, and the boat, now a steamboat, stopped shaking.

A couple of minutes passed, then Aybek yelled down, "Skipper says all ahead slow."

Fedot adjusted the steam to the engine to slow, then reengaged the prop. This boat only had one prop, so the "all ahead" was just silly. You were only supposed to use that when you had two props.

The *Aya* pulled away from the dock at Alty-Kuduk and steamed out into the bay. And Fedot thought about how his life had changed since his first steam engine almost four years ago. God, what a horror that monster had been. It had had a pot boiler that was literally an iron pot and a steam engine made of wood by the village barrel maker. Then he looked at his present engine and wanted to kiss it. Would have, if it wasn't hot as a demon from hell. It was a tube boiler with a proper firebox, with steel piping to precision-cut cylinders. It was a thing of beauty and it was all his, now that he'd worked his way up to chief engineer on the *Aya*. It was also efficient in its use of fuel. Efficient and flexible. It could use oil or coal, charcoal, or even wood.

The skipper stuck his head in the hatch. "How confident are you that that monstrosity of yours will keep working?"

"If anything goes wrong, I can fix it," Fedot half shouted. The engine room wasn't quiet.

"Come up here, you crazy Russian," the skipper more than half shouted.

Fedot waved Aybek over and told him what to do. Aybek nodded. It wasn't new. They'd been going over what to do since Fedot had arrived two weeks ago. Then Fedot went up onto the deck of the riverboat. The boat was wide and flat bottomed. At the moment it had twenty-two barrels tied down on it, so there were walking paths, but that was it.

"The khan wants the oil in Shavgar as soon as possible. When can we go?"

Fedot shrugged massive shoulders. "Now, Skipper. Like I said, anything goes wrong, I can fix it, and mostly nothing's going to go wrong. The cylinders were cut in Murom. Ain't none better, not even from Grantville itself." Fedot had never been to Grantville. He'd never even seen anything made in Grantville, but Murom had an excellent reputation for top-flight precision steel work. At least, it did in Russia.

The skipper nodded and shrugged his much smaller shoulders, then turned to the pilot and said, "Make for the Shar Dia River."

Alty-Kuduk wasn't on the Shar Dia. It was located in a bay at the very top of the Aral Sea. While the Shar Dia entered the Aral Sea on the upper east side, it was a hundred and twenty miles along the coast of the Aral Sea before they would get to the Shar Dia, and after that another three hundred miles to Shavgar.

On the other hand, at full steam the riverboat did about ten knots per hour. At two hundred and forty knots per day, they would reach Shavgar in two to three days, even going up the slow-moving river.

Tsaritsyn, on the Volga
September 14, 1637

In their stateroom on the *Ilya M.*, Bernie read over reports while sipping Turkish coffee.

After several days in Samara accomplishing very little beyond getting to know the situation, Bernie and Natasha had proceeded to Tsaritsyn, where they were accomplishing about the same nothing. Still, getting to know the situation had its own value. Colonel Ivan Greshnev was an older man whose clothing was tightening as his waist expanded. He was of good family but not overly competent, which was why he was posted here in what until recently was something of a backwater.

That wasn't how Colonel Greshnev saw it. To his way of thinking, he'd been mistreated by fate and Russian politics. He'd supported Ivan Romanov's bid for the crown as a young man, and his career had never recovered. He'd mentioned the fact several times since they'd arrived.

The situation in Tsaritsyn was complicated by how near it was to the Don River. Kalach, a settlement on the Don River, was only about fifty miles away as the crow flew, but closer to a hundred by a combination of river and trails that was the present route. Boats were actually portaged from a tributary of the Don to the Volga and back. Whole boats, not just their content. A rail line, especially one that was designed to take boats, could connect the Don to the Volga and allow much more efficient trade with the Ottomans and the Mediterranean states. The town was actually run by a group of wealthy *streltzi* who were making a fortune out of the cross-river trade between the Don and the Volga. That group was headed by Ignat Vitsin.

There was a knock at the door and Natasha opened it. It was Radomir Ivanovich Greshnev, the son of Colonel Greshnev, and at least nominally in charge of the Tsaritsyn militia.

"Good afternoon, Radomir," Natasha said with a lifted eyebrow. "What brings you to the docks?"

"The Cossacks!" he blurted. "You have to do something about the Cossacks." The population of Tsaritsyn had increased, but not as much as Samara and not quite the same way. A lot of Don Cossacks had migrated east as the news of the constitutional convention reached them. They now represented an armed minority of the population of the city and surrounding countryside, and were making the local government quite nervous.

"Really? I *must*?" Princess Natalia Petrovna Gorchakov asked. Radomir's family had some rank, but not nearly as much as Natasha. Especially now, having served in the constitutional congress. There weren't a lot of people in Russia who could compel Natasha to do anything. Bernie knew that because he wasn't one of them.

Radomir turned red under his tan. "They want to make Tsaritsyn part of the Don State." The Don State was the notional state that covered the Don River, or at least a good chunk of it. And, as Bernie heard the demand, he was mostly impressed by Vladislav Golovin's astuteness. Golovin was the leader of the Don Cossacks in Tsaritsyn, and he wasn't fond of the borders that Tsaritsyn's council were insisting on, since they included that bit of the Don River that was closest to the Volga. The Don Cossacks were looking at their main trade corridor being in another state. And while states weren't supposed to be able to tax interstate trade, that didn't necessarily mean that none of them were going to come up with ways to charge people fees that weren't quite legally taxes.

As of this moment neither the Don Cossacks nor the government of Tsaritsyn had ratified the United Sovereign States of Russia's constitution. And both sides were trying to get the federal government to come down on their side without actually ratifying the constitution.

"That's an interesting proposal," Natasha offered. "Bernie, do you think that the Don Cossacks would ratify if we gave them Tsaritsyn?"

"They might, but I'm not sure that would be a great idea. I mean, the Don State is pretty big as it stands. If we give them this section of the Volga too, they might get arrogant."

"I assure you, Gospodin Bernard," Radomir insisted stiffly, "this is no laughing matter."

"No more than your insistence that part of the Don River should be in your state," Bernie agreed. "And worse, as the federal government sees it, insisting on that grant of territory you don't actually control without ratifying the constitution."

"Are you going to let the Cossacks loot Russians?"

"Are you a part of the United Sovereign States of Russia?"

"Perhaps we should see what Moscow is offering."

"Perhaps," Bernie agreed. "I know. Why don't you send an emissary up the Don River, then across to Moscow? I'm sure the Don Cossacks will give him safe passage. Then you can talk to Sheremetev. No, he's missing. I guess you can ask Mikhail's uncle, Ivan. I'm sure he'll give you the Don's lands. After all, he has no need for troops." Bernie's voice had started out whimsical, but it was hard by the time he finished. "Look, Radomir, the function of the federal government is to keep all the states safe, not just yours. Yes, the portage between the Don and the Volga is vital to Russia. But you, in fact, only hold one end of it. It's not *that* vital, and when we take Moscow back, it will become less vital. Also, as the railroads come, it will become still less vital. It may seem to you and your father that you have Czar Mikhail over a barrel, but it only seems that way."

"For which you should be grateful," Natasha chimed in. "Mikhail doesn't care for being coerced. He's had enough of that. If there was no way around you, we wouldn't be talking. We'd be shelling." The *Ilya M.* had steel breech-loading cannon, and the river here made a smooth, flat gun platform. They probably couldn't knock down the walls of Hamburg, but Tsaritsyn's walls were wood and quite thin.

Radomir bowed stiffly and departed.

"We'd better go have a talk with Golovin," Bernie said.

"Yes, and radio Czar Mikhail about this development. Then I think we should proceed to Astrakhan to complete our survey."

"Do you think that will help?"

"It might, if the government of Astrakhan is reasonable. We will be in a much better bargaining position if they decide to ratify. It's good that we have the *Ilya M.*'s guns, but it will be better if we don't have to use them."

"We can hope," Bernie agreed, but he didn't sound all that hopeful.

Ufa Kremlin
September 15, 1637

Czar Mikhail looked at the thing on his desk. It was eight inches tall and if it glowed no one could see it because the casing of the tube was ceramic-coated steel and it was made right here in Ufa. A great deal about how to make radio tubes had been learned in Grantville and Magdeburg in the last six years. A lot of the blanks had been filled in and the tools to build the tube had been produced, tried, failed, and new ones produced. And at least one of the companies that was doing that learning was partially owned by Vladimir Gorchakov. So when he'd arrived here last winter, he'd brought with him not just tubes, but the tools to make more. And here before Mikhail was the "more." At least the first of them. "And how many can you produce?" he asked, looking up at the Dacha-trained *streltzi* electrical engineer.

"We don't know yet. We can scale up, but it depends on how many we can have on the assembly line. The biggest bottleneck is still the vacuum and waiting a week after the tubes have been sucked down to vacuum for the oxygen caught in the walls of the tube to be released. And the more tubes you hook up, the more likely you are to have a leak. It's going to be a balancing act and we're going to have problems. We just don't know how many."

Czar Mikhail nodded at the man. "Do your best. We need radio stations to tie the United Sovereign States of Russia together. And I don't want to be dependent on the USE for them."

New Ruzuka
September 15, 1637

The New Ruzuka farms were being harvested and facilitating that was a horse-drawn harvester. And as Vera Andreevich looked out over the fields, she saw a lot of well-fed children following the harvester picking up what it missed. There was a new priest in New Ruzuka who didn't share Father Julian's views. He was an older man, happily married, and though literate, he wasn't the self-educated scholar that Julian had been. So New Ruzuka was looking to hire a new school teacher.

All of which made New Ruzuka not that different from the rest of her district. Mostly farmers, mostly very loyal to the czar, but also mostly about full up on change for now. She was finding being a congressperson a bit of a challenge. "Do you object to the reaper, Father Grigori?"

"No, of course not. But that is not the same as women and children voting. They lack the maturity to understand the issues." He looked her in the eye. "Women inherently because of their sex, and children because of their lack of experience. It's God's will that the man should lead and the woman follow."

"So you would have New Ruzuka have fewer voters and fewer votes in the House of Representatives?"

"If need be, to have better ones."

He wasn't backing down an inch and it wasn't just him. A lot of the women in New Ruzuka were not going to vote in the upcoming election because they accepted their role as "lesser vessels."

What amazed Vera was how many of the women of New Ruzuka and the other villages in District Two agreed with him. Enough of them so that if an even slightly viable male candidate showed up, she was likely to lose her seat. The good news was that while there were locally viable male candidates, most of them were not known outside their individual villages. This was why she was making this trip. She was introducing herself to the people of her district. All they knew of her so far was that she'd been in the constitutional convention and that her husband Stefan had killed a man with a single blow of his fist and managed to get made a member of the lower nobility out of it. What she needed was a way to change the discussion. Vera started to smile.

That evening as the sun was getting low and the people gathered round in the town square, Vera climbed to the small impromptu stage, shoved her fist into the air, then she looked at it and sighed loudly. "This sure isn't going to kill anyone with a single blow," she said, and the villagers laughed. She looked out at them, some of whom she knew and many of whom she didn't

"The truth is Stefan wasn't trying to kill the man either. I know. He told me about it, had nightmares about it, if you want to know the truth. He was defending Ufa because someone had to and he was there. Also because, in spite of what he thinks, my husband is a natural leader. He knows what needs to be done and when he sets about to do it other men follow him.

"I know that Father Grigori here would be happier if Stefan was running for the second district seat in the congress instead of his wife. Because Stefan is a leader and we need leaders."

There was considerable applause for that view.

"But, with all due respect for Father Grigori, that's not what congress is for. I know. I was in the constitutional congress. In fact, that's where I was when Stefan was defending Irina Way against the Kazakhs. The Kazakhs who are now on our side because Czar Mikhail knew when to fight and when to deal. And that's what you do in congress. You don't lead, you bargain, like wives on market day.

"Now some of you know my husband." Vera grinned at some of the people who were from old Ruzuka. "A good blacksmith, a generous man but one who doesn't bargain. Never in his life has Stefan used two words when he could get away with one. You know what Stefan does when someone comes into the foundry to bargain for a load of chambers or a tube boiler?"

She looked around and saw grins on the faces of some of the men and a lot of the women. They remembered from back in old Ruzuka, from the road, even from the last fall before they set up the foundry in Ufa.

"He sends them to Izabella Utkin and lets her bargain. Just like back in old Ruzuka, he had me do the bargaining. Not because he was lazy. He's not. Or even because he didn't like bargaining. He doesn't. But that's never stopped him from doing something. It's because, for all his other good traits, Stefan is not a good bargainer.

"So, as much as I love and respect my husband, he shouldn't be in the congress. What you need in the congress is someone who knows when to stand firm and when to compromise. It doesn't get you the best laws maybe, but it gets you the laws that everyone can live with, so we don't have to worry about the Kazakhs attacking, or the nobles from the northern states. You don't need a leader in congress. You need a bargainer."

She sat down and Father Grigori was glaring thunderclouds at her. He knew she was right. He wasn't stupid. But in spite of everything, he didn't want her to be right.

The next morning, Vera and a couple of aides got on their horses and headed north to the next village. Over the next few weeks, she refined the speech, polished it until it shone like a gold coin.

New Ruzuka Foundry, Ufa
September 16, 1637

Stefan missed Vera, but other than that he was content. The explosion at the chemical plant had produced an odd result. At least it was odd to Stefan. As of now, Stefan's designs for fireboxes were considered the best in Ufa. Well, they were. But why people would think they were because of the blast was beyond Stefan. The thing hadn't even been in use when the blast and the fire happened. If it had been, they couldn't have used it.

That didn't appear to matter. Over the last two months, they'd received orders for ten more of the things. And Izabella had gotten really high prices for them. The New Ruzuka Foundry & Machine Shop was a going concern, with more business than it could handle.

There were a lot of new projects and they were all interesting and challenging. And they were a lot of work. The sort of work that gave a man like Stefan a deep satisfaction. The steam whistle blew, which was the signal for the end of the first shift, and Stefan looked up from the clay model he was working on, and checked the clock to see that it was indeed six in the evening. He looked back at the model and considered putting in another hour, but no. With Vera out of town, the children would expect him. They were both in the Dacha school now. Pavel was nine and Luiza eleven. Their aunt, Nadia, looked after them most of the time, and now there were servants in the house, but they wanted and deserved to see at least one of their parents most days.

Besides, Luiza was taking the junior engineering courses at the Dacha and she usually had interesting homework.

Today's homework was interesting. Luiza's class was learning about tube design and vacuums. Pavel at nine was taking reading and writing and rhetoric, standard fare for the son of a member of the lower nobility, at least in this part of Russia. But at nine, Pavel was mostly interested in the war games, and General Tim. In all honesty, while Stefan tried to listen, he was more interested in the triode tubes that would be used to amplify a tuned signal for broadcast.

After homework, they had dinner. It was fish from the Caspian Sea, shipped up the Volga in refrigerated steamboats. And expensive. But Nadia insisted that as members of the lower nobility, they had standards to maintain and they could afford it.

They listened to the new broadcast on their crystal set, which required that they all be quiet, because it wasn't loud even with the horn.

It was still strange to Stefan how they had become a prominent family with friends of great rank. He thought about Bernie and Natasha and wondered where they were now.

CHAPTER 7

𝔗𝔥𝔢 ℭ𝔞𝔰𝔭𝔦𝔞𝔫 𝔖𝔢𝔞

Astrakhan, mouth of the Volga River
September 17, 1637

Bernie looked out on still waters. The Volga, at this point, was as wide as a lake, but they were still some distance from the Caspian Sea. And here they'd been welcomed with much more joy than concern. For one because, with freedom of religion as part of the United States of Russia constitution, the Muslims were confident of their ability to make pilgrimages that their religion demanded of them; but also because the gunboat represented proof that Czar Mikhail wasn't leaving the city to the Ottoman Turks.

This was a more cosmopolitan city than any in the United Sovereign States of Russia, more than Ufa, Kazan, even more than Moscow. Here the Volga trade reached the Caspian Sea, where the Safavid Empire, Russia, and the Kazakhs all met and traded with one another. There were even merchants from China and India here. So the *Ilya M.* was considered more a demonstration that the United Sovereign States of Russia really was developing into a powerful industrial nation than a threat.

The only concern that the city, soon to be state of Astrakhan, had about ratifying the constitution was the duties that the federal government was going to impose on the Caspian Sea trade.

The city council was negotiating for all it was worth, but ratification was assured.

"Mister Zeppi..." The voice had a Chinese accent and it went with the face of the Chinese merchant who had moved here ten years ago, before the Ring of Fire had happened.

78

Bernie turned. "Yes, Wong?" Chao Wong was a short, chubby man in silk.

"I wanted to try again to persuade you to take this lovely ship on a trip around the Caspian Sea." He held up a hand. "Yes, I know the decision will be made by Czar Mikhail. But he listens to you. It's well known."

"Very well. Explain to me why, when we need to return upriver to persuade the other Volga states to ratify, we should take this lovely persuader on a pleasure cruise around the Caspian Sea to visit countries which are not now and are not likely to become Russian states."

"Trade. Such a trip would accomplish two things. First, it would act as a reminder to the Ottomans and the Safavids that Russia has the means to defend the city. And, second, it will show the whole Caspian Sea that Russia can provide them with the tools they need to build their own steamships and factories. A source that is not the USE. A source which includes Muslim states, so will respect Islamic tradition and law. A source of safe and morally acceptable change." Chao Wong was a Buddhist, not a Muslim, but he'd been dealing with Muslims for his whole career, and knew their wants and concerns. And most of the coast of the Caspian Sea was Muslim.

"I am particularly concerned that Grand Vizier Saru Taqi be made acquainted with Russian technology. He has a great interest in building and technology."

Bernie turned back to look at the Caspian Sea. The waters were still here, but in spite of the fact that it was less salty than the Mediterranean, it was a sea. Smaller than the Mediterranean, but bigger than all the Great Lakes combined. It wouldn't be like trying to cross the Atlantic in a riverboat, but a storm on the Caspian could sink the Ilya M. And that wasn't the only danger. Bernie considered the Kalmyk Khanate.

The Kalmyk were much like the Kazakhs in that they were herders, but they hadn't yet signed on with the United Sovereign States of Russia and it wasn't beyond the realm of possibility that the local sultan would decide to prove his strength by taking the steam-powered gunboat. It was unlikely that such an attack would succeed, but Natasha was on the boat and he didn't like the idea of her being in the line of fire.

Not that he was ever going to admit that out loud. Natasha wouldn't appreciate it.

Then there was the Safavid Empire. It was a big, powerful state, even if Murad had taken Baghdad away from them a couple of years ago. He'd also taken Vienna away from the Austro-Hungarian empire just about as easily. And Grand Vizier Saru Taqi was indeed interested in building and new tech. But the guy was, according to the Embassy Bureau, also crooked as a dog's hind leg and not averse to stealing what he wanted.

Bernie turned back to Chao Wong. "Not this trip, sir. You're no doubt right about the need for such a mission, but if we're going to do it, we should do it with a half a dozen gunboats and a thousand troops carrying AK4.7s, not the hundred we have with us. What we need, sir, right now is to stabilize our control over the Volga and Don rivers. For that, we need to be ratified by Tsaritsyn. And, for that, we need to be ratified by you folks here in Astrakhan. Once that's done, we can revisit the idea of diplomatic missions to truly foreign powers."

"I was afraid you'd say that," Chao Wong said. "May I have the use of the radio?"

"Going over my head, sir?" Bernie grinned, but authorized him to use the gunboat's radio. It was a big one with a directional antenna.

Ufa Kremlin
September 17, 1637

Czar Mikhail and Evdokia were in his private office having tea when the radio message from Astrakhan arrived.

Mikhail read it, then passed it over to his wife. Evdokia read it, grinned, and said, "Bernie's worried about Natasha."

"What? Where do you get that?"

"Think, husband. If it were just Bernie, would he be telling you that we should wait? Or would he be raring to go? And don't you doubt for one minute that Natasha won't realize it."

"I think it's a perfectly reasonable position," Mikhail said.

"Yes, dear. I know you do, and you're right. But you're a czar, not a former football jock. Trust me. If Natasha wasn't in the boat, Bernie would be all for trying to sack the quarterback."

"And that's what worries me about the mission that this Chao Wong wants. Safi is going to be worried that we're getting ready to incorporate Iran as another state."

The Safavid Empire's official name was Iran. Its borders weren't all that different from the borders of Iran in the atlases from Grantville. They extended from the Caspian Sea to the Persian Gulf.

"Safi is too busy with his booze, drugs, and women to notice. What you're worried about is Grand Vizier Saru Taqi. There hasn't been a more conniving eunuch since Narses."

"Who?" Mikhail wasn't nearly the student of history that his wife was. It was the influence of Natasha and Brandy Bates.

"He was one of Justinian the Great's generals and, according to Procopius, a conniver second to none."

"All right, if you say so. But he can't have been as much of a conniver as Saru Taqi. The only reason that Safi is still alive is that he spends his time drunk, stoned, or getting laid, and leaves governing to Saru Taqi. And Saru Taqi is going to see Bernie and the *Ilya Muromets* as a threat to his power. I don't need a war with the Safavid Empire."

"You won't get one, not with Murad to their west. I'd be more concerned about Saru Taqi deciding that he can take the *Ilya Muromets* and apologize for it later. So what we should do is make the expedition too big for that."

"How big?"

Ufa, as it happened, wasn't short of riverboats. Over the past four years, and especially over the last two, river traffic had become steam powered on the Volga, and to an equal extent on the Don River. The change had started slowly, but had been growing exponentially as the presence of steamboats had demonstrated their utility.

Any riverboat owner who had the money converted their boat to steam. The rest just wanted to. Of course, many didn't have the money, but having to compete with steamboats was putting them out of business, and their boats were being bought up by those who did have the money to convert them to steam. And in the last few months more and more of the steam riverboats had switched their allegiance to Mikhail as life around Muscovy got scarier and scarier.

"We have a couple of months before the Volga starts to freeze, but wouldn't it be nice to have all those riverboats or at least a good number of them on the Caspian Sea when the ice makes the Volga impassable?"

"The Caspian Sea freezes in the winter," Mikhail said.

"Only the northern part of it," Evdokia returned.

In any case, it was true that most of the riverboats in the Volga wintered at Astrakhan because the Caspian froze a bit later than the Volga and thawed a bit sooner. So even before steam was added, a lot of the riverboats would keep working by migrating south, then would put up for the winter in Astrakhan. Which meant they were pulled up onto the shore at fairly extensive drydocks in Astrakhan, and sat there for the eighty to a hundred forty days that the river and northern Caspian were frozen. With the advent of steam, that had become even more pronounced. A steamboat was more profitable both because it was generally faster and because wood was less expensive than food for a couple of hundred people that you tied to the boat to pull it upriver.

There were a lot of former Volga boatmen in Ufa acting as stevedores and general workers. And most, though by no means all, of them considered their situation an improvement over their previous job. It did mean that there were plenty of people to operate spinning wheels and steam-powered lathes and drill presses, and all the other devices that now filled new factories and shops and every nook and cranny they could be fitted into. And production levels in Kazan were even higher.

Mikhail pulled his mind back to the problem. He really didn't want the *Ilya Muromets* sitting in Astrakhan over the winter. It was a waste of resources. And even more, he didn't want the other riverboats laid up for the winter. Especially the armed riverboats.

"How will we supply them?" Evdokia asked.

"That's the problem," Mikhail agreed. "They will need a supply base somewhere where the Caspian doesn't melt."

Evdokia considered. "We can't do it anywhere on the west coast of the Caspian, not south of the winter ice, that's all the Safavid Empire. And the east coast is all desert with no freshwater."

Mikhail smiled at his wife. "Would you mind running over to the Dacha and seeing what they can offer in the way of a desalination plant?"

With Bernie and Natasha in Astrakhan, the Dacha was run by Anya, the former slave who had shot Cass Lowry when he tried to rape Natasha. Anya worked from an orderly office about fifteen by twenty feet long. It had an up-time-style desk that had an in-basket and an out-basket. Anya spent her days emptying the ever full in-basket and filling the out-basket.

As Evdokia opened the door to Anya's office, Anya was seated in her office chair with her feet on the desk, reading a file with a pencil in her hand. She looked up as the door opened and when she saw who it was, her feet came off the desk, but at Evdokia's wave she didn't start to stand. She did drop the file she'd been reading on the desk between the baskets and sat up. "Welcome to paperwork central, Your Majesty," Anya said, waving to the couch along one wall.

"Not even close," Evdokia said. "Tell me about desalination?"

"That's just one aspect of water purification," Anya said. "And that's something we've been working on since Bernie met the slow plague in Moscow." After Bernie Zeppi was recruited to be a translator of books at the Dacha, he'd learned of the slow plague that hit Moscow every summer. It was a consequence of a waterborne disease, and because of that the Dacha had been deeply interested in water purification.

"Up-time they could do reverse osmosis, but we can't. Though there is good work being done, we aren't there yet. We have to do it the hard way. We boil the water, collect the steam and end up with distilled water. These days, we avoid doing it when we can.

"For river water, just getting the water hot enough to kill the microbes is plenty, so that's what we mostly do. The killing of the microbes is why the Dacha has been actively encouraging the drinking of hot tea. When you boil the water to make the tea, you're killing the bugs.

"For seawater or any water with dangerous elements, you need to collect the steam and that takes a lot more energy, because you have to turn all the water into steam. I assume that's what this is about?"

"No, it's about having drinking water on the east coast of the Caspian Sea. We want to put a supply base somewhere on the east coast so that... Never mind. But we want something that will provide water for a few dozen people over the winter."

Anya chewed on the pencil as she thought. Part of why a woman who'd been essentially illiterate five years ago was now in effective charge of the United Sovereign States of Russia's premier research and development center was that Anya had a phenomenal memory. It wasn't eidetic, but it was very good.

"There was something in one of the magazines. *Good Earth*, I think, or maybe *Mother Earth News*. It had something to do with sunlight."

Vladimir Gorchakov had, as part of his mission in Grantville, managed to have just about every book and periodical in Grantville copied and sent to Moscow. Not translated, just copied. And even that cost a great deal of money. But by now both dachas, the Moscow Dacha and the Ufa Dacha, had fairly complete copies. And the *Mother Earth News* was right up there with the encyclopedias, at the front of the line to be translated.

"I'll put a team on it, Your Majesty. When do you need the results?"

"As soon as possible."

Astrakhan, mouth of the Volga River
September 18, 1637

The radio message that came back from Ufa the next day was long. Bernie considered it as he read it. Then he had one of the military aides the captain had assigned him find out where Chao Wong was.

Natasha had already read the message and was going to be busy for the rest of the day putting things in motion.

Chao Wong's business was on the ground floor of his house. He was an importer/exporter on this spur of the Silk Road. There were caravans, mostly Kazakh caravans, that brought goods from China and took other goods back the other way. In fact, one of Wong's main concerns was the rail line from Ufa to the Aral Sea because that rail line threatened his business. However, there was absolutely nothing he could do about it, and Wong was a realist. The business consisted of an office and a shop where silk, tea, lacquered woods and Chinese porcelain were on offer, as well as furs from Russia and a new product, canned caviar. The Volga was rich in sturgeon and in the seventeenth century probably the best source of caviar in the world.

Bernie didn't have a lot of time to look at the goods Chao Wong had on offer, because as soon as he arrived Wong broke off whatever he was doing and came over to ask Bernie what the czar had said.

"You're going to get what you want, but not for a couple of weeks. We're going to be going back to Ufa first, to collect some more armed riverboats, and some supplies, and then we're going to want you to arrange a lot of supplies for..." Bernie trailed off. Chao Wong was one of the leading figures in Astrakhan, even though he wasn't officially part of the city's government. They were going to need him and his connections for supplies, though once the winter closed in, they weren't going to be able to get supplies from here. He didn't need to know where they were going, or what they were doing. "We're going to need a lot of grain and preserved fruits and vegetables and a fair amount of preserved meat."

"What for?"

"Something Czar Mikhail wants us to do."

Ufa Kremlin
September 21, 1637

"How was your trip?" Czar Mikhail came around his desk and took Bernie's hand.

"Confusing, Your Majesty," Bernie said, shaking the proffered hand. "We got to Astrakhan and someone changed our mission. What's this all about?"

Mikhail waved Bernie to the couch. "Oil. We've been putting together what the twentieth century knew about Russia, and what our friends the Kazakhs are telling us, and we are pretty sure that there are extensive oil fields on the east coast of the Caspian Sea. We don't think that the Safavids know that yet, though they are already exploiting oil wells on the south end of the Caspian. Right now, no one lives on the east coast of the Caspian Sea. There's no freshwater, no wells, no rivers. It's desert, and cold desert, at that. But under that desert, there is probably a lot of oil. We want to already be there when the Iranians, the Bukhara Khanate and especially the Khiva Khanate, realize that there is something of value under all that sand. Right now, no one actually owns the place. Arap Munhammad died in 1623 and they haven't had a stable government since. Besides which, ninety percent of their population is centered in the oasis south of the Aral Sea. Like I said, there is no one there. Because there's no water, so no food, there."

"Well," Bernie said, sounding disgusted, "if you're going to catch the imperial bug and start seizing territory, at least you're not seizing land other people are living on."

"The imperial bug, as you call it," Evdokia said, "isn't a disease. It's a job requirement. We, our people, are going to need that oil, and we don't want the Iranians to be able to jack up the price. We have the beginnings of the industrial revolution going on here in Russia, Bernie, but that revolution needs oil just like it did in your timeline. I don't want our people sent back to subsistence farming and serfdom because we can't run the machines that release them from the land."

Bernie looked at her, then stood and bowed. "You're right, Your Majesty. I spoke without thinking. So what do you want us to do?" He sat back down.

"Just what I said. I want you to put a well-supplied and defensible base on the east coast of the Caspian, below the freeze line." There wasn't a firm freeze line per se. The northern third or so of the Caspian Sea froze in winter, and there were chunks of ice all over the Caspian, but it was generally safe to run boats over the southern two-thirds or so. Mikhail waved Bernie over to his desk, where there was a map of the Caspian Sea. That map was based on up-timer maps, but also on what they already knew. Mikhail pointed at a place on the map where a city named Aktau was located. "There is nothing there now, from what little we can discern from encyclopedias. The up-time USSR established a city there after they found uranium in the area. But by the late 1990s, it was the prime location in Kazakhstan for the support companies for oil drilling.

"I don't insist that you put the base there, but find some place around there where you can build a base. Docks, distilleries for distilling water, facilities to store and refine oil, eventually all that. For right now, I want enough of a presence there so that we can accept a petition for statehood from the residents."

After that, they got down to planning.

CHAPTER 8

𝔖𝔱𝔢𝔞𝔪 𝔗𝔯𝔞𝔦𝔫

Shavgar
September 21, 1637

"The big difference between a steam train and a horse-drawn train," Ivan Maslov said as he stood in the khan's conference room, "is that the steam train doesn't have to rest after galloping for a few minutes. You can, by changing gaits, keep a horse going for a couple of hours, but if you want it to pull a wagon, that's about it. A steam train, even if it's only going at the equivalent of a canter, say fifteen miles an hour, it can keep going at that speed for twenty-four hours a day, assuming you have light to see by. But even at ten hours a day, that's still a hundred and fifty miles a day, and that's four and a half days from Ufa to Alty-Kuduk. Which is about what they are managing now, and they're going to get faster as more of the way is tracked.

"I want to keep one of the trains going back and forth on that route, moving guns, powder, canned and dried foods, and whatever else your army is going to need from Ufa to Alty-Kuduk, but I want the other one here." He knew the speed of the trains because the straight-line distance from Alty-Kuduk was less than three hundred and fifty miles, which should put it in range of the Hero-class aircraft. As it was turning out, with the steam leakage, it was barely within range. Steam planes didn't have as much range for a given weight of fuel as internal combustion. At least theirs didn't, but that mattered less at the moment than the fact that the *Nicky* had made two trips to Alty-Kuduk since their arrival. The last had landed about an hour ago, so Ivan had very up-to-date information on the logistics train.

"We haven't seen a lot of your mythical logistical support so far," Aidar Karimov said testily. "Mostly just fuel for your aircraft."

"That's because so far we only have the one steamboat, and it's not as fast as a train. It can carry a bit more and it uses less fuel to do it, but it takes it a couple of days each way to get from Alty-Kuduk to here and back. It should be arriving tomorrow with a load of AK4.7 chamber loading caplocks."

Aidar Karimov snorted. The most irritating thing about the old bastard was that he was smart. It wasn't that he didn't understand what Ivan was saying. He just didn't approve of it.

Ivan had been thinking about those trains from when he was working on the logistics design back in Ufa. He remembered Tim's use of the *golay golrod*, the walking walls in Rzhev. For that matter, the way Russians had been using the things for a long time before that. The Kazakhs had their own version, but they were wagons pulled by horses, sort of like what Bernie talked about in "Westerns," but with heavy wooden walls strong enough to stop a bullet. That extra weight was hard on the horses. It wore them out and beat them down so that such armored wagon trains had to move slowly to conserve the horses. That, in turn, decreased their utility in terms of putting a fort where you wanted it and moving it as the strategic situation changed.

But with steam that restriction might disappear. With steam, if it worked, they might be able to actually move a wooden fort ten or even twenty miles in a day over basically flat terrain and that would really allow the strategic offense/tactical defense doctrine to work.

"Look, Sultan Karimov," Ivan continued. "Even just the aircraft gives you a massive advantage against the Zunghars."

"Again, I will believe it when I see it." Aidar Karimov held up both hands in a "wait" gesture. "Yes, I do understand their utility, and I understand the need for fuel. But while they are very fast and I personally love to fly, their dependency on special fuel that needs to be shipped in from the Safavids is a real vulnerability. A raid on horseback to strike a fuel depot with flaming arrows and your airplanes are useless."

"Not entirely," said Vasilii. "Steam has several disadvantages compared to internal combustion, but it has three advantages that for us makes it much superior. It works at lower temperatures, so the materials don't have to be quite as high tech. You don't need to generate sparks because you're using continual flame, and you can use anything that will burn—oil, alcohol, even charcoal or wood in theory. That makes them simpler and easier to build, but, more important in this case, means that we can, if need be, convert the plane to operate without oil. At least the steam planes. Not the smaller Scouts, with their internal combustion engines, but the *Nicky* and the other planes of the Polianitsa class."

That was the first Ivan had heard about this. "How much of a loss of efficiency are you looking at if you make the conversion?"

"I have no idea. I'm pretty sure we'll have enough steam to get into the air, but how long we'll be able to stay up? That's anyone's guess until we make the conversions and try it."

The khan coughed, and once he had their attention, he said, "Before Vasilii takes us all on an exploration of mechanical engineering, I think we need to address the issue of guns. Specifically, the AK4.7s that we were promised. And the chambers for them?"

"The first load is on the steamboat now, Salqam-Jangir Khan. It's five hundred AKs, five thousand chambers and fifty thousand caps. There is also a lot of black powder and canned scrambled eggs."

"Canned scrambled eggs?" Sultan Karimov asked.

"Yes, sir, and the council in Kazan have examined the factory and assure us that the canned eggs are *halal*. The eggs are beaten, seasoned, and injected into the containers, then cooked in the container and the container sealed to prevent spoilage. They're good for at least a year if the containers aren't opened."

"Sounds disgusting," Salqam-Jangir Khan said.

Ivan shrugged. "They will feed a man and can be eaten cold if needed."

"That sounds worse," Togym said.

"We're also sending dried beans and freeze-dried vegetables. But they will be coming on later boats, as the harvest comes in and is processed."

"And where is the rice that your rich landowners have promised us?" Sultan Karimov asked.

"That too is waiting on the harvest, and processing," Salqam-Jangir Khan said. "We will wait for the next riverboat. And I approve General Maslov's request to have the second train brought overland to us here as soon as it's ready."

The discussion continued as they worked out the logistics of the campaign. The real issue was the same as it was at the beginning of the discussion. It was simply going to take time to put all the parts in place, and none of them were sure that they would have the time.

Ufa
September 21, 1637

Bang! The wrench slipped off the nut and slammed into the pipe and was accompanied by a great deal of Russian cursing. The pipe was part of a two-cylinder steam engine. The cylinders were the better part of a foot wide and a yard long, and getting the valves to open and close just the right amount at just the right time was proving decidedly difficult. But once they did, this engine would produce an amazing amount of torque.

There were by now quite a lot of steam engines in Ufa. They were in factories and shops. There were two in the Kremlin and four in the Ufa Dacha. And they were, in many varieties, installed in riverboats that plied the Volga and its tributaries. There were even a couple of steam tractors pushing or pulling implements to help build the walls that were going to defend Ufa if Sheremetev's forces were to attack.

However, a railroad engine was a different kettle of fish. It had to produce a *lot* of force. It had to produce it over a long time, and it had to do all that in a container that couldn't be much wider than a standard wagon.

Making everything work and fit was proving to be a knuckle-scraping pain.

Alla Lyapunov listened to Vadim Ivanovich's cursing with amusement before proclaiming, "How rude!"

Alla was playing hooky. Alla wasn't the family geek, but as soon as they got back to Ufa, her "father" had stuck her in the Dacha school to "catch up with her education." He'd pointed out that she'd spent the previous year as an undercook or scullery maid and needed to learn, well, everything.

Alla hadn't ever been a particularly studious child. She could read and write, which was more than most people could, but in the Dacha that wasn't considered nearly enough. At least one of her teachers had made her feel like an idiot every day since Vasilii and Miroslava had left on their mission to Shavgar. Right now she was supposed to be learning up-timer English. It was the new "language of scholarship," so everyone told her. It was incredibly boring and the language made no sense at all. So she'd cut class and come here to watch them building the new locomotives.

A locomotive was the engine part of a train. She would have gone out to watch the workers building the tracks, but they were too far away by now. So rather than watching young men lifting heavy wooden beams into place and topping them with thin steel tape, she was watching an old fat guy twisted under a train locomotive trying to attach a pipe in a place where her new adoptive father should never have put the connection.

"What? Who's that?"

"It's me," Alla said. "And I'm going to tell Vasilii you said that."

"Tell him anything you want," Vadim Ivanovich said as he wormed his way out of the innards of the steam locomotive. "But I suspect that what he's going to care about is that you weren't in class."

Alla pouted. That was mean, but probably true. "It's *English*!" she cried.

Vadim snorted a laugh. "I can't argue with you about English. Silliest way of talking ever invented by man. 'Course I'm not a *polymath* like your papa." He used the English word polymath. "Just an old smith turned mechanic. But if anyone has to repair the hydraulics on this monster in the field once we have the body on her, they are going to need a special tool."

"Why does it need hydraulics in the first place?"

"Because the drive wheel weighs three hundred pounds and will have to be lifted when this thing isn't traveling on its track."

"When's it going to be done?"

"Sooner than you think. This is the second one and we'd been working on models since before the move to Ufa." Vadim was one of the "steamheads" from the original Dacha, the one located outside Moscow by the Gorchakov family just after Bernie Zeppi arrived from Grantville. "Steamboats were the first steam engines designed by the Dacha, but steam locomotives were the third. And the problem wasn't the locomotive. It was the rails. It still is. Czar Mikhail and Togym Bey are spending a fortune putting in the rail line from Ufa to Alty-Kuduk."

"Now you sound like my economics teacher," Alla complained. Czar Mikhail was, according to at least one professor in the economics department, spending way too much money on things like the railroad, the airplanes, and so on. Alla had asked what he should be spending it on, and the professor had spent an hour explaining that he didn't have the money and shouldn't be spending it on anything. Partial reserves and gold-and-silver-backed paper money was fine, but he should have a larger reserve than he was keeping. It gave Alla a headache just thinking about it.

"Never mind. What's sooner than I think?"

"Another three days and we'll be ready for the high-pressure steam test. If that goes well, and it should, we'll have the engine on the road in another two weeks."

"So it's going to be October before you're ready to go."

"For this train, yes. But we've ordered two more boilers from Murom."

Alla shook her head. The Russian civil war was strange. Or maybe it wasn't. But in spite of the fact that the United Sovereign States of Russia were at war with western Russia, which was controlled from Moscow, there was regular trade between the two. Canned caviar from the lower Volga was for sale in Moscow, and steam boilers from Murom, which was in the Muscovy-controlled part of Russia, were routinely transported to Ufa. For that matter, silk from China could be bought in Moscow cheaper after traveling through Ufa than you could get it traveling by sea. The war was going on and serfs were still escaping from Muscovite Russia to the Sovereign States, but trade went on. If there was a way to make money, someone would find it.

Siege lines outside Kazan
September 21, 1637

General Birkin sipped tea from China shipped through Ufa and looked out a double-paned window. The window unit was made in Kazan, the city he was besieging, from an idea brought back in time by the up-timers. And aside from the joy that he would be warm this winter, he didn't think about it at all. What he thought about was the fact that he was going to have to wait for the winter to close in, because the summer campaign season was over. It ended about the same time that harvest season ended. Now they were into the fall wet season, when the world turned to mud before it turned to ice. And Birkin wasn't quite ready to move yet.

By now the siege lines to the north of Kazan were a city in their own right. A walled city and a well-supplied one. Not an easy nut for General Lebedev to crack. General Birkin had a lively respect for Boris Timofeyevich Lebedev, but there was no way that he was going to call him "General Tim" like the broadsheets did. So if he couldn't move his army around Lebedev, well, the same was true the other way. Lebedev couldn't move his army around Birkin. The stalemate let both armies rest and refit. But the stalemate was all on the side of Czar Mikhail. The longer it lasted, the stronger the Sovereign States got and the weaker Moscow looked.

Birkin knew that and so did his boss in Moscow. And his boss, after the latest shake-up, was Ivan Romanov and it was looking like it was going to stay that way. Birkin shook his head. One way or the other, Russia was going to be ruled by a Romanov. Maybe even two. There was a faction in the Moscow Kremlin that wanted to make peace with the Sovereign States and let there be two Russias.

However, Ivan Romanov wasn't part of that faction. Birkin had his orders, and as soon as the world froze, he would carry them out.

He went over to the desk and opened a panel, revealing a map of Perm, the city and the region. Perm was a new city. There'd already been a town there, but with the knowledge from the up-timers, the copper deposits in the area had been found and the new city of Perm was busy mining, smelting, and exporting copper ingots. Those ingots went down the Kama River to Kazan, where the copper was electrically purified, which produced small amounts of silver and gold, as well as very pure copper, just right for making wires and all sorts of modern products.

Not that Birkin cared all that much about Perm. Birkin cared about the Kama River. The Kama River, which joined the Volga, downriver of Kazan. Taking Perm would let him move down the ice-covered river and go all the way to Ufa, without Lebedev being in a position to stop him. It was a risky move, and one that Birkin had been convinced would fail until just a short while ago. Because, if he could move his army to Perm, General Lebedev could do the same. And probably faster.

General Birkin looked at the map and smiled. General Lebedev couldn't move an army he didn't have, and Czar Mikhail had borrowed the boy's army to go rescue the Kazakhs. *You just keep on moving your troops southeast, all the way out of the theater of operations,* he thought happily.

In the air over Ufa
October 14, 1637

General Ivan Maslov sat in a seat in the passenger section of the *Nicky*. He'd been in Shavgar this morning when the radio message that the second steam train was ready reached them. Brandy had volunteered to bring him back so that he could see about setting up. It was raining, lowering visibility, which lowered their altitude. Brandy needed to be able to see the ground to navigate. They were following the rail line from Alty-Kuduk and while not flying at treetop level they were lower than Brandy liked to be. Sultan Aidar Karimov was in another seat and one of Vladimir's scouts was acting as Brandy's navigator and Vasilii was acting as the aircraft engineer. Vladimir was still in Shavgar.

Brandy put the plane in a ten-degree bank and circled Ufa as she lined up on the Ufa River to land. The landing was smooth and they pulled up onto the shore, cut the steam to the engines and the fans that inflated the ACLG, and settled gently onto the *Nicky*'s accustomed spot.

General Maslov stood and moved to stand on the lower wing. He didn't wait for the stairs to be placed. It was only a four-foot drop, so he jumped down and his shiny black boots sank to the ankle in the muddy ground. Ivan was off-balance and landed on his face in the mud.

One of the flight crew sloshed over to help him stand up, but he was covered in cold, wet, and exceedingly embarrassing mud.

He looked back to see Sultan Karimov grinning. "It's often best to wait before jumping, General Maslov."

"Yes," Ivan said as he used a dirty kerchief to wipe his face.

"It's been raining off and on for four days, General," said the aircraft maintenance worker.

"So I gathered," Ivan agreed. "A little too late."

Three hours later, in a different uniform, Ivan walked around the steam locomotive. It wasn't a copy of one of the early trains built in the first half of the nineteenth century, nor of one of the last steam trains built in the first half of the twentieth century. It was a compromise between the two, but not something like they would have built in the 1880s either. This was a new design based on what they'd learned up through the twentieth century, but using the materials they could produce in the here and now. The tube boiler was good steel, but not one of the up-time computer-designed alloys that were used on the space shuttle or whatever. It was just your good, solid, medium carbon steel, strong enough and heat resistant enough to work at the few hundred degrees that this train would operate at.

It was also heavy. The engine weighed the better part of twenty tons. And after his experience earlier, Ivan realized that his plan to use this locomotive pulling a train directly to Shavgar and from there to points east wouldn't work, at least not during the rainy season. Ivan looked from the train to the railroad track. This too was different from pictures of steel rails he'd seen. The rail itself was at least three times as wide as a steel rail would have been, with a curved steel cap that covered the top and some of the sides of the curved wooden rail. The rail was curved so that a cart or wagon could climb over it with relative ease. Surrounding the rail was a tarmac road. The weight of the train was carried on the rail wheels. The outer wheels were there for balance only, as long as the rail was in use. It was only after the train left the railroad that the outer wheels would actually carry a load.

That was what the rail was for, to support the weight on a smooth surface. The weight was supported by the rail and bumps in the road were for the most part eliminated. That was why the steel caps on the rails extended between one section of rail and the next. With ninety percent of the weight of the train on the rail, friction was drastically decreased and the top speed was drastically increased. That was also the reason for the tarmac surface supporting the wheels that took the other ten percent of the train's weight.

Once the ground froze, it would take the weight, but not until then. For that matter, the train wouldn't be able to travel on the stretches of the Ufa–Alty-Kuduk line where the rails weren't in place yet. Of course, even after the ground froze the rough terrain would keep the speed of the train low, preventing the incredibly high speeds that the steel-topped rail and the tarmac allowed.

Ivan didn't curse. Sultan Karimov was here, and he was

embarrassed enough. At least here in the engine house, the weight of the massive locomotive was supported by the steel-topped wood rail. The power wheel and support wheel were both lowered, so the weight of the massive locomotive was well supported.

"Would you like to go for a ride?"

Ivan lifted an eyebrow. "Is there enough track?"

"Sure, General. The crews are adding a mile a day. There's a factory just out of town that makes the rails, steams the wood, straightens it, cuts it, soaks it in tar, and attaches the steel strips and the supports. All the workmen at the railhead have to do is flatten the land, lay the gravel, put in the rail, and cover the gravel with tar. It's still a lot of work, but they are pushing the line out."

They climbed aboard, and Vadim Ivanovich showed them around the cabin. He showed them the steam gauges and the controls, then they pulled out and the train followed the track to the bridge over the Ufa River at a sedate speed of about eight miles per hour. Once they were over the bridge, Vadim blew the steam whistle and opened her up. They hit forty miles an hour, then fifty before they started slowing down. The *Nicky* was faster, but the *Nicky* flew at a thousand feet or more over the land. It felt slow. This felt fast. Terrifyingly fast. But Vadim was grinning like a loon the whole distance to the railhead.

If this had been an up-time train that traveled on two tracks and didn't have other wheels, they would have had to pull onto a siding, or go backwards to get back to Ufa. But it wasn't. When they got to within a quarter mile of the railhead, they stopped. Vadim pulled a lever and a hydraulic system lifted the guide wheel and the power wheel, leaving them in a large, heavy steam car. They pulled off the rail onto a temporary platform, where they turned around and stopped.

"Come look at the work crews," Vadim said.

It was still raining. Not hard, but the sort that soaked into the ground and caused plants to grow with profusion. In spite of the rain, there were fresno scrapers piling up earth, smoothing out the top, and covering that with gravel, using heavy rollers to compress the earth, then covering that gravel with finer gravel. And for right now that was all they were doing. The rest would wait till the rain stopped and the subgrade, the subbase, and the base had a chance to dry. Once that happened, they would add a layer of tar. Then another layer of fine gravel. Then another team would pull a rail section from a train car and carry it to the railhead, where they would place it on the gravel, making sure that it was straight and even. Then more gravel would be pushed over it so that only the rounded top of the rail stuck up above the roadbed. Then onto the next section. The foreman told them that they wouldn't add the tar until the rain had stopped and the bed had had a chance to dry a little. What they would have at the end of the process was a tarmac road.

"This is a raised road," Sultan Karimov said. "It's a good two feet above the land around it, and you're pulling that earth from the ground right around the road." He pointed at the wide, shallow ditches on either side of the road. "The water's going to build up on the uphill side of your road and sweep it away."

"We've thought of that. We've surveyed the route carefully, and we're installing culverts under the road as needed to let the water flow under the road without damaging it. It will also let the roadbed drain and, once the tarmac is on, it should stay dry."

Sultan Karimov nodded thoughtfully. "I almost wish this rail line was going through our lands."

"In spite of the gold mine?" Ivan asked.

"Yes, in spite of the gold mine." The gold mine in their clan lands had been discovered while the rail line had been being surveyed and had led to quite a bit of trouble. But it was operational now and Karimov's clan was shipping gold to Ufa, and had a solid account in the Sovereign States central bank. Which was the other reason that Karimov was here. He wanted to see for himself just how spendable that money was.

Finally, they finished the sightseeing tour and got back on the locomotive. The locomotive pulled back onto the track, and away they went, steaming back to Ufa, satisfied with what they'd learned.

New Ruzuka Steel Works, Ufa
October 15, 1637

Stefan looked up as the sultan walked in, escorted by Izabella Utkin. He recognized the sultan by his outfit, but wasn't sure if he'd ever met the man before.

"This is Sultan Aidar Karimov," Izabella said. "You know, the clan with the gold mine."

"Yes, what can I do for you, Sultan Karimov?" Stefan walked around his desk and held his hand out.

The sultan looked at the outstretched hand, and after a moment, took it. "I wish to buy AK4.7 caplock rifles."

By now the steel works, mostly at the urging of Izabella, had expanded. Not so much by building more businesses as by buying them, or entering into partnerships with them. The barrels for the AKs were made in Kazan. Stefan still had the assembly line for the chambers and the chamber clips, and the caps were made by a chemical plant that was located six miles up the Ufa River. The chamber locks, stocks and assembly were done in Ufa. They sold the finished rifles in both Ufa and Kazan.

They arranged to sell three hundred fifty AK4.7s for seven rubles each, with each ruble being roughly equivalent to eighty USE dollars, at least according to the United Sovereign States of Russia bank in Ufa. The exchanges in Grantville and Magdeburg had rubles worth rather less than that.

Overall, the sultan was pleased, or at least that was Stefan's impression.

In fact, Sultan Aidar Karimov was pleased, sort of, in a way. Partly because the price was fair, even perhaps a bit generous. Certainly less than he'd be paying a gunsmith to build the rifles individually. But more than that, he was pleased by the ready way that the merchants in Ufa were willing to take his check on the bank of the Sovereign States. No fuss, no discount required, nothing. And it wasn't just here. All the merchants in Ufa were happy to take a check as soon as he pulled out his bank book, which had an image of his face on the first page. People were happy to take his check. And he was getting better prices for cloth than he would have in Shavgar.

Yes, everything the Russians claimed about their money seemed to be true, or at least the merchants here believed it. And their manufacturing capability was even greater than advertised.

And that was utterly terrifying.

Laying track a mile a day, and that was just one team, the rail-laying team out of Ufa. There were other teams, one moving north from Alty-Kuduk, and Togym had several teams working. They probably weren't matching the Ufa team. They didn't have Ufa's support, but they would be doing at least a quarter mile a day, and there were several teams.

Once the rail line was in, Togym would be selling beef and mutton in Ufa and Moscow and everywhere on the Volga, and getting top dollar in good money. Aidar looked at the bank book in his hand. Money as good as, or better than, gold.

Steam train leaving Ufa
October 16, 1637

The Nicky *would be halfway to Shavgar by now,* Sultan Aidar Karimov thought as he boarded the train. He was accompanying the rifles back to his clan. He settled into the seat in the one passenger car of the eight-car train and felt the jerk as it started on its trip. He'd be to the railhead in less than an hour, but after that, packing the rifles to his clan lands would take a week. Horsemen were no longer the fastest men on Earth, and his way of life was going to die.

CHAPTER 9

Getting There

Shavgar approach
October 16, 1637

Brandy turned onto final approach and looked over at "General" Ivan Maslov. He wasn't enjoying the flight. He was conscientiously using the navigational instruments and learning how to operate them. And he wasn't frightened, but he wasn't taking any joy in flying. That was what happened when you made a twenty-year-old kid into a general. "Relax, Ivan. We're landing."

"Yes, Princess," Ivan said, never taking his eyes from the ground scope. The ground scope was a set of binoculars which were built into the plane and looked straight down, or down and to the front, at least when the plane was in level flight. They were used to measure height above ground, and ground speed. It took practice and math, and while Ivan had the math, he didn't have the practice to do it well.

"We're not in level flight; those instruments aren't going to give accurate readings."

"I know. I'm trying to determine if I can tell from the instruments that we're not in level flight."

"We have other instruments for that," Brandy muttered. Most of her attention was now focused on their glide path. They were getting close now. She adjusted the flaps and brought the nose up a smidge to make the most of the ground effect as they came in. Then she shifted some steam to the fans for the ACLG, and a few seconds later they settled gently onto the river and started their taxi to shore.

✧   ✧   ✧

Vladimir was there to meet them. He kissed Brandy quickly, then said, "You need to get in the Scout. We just got a pony express rider from Almaty. The Zunghar are on the move. Erdeni Batur has apparently decided to take Almaty. And Salqam-Jangir Khan has decided to go to Almaty to take control, and we're going to take him there. We'll need the Scout, and the *Nicky* is going to be busy ferrying fuel to way points.

"I'll be taking the *Nicky* as soon as it can be refueled."

Ivan heard and asked, "Couldn't you talk him out of it?"

"No, I couldn't. And in political terms, he's right. He needs to be there."

"But in military terms, it's exposing your king to protect a rook," Ivan answered.

"The decision has been made and it's above your pay grade, General. In fact, it's above mine."

Lake Kyzylkol
October 16, 1637

The lake was about one hundred thirty miles not quite due east of Shavgar, and it was surrounded by desert. There was grass in some places, but the lake itself was salty and there were salt flats around it. It was not, as it turned out, too salty for plants and other animals to live in. As he circled over it, Vladimir determined that it was just about perfect. The *Nicky* landed on the water, pulled up onto the shore, and the crew started unloading fuel while Vladimir went over his notes on the flight and the landmarks spotted. Two hours flight time here, an hour to unload, and two hours back. He could make two, maybe three, trips before sunset.

The crew was Vasilii, Miroslava and Ariq Ogedei. Ariq volunteered to stay here while Vladimir and the rest went back.

"I'll set up the distillery and do some fishing," Ariq said.

The distillery wasn't the one they'd hauled. This one was made in Shavgar by local crafters. It consisted of a copper pot over a firebox with a copper tube coming out the top. The tube went down the side of the firebox to another container that was also filled with water. The tube coiled through the water in the second container while the steam cooled and condensed, then extended out of the water box to an empty pot that gradually filled with distilled water. The cooling box cooled the steam and at the same time warmed the water that went into the boiling pot. It wasn't really complicated and it wasn't super efficient, but there was a lot of grass, weeds and other burnables around here, even a fair amount of scrub wood. Plenty enough to turn the salty lake water into distilled water suitable for drinking.

Back at Shavgar, Vladimir showed the coordinates to Brandy, and the markers to the khan's officers, one of whom knew the place. Or thought he did. A caravan with food and supplies would leave tomorrow. Meanwhile, Brandy would follow him on the next trip, then scout east from there. The Scout had less range, but that was because it had a much smaller fuel tank. One load of fuel carried by the *Nicky* was ten tankfuls for the Scout. And for his next flights, Vlad would be flying with only Vasilii on board. The rest of the weight would be the extra fuel.

Brandy headed for the plane.

Taraz, Kazakh
October 16, 1637

Brandy circled the village. There were visible ruins where a larger town had once been. There were also fields and animals, horses and cattle, surrounding the town, and the river which, according to the other scout, was called the Talas River. People were coming out of the town and staring, and Brandy decided that the better part of valor in this case was to go back and get the *Nicky* and Salqam-Jangir Khan before landing among strangers.

She made note of landmarks and headed back to Lake Kyzylkol.

Shavgar
October 17, 1637

The *Nicky* was full of fuel, Salqam-Jangir Khan, Sultan Togym, two men at arms and supplies that would go to Lake Kyzylkol or on to Taraz and points east. The *Nicky* was starting a busy day.

From Shavgar to Lake Kyzylkol to top up, then on to Taraz, where he would drop off Salqam-Jangir Khan, Sultan Togym, the two men at arms and supplies, then back directly to Shavgar for another load of fuel. Straight back to Taraz to unload, back to Shavgar for more fuel, and so on all day long. Shavgar to Taraz was a straight shot, two hundred forty-two miles. With a stop at Lake Kyzylkol, it was two hundred forty-five. Not much difference, only three miles, though it did take extra fuel to land and take off again. But the *Nicky* was proving herself thirsty. She was drinking thirty gallons an hour. That was around one hundred ninety pounds of fuel per hour of flight, and Shavgar to Taraz was four hours. And with just Vlad and Vasilii on board, the Nicky could only carry two tons or four thousand pounds of fuel or twenty-one hours' worth.

If the maps were right, Almaty was another three hundred miles or so. Though by now Vladimir's faith in up-time maps of places in Kazakh was being greatly revised. The up-time maps from Grantville didn't show the town of Taraz, and Taraz was a good twenty miles south of where they'd thought it would be.

Finally Station
October 21, 1637

Brandy circled, then landed on the creek. It wasn't near being a river, but there was water, and there was a flattish piece of land. No one was here, and it had no name. And it had taken three days of recon flights to find it. So Brandy named it "Finally." They were flying over the northern edge of the Tian Shan Mountains and there was a dearth of what Brandy considered good landing sites. Not that there weren't places to land. Both the Scout and the *Nicky* were quite flexible when it came to landing. All they needed was someplace flattish. But for a station, a depot, water was also necessary and there wasn't a lot of water locally. Nor an overabundance of flat spots. Finally Station was about ninety miles east of Taraz and it would do. Barely.

The only good news was that while she'd been searching high and low for some place to land, Vlad had been shifting fuel to Taraz.

Pishpek
October 22, 1637

Brandy circled the collection of small buildings, then flew to the Chu River nearby. They could use it as a landing area, but it would be a bit tight for the *Nicky*, which had a wider wingspan.

They were getting close, if the Grantville maps were accurate, around a hundred miles from Almaty.

Salqam-Jangir Khan arrived on one of the later flights and was consulting with the scouts. Salqam-Jangir Khan was trying to determine where they actually were according to the up-timer maps, while Brandy and Miroslava looked on. The issue was that, to a great extent, the up-timer maps of this part of central Asia were evidently blank. Not so much "here there be dragons" as "here there be nothing much worth noticing." There were mountains. The maps sort of showed that, but the sort of long, brown blob on the map labeled "Tian Shan Mountains" didn't even begin to describe the beautiful vistas that Brandy had spent the last several days flying over. They were near the northern edge of the Tian Shan, but not that near it and they weren't all that sure just how far south of Almaty they were. They were pretty sure they were south of it.

"Go to Issyk-Kul," Miroslava said.

"What?"

"Why?"

"It's out of the way."

Issyk-Kul was an inland mountain lake that was one of the largest inland bodies of water by volume in the world, because it was deep. But it was pretty big even in terms of surface area. It had to be, or the map wouldn't show it.

The map was from "the atlas." Which had been made in Grantville based on some half a dozen atlases that had come back through the Ring of Fire. The truth was that the mapmakers in America up-time just hadn't cared all that much about this part of the world.

But, Brandy realized, Miroslava was right. "It's big," she said. "All we have to do is get some altitude and head east and we'll see it."

"Use the *Nicky*, not the Scout," Miroslava said.

"Why not use the Scout?" Brandy asked.

"Carburetion," Miroslava said as though that explained everything.

Brandy looked at Miroslava in confusion, which made her no different from Salqam-Jangir Khan or the two scouts. But Miroslava was looking at Brandy like she should understand.

"What about carburetion?" Brandy asked, wondering if dealing with Conan Doyle's Sherlock was this irritating.

"Air pressure decreases with altitu—"

"Got it!" Brandy said, realizing that as planes got higher not only did it get harder for the people in them to breathe, it also got harder for the engines to breathe. As the air pressure decreased, you got more gas and less air to the cylinders, and that decreased engine efficiency. You could sort of compensate by adjusting the carburetor settings if you could do that while in flight, which you couldn't. "But the same thing would... Wouldn't it?"

"No."

"Why not?" *It's like pulling teeth*, Brandy thought.

"Steam planes don't have carburetors," Miroslava said, and it was true. A steam plane had a nozzle that sprayed a fine mist of gasoline or fuel oil into the combustion chamber which was open to the air, and after the initial spark, it was a continuous flame that could be adjusted by adding more or less fuel into the chamber. Even if you turned off the fire entirely, the steam engines would continue to work for a while as the steam already in the system was used. There was plenty of oxygen to burn at altitudes greater than a human could survive.

"I wonder how high you could take a steam plane?" Brandy asked.

"According to Vasilii, higher than a human could survive, even using oxygen," Miroslava said. Brandy realized that this wasn't Miroslava's weirdness. It was Vasilii's. *The pillow talk between those two has to be really outlandish. Murder and machines.*

Meanwhile, Salqam-Jangir Khan and the scouts were still looking confused and the khan was starting to look irritated as well. "Ah. Miroslava's right," Brandy offered.

"She usually is," Salaam-Jangir Khan said with a sort of half smile. "But there is usually Vasilii to explain what she's talking about, and he's not here now, so would you like to give it a try?"

"Internal combustion engines have a ceiling..." Brandy trailed off at the blank looks, and got just a touch of what it felt like from Miroslava's end. It wasn't that Brandy was smarter than the khan. There was a reason that his people were already starting to call him "the Great." He was a smart young man. It was just that she was looking at the world from such a different place that it could be hard to describe. "When you climb a mountain, it can be hard to breathe. The same thing happens to an internal combustion engine. If you fly high enough, the engine stutters and dies. But external combustion works differently, and will keep working even as you go higher. That means that the *Nicky* has a higher ceiling, can fly higher than the Scout."

"How high?" Salqam-Jangir Khan asked.

"High enough to cause hypoxia," Brandy said without any doubt at all. "High enough so that the passengers would suffocate while the engine was still working."

"Well, let's not fly it that high," Salqam-Jangir Khan said with another of those half smiles.

One of the scouts said something in Kazakh that Brandy didn't understand, and from his expression, she felt that was probably best.

Issyk-Kul
October 23, 1637

The *Nicky* was at fifteen thousand feet and Vladimir was afraid that that was too high. The ceiling that Hal Smith back in Grant-ville recommended was ten thousand feet above sea level. So, at around three miles high, Vlad and Vasilii were well into the range where supplemental oxygen was recommended. But they didn't have supplemental oxygen.

So far, everything felt fine. But, again according to Hal and his son Farrell Smith, that didn't mean much. People suffering from hypoxia often felt great, even while their mental abilities were so degraded that they couldn't sign their name.

Given that, they'd worked out a plan. They'd flown at three thousand feet for half an hour, then gone up, not quite as fast as they could, but close to it. Now they were leveled out and looking around. And, at a guess, thirty or forty miles to the southeast was what just about had to be Issyk-Kul. It was huge.

"Vasilii, get us a bearing."

"I am. The good news about hypoxia is it generally takes it a while. Yaw us right."

Vlad snorted, then said, "Slew turn to the right."

"Almost," Vasilii said, then, "There." Then he looked at the compass and made a notation.

Twenty minutes later, they landed in a small bay on the north shore of the Issyk-Kul. It was beautiful, with the mountains to the north and the huge lake to the south. But where they were was desert. Sand and the sort of desert shrubbery you would expect, and it was flat as well.

They settled on the beach and spent an hour making a careful survey of the surrounding peaks and prominent terrain features. While relatively flat on the shore of Issyk-Kul, they were surrounded on three sides by hilly terrain. The Tian Shan Mountains were beautiful and lush. A couple of hundred years ago, this had been a major stop on the Silk Road, but as trade dried up the population moved elsewhere. But there were wild groves of apple trees as well as other fruit and nut trees. It was 76 degrees, with a breeze coming off the water.

It was a beautiful place and Vladimir was in no hurry to leave. Vladimir wrote on the location form: "Brandy's Cove."

Still, after they'd made their observations, they climbed aboard and started the fire in the boiler. Ten minutes later, with the steam up, Vlad fed steam to the fans and the ACLG inflated. Then, feeding steam to the props, Vlad took off from the beach, brought the compass to a heading of 290 degrees, and set off back to Pishpek.

Pishpek
October 23, 1637

By comparing the maps from Grantville and what they knew, they had a good vector and distance from Brandy's Cove to Almaty, and while the straight-line distance from Brandy's Cove to Almaty was only sixty-two miles, it was sixty-two miles over a mountain range. Even if the Zunghar knew where their airbase was located, it would take his army a week of hard travel to get there. And now that they knew with confidence where Brandy's Cove and Almaty were relative to each other and Pishpek, they could see routes that didn't require flying quite so high. There were routes between mountain peaks, after all.

"What I recommend, Salqam-Jangir Khan, is that we spend a few days moving fuel to Brandy's Cove, and then start reconnaissance over Almaty," Vladimir said.

Salaam-Jangir Khan looked at the map and slowly shook his head. "I know that you must be concerned with fuel and equipment. And I know that the *Nicky* is using more fuel than you expected. But we can't wait. My people in Almaty are convinced that I am still back in Shavgar. Even killing horses by the score, I can't be anywhere near Almaty yet. But we are. Yes, move the fuel and the pistols to Brandy's Cove, and do all that is needful to prepare the place. But, in the meantime, today Brandy and I will take the Scout to Brandy's Cove, refuel and then fly over Almaty and determine what the situation is there."

The pistols were copies of the Colt Dragoon caplock revolver and were for cavalry use. The AK4.7 rifle had excellent range and relative to a muzzle-loading rifled musket, a tremendous rate of fire. But it was big and heavy, and even the carbine version, the AK4.9, was heavy and hard to use effectively from horseback. The Colt Dragoon, however, could be fired readily one-handed, fired six shots about as fast as you could pull the trigger, and was, in general, a much better weapon. However, they had made changes even here. The revolvers had the loading lever of the Dragoon, but they were also designed to allow the quick removal and replacement of a loaded cylinder, meaning that by switching out the cylinder, they could fire six more shots, assuming the gun didn't hang up or get clogged with powder residue.

But the big reason that they were carrying pistols, not AKs, was simply that they were smaller and lighter, so the *Nicky* could carry more of them.

"Salqam-Jangir Khan," Vladimir started.

But the khan held up his hand, and looked not at Vladimir, but at Brandy. "Will you carry me to Almaty, Brandy? In spite of your husband's fears."

"Yes, Salqam-Jangir Khan."

CHAPTER 10

Guns for Almaty

In the air, over Almaty
October 23, 1637

Almaty had a mountain range to its south, and not very far to its south, but the land right around the city was flat. The city was walled, and a hundred years before had been a large and prosperous place, a major stop on the Silk Road. The Esentai River, a bit more than a creek, but not much more, ran through Almaty, and on both sides of the city, parts of it were diverted for irrigation purposes. As Brandy and Salqam-Jangir Khan flew over the city, they could see a place on the river that was actually within the walls. It wasn't large enough to let the *Nicky* land, but the Scout could fit. At least, Brandy was pretty sure that the Scout could fit.

On the other hand, the sun was getting low in the west. And it was clear that Almaty was under loose siege. There were camps of Zunghar just out of musket shot of the city. And it was rifled musket shot, not bow shot. Apparently there were snipers in Almaty.

"It's a shame we don't have a bomb," Salqam-Jangir Khan said.

"Yes, it is," Brandy said. Both of them were wearing headphones because the engine noise from the Scout would make conversation impossible without it. "How would you feel about doing something stupid?"

"What?"

"It's just that I'm wondering how the Zunghar horses would respond to being buzzed."

"Buzzed?" Salqam-Jangir Khan asked. "What does buzzed mean?"

Brandy grinned. "You want me to show you?"

There was silence for a moment, then Salqam-Jangir Khan said, "Yes, I do believe I do. Show me!"

The Scout was a light, low-speed aircraft. Its cruising speed was just seventy miles an hour, but that was cruising speed, not even the top speed in level flight. An airplane in a dive goes much faster. Suddenly, Salqam-Jangir Khan's hands were locked onto the armrests of his seat.

The arrangement of the Scout was the navigator in front and below the pilot. So Salqam-Jangir Khan had an excellent view as the Scout heeled over and dropped into a dive. With the engine and gravity in accord, the aircraft accelerated to just under two hundred miles an hour before Brandy started a slow pull out at six hundred feet.

By the time they were in level flight again, they were barely twenty feet above the ground and traveling at just over one hundred twenty miles an hour. And the unmuffled radial engine was loud. It wasn't as loud as a gunshot, but it was continuous, and it looked to the horses like the biggest eagle in the world was looking for a snack.

A big, angry, noisy eagle.

The horses, with no consideration of bridles, riders, or anything else decided to be elsewhere, just as fast as they could gallop.

Surprisingly, a number of the Zunghar warriors were cool-headed, and quick-witted enough to actually use their bows. Or, in one case, his prized *rifled* hunting musket. But they had never shot at something as fast as the Scout. Every shot missed.

After they'd passed over the camp Brandy pulled up and in seconds they were at five hundred feet and back down to sixty mph in a climb. At eight hundred feet, they leveled out, flew over Almaty and wiggled their wings at the town.

Then they headed back for Brandy's Cove.

Almaty
October 23, 1637

Sultan Aidan Karimov, the mayor of Almaty, watched the thing fly over the town and reconsidered. At least some of the stories were true, after all. But what did that mean for Almaty and for his clan?

A hundred years ago, Almaty had been a thriving city and

center of trade. Even fifty years ago it had been a good-sized town. Now, with so much of the trade from China going around the Cape of Good Hope, it was a sleepy little backwater surrounded by relatively rich farm and pasture lands, but no trade worth mentioning. His clan owned a lot of land around here, farms and ranches, mostly worked by tenants and slaves.

Normally worked by tenants and slaves. Now those tenants and slaves were crowded into town eating the city's victuals while the ranches were emptied of stock and the farms burned.

The mechanical eagle was out of sight . . . no . . . heading south toward the mountains. Yesterday he'd been wondering if . . .

"We should sortie." His grandson Baurzhan interrupted his thoughts. "While Salqam-Jangir Khan's jinn distracts the Zunghar."

"No!" Sultan Karimov's response was instant and certain. And he was tempted to leave it at that, but the young men of the village were getting restive. As young men often do when they didn't know what to do, they wanted to fight someone. He looked at his grandson. The seventeen-year-old was looking back at him belligerently, and Aidan decided that he had to explain. Which meant that he had to figure out why he was opposed to a sortie.

"That"—he pointed in the direction that the mechanical eagle had gone—"was Salqam-Jangir Khan telling us he's coming. Telling us not to lose hope. *Not* telling us to be idiots. Yes, he scattered one of the Zunghar camps, but there are two more. If we sortie against the one disrupted camp, we expose ourselves to the other two. Besides, that"—he pointed again—"will be coming back . . . Soon. Perhaps tomorrow, or perhaps in a few days. And when they come back, what else are they going to bring?"

Baurzhan had to be content with that answer. For the time being.

Brandy's Cove
October 23, 1637

They left it a little too late, failing to give proper consideration to the fact that there were mountains to the west of Brandy's Cove. It was still dusk at a thousand feet, but at lake level it was full night. Brandy got on the radio. "Scout to *Nicky*. Over."

"*Nicky* to Scout. You're late!" Vladimir didn't sound particularly happy.

"It's earlier on the other side of the mountain," Brandy sent. "You want to put out a light?"

"I'll start the torches." The torches were placed in a line a specific distance apart, so that the plane could tell their angle by how far apart they were. If you came at them straight on, the closer to the ground you got, the closer together they were. The problem was that though both Brandy and Vladimir had completed ground school and knew the theory, neither one of them had ever actually made a night landing.

The good news, such as it was, was that the Scout would be landing on the lake. There was no way they were going to miss the runway. The bad news was the lights weren't going to be on the lake, but on the shore.

Vladimir called out of the side of the plane, and Vasilii, Miroslava, and the two guards who accompanied Salqam-Jangir Khan, lit the torches soaked with fuel oil and wrapped with cloth, to create a row of fires thirty feet apart.

Then he got back on the radio. "Turn on your lights, Brandy." Both the Scout and the *Nicky* had electrical systems. They needed them for the radios, and since they had the electrical systems anyway, they made wingtip lights. Those lights weren't bright enough to light the Scout's way, but they made it visible to Vladimir in the *Nicky*.

Brandy flipped a switch and a red light came on on the left wing, and a green light on the right wing. That was a standard from up-time and it was so that an observer could tell which wing was which, so which direction the airplane was moving in.

Once the lights were on, Vladimir could see them and direct them onto the glide path and tell them if they were high or low. It took about ten minutes and one aborted landing that ended in Brandy overflying the beach and circling around again. But they finally landed on the water about fifty yards from shore and taxied in.

Brandy's Cove
October 24, 1637

The next morning at breakfast in the large yurt-style tent, Salqam-Jangir Khan broached the question. "Not today, but soon, I must learn to fly. I will need to be trained to fly both the scout and the larger Hero aircraft, the *Nicky*. Further, I will want an aircraft factory in Shavgar. Again, this is not urgent, but is necessary." He looked from Vladimir to Vasilii and back.

"Certainly as a state in the Sovereign States, Kazakh can build airplane factories if it chooses to," Vladimir said. "You can build them, your merchants can build them. It's up to you. However, the design of the Hero-style aircraft was developed by the Ufa Dacha in large part from plans I either sent to the Moscow Dacha or bought in the Netherlands and brought with me. Those designs are the property of my family."

Salqam-Jangir Khan smiled and nodded. "I would like to acquire a license to construct Hero-style aircraft and the technical expertise to put those plans into practice." While not a wealthy nation by up-time or even down-time standards, the Kazakh Khanate had been a nation before it joined the Sovereign States, and the khan was, by any reasonable standard, quite rich. There was, at this point, no real difference between the national, now state, treasury of Kazakh and the private treasury of Salqam-Jangir Khan. "We can talk about it later, but not much later. In the meantime, we need to take the pistols to Almaty, and having done that, you will leave me and my guards there, and start shipping more supplies and fuel to Brandy's Cove."

Then he grinned. "Consider making Brandy's Cove Brandy's cove in fact, rather than in name. Part of the property of the Gorchakov House."

After breakfast, they loaded the *Nicky* with the crates of pistols and caps and with Salqam-Jangir Khan and his armsmen. Both planes set off over the mountain to Almaty.

In the air, over Almaty
October 24, 1637

Vladimir cruised over Almaty and realized that he wasn't going to be able to land in the city. There were two problems. One was the *Nicky*'s wingspan. It was a hundred feet across, and would need triple that to land safely. In other words, its landing field needed to be as wide as a football field was long. With the *Nicky*'s props being able to be reversed, it could land in a short distance, but it still needed a fair distance to take off. So even if he'd been able to land inside the walls of Almaty, he couldn't take off from the city. Vladimir got on the radio. "You were right, Brandy. I won't be able to land in the city, but after a bit of work, you ought to be able to land and take off from inside Almaty."

He looked over at the khan, who was standing in the cockpit, looking over Vasilii's shoulder. "I wish you would reconsider. We can wait until we've established contact and gotten a field established in the city, then you can fly in, in relative safety. There is room for a small landing strip."

The Scout wasn't an ultralight, but neither was it a Cessna. It was a small, relatively short-ranged, and very light plane that required three hundred feet to land and half that to take off. Part of the short landing requirement was accomplished by feeding less air to the air cushion. Less air meant more drag.

For its size and weight, the *Nicky* had the same advantages, but it weighed a lot more. In fact, it weighed almost a thousand pounds more than the Jupiter Five. It needed eight hundred feet to take off, and its lack of power meant that it didn't have a lot of lift after takeoff, so if there was a wall in the way, it needed even more takeoff space.

They'd talked about all that before they took off this morning, and Salqam-Jangir Khan had known it all before that. But Vladimir still tried one last time to get his royal stubbornness to reconsider.

Salqam-Jangir Khan smiled and reached for the radio's mike. "We're about to land at the north gate, Brandy. Be ready to cover our dash."

It was, Vladimir thought, a stupid plan. But as the khan went back to his seat in the passenger compartment, he brought the plane around to the desired heading, west to east, just north of the city. Then, starting at two thousand feet, he put the *Nicky* into a shallow dive that brought their airspeed up to one hundred forty mph, and much more gradually than Brandy had the day before. He flattened out to fly east at a height of less than thirty feet for the better part of half a mile. By the time they were getting close to the north gate, they were down to sixty-three mph. That was when Vlad reversed the thrust on the engines and the speed dropped to thirty-four as the plane dropped onto the air cushion, which was running flat out. The *Nicky* bounced on a cushion of air and Vlad let it skim until they were just in front of the north gate. He reversed the fans to the air cushion landing gear.

Then he grunted as the *Nicky* went from twenty mph to zero in less than a second. He wasn't the only one. He could hear grunts from all over the plane as the seatbelts kept people from flying out of their chairs at the cost of bruised bellies.

It was only a couple of seconds later that Salqam-Jangir Khan was up and at the door, followed swiftly by his guards and Sultan Togym.

Each of them grabbed a backpack full of pistols, shot molds, and caps, shrugged them on, and headed for the door. They flung open the door, ran out onto the lower wing and jumped down onto the field about eighty feet from the north gate of Almaty.

Vasilii had gotten up as they were running out and closed the door as the last of them exited. "They're out," he shouted. "Hit it!"

Vladimir hit it. He slammed the lever over to feed full power to the fans that inflated the ACLG, and then put the engine back to full. It took about fifteen seconds for the ACLG to inflate enough for them to start losing traction and begin to move. Then he reversed the left-side engines to spin the *Nicky* to the left, set them back forward, and started the *Nicky* straight toward a hastily assembled troop of Zunghar horsemen. The upper wing of the *Nicky* when at full stop was fourteen feet above the ground. With the ACLG inflated, it was fifteen feet above the ground. Even on horseback, the Zunghars would have to reach up to hit the wing, and might not make it.

The forty-foot lower wing was another matter. While on ACLG, it was a foot and a half above the ground, but it was also pretty solid. What really concerned Vladimir were the struts from the outer edges of the lower wing. Two struts extended outward to two points about thirty-five feet out from the centerline of the plane. If a horse or rider hit that hard enough, he might well break one of those struts. And without those struts, there was a very good chance that the *Nicky*'s upper wing would come loose.

On the other hand, it wouldn't do the horse and rider a lot of good either.

In any case, the horses more than the riders saw the *Nicky* coming at them and decided that anywhere other than in front of it was where they wanted to be. They scattered. Except for three unfortunates whose horses had decided to run directly away from the *Nicky*, convinced that they could outrun it. Which they could at first. In the first few seconds, they were galloping at thirty to thirty-five miles per hour, and the *Nicky* was accelerating from a dead stop. But within seconds the *Nicky* had sped up to forty-five miles per hour and Vlad pulled up the nose, the lower wing changed angle and went from air cushion to ground effect, and they were flying. Not very high, but by the time they clipped a horseman, the lower wing was six feet off the ground and traveling at sixty miles an hour.

The bag of the ACLG cushioned him a little, but that didn't matter, because the impact caused his horse to fall and roll over him.

Then they were up and away. Vlad turned the *Nicky* to try and see what was going on with Salqam-Jangir Khan.

"Open the gate for Salqam-Jangir Khan!" shouted one of his guards.

"Shout a little louder, Dilnur!" Togym shouted. "I don't think all the Zunghars heard you the first time."

Salqam-Jangir Khan laughed out loud. "You really think they'll leave us alone if they don't know who I am?" He watched the *Nicky* hit the galloping Zunghar and fly away, then he looked around.

The Zunghar were nicely disrupted, and even as he watched, Brandy flew the Scout down to buzz a group of horsemen who were trying to get organized, but there were a lot of groups of horsemen. And one of them was heading right for them, eight men with sabers out riding-hell-for leather.

"Idiots!" Dilnur complained. "They should be standing off and peppering us with arrows."

"Dilnur!" Togym almost whined in frustration. "Do you have to tell the enemy how to fight better?"

"He can't help himself?" Miras said. "Man told his momma she was doing it wrong when she birthed him."

"Well!" Dilnur said. "She was."

Salqam-Jangir Khan laughed at the oft repeated joke, then took aim at the approaching cavalry. They were about sixty feet away now, not really within range for someone with Salqam-Jangir Khan's limited experience, but he had nine shots before he had to change the clip and two spare clips. He started shooting and beside him the two guards opened up with their black-powder revolvers. They fired bullets down a rifled barrel, so the limitation on accuracy was primarily the accuracy of the shooter, not the gun.

And they were experienced men, so like Salqam-Jangir Khan and Sultan Togym, they shot at the horses, not the men.

One horse went down, then another, a third, then a fourth, all while the Zunghars were getting closer. But getting closer to men carrying accurate pistols is not a good thing. Two more horses went down, and one peeled off, leaving the last of them leaning over his pommel and lifting his sword. Four bullets ripped into him and he went off the back of the horse, which ran by them riderless.

Salqam-Jangir Khan turned back to the gate. "Would you get a move on in there?" he shouted. "It's getting hot out here."

And it was too. Someone was following Dilnur's excellent advice about how to kill pistol-armed men caught in the open.

Arrows were starting to come in from long range. The thing about arrows at long range is they are an area-effect weapon. Each individual arrow has a poor chance of hitting, at least in combat. Hunting was another matter.

However, there were only four of them standing out here in the open. And there was some distance between them. Also, there were only a few archers firing at them so far.

The north gate started to open and the four men ran inside.

Sultan Aidan Karimov had been called as soon as the guards on the walls saw the airplanes, and after yesterday the guards had been looking for airplanes. But the north gate lacked a sally port, and was heavily barred. It took them no more than a minute to get it opened, but Sultan Karimov knew from experience just how long a minute was in the middle of a battle. Besides, the main gates were the east and west gates, not the north gate. And that was where most of Almaty's remaining cavalry was located, waiting for the opportunity to sally after the mechanical eagle disrupted the troops and Sultan Karimov had been with them. So he was just getting to the north gate as it opened and four men came in.

He didn't recognize them. He'd never been to court and was a sultan mostly by courtesy, since he was the mayor of Almaty. He was a Kazakh, but his family had been townspeople for the last three generations.

The youngest of the four men looked around, saw him, and walked over. "I am Salqam-Jangir Khan and I'm here to help."

Sultan Karimov noted that there were just the four of them, then he remembered the mechanical eagles, and bowed as a sultan should bow to a khan. "We are ready to sally," he said, standing back up.

"Don't. At least not yet. We need to get your men armed first. Do you have black powder? Do you have lead?"

"A little. There is excellent hunting in the mountains and many of our young men use rifled muskets to hunt. They have been hunting other game from the walls since the siege started."

"We're going to need more than a little." Salqam-Jangir Khan pulled his backpack off and opened it. He pulled out a thing from the pack and handed it to the sultan. "This is a pistol."

"What's that?" Sultan Karimov had been riding from the east gate to the north gate while Salqam-Jangir Khan and his companions had fought outside the gate. Chinese muskets were as tall as a man. This wasn't a musket.

His grandson, Baurzhan, Karimov had put on the north gate to keep him out of trouble, had seen the skirmish. He'd been in the gate house. "How do they shoot without reloading?"

"Baurzhan! Wait until the khan asks you a question. Don't interrupt."

The khan handed Baurzhan a pistol. "See the rotating cylinder? Now, you have to half cock the hammer to rotate it. I'll show you." He took the "pistol" back, moved a lever and spun an iron container that had several holes. Suddenly Karimov looked down at the thing in his hand, not at all sure if it were a pound of gold or a spitting viper. He realized what those holes were for. You loaded them like you loaded a musket by pouring the powder in the hole, then putting the bullet in on top of it. He counted the holes in the cylinder. Six times. You could load it six times, then fire it six times.

It was almost more than the mechanical eagles had been.

"No. We use percussion caps to ignite the powder. Loading a pan for a slow match would defeat the purpose of the revolver," Salqam-Jangir Khan was saying.

"Will you let me shoot it?" Baurzhan asked.

"Baurzhan!" Karimov almost shouted at his grandson and Salqam-Jangir Khan laughed.

"Dilnur, take Baurzhan up on the wall and show him how to load and shoot the revolvers while Sultan Karimov, Sultan Togym, and I have a talk."

The talk took place in Sultan Aidan Karimov's home, and took the better part of an hour. It was only the first talk, but Salqam-Jangir Khan needed to get started as quickly as possible to clear the ground to let the Scout land in and take off from Almaty.

Almaty in 1637 was a walled city with a small river running through the center of town. The walls were mud brick, about twenty feet high, and had been built when the city was more prosperous. Since the siege had started, they had been working frantically to strengthen the somewhat decayed walls.

They were quite effective against the siege. There were three camps of Zunghars in armor, equipped with bows and swords, who patrolled around outside the city. And with the Kazakhs all the way over to the Aral Sea, that was all they figured they needed, since the main goal was to draw the Kazakhs out into the open so that they could be met in the field and crushed.

Almaty was the better part of a mile long, but less than half that wide, and the creek was shallow and about thirty feet wide. It had also been straightened by human labor at some point in the past. The walls were banked so that the creek narrowed as the water level lowered. Just at the moment, the creek was fairly close to full from the fall rains. There were streets on either side of it, and shops on the streets. Some of those shops would have to come down to provide room for the Scout to land, but other than that it was an excellent place to land. And once it landed, people, at least a few people, would be able to move in and out of Almaty at will.

Sultan Aidan Karimov, after looking at the map, said he would have it done in a couple of days. "What about the big one?" he asked. "We can take down more buildings here and here." He pointed.

Salqam-Jangir Khan shook his head. "The *Nicky* has less power for its weight than the Scout. That means it can't climb as fast. Yes, if you removed those buildings, it could get off the ground, but it couldn't get above the walls in the range you have available."

On the wall, standing behind the outer curtain, Dilnur opened his pack and pulled out several pistols. Then he pulled out a mold.

It had two sides and when you put those two sides together, it had six bullet-shaped holes and channels for the lead to get to them. He showed the kid, Baurzhan, the mold and a pouch full of lead bullets. He also showed the kid the powder horn and the caps. Then he handed the kid an empty pistol.

Baurzhan took the pistol and lifted it.

"Stop!"

"What?" Baurzhan looked at him and without thinking, pointed the pistol in the direction he was looking.

Dilnur reached out and jerked the pistol out of Baurzhan's hand and as he did, the hammer fell.

"Hey, what do you think you're doing!" Baurzhan demanded.

Dilnur pulled his own pistol and pointed it at the kid. "Two things, boy. Learn them now and learn them well. The next time you take a gun, any gun, anytime, anywhere, under any circumstances, and fail to check and see if it's loaded, I will shoot you myself. And if you ever point a gun at me again, it had better be loaded and you'd better shoot to kill, because if you don't, I'm going to take it away from you and beat you to death with it."

There was a small group of soldiers who had gathered around to watch the demonstration, and there was some angry muttering, then someone shouted, "Silence!" and there was silence.

A grizzled old sergeant—the man must have been sixty—looked around the small group. "When a man is teaching you how to deal with an angry cobra, listen to him!" He looked around to make sure he had everyone's attention, then looked at Dilnur. "Two things! Always check to see if it's loaded, and never point it at someone you don't want to kill. Got it. Next?"

Dilnur still had Baurzhan's pistol. He handed it to the old sergeant.

"How do I check to see if it's loaded?" the sergeant asked, pointing the pistol at the floor.

Dilnur explained and added calmly, "It's better to point it up if it's a stone or brick floor. The bullets will ricochet and can still kill you."

The lesson continued. Baurzhan and the sergeant got to dry-fire their pistols. Dilnur gave Baurzhan another one, and finally Dilnur walked them through loading the pistols, saving putting the caps on for last.

The parapet of the city wall rose about four feet above the

wall. So, standing and facing out, the parapet covered them to chest height.

Dilnur pointed out at the closest enemy camp, which was the better part of a mile from the wall, and fired, saying, "It would take a miracle to hit anything at this range, but the bullets will go that far and still be deadly when they get there." He showed them the proper firing stance for firing from a wall. One hand holding the pistol out at arm's length, and the other hand supporting the first. It was something Brandy had told him about from police shows. Whatever those were.

Then he showed them how you used the pistol in a cavalry battle, firing it with one hand. "It's not as accurate this way, but it works. And you'll probably be a lot closer."

Aside from the pistols for Baurzhan and the sergeant, he didn't give out any more, though he did let most of the guards fire a pistol at least once. By the time they got done, the sun was starting to set and workmen were tearing down buildings near the creek.

It was a good start.

CHAPTER 11

Almaty

Zunghar camp one outside Almaty
October 24, 1637

Sultan Soqay stood at the edge of the camp and watched the puffs of gun smoke from the walls. And listened to the *crack, crack* of the...? The *things* over there.

There were two rifled muskets in his camp.

Two!

And the other camps had none.

The Kazakhs had at least ten and possibly twice that. It was the fear of those rifled muskets that had decided him that a siege was better than an assault. The walls and the fact that he lacked scaling ladders or any other siege equipment had also contributed to his decision. But knowing that he was likely to lose most of his top officers in the first rush had undeniably been a factor. And, though he would never admit it publicly, knowing that he would probably be among the casualties played a role as well.

Then the little flying thing yesterday. Little. He snorted to himself. It hadn't seemed little yesterday. It had seemed huge. It wasn't until the big one landed today that it became little by comparison.

The Kazakhs could fly! Like gods!

Sultan Soqay jerked his mind away from such thoughts and went back to the puffs of white smoke and the *crack, crack, crack* from the walls. That, he could almost understand. He was familiar with Chinese muskets, after all, and Erdeni Batur's spies had reported that the reason that Salqam-Jangir Khan had attacked the Russians, then joined them, was to get a new type of muskets that were said to be much better than the Chinese muskets the Zunghar were familiar with. Apparently that wasn't all they'd gotten, but the short muskets were enough, never mind how they were delivered. Four men caught out in the open, armed only with the short muskets, had killed six horses and four men. Behind the thick walls of the city, with who knew how many of the short muskets, they would destroy his army. Not just his officers, but his army. His clan would die trying to take Almaty and he wasn't prepared to do that, not for Erdeni Batur.

On the other hand, if he were to abandon the siege, Erdeni Batur would have him killed. He looked around at his officers, brothers and cousins all, and decided. "We'll maintain the siege, but that's all. If Erdeni Batur wants Almaty taken by storm, let *him* storm the place."

Brandy's Cove, Issyk-Kul Lake
October 24, 1637

They had landed under lowering clouds, and were socked in for the next three days, which gave Vladimir, Brandy, Miroslava, and Vasilii plenty of time to worry over how they were going to deliver supplies to Almaty. The hard landing outside of Almaty had trashed the air cushion skirt on the *Nicky*. They had a spare, but that sort of maneuver was to be avoided as much as possible. It was hell on the skirts. The good news was that even with the skirt in tatters, they got enough of a pressure differential to get the bottom wing off the ground, which was all they had to have to take off. But it was bad for the plane.

It was on the second day that the idea of parachutes was brought up. And it wasn't even in the context of supplies. It was Brandy telling Miroslava about Valeriya Zakharovna, a woman who'd parachuted from the *Czarina* several times before the dirigible crashed in Berlin.

"Could we do that with supplies?" Miroslava asked.

"Yes. They dropped supplies in World War II over Bastogne. Of course, the supplies landed in places the Germans held. So we'd have to be careful. We don't want to deliver a bunch of AKs to the Zunghars."

The AKs had longer effective range than the pistols by an

order of magnitude. If they could get a couple of hundred AKs into Almaty with ammunition and good firing platforms, no place within half a mile of the city would be safe for the Zunghars, and at that point landing the *Nicky* might become practical. *Might*.

Meanwhile, they were still socked in, so they spent their time fishing, purifying water, eating freeze-dried stew, and wondering how things were going in Almaty.

Almaty
October 25, 1637

"Where are your airplanes, Salqam-Jangir Khan?" Sultan Aidan Karimov asked, not in censure, but clearly concerned as the sun set in the west. It had been a clear day.

The radios were heavy devices and the ones used for ground stations were heavier still. Not the sort of thing you carry in a backpack. Not even the sort of thing that the Scout could carry in a single trip over the mountains. All of which meant they were out of communications for now.

Which was already something that bothered Salqam-Jangir Khan. "I don't know. I wish we'd been able to bring a radio."

"Do airplanes come up lame as horses do?"

"No, but they can have mechanical problems. But that can't be it. Not with two of them. They can't fly in bad weather, but—" He waved at the clear sky.

"Your camp is on the other side of the mountains. The weather could be different there," Karimov said. "It's a week's travel on a good horse, but I've hunted across the mountains and the weather can be different."

"I hope that's it," Salqam-Jangir Khan agreed.

"It could be," Karimov said cautiously. "It rains often around the lake."

Brandy's Cove, Issyk-Kul Lake
October 28, 1637

The weather was clear and the *Nicky* was going to fly back to Pishpek to start the process of getting silk for parachutes. Silk was the lightest fabric available, and if woven tightly was among the best for holding air, so made the best parachutes.

Brandy would go to Almaty, in hopes that there would be a clear space to land the Scout.

"Don't land unless you're sure you'll be able to take off," Vladimir told her.

"I'll be fine, Vlad. You just see that you don't get lost." They kissed and climbed into their respective planes.

Almaty
October 28, 1637

Brandy's flight path was partly cloudy, but not that bad and it cleared up near Almaty. Brandy made a pass and then brought the Scout in on the canal. It was long and straight, and the buildings around it were far enough away for her wings to be safe. The two buildings that had butted up against it were gone now.

The landing wasn't difficult. The Scout was a slow plane to begin with, so it had a low stall speed. She couldn't do the reverse thrust on the fans that the *Nicky* did, but she did reduce power to the ACLG as soon as she was down and floated over to the edge of the canal. She didn't have a passenger this trip. Instead, she had a hundred-pound barrel of corned powder.

She opened the door and climbed out to see the citizens of Almaty staring at her in shock. Specifically staring at her chest, then her hips, and finally to her face. She looked at their expressions, which were going from shocked to outraged, and realized that Salqam-Jangir Khan had failed to mention that the pilot of the Scout was a woman. Luckily, he was right here to introduce her.

"This is Princess Brandy Bates Gorchakov," Salqam-Jangir Khan said. "She's from Grantville, the town from the future that arrived in Germany in 1631. Later she married Prince Vladimir Gorchakov, one of Czar Mikhail's closest advisors."

And Brandy realized that the omission had been intentional. What she didn't know was why. Brandy had a PPK, just like Miroslava and Salqam-Jangir Khan. The guns were about twice as expensive as the revolvers, but the real expense was the brass rounds full of smokeless powder. They cost a lot. Way too much to equip an army with, but not too much for a few wealthy individuals. And by now Brandy was very wealthy. Now, she casually dropped her hand to the PPK in its holster on her hip.

A few expressions got even more disapproving, but they all

got more cautious. She looked at Salqam-Jangir Khan. "I brought some black powder. We were socked in at the cove the last couple of days. And Vladimir is on his way to Pishpek to get silk for parachutes." Brandy was speaking in Russian. She didn't speak Kazakh well enough to make herself understood, and Salqam-Jangir Khan was quite fluent in Russian.

However, his fluency wasn't shared by the people of Almaty, at least not most of them. Only a few Russian explorers had gotten this far east, and most of those had been well north of here. There were a lot more people here who spoke some variety of Chinese than who spoke Russian. That would change, or would have, in that other timeline, but for now Chinese and Tibetan were the main influences on the Kazakh these people spoke.

"What about a radio?" Salqam-Jangir Khan asked.

Brandy shook her head. "Too heavy. Not the radio itself. The antenna and power supply."

"Isn't there a radio in your airplane?" a young Kazakh asked in accented Russian. She looked at Salqam-Jangir Khan, who nodded.

"This is Baurzhan Karimov, Sultan Karimov's grandson. I imagine he's been talking with Dilnur and Miras." Salqam-Jangir Khan grinned, and Brandy rolled her eyes. The khan's bodyguards were an "interesting" pair.

She figured she'd better explain. She pointed at the wing of the Scout. "The antenna in the airplane is built into that; it's actually laminated into the surface. The power supply runs off the Scout's engine. Again, it's built in, and the radio itself is a version that's stripped down for weight," she told the young man, who looked more confused than enlightened.

"Never mind. Get some help and unload the corned powder. Then set guards around the Scout. Princess Gorchakov, as soon as you're done supervising Baurzhan here, please join his grandfather and me for tea while we discuss the reinforcements that Czar Mikhail is sending us."

Brandy looked around and a part of her thought that maybe leaving a lone woman in an Islamic crowd wasn't the best idea in the world. But she'd felt the same thing before and she knew what Salqam-Jangir Khan was up to, and she approved of it. She was flatly unwilling to be sent to the harem to adhere to down-time Islamic notions of propriety. So she went about her business mostly ignoring the crowd.

✧   ✧   ✧

About twenty minutes later, Brandy was escorted into a nice room with walls inlaid with blue and white designs. Tea was brought and the women who brought it retreated. Brandy didn't know if they were servants or the sultan's wives. Brandy's West Virginia sensibilities had been widened a bit by her travels, but she still wasn't comfortable with the situation. Her inclination was to be belligerent, but a look from Salqam-Jangir Khan was enough and she decided that, for the moment, she would be diplomatic.

"So where is Brigadier Maslov?" Salqam-Jangir Khan asked, after taking a sip of the hot tea.

"The last word we have is that he's stuck in the fall mud, halfway to Shavgar. Trains are heavy. They don't do well in mud." She looked at Salqam-Jangir Khan, still unsure what he wanted her to say. But he nodded and waved for her to continue. *Okay, screw it,* she thought. "Frankly, Salqam-Jangir Khan, I think we messed up. By the time Ivan gets here, it's going to be all over but the shouting. At least, it will unless this Erdeni Batur has more than a bunch of bow-wielding horsemen in his army."

Salqam-Jangir Khan leaned back on the pillows, grinning, but he said, "Not at all. Oh, I don't disagree with you about the final outcome, but the real point of Ivan's train has more to do with my Kazakhs than Erdeni Batur's Zunghars."

That was less of a surprise to Brandy than the fact that Salqam-Jangir Khan would say it here in front of the Sultan of Almaty.

"Is the Russian czar so wise?" Sultan Karimov asked.

Salqam-Jangir Khan grinned at the old man. "Mikhail Romanov's biggest problem is that he is a bit too smart for his own good. He has a tendency to overthink things. Which is why Bernie Zeppi was such a gift from Allah."

"How so?" Sultan Karimov asked.

"Bernie is a good man and not really stupid, but he is no mental giant. What he is good at is cutting to the heart of the matter. 'Sacking the quarterback,' as he would put it."

Sultan Karimov was now just looking confused and Brandy was reminded that Salqam-Jangir Khan had been in the room when such things as the slavery issue had been decided in the constitutional convention. "Three fifths of a man." At least they were spared that abominable compromise. Suddenly Brandy was grinning as she remembered that if they wanted representation in congress, the women of Kazakh would have to be given the vote.

Moreover, would *have* to vote. And their men weren't allowed to tell them how to vote.

And she realized why Salqam-Jangir Khan had failed to inform them that Brandy was a woman or an up-timer. He wanted the full impact of her climbing out of the airplane, a woman, face uncovered, flying a plane and bringing them gunpowder, before they got to the bit about her being an up-timer.

"To answer your question, yes, Mikhail does know that Ivan Maslov's war train, with its cannon and its armor, and the ability to roll up a hill and have a fort in place in minutes, will have as much of an effect on the Kazakhs, whose territory he runs that train through, as it will on the Zunghars in battle. His problem is that he is afraid that they will feel that they are being invaded. And some of them will.

"But my people are a practical people. They will feel like it is an invasion, but they will know that if I hadn't made the deal, if we hadn't joined the United Sovereign States of Russia, sooner or later, that train would be coming anyway, and it wouldn't be coming to save them from the Zunghars. It would be coming to take their herds.

"And they will realize that a train that carries cannon can also carry cattle to market, and goods back from that market to make their lives better." He gave the sultan a straight look and went on. "That's what I wanted you to see when Brandy, here, climbed out of the airplane. Change is coming whatever you do. Embrace it, and it can restore the Silk Road and make Almaty greater than it ever was before on the wings of airplanes. Reject it, and it will come anyway. It will just crush you under the wheels of armored trains."

The look Sultan Karimov gave Salqam-Jangir Khan wasn't happy. And the look he gave Brandy was worse. But, finally, he bowed his head. "It will be as the khan commands."

Brandy wondered when Ivan would get here.

On the rail line
October 24, 1637

Ivan Maslov climbed into the car and looked at the rail line. This section had about four miles of track, then they would be back to mud. But the mud was starting to dry. It would be frozen in a month, and once that happened, the train would be very fast. The rest of the men climbed back aboard. They were happy to get off while it switched from land to track, a process that had to be done one car at a time. It was good to get away from the vibration for a little while. They moved best just after dawn, when the ground was better than half frozen, but they had light to see. They'd been making steady progress since the twentieth and there was only one more untracked stretch before Alty-Kuduk.

Ivan heard a noise, and looked up to see a Hero-class airplane. He waved, and the plane wagged its wings.

An aide called, "General, we have a radio message from the *Valentina Vladimirovna Tereshkova*. They want to know if we want them to land?"

"Why would we want that?" Ivan asked, then shook his head. "Never mind. Tell them to go ahead and land. I'll find out in person."

A few minutes later, the plane landed and a middle-aged woman got out. She hopped off the lower wing, which doubled as the air cushion platform, trotted over, and saluted.

Ivan returned the salute. "Captain Novikov, nice landing." Which was generous. The landing had been hesitant and she'd overshot and had to turn around and come back.

"Thank you, General, but, no, it wasn't," Captain Novikov admitted. "And the truth is, that's half the reason I wanted to land. We need the practice. Especially we need practice landing in the field, where we don't have the tower telling us we're too low or too high, at the wrong angle or off our glide path." She shook her head. "We need the practice on everything. The other reason is we could use some fuel oil. The *Tina*'s proving to be a thirsty lady."

The train had a whole train car full of fuel oil. It was right behind the engine and the engine used a lot of it. But topping up the *Tina* would make no material difference in their range.

"Certainly, Captain. Are you heading for Alty-Kuduk?"

"I would have been if I hadn't seen you, but I think I'll head straight for Shavgar."

"Is that in range?" Ivan asked as Gregory Petrov jumped down from the *Tina*'s lower wing with a jerrycan. He was wearing a sublieutenant's uniform with an Air Corps tab on his left shoulder. The uniform was new, but then again all uniforms in the Sovereign States armed forces were new. They were the result of the introduction of sewing machines after the Ring of Fire, making uniform clothing practical for governments to buy for their soldiers. In the spirit of newness, the Air Corps had gone with zippered jackets rather than buttons.

Gregory Petrov carried the jerrycan over to the tanker car and, under the direction of one of the train crew, filled it with fuel oil. Then he ran back to the *Tina*, opened a cover, unscrewed a cap, and poured the fuel oil in, and started another trip.

Watching, Ivan said, "This is going to take a while, Captain. Why don't we go look at maps?"

In the car, Ivan pulled maps out and between him and Captain Novikov, they refined their present position, the distance and direction of Shavgar. "I make it four hundred and thirty miles, Captain," Ivan said. "The Jupiter Fives have a range of around four hundred miles. And if the Hero class is proving to have less range..." He shook his head. "I can't approve such a risk, Irina. Get more practice landing at Alty-Kuduk."

She looked stubborn and Ivan said, "That's an order, Captain. We need that plane in operation, not sitting on the river waiting for a fuel barge." They did, too. Even after hard winter set in sometime in November, it was going to take a month to get the war train to Almaty. And even then, there was going to be Almaliq. "We are going to be doing the Berlin Airlift into Almaty for months before the train can get there."

Captain Novikov looked confused. It was understandable. Captain Novikov was out of the Ufa Dacha and the widow of a *deti boyar* who looked to the Gorchakov family. She was involved in designing the airframe and with Czarina Evdokia, Brandy Gorchakov, and Princess Natasha all pushing, she'd gotten a commission in the army as a captain in the Air Corps. And still a lot of the officers were very unhappy about it. They were sort of okay with Brandy flying. She was an up-timer and the standard rules didn't apply. But that attitude didn't apply to Irina Novikov. She was just an ordinary Russian widow with an engineering turn of mind.

Ivan was okay with her, except he wished she was designing new airplanes, not wasting her intellect flying them. She was, after all, about the best aviation engineer that Russia had. But he spent an hour explaining about the Berlin Airlift after World War II, and explaining what World War II was, and then the Cold War. Irina had an engineering turn of mind, but very little interest in military history or history in general. Especially not that other history that now would never happen.

But she got the idea that she would be spending long hours flying for the next several months, which almost made her okay with skipping the shortcut.

"Very well, sir!" she said stiffly. "But we need better maps and we aren't going to get them flying back and forth over the same ground."

"Isn't that the Scout's proper job?"

"Not really, sir, no."

Apparently she wasn't going to drop the "sir." Ivan was just past twenty and Captain Irina Novikov was rapidly approaching forty and she wasn't thrilled to be taking orders from boys barely old enough to grow a beard. Well, Ivan wasn't thrilled to be giving orders to women older than his mother, but that was the job.

"Why not, Captain?"

"The Scouts have less range, and they lack the mapping facilities available on the Hero class. The only reason we're making them is for their tactical utility. They aren't strategic."

Ivan nodded. She was right. The Scouts could go out a few miles, spot the enemy, and let the commander in the field know where they were. And they could land and take off in short little hidden places, while the Hero class needed more space, and apparently more fuel as well.

"I'm afraid the mapping is going to have to wait a few months until we have more of the Heroes in the sky."

Finally, Gregory Petrov knocked on the door and told them that the *Tina* was fully fueled. His bright red face testified to the weather. It was 30 degrees Fahrenheit outside, but their discussion in the train car had been held in comfort.

Ivan was thankful for the cold. The train was much less likely to sink into ice than mud.

The *Tina* would be in Alty-Kuduk in half an hour. It would take the train the rest of the day.

Ivan had his radio team report back to Ufa through the radio network.

Ufa Kremlin
October 24, 1637

Czar Mikhail took the memo, read it quickly, and passed it to his wife, who read it, grinned, and said, "I told you she was a pilot."

Mikhail snorted, and waved for the boffin from the Dacha to continue.

"This is the new radio system, Your Majesty."

It was set out on a table in several metal boxes with leather padding glued onto the corners. He pointed to the first box. "This is the transmitter receiver. It uses three tubes for tuning and signal amplification. We've had the design for years, and were just waiting for the tubes." He pointed to the next box. "This is the aqualator. It converts text into binary code for transmittal and sends the binary to the transmitter in blocks. The receiving station uses its own aqualator to run a check sum and inform the sending unit if a block has to be resent."

"How big are the blocks?" Evdokia asked.

"One K, that is one kilobyte, eight thousand bits held on the magnetic disk." He pointed to the aqualator which included a steel disk and a read-write head, none of which required complex electronics. Though the electromagnet of the read-write head did require the craftsman who made it to be working through a powerful magnifying glass and using gold thread thinner than a human hair. Then he pointed at the radio box. "Which takes the radio about three seconds to send. We considered using smaller blocks, but we are hoping for better signal strength as time goes on, and the aqualator can output or read at a kilobyte a second now. It's signal degradation in the radio transmission that is the problem."

Evdokia nodded and he went on. "This is the basic antenna. We adjust this for each installation. But this is the field expedient system and it's essentially just a long wire. On an airplane we build the antenna into the wings, and in a station we usually build an antenna tower and put a directional antenna up to increase the range. We can send the signal at sixty miles over flat land and thirty-five over hill country."

"Then we have the power supply, lead acid batteries and some sort of a generator. For field stations like this one, we use a pedal-powered generator. Permanent stations, we use a steam engine. Right now, we're using reciprocating steam engines, but we would like to switch over to steam turbines after what we've learned making the turbines for the Hero-class aircraft engines. They are a simpler system."

It was clear from the boffin's tone that he thought they never should have made reciprocating steam engines at all.

He was probably correct. Even here in Russia, it was amazing how much they copied the mistakes of the up-timers. "The up-timers used reciprocating steam engines first, so that must be the simplest way to do it." It was a common problem, more common in the USE than in Russia. Either Russia.

"In the aircraft; that's the *Princess Anna* in Hidden Valley, and the new heavier-than-air aircraft; we build the antenna into the structure of the vehicle and make them directional, so that you can adjust the signal strength by turning the aircraft. This allows the aircraft to point at the signal in flight and take a compass heading, so that they can use radio stations to get their bearings and calculate their location. It's not as accurate as we would like, but it does work."

The briefing went on and much of it was stuff that they already knew. This system hadn't burst full grown from Zeus' head, or even the library at Grantville. Instead, it had been developed gradually over time, partly in the original Dacha outside Moscow, partly in Grantville, and partly here in the Ufa Dacha. A lot of the how-to had come from Grantville, but actually implementing it was the work of the scholars and craftsmen of the Russian Dachas, who were becoming an increasingly influential class within Russian society.

Ufa Dacha
October 24, 1637

"Okay, Yuri, let's run it."

Yuri pushed the button and the punch cards started feeding into the punch card reader. Each punch card represented a single line of code. And they were feeding the program into a set of aqualators, which, taken all together, had almost as much power as a laptop from the 1980s.

Of course, they couldn't be taken all together. They didn't run fast enough to be integrated into a single computer, so the program had to be designed to operate on several distinct aqualators. Each aqualator did the calculations for one part of the program, then fed the data to a different aqualator, which combined the results with others, set new parameters, and then fed that data back to the start to run the whole thing again.

Twenty minutes later, the run finished and the bank of aqualators spit out a weather prediction for this part of the world. The prediction wasn't going to be great by up-timer standards, but that was only partly the fault of the primitive computing system and the still-learning programmers and meteorologists. Mostly it was due to the fact that they didn't have enough weather stations. By now most of the stationary radio telegraphs had weather-measuring equipment too, and reported readings at dawn, noon, and dusk. And a lot of them at midnight, if they had someone covering the night shift, but that was still a tiny fraction of the weather reporting they'd had up-time, and there were no satellites in orbit. Still, what they would be reporting on the Ufa broadcast tonight was much better than anyone had ever had before. When you had planes in the air, you needed accurate weather predictions.

CHAPTER 12

Gunboat Diplomacy

The Ilya Muromets, Caspian Sea
October 24, 1637

Captain Leonid Belyaed looked at the weather report. The radio teletype message was an indication that they were getting close to Astrakhan. Astrakhan had a good radio station with a broadcast range of about a hundred miles into the Caspian Sea, so they should be back to the port city by tonight. He handed the sheet back to the radio man. "I assume you sent them our data."

"Yes, sir. Winds, barometric pressure, humidity, our estimated location, the works. They said they would forward to Ufa."

This was the return leg of their third trip to Base One, the secret base on the Kazakh side of the Caspian Sea. There was a team of thirty people living there now. It wasn't a preferred duty station. The only water they had was distilled, and the only food they had was fish and what they had brought with them.

Leonid Belyaed was expecting to load up on canned goods and dry foods in Astrakhan and then make a fourth trip. It was moderately boring, but only moderately. The Caspian Sea was a sea, after all, and the *Ilya Muromets* was a riverboat. Astrakhan was the Sovereign States' largest seaport on the Caspian Sea, and food, as well as other goods, from the entire Volga River system was available there.

And it was part of the Sovereign States because the state of Astrakhan had quietly joined the United Sovereign States of Russia two weeks ago. That had pissed off Tsaritsyn and Saratov, who'd been counting on the four southern Volga states acting as a block.

Leonid nodded to the radio man and went back to his breakfast. It was eggs and Caspian sturgeon caviar and fresh bread. Leonid liked being captain of a gunboat.

If Leonid Belyaed was happy with his job, that made him no different from Bernie and Natasha. Who, over the last two months, had had plenty of privacy and no interruptions worth worrying about. The two were having breakfast while Natasha read a report on the advances in computers, and Bernie read a mystery novel.

The protagonist of Bernie's novel bore a marked resemblance to Miroslava Holmes in background and appearance, but was highly fictionalized. Of course, the name had been changed so that Miroslava couldn't sue over the use of her name or damage to her reputation. Not that she would anyway. Miroslava didn't care much about money or her reputation. She liked solving problems. Besides, she was off in Kazakh, not sneaking around in Nizhny Novgorod on a secret mission for the czar to catch the Muscovite spy, Med Nayezdnikovna. To the best of Bernie's knowledge, Miroslava didn't even *have* a secret decoder ring.

He snorted a laugh and Natasha looked up from her report. "Those things will rot your brain, Bernie."

"Too late. It was already completely rotted away by MTV before the Ring of Fire. Ask any of the geeks at either Dacha."

"Filip actually thinks you've done quite well," Natasha said, then paused before adding, "considering your limitations." Filip Pavlovich Tupikov was one of the scholars of the Dacha, both Dachas, who'd been involved in the development of everything from indoor plumbing to airplanes, and, quietly behind the scenes, the development of the Sovereign States and was the actual writer of the Flying Squirrel pamphlets that still circulated in both Russias. Russia's Benjamin Franklin and Thomas Paine rolled into one, except he avoided the limelight like it was sunlight and he was a vampire. He was also Anya's present squeeze, and probably future husband. Anya preferred geeks to former football stars. She insisted geeks were at least trainable.

Bernie stuck out his tongue, and went back to his novel. There was no TV in the seventeenth century, at least outside of Grantville, so the simple lack of other options had turned Bernie into a reader. And the many improvements in the art of printing and preparing a manuscript for publication that had been developed or copied from the tag end of the twentieth century made paper books inexpensive enough to be readily available. Even, these days, to the poor. So books like this one flowed down the Volga by the crateload and were sold in shops from Moscow to the southern Caspian sea. They weren't all that flowed down the Volga, with the manufacturing centers in Murom, Moscow, Nizhny Novgorod, Kazan, and Ufa. Russia—both Russias—were developing their own golden corridor. Not quite as robust as the Elbe corridor in the USE maybe, but getting there. And the civil war had barely even slowed things down.

That was half the problem. The cities of the southern Volga River, Samara, Saratov, Tsaritsyn, and Astrakhan were looking at all that improved trade running down the Volga on steamboats, and all too often going right by their towns without stopping to give them what they considered was properly their share.

It was also why Astrakhan had signed up. Even with the steam power of the riverboats, they still had to stop at Astrakhan to transfer their cargo to sea-capable ships. The *Ilya Muromets* wasn't really suited to its present mission, but it had higher gunnels than most riverboats to protect its guns and the gunports were watertight when closed, so it could handle the rougher seas of the Caspian Sea better than the average. But most Volga riverboats were taking major risks if they ventured into the Caspian.

All of which left the other southern Volga states in an unenviable position. And Bernie was confident that they were going to sign on simply because they had nowhere else to go.

There was a knock at their door and Bernie called, "Come in."

The door opened and a petty officer in a blue navy tunic with a brass zipper on the front came in. The zipper wasn't hidden behind a flap of cloth. It was displayed as though it was a set of fancy brass buttons which, in a sense, it was.

It was proof that the Sovereign States industry was up to making zippers. An advertisement that the Sovereign States was a modern nation as much as the USE. Which wasn't true yet, but they were trying.

He handed Natasha the note from the captain. She was a princess, after all.

"We're in radio range," Natasha said, and Bernie frowned. The real limit on radio range was Earth curvature, though there was some "bend," but not all that much. The new station at Astrakhan had its radio tower set on top of a tall building, and between the two it had excellent height and the *Ilya Muromets* could raise an antenna to give it extra range. Which it did, except in bad weather or combat.

Between the two, the range of the radio telegraph system was around a hundred miles on the Caspian Sea. Lower on land, but they had multiple stations on land. All that meant that Base One was going to be out of touch with the rest of the Sovereign States until they got a radio linkage through Kazakh. And the people of the great state of Kazakh had better things to do than set up a bunch of desert radio repeater stations to keep in touch with an oil exploration station that most of them didn't even know about.

"They'll be fine, Bernie," Natasha said. "We survived for centuries without instant communications. For that matter, you survived just fine for the last few years with nothing faster than a sailing ship to take your mail to and from Grantville."

She was right and he knew it, but it still felt like they were leaving their guys out on the end of a very long limb with no way to call for help once the ice closed the northern Caspian Sea.

Astrakhan docks
October 24, 1637

The sun was setting as they tied up, and Chao Wong was standing on the dock waiting for them. He didn't look happy. As soon as Bernie and Natasha were at the bottom of the gangplank, he leaned into them and spoke quietly but urgently. "The Tsaritsyns have gone crazy. We need to talk, but not here."

Once in his shop, Chao Wong said, "Colonel Greshnev has declared for 'Czar' Ivan Romanov."

"What?" Bernie asked. "Has Uncle Ivan declared then?"

"No. As of the latest report from Moscow, he's still calling himself Assistant Secretary General. He does have the dog boys on his side, and most of the remaining Boyar Duma. What's left of it after the purges."

After Sheremetev went missing, there was another set of purges with Ivan Romanov mostly tonsuring boyars rather than killing them. That is, he forced them to take holy orders, which made them ineligible to be part of the government. Exactly as had happened to Mikhail's dad.

"Then what is Greshnev thinking?"

Chao Wong shook his head. "Honestly, I think it's a ploy. He thinks that Mikhail lacks the will to go to war. Even with a small city state that doesn't actually control most of the territory they are claiming." Chao tugged on his beard in thought. "When Czar Mikhail and the *Czarina* first arrived here on his goodwill tour after they got to Ufa, we were overawed by the dirigible. A flying whale is an impressive sight. Especially if you don't understand the science behind it. But time passes, and the Ufa Dacha isn't much for keeping secrets. Then when the *Czarina Evdokia* was lost in Germany and the *Czar Alexis* was shot down so easily by the rocket men of Ufa, the awe faded."

"And the fact that we hold the Volga from the Caspian to Kazan doesn't impress him?" Bernie shook his head.

Chao Wong lifted open hands. "That was accomplished by politics and compromise. Czar Mikhail has given much of his power to the congress. He bought off the Kazakhs with the promise of aid against the Zunghars, and now the better part of his army is off in Kazakh, and the rest is tied down holding the Volga at Kazan. I think that Greshnev and his allies think that Mikhail is overextended and will be forced to give them whatever they want if they threaten his flank."

Natasha asked, "What have they done, other than declare for Ivan?"

"They've seized riverboats, mostly unarmed steamers, for taxes and duties, they say. Oh, and they are refusing to retransmit anything not sent in clear."

The radio system sent digital signals, so technically everything was encoded, but there was a standard code that anyone could read, so it was easy enough to sort everything by the way it was encoded and pull anything you didn't want out of the stream.

"The radio team at Tsaritsyn is ours," Bernie said.

Chao Wong nodded. "My impression is that they are under duress."

"Which means we're out of touch until we get near Saratov. Do they hold all the stations or just the one at Tsaritsyn?"

There were five radios along the Volga that were in the territory that was nominally the state of Tsaritsyn. There was another on the Don River, but that was controlled by the Don Cossacks.

"And what about the Don station?" Bernie asked.

"Tsaritsyn holds the radio nearest our border. As for the Don's radio, I don't know."

"I wish we had a Hero," Bernie muttered.

"We do, dear," Natasha said. "*You* are my hero."

He grinned at her. "Thanks, but I meant the airplane." Then he paused. "Why don't we have an airplane? Why didn't Mikhail divert one?" He turned to Chao Wong. "When did this happen?"

"Yesterday afternoon is when we heard about it. We had a boat return after being ordered to heave to for boarding near the state border.

"Then we sent a set of radio messages and we were informed of the change in allegiance. But they didn't announce it until the riverboat returned, and there are at least two more that may have been boarded and seized. As to when Mikhail found out about it, I don't know. For all I know, he doesn't know about it yet."

Bernie looked at Natasha "Do we wait?"

"No, Bernie. Mikhail sent you here. He knows who you are."

"Sent *us* here, love. He also knows that you're smarter than me and understand Russian politics in your bones. So I ask again, do we wait?"

Natasha considered. "No. We teach Tsaritsyn a lesson and a hard enough lesson that the others will learn it as well."

Bernie gave her a formal salute. "Aye aye, ma'am." And it wasn't a joke.

"Okay, we're going to need to top up on ammunition and fuel."

That took some time. While the *Ilya Muromets* was an excellent vessel, it wasn't the only armed riverboat on the Volga. Most of them had some armaments.

While Natasha and Captain Leonid Belyaed were organizing supplies and troops, Bernie considered the tactical situation. If Czar Mikhail hadn't heard about it yet, he would soon. And that meant Tim would be running the fight from upriver.

Ufa airport
October 25, 1637

General Boris Timofeyevich Lebedev climbed out of the Scout's front seat smiling. Tim had just learned that he liked flying in airplanes even better than flying in dirigibles. He did wish the

Scouts were a bit quieter, but the view was outstanding, especially on takeoff and landing.

He thanked the pilot and mounted the horse that a soldier was holding for him, and five minutes later, he was at the war room in the Kremlin.

"Can you pull more troops from Kazan?" Czar Mikhail asked as Tim entered the room. The map showing on the wall was of the Volga from Kazan to the Caspian Sea. The map table showed the map that included all of Russia, including Moscow and the state of Kazakh. And his army, as well as Ivan's, which was in Kazan.

"I'd rather not, but I could," Tim said as he headed for the stove in the war room. It was a chilly day out. "Honestly, it's not Kazan I'm worried about, but an end run of some sort around Kazan." Between Bernie and Cass Lowry, football terminology had made its way into the Russian military lexicon. "I have agents in Iakov Petrovich Birkin's army and I'm sure he knows it. The problem isn't what I'm hearing. It's what I'm not hearing. He's planning something. I'm sure of that, I'm just not sure what."

"Tsaritsyn has declared for *Czar* Ivan Romanov." Mikhail's emphasis on the czar was pointed.

"Well, your uncle didn't ask them to."

"I know that. Uncle Ivan may be a worse crook than Sheremetev, but he's not an idiot. On the other hand, if they make it stick, it could help him a lot. If he can start seizing territories without firing a shot, that will strengthen his position drastically."

Tim nodded thoughtfully and Czarina Evdokia put his thoughts into words. "People might think that Mikhail isn't the only Romanov who can gain territory without having to take it by force."

Tim didn't nod, but Mikhail did.

"What about Bernie and Natasha?" Tim asked.

"Out of touch. The radio network doesn't have much spread down the Volga. And Greshnev has seized the radios in the state of Tsaritsyn, so we don't know what's going on in Astrakhan either. For all we know, they've agreed to Greshnev's scheme or been conquered. The same thing is true of the Don Cossacks. We don't know if they are on Greshnev's side or our side, and they have a radio chain that goes to Moscow without going through our network."

"Why not use that? We have tie-ins to the Russian network."

"Gee, why didn't I think of that," Czar Mikhail said rather sarcastically. "We've sent messages up our chain, but haven't heard back yet."

The map on the wall was of the territory in question, showing just the western edge of Kazakh and the top of the Caspian, but also the top of the Black Sea. Tim looked at it and thought about what he knew about Bernie Zeppi, Princess Natasha and, especially, about Captain Leonid Belyaed. Bernie had proved that he kept his head in a battle. His ability to command others was less proven, but he knew enough to let the professionals do their jobs.

Again, for just a moment, Tim wondered when he'd become one of those professionals. But he knew the answer. Gradually, over the last couple of years. He really was General Tim now. And Captain Leonid Belyaed was a professional, one who'd been at Regev and learned its lessons well.

"I'll take a riverboat back. Send the Scout to establish contact with the *Ilya Muromets*, but I honestly think that Princess Natasha, Bernie, and Captain Belyaed will be able to handle it."

In the air, south of Saratov
October 26, 1637

The weather was closing in a little as the second Scout made its way south from Saratov. Saratov didn't have an airport, but it did have a river and a stock of fuel, the gasoline-alcohol mix that the Scout's engines preferred. The alcohol wasn't added because of a lack of gasoline. It was added to push up the octane and avoid backfires. On the other hand, it did reduce the power output a fair amount. Today, Konstantin Golov was piloting the Scout and Yakov Davydov was the spotter.

The Scout had a chain drive from its engine to the fan for the air cushion landing gear, and it had a radio and headphones for pilot and spotter. But it was a simple plane, designed to fly slowly and to look around for enemy forces. It had nothing approaching a pressurized cabin, which gave it an effective ceiling of around twelve thousand feet, but that didn't matter. Its carburation was also iffy, so the single 110 hp engine started losing power at about eight thousand feet.

Konstantin Golov had it at nine thousand to try to give Yakov the best view. They were looking for riverboats.

"Come in, Astrakhan," Konstantin heard Yakov say. Then the click as Yakov took his finger off the send button, then nothing but static. "Come in, *Ilya Muromets*." Click. Static.

"You see anything, Yakov?"

"Nothing, and the weather's closing in. We should head back."

Konstantin looked around. The clouds were closing in, but they were pretty and it was darn cold, so Konstantin figured they were probably snow clouds, not rain clouds. So he wasn't all that concerned with icing on the wings. Konstantin was bright, cool headed, and exceedingly well read on the subject of flight. What he wasn't was an experienced pilot. He had experience in dirigibles, but his total time at the stick of a Scout was seven hours. He could take off. He could land. He could navigate, turn and bank, all the things that, according to the book, meant you were a pilot. But seven isn't five thousand, and all the book learning in the world won't make it so.

He knew from his books that snow pulled water from clouds, making them less likely to cause icing than the lower, warmer, rain clouds. And besides, it was important to restore communications between Ufa and Princess Natasha. So they kept going south for another ten minutes until the snow clouds had closed in. But with the clouds closed in, he wasn't quite as sure of his airspeed, and he fiddled a bit until he thought he had it right.

He almost did.

But though the nose was a touch above the horizon, he was actually losing altitude gradually, and as he sank through the cloud, it went from a snow cloud to a slush cloud. That is a cloud with quite a few snowflakes, but also quite a bit of the sort of supercooled water that forms sleet and ice on wings. As the thin sheet of ice formed on the wings, the aircraft got heavier and sank faster and Konstantin Golov still couldn't see crap except a pale gray soup all around his plane.

His instruments told him he was mostly level, and the Scout had 5 degrees of dihedral, so it ought to self-level, but it didn't *feel* level. He made an adjustment, then another.

And the ice on the wings was changing the flight characteristics of the wings, and not in a uniform manner.

Fifteen minutes later, they came out of the clouds, a thousand feet of height above ground, and in a bank of about 30 degrees, losing about thirty feet a second.

They came out over open prairie, and that should have saved them. The Scout was a forgiving plane, and the air cushion landing gear made it even more forgiving. But it wasn't just the upper wings that were covered in ice. It was the lower wings and the skirt. With a coating of ice, the skirt couldn't inflate. And, worse, it blocked the flow of air, so there was no air cushion. Which would have led to a belly landing if the pilot was more experienced, or if the wings weren't covered in ice.

Instead, Scout Two hit the ground at a 15-degree down-angle, traveling at just under two hundred miles per hour. It spread over about a hundred feet of prairie and wouldn't be found until after Konstantin Golov and Yakov Davydov were nothing but bone.

CHAPTER 13

Most Successful Failure

Saratov
October 26, 1637

Aviv Yeltsin looked up as the radio man came in. Aviv was mostly a farmer, but his brother had gone upriver and sat in on the constitutional convention and, by Saratov standards, the family was quite well off. In preparation for maybe becoming a state in the Sovereign States, they'd held elections in the town and the villages and Cossack camps around, and Aviv had ended up "Governor," whatever that meant, of the not-yet state of Saratov. The state legislature, a couple of dozen drunken Cossacks, had yet to decide if they were actually going to join the Sovereign States. And Aviv wished they would make up their minds.

Especially since the idiots in Tsaritsyn looked to be trying to drag the whole southern Volga into a war with Czar Mikhail.

There weren't a lot of serfs in Saratov. The Cossack tribes were violently opposed to serfdom and had a habit of burning farms that held serfs to the ground, and stringing up the serf holders. If Saratov joined the Sovereign States, it would be a free state.

"What is it, Kirill?"

"We got a distress call from Scout Two, then nothing."

"Where was it?"

"We don't know. South, but that's it."

"Damn!" Aviv Yeltsin was about half Cossack himself. His father had been a minor Russian noble in the service nobility, and he'd been sent down here by Czar Fyodor Ivanovich and married the daughter of a Cossack chieftain who had started life as a runaway serf. So, technically, Aviv was a member of the service nobility, but he wouldn't be in charge unless his neighbors wanted him in charge. He knew that, and the truth was he'd always been more of a politician than a war leader.

"Run over to the tavern, Kirill, and tell those drunken louts that I need to talk to them."

Kirill grinned and left. And Aviv shook his head. Kirill was a good kid, down here from the Ufa Dacha with certificates in radio and aqualator science. He ran the radio room, and wasn't averse to using the aqualator to print out reports and do necessary calculations. Aviv hoped he'd be diplomatic with the Cossacks and not get himself beaten up.

Fifteen minutes later, Aviv was in the tavern where the legislature of Saratov met. "Listen, you drunken louts."

"Boo!" was followed by other expletives, most of them scatological in nature, and a few disparaging his ancestry. Mostly complaining that he wasn't drunk enough to be listened to. Aviv waited for them to quiet.

"That airplane that landed here last night and took off this morning has gone missing and whether it's Tsaritsyn's fault or not, Czar Mikhail is going to be upset. We're out of time. You need to make up your minds."

Of course, the problem was they had made up their minds. But of the twenty-four Cossack legislators, eleven wanted to join the Sovereign States, six wanted to stay independent, and the rest wanted to join the Muscovites.

The Muscovites were promising to make the chieftains Registered Cossacks, which was an important distinction in Poland, but less so this far east.

There was silence, then Iosif bellowed, "Have a drink, Aviv, and tell us what you think!"

Aviv didn't like to drink. He watered his beer and avoided wine, but he went to the bar and the bartender gave him a mug of the black beer that he made. Aviv choked it down, all of it, to prove to the "legislators" that he was serious. "I think that with the steamboats, Ufa is three frigging days away. With the radio, it's three minutes away, and with the factories, it's armed to the teeth. I think there are copper mines in the Urals and sturgeon in the Caspian, and we can sell them wheat and rye, and buy both those things. I don't care if *Assistant* Secretary General Ivan promises to make us Registered Cossacks. *Czar* Mikhail has already promised to make us full citizens if we join the Sovereign States. And he can get to us faster and easier than his Uncle Ivan can."

"You make us sound weak," Iosif complained.

"Iosif, you're a tough son of a dog, but I own an AK4.7, and two months ago I shot a bear with it. I shot that bear from over a hundred yards away, then I shot it again before it could get away. Iosif, you're not as tough as that bear. And it's a rug on my floor now."

Iosif stood up, pointed at the ceiling with a finger, and said, "I'm tougher than any bear." Then he sat down. "But I understand. They shoot us enough times and it doesn't matter how tough we are. But Uncle Ivan is making guns too. Lots of guns. And the iron mines...well, some of them are in his territory."

"Steamboats down the Volga," Aviv said. "I say we join the Sovereign States."

They argued for another hour, then voted. Fifteen votes to join the Sovereign States, nine opposed. Good enough.

When Aviv reported to Ufa that Scout Two was out of contact, he also sent word of the state of Saratov's formal desire to join the Sovereign States with the borders as specified in the constitutional convention.

Samara
October 26, 1637

Timofey was sipping beer in his room. "Office" was a bit too grand a title for the place. It had log walls with a ceramic stove in one corner, and at night doubled as his bedchamber. It had kerosene lamps with glass chimneys, though. And it was a comfortable place to sit with a beer and consider the situation.

The clerk opened the door, stuck his head in, and said, "Boss, Saratov has joined the United Sovereign States of Russia."

"Bear crap!" Timofey Razya was a Cossack. In fact, he was a Don Cossack. He'd moved here in 1634, and he had a seven-year-old son, who, it turned out, had made it into the Grantville history books as a rebel leader. Timofey had been half hoping that the southern Volga states would rally around Tsaritsyn, but Astrakhan had pretty much killed that idea. Now, with Saratov joining the Sovereign States, it was a choice between being a state in the Sovereign States or a bandit chief in the state of Ufa. And Ufa was already too big for his peace of mind.

"Okay. Get the men together and tell them we're joining the Sovereign States, and Fedor is going to be our senator."

Timofey wasn't the same sort of leader that Aviv Yeltsin was. His people voted, but they voted publicly with his men watching each vote. One of the reasons that he'd hesitated to join Mikhail's new union of states, was that he really didn't want the up-timers' notions of poll watchers involved in his elections.

He might lose.

But, officially, he'd held elections and everyone over ten had voted.

Tsaritsyn
October 26, 1637

Colonel Ivan Greshnev of Tsaritsyn was not a Cossack. He was a Russian *deti boyar* and an officer in the Russian army. He wasn't one of Russia's better officers, but he thought he was the second coming of Ivan IV Vasilyevich, and this conflict between Mikhail and Sheremetev, now Mikhail and his Uncle Ivan, had seemed like an excellent opportunity to carve out his own kingdom.

Had seemed like.

Now it was all going to crap. Those gutless wonders in Astrakhan had betrayed him, and now Saratov and Samara had betrayed him, as well. But they would get theirs. The Sovereign States couldn't access the Caspian Sea without him, and he would get Ivan Romanov to support him.

He would make it work.

The rational part of his mind knew better, but he'd already gone too far to back down. He'd had Ilya Blatov killed for insisting that they join the Sovereign States, and he'd placed armed guards on the radio operators in the state of Tsaritsyn. That was five radio telegraph teams and three of them were from Ufa, a total of seven soldiers of the Sovereign States, who were his prisoners. And one of the fools had resisted and died while he was being "persuaded."

Worse, there were fools who thought this ended things and would want to yield to Mikhail the Weakling now.

He gave his closest aides new orders.

All voices of dissent in Tsaritsyn were to be silenced.

CHAPTER 14

𝕽𝖎𝖛𝖊𝖗 𝕱𝖎𝖌𝖍𝖙

Ilya Muromets, *Volga River*
October 27, 1637

Captain Leonid Belyaed still liked his job. Not quite as much as when he was ferrying troops to Base One, but he still liked it. He still had hot, sweet black tea from China to sip as the *Ilya Muromets* steamed up the Volga.

They rounded the bend in the river and saw the "customs boat" right where the reports said it would be. It was a riverboat, converted from sail and human power to steam, and now with two brass cannons on platforms on the deck. Leonid looked through his binoculars and wanted to laugh. They were muzzleloaders. They had to have been made before Bernie Zeppi got to Russia in 1632.

Actually, looking at the things, he thought they'd probably been made at least ten years before Bernie got to Russia. On the other hand, the *Ilya Muromets* had four breech-loading four-pound guns with powder in bags and fired using percussion caps.

The *Ilya Muromets* also had a bull horn, and this was an excellent time to use it. He flipped a switch and spoke into the headset. "In the name of the United Sovereign States of Russia, I call on you to surrender your vessel." Using the same amplifier that the ship's radio used, his voice boomed out of the bull horn located on the prow and there was only a little feedback squeal.

The response was a blast of grape. Since the men were under cover, little actual damage was done, but some of the expensive glass was broken.

Leonid looked over at Bernie and Natasha, who'd joined him on the bridge for this, and said, "Permission to engage?" He didn't really need it. He was in command, but he was very much aware that what he was about to do was technically an act of war, since Tsaritsyn wasn't legally a state yet.

"In the name of the Czar, permission granted," Natasha said.

"Take them out," Bernie said.

"Right full rudder," Leonid told the pilot. He flipped the switch that would send his orders to the port gun deck. "Fire as you bear."

The gunner watched through the periscope, less for safety than for accuracy. The periscope was designed to let him see just where the shot would go. It wasn't perfect, but it was way better than looking at the cannon, then looking at the target, then holding your head next to the barrel, then standing back up and guessing.

He watched as the bow of the customs boat came into view, then as it moved out of sight until the cannon was pointing amidships at the customs boat. Then he pulled the lanyard and the hammer fell on the cap and the cannon went off. The customs boat wasn't armored. The hull was moderately thick, but the cannonball didn't even slow much. Not until it hit the support for the mast that still stood. It shattered the mast, but was deflected forward and down, so that it went through the hull well below the waterline and about five feet forward of the mast.

Not that that mattered. The second cannon's shot hit the custom boat's powder magazine.

Back on the bridge, the *whump* and the geyser were quite impressive. At Bernie's insistence, they stopped to pick up survivors. There weren't that many. No one from the black gang had survived.

Then they went on. The next stop was the radio station closest to Astrakhan. The entire radio chain from Kazan to Astrakhan was placed along the river to make resupply easy.

It also meant they were easy to take. They were small settlements, a radio tower—which looked to Bernie like an up-time wooden oil rig tower with a long pole sticking out its top—a building to house the radio, the aqualator, the generator, and the batteries and usually a few other houses to house farmers or, in this case, fishermen.

The fishermen were staying out of it. There wasn't a person on the street. Heck, there wasn't so much as a cat on the street. The fishing boats were pulled up on shore, not tied up to the dock, leaving it clear for the *Ilya Muromets*. The radio tower was located about the length of a football field from shore, and it was pretty clear it was only that far back to avoid the spring floods. It did have a stockade around it, perhaps ten feet tall. It wasn't on a hill for the simple reason that there weren't any hills. The ground here wasn't as flat as a tabletop, but flat as a pancake might well fit.

They pulled into dock and the crew put out the gangplank and then Royal Russian Marines went down the gangplank and formed up on the dock. They weren't all that good at it. At least not to Bernie's up-time movie-based notions of forming ranks. They milled about, found their place in formation, and when they started marching up the dock at least one in three was out of step.

Natasha squeezed Bernie's arm and said, "Don't they look professional."

Bernie just nodded. Partly that was politeness, but he could see what she was talking about. They were in uniform. And that was new. They had red coats, black pants, and white shirts. They each had a bandolier for AK4.7 chambers and most of them had chambers filling their bandoliers. They were all wearing the fur-lined brimmed hats that Bernie thought of as baseball caps. After General Tim adopted that sort of cap, it had become the standard for the whole army. And they were all wearing leather boots. Their AK4.7 carbines were at shoulder arms as they walked up the dock to the main road of the village.

Bernie and Natasha walked down the ramp and followed them up the dirt track that was the main and only road of the fishing village. It went from dock to stockade, and that was it.

The stockade gate was closed and barred. Major Ivan Kalashnikov got the men in formation, then looked to Natasha.

Natasha stepped forward and shouted, "In the name of Czar Mikhail of the United Sovereign States of Russia, I order you to open the gates."

"You aren't in the Sovereign States," a shouted voice came back. "You're in the free state of Tsaritsyn. You have no authority here."

"That radio belongs to the United Sovereign States of Russia, and the people manning it are her citizens," Natasha said. "As to the 'free state' of Tsaritsyn, I doubt it's going to exist much longer. But even if Czar Mikhail decides to let Tsaritsyn remain independent, I guarantee he's not going to let you cut off trade and communications down the Volga. And the radios *are* trade and communications. So open the gates, and let us talk to our people before things get ugly."

"Or I could just shoot you!" the man shouted back, and someone stuck a rifle barrel up over the stockade and marine carbines started to shift.

Bernie shouted, "Attention!" and a heartbeat later he was echoed by Major Ivan Kalashnikov, who echoed the order, then gave Bernie a dirty look for ignoring the chain of command. The Marines came to attention.

After being told about the up-time confusion of ranks when a marine captain was onboard a ship with a navy captain, Czar Mikhail had solved the problem for the Russian Marine Corps by the simple expedient of eliminating the rank of captain from the RRMC, Royal Russian Marine Corps. Russian Marines had junior lieutenants, senior lieutenants, majors, junior colonels, and senior colonels, but no captains.

"Then I would die, and shortly after that you would die, and everyone with you would die as well," Natasha said calmly, as calmly as you can shout something. "If you were to try it, the smartest thing your fellows could do is shoot you first. Because at that point, it wouldn't matter at all who won in the end. None of your people would live out today. So, don't be stupid if you want to live to see another sunrise.

"Now, I'm getting tired of standing out here, so open the *damn* gate!"

There was a silence, then the noise of a bar being removed, and the palisade gate opened. The radio team, at least this radio team, was bruised, but not seriously injured, so the garrison that Colonel Greshnev commanded were simply disarmed and sent on their merry way, after being questioned about what was going on in Tsaritsyn.

A platoon of Marines was detached as guards for the radio station under the command of Lieutenant Eduard Vetrov.

Lieutenant Eduard Vetrov was a junior lieutenant, one silver bar on his baseball cap. A senior lieutenant had railroad tracks, and a major an oak leaf. He also, to Bernie, looked like a kid in his shiny new uniform, with his shiny new brass zippers. Fortunately, there was a forty-year-old *streltzi* sergeant as his platoon sergeant. An old bruiser with a busted nose and several missing teeth, who was actually running the platoon while he taught his young gentleman how to be an officer.

Russia was modernizing just as fast as it could. Both Russias were. There wasn't any choice. But it had only been six years since the Ring of Fire.

The same thing happened at the next station and the one after that. Then they came to the city of Tsaritsyn. In that other timeline it would be renamed Stalingrad, then after the fall of the Communist party, Volgograd. This, to a great extent, was the bite that broke the Nazis' teeth in World War II, or it would have become that anyway. Two and more centuries earlier, it made Grantville before the Ring of Fire look prosperous. There were six hundred soldiers in the garrison and perhaps two thousand citizens, most of whom worked as porters in normal times.

These weren't normal times. The city was locked up tight. The houses beyond the walls were abandoned.

But it wasn't because they were afraid of Natasha and the riverboat. No, it was the Cossack army on the landward side of the town that had them locked behind their walls.

Tsaritsyn docks
October 29, 1637

Bernie stood on the roof of the second floor of the riverboat and used his Russian-made binoculars to look at the city of Tsaritsyn and the Cossack camp on the far side of it. There were actual hills of a sort at this bend of the Volga. Not big hills, but big enough to make it an uphill slog through enemy fire to take the Tsaritsyn Kremlin. And Bernie knew that the garrison at Tsaritsyn was equipped with at least AK3s and probably at least half of them would have AK4s.

The guns on the *Ilya Muromets* were rifled breechloaders and the Kremlin walls were still mostly wood, but they were light guns and it would take them a while to punch breaches in the walls. And Tim's insistence that the defense had gotten a lot stronger with the introduction of new weapons systems had just bitten the Sovereign States on the butt.

That was something that the Don Cossacks had found out the hard way, apparently in the last couple of days. There were still bodies outside the Kremlin walls. Meanwhile, though they hadn't fired yet, the *Ilya Muromets* was within range of the muzzle-loading twelve-pounders located in the Tsaritsyn Kremlin.

"Gunboat diplomacy, you told Mikhail," Bernie muttered to himself. "When are you going to learn to keep your big fat mouth shut?"

The Volga, this far downriver, was huge. Not quite Mississippi huge, but bigger than anything in West Virginia, that was for sure. It was perfectly possible to sail right by this bend in the river in relative safety. The smooth bore brass cannon in the Tsaritsyn Kremlin could reach the far side of the river, but if they hit anything at that range, it would be the next best thing to a miracle. And they only had four of the things with a rate of fire that meant they would still be reloading from the first salvo when the boat they were targeting steamed around the bend and was lost to sight.

On the other hand, Tsaritsyn could put boats on the river and interdict traffic that way. So they couldn't take the *Ilya Muromets* home and just ignore Tsaritsyn. As long as Tsaritsyn was hostile, they were a threat.

Bernie was still examining the tactical situation when Natasha's voice came over the bullhorn. "To the commander of the Cossacks, we'd like to talk."

Bernie stood up and went down the ladder to join Natasha and see how things developed.

A few minutes later, what looked like a Polish hussar, complete to the wings on his horse, came riding out of the Cossack camp, rode around the outskirts of Tsaritsyn, keeping at least a hundred yards from the Kremlin walls, rode up to the dock, rode out on the dock, and up the gangplank.

He almost got shot for his trouble by the Marines on duty, but he was grinning through a graying blond beard when he dismounted. "I'm Gregori Denisov, registered Cossack and leader of that group of hearty fellows over on the other side of Tsaritsyn. Now, where is the beautiful woman who wants to talk to me?"

Natasha grinned. "Welcome, Gregori Denisov. I am Princess Natalia Petrovna Gorchakov. My friends call me Natasha."

"Ah, Natasha. The famous princess who married an up-timer and can enchant any man with a glance. The woman who turned a mouse into an emperor, and pulls steam engines out of her sleeves."

"It's getting deep in here," Bernie muttered, and Natasha elbowed him in the ribs.

"I said it in English," he complained, still in that language.

"Then this must be the famous up-timer wizard who conquered the slow plague in Moscow and taught the Russians to fly. I saw the *Czar Alexis* before it had its unfortunate encounter with the rockets from Ufa.

"So, tell me, great wizards, what is your plan to school this traitorous officer?"

"Good question," Bernie muttered. "Tim says that the defense, especially a well-fortified defense, has a ten-to-one advantage over offense."

"Tim?" Gregori Denisov's smile was gone. "Oh, your famous boy general. I wish he'd been here yesterday." He shook his head. "I probably wouldn't have listened anyway. Five hundred dead, and we never even reached the Kremlin walls. How can an army of brave men be stopped by a bunch of garrison troops?"

It was a serious question, with a lot of anger behind it. Gregori Denisov's bluff good humor was an act that he was maintaining with difficulty after the drubbing his army had taken. Behind that mask was a man who'd lost friends and allies and whose anger was just barely held in check. Bernie could see a carbine, a flintlock carbine, on the saddle of Gregori Denisov's horse. It was an AK3 . . . no, it was an AK2.

The AK rifles, like buggy software up-time, had gone through generations. The AK1 through AK1.9 were basically experimental guns. The AK2s were the first to go into production but they hadn't been in production long. By 1634, no one was making them anymore. They'd been replaced by the AK3s, which had lighter chambers, a lever action to pop a used chamber from the gun and make it ready to take a new chamber. The AK4s made the change from flintlock to caplock and a sealed system that could be fired in the rain.

This was a registered Cossack, which meant he was a leader. What the hell was he doing with an AK2?

Bernie looked over at Major Kalashnikov, who'd joined them. "Major, please let Colonel Denisov examine one of your men's AK4.7s."

"Vetrov, front and center," Major Kalashnikov ordered.

Vetrov, a short, broad man with a thick black beard starting to go gray and two rockers under the three chevrons on his hat and sleeves, stepped forward smartly and brought his AK4.7C to present arms. It had a walnut stock polished to a high sheen with a thick leather butt, and you could see the chamber clip sticking out the side. The pump was also walnut and highly polished.

Major Kalashnikov took the presented carbine and showed it to Colonel Denisov, pointing out the salient points. "The AK4.7C—the C is for carbine—is the Marine's issue weapon."

Bernie knew that the major was bragging. Even with the factories running full tilt, which they were, less than half the Royal Russian Marines had actually been issued AK4.7Cs, but this was a diplomatic mission, so all *their* Marines had them.

"It is a light weapon, easily maneuverable on shipboard. And the tight rifling and high spin give its rounds an accuracy greater than longer guns with looser rifling."

That part was true, and Sergeant Vetrov was the best shot in the company.

Holding the carbine up, he pulled the pump and the first chamber was pulled back and to the left. Then he pushed it forward and the second chamber was slotted into place, while the first stuck out to the left of the carbine, still unfired. He repeated the action six more times, catching the clip of chambers as it fell out the right side of the carbine at the end. Then, pulling the pump, he slotted the clip back in the left side.

"These are still black-powder weapons though the eggheads at the Dacha keep insisting that they are only a few months away from large-scale smokeless powder production," Major Kalashnikov said. "Fortunately, the chambers are enough heavier to absorb the added force, so we will probably continue to use the same design when we get smokeless powder. Perhaps with a longer, heavier bullet."

Bernie snorted at that. The bullets they were using now weren't light. The AK4.7, carbine or not, had a .45 caliber bullet and the present black-powder charge would punch that bullet right through a steel breastplate at a hundred yards.

"If you would care to pick a target," Major Kalashnikov finished, "we can have Sergeant Vetrov demonstrate rapid aimed fire for you."

Colonel Denisov looked at the carbine, then he looked at the AK2 still riding in the holster on his horse's flank. His eyes had gotten big as he saw the chambers automatically moving from the right side of the carbine to the left as Sergeant Vetrov pumped the carbine. After a moment he nodded and looked around for a target. There were some trees about sixty yards away, just the far side of one of the fishermen's cottages that lined the river bank.

"One of those trees?" Colonel Denisov pointed. "Or you could just shoot up the fisherman's shack. This side of them."

"Let's not damage anyone's property unnecessarily," Bernie said.

"Not much of a challenge," muttered Sergeant Vetrov in a voice that Bernie knew was meant to be heard. Pavel Vetrov was an excellent shot, a good sergeant, and about as arrogant a man as Bernie had ever met. He was also right. Bernie knew the man could put a seven-round clip into a five-inch circle at one hundred fifty yards.

Colonel Denisov looked at the sergeant, then at the grove of trees. "See that pine there on the side? The one with the single limb lower than the others. Think you can put one of your bullets into that particular tree trunk?"

The trunk was about a foot wide, maybe a bit less.

"Kneeling, aimed rapid fire, Sergeant," Major Kalashnikov said. "Whenever you're ready, Sergeant."

Sergeant Vetrov took two quick steps to the railing, knelt, put the carbine against his shoulder, and proceeded to put all seven rounds into the trunk, right next to the low-hanging limb.

Colonel Denisov sighed.

"The men behind Tsaritsyn's wall mostly have AK3s, but some of them have AK4s," Bernie said. "I don't actually know how many of them have AK4s. The gun shops in Ufa, Kazan, and in Muscovy-controlled Russia are, for the most part, privately owned, and Tsaritsyn's right on the Volga. Buying an AK4 there is simply a matter of having enough money."

"And if we'd had those AK4.7C like that?"

"It would have made very little difference," Major Kalashnikov said grimly. "They were behind walls. Not great walls, but walls, with ninety percent of their bodies hidden from view and protected from shot. While your men were charging forward en masse in the open, where someone with much less skill than the sergeant there would have hit the man next to his target or the man behind his target, even if he missed the man he was aiming at."

"Then what are we going to do?" Colonel Denisov demanded. "My men are Cossacks, not siege engineers."

"For right now, I think a siege is what we should be doing. At least until I can get back in radio communication with Ufa and Tim in Kazakh. He may have some idea what to do about this thorn in both our sides."

It took a bit more negotiation, but he got Colonel Denisov to agree to keep his men camped just out of rifle range of Tsaritsyn, while the *Ilya Muromets* retook the radio stations upriver.

Dubovka radio station
October 30, 1637

The radio station was trashed. The oil-rig-style tower was burned. So was the radio building. The radio itself, along with the aqualator, the teletype machine, and the batteries, as well as the generator were all gone.

The radio team was still there, as were the four fishing families that had set up around the radio station.

"At least they didn't kill you guys," Bernie said.

"They were going to, at least the radio operators. Those were the orders they got from Tsaritsyn," the head radio guy said. "But I pointed out that the villagers were witnesses, and even if they killed them, who was assigned here was a matter of record and they knew it in Ufa." He grinned. "I told him I'd radioed the whole unit roster to Ufa the day we set up."

"Had you?"

"Nope, but I figured 'what do I have to lose?'"

"Well, in the future, that's going to be standard policy," Bernie said. "And we'll get you a new radio out here within a couple of days."

The next station upriver was close to the border between Tsaritsyn and Saratov, and the troops there decided that they were going to switch to the Saratov militia. The radio stations down the Volga from Kazan were joint endeavors between Czar Mikhail and the locals. The czar provided the radios and the radio operators, while the locals provided the guard force and the farmers and fisherfolk who set up villages around the radio stations to supply them. It worked other ways in other places, but that was how it worked here.

The Tsaritsyn garrison here had obeyed the orders of Colonel Greshnev. But the Tsaritsyn garrison farther upriver had gone the other way. They'd figured that Colonel Greshnev was going to lose, so when they got the orders to kill the crew and steal the radio, they decided to turn their coats. The decision might have been influenced by the fact that the sergeant of that group was walking out with one of the radio techs, a woman of thirty-five who had a nice smile and liked bawdy jokes.

So the radio station at Kamyshin was now in the state of Samara, which was about fifty square miles bigger, while the state of Tsaritsyn was smaller by an equal amount. Actually, when this all played out, the state of Tsaritsyn was probably going to end up two thirds to half the size it had been at the beginning of the process.

"Czar Mikhail has been informed of what's been happening out here, and another Scout plane is being sent out," Bernie continued. "Also, we've called in the big guns. General Tim is on his way."

The radio tech looked more relieved after hearing that than he had all morning.

CHAPTER 15

𝔅𝔶𝔭𝔞𝔰𝔰 𝔖𝔲𝔯𝔤𝔢𝔯𝔶

Tsaritsyn docks
November 4, 1637

There were four gunboats steaming down the river to Tsaritsyn and Tim wasn't the only person on them. Czar Mikhail and Czarina Evdokia were there as well.

"It wasn't my idea," were the first words out of Tim's mouth as he came down the gangplank.

"That's right!" Czar Mikhail said gaily from behind him. "And consider yourselves lucky we didn't bring the kids. They wanted to come, you know. Raised an unholy ruckus about the whole thing."

"Congratulations on your success," Bernie said, paused a beat, and added, "Czarina Evdokia."

From behind Czar Mikhail, the czarina grinned.

"I do believe my royal self has been offered insult."

"No, Your Majesty," Natasha said. "Just knowledge of the inner workings of the royal household."

"Even more dangerous," Mikhail said, grabbing Bernie and giving him a bear hug. "Off with his head."

"I really wish you wouldn't say things like that, Mikhail. Someday, someone isn't going to realize you're joking."

All this was happening on the Tsaritsyn docks in full sight of at least a hundred people, including Colonel Denisov, who commanded the Don Cossacks investing the city, and several of his captains. It was also in full view of the city walls, though far enough away so they probably couldn't hear.

Mikhail looked around and said, "Let's adjourn to the imperial steamboat. We have excellent maps, and a meal, and it's warm." He shivered rather theatrically. It was a cold day. Cloudy with ice on the ground, reminding them all that the Volga was going to turn into a sheet of ice over the next couple of months. It would be late December before it froze around Astrakhan, but here it would be unnavigable by steamboat by mid-December. They adjourned to the large and windowed dining hall on the czar's steamboat in time to look out its windows and see a Scout circle over Tsaritsyn and land on the Volga. It tied up to the dock and they were shortly joined by the pilot and the scout.

While Czar Mikhail, Czarina Evdokia, Bernie, Natasha, General Tim, Colonel Denisov and his second-in-command, Major Simeon Platov, dined on sturgeon steaks with a dill sauce and tomatoes from the czar's greenhouse, the pilot and the scout added details to the map of Tsaritsyn.

Tim put down his napkin, looked over at the map table, and Czar Mikhail waved at him. "Go ahead, Tim. I know you won't be happy till you've pored over the latest additions, not that they are going to change anything."

"Probably not, Your Majesty," Tim agreed. And he was almost certain that the czar was right. He'd been thinking about this problem for a week, but in a larger sense, he'd been thinking about this problem from the other side for more than a year. And he had the experience of fighting a siege just like this one for that year, from the besieged side. Of course, he'd had a better situation in most ways, but part of what General Birkin had done by accident was effective. That was why Birkin still technically had Kazan under siege. He'd effectively built his own city outside Kazan, just upriver from Kazan, between Kazan and Kruglaya Mountain. Birkin couldn't successfully attack Kazan or Kruglaya Mountain, but Tim couldn't take Birkin's city either. Over the last year the men on both sides had started calling it Birkingrad, much to Birkin's annoyance. Birkin was smart enough and politically savvy enough to realize that building a city named after himself when he was supposed to be conquering Kazan and moving on to Ufa wasn't designed to make him popular with Sheremetev or Ivan Romanov.

At the table, it turned out that Czar Mikhail was right. The walls were mostly wooden stockades, but Colonel Greshnev, while not the greatest strategic thinker Tim had ever met, wasn't a total idiot when it came to tactics. He had workers building a second wall behind the first and filling in the space between them with earth, making breaching the walls a lot more difficult. Tim could still mortar-bomb the city. Or, using one of the Heroes that were under construction in Ufa, literally bomb the city, killing hundreds of people. That was militarily possible. It wasn't politically possible, not under Czar Mikhail. There was no way in hell that Mikhail would stand for carpet-bombing a city full of civilians.

Tim smiled slightly. People didn't understand Czar Mikhail, which was probably a good thing. Czar Mikhail wasn't in any sense a personal coward. But he was a man who saw the consequences of his actions perhaps a little too well, and was utterly unwilling to kill the innocent along with the guilty. He had enough trouble killing the guilty when they needed it. In that other world, he would have been standing right next to Gandhi or Martin Luther King. It made him a difficult monarch to work for, but at the same time, it made him more worthy of Tim's loyalty than anyone Tim had ever known.

Along with his studies of the tactics and strategy of people like Rommel and Patton, Marshall and Eisenhower, Lee and Grant, Tim and his friend Ivan Maslov had also studied the battles, tactics, and strategy of this universe and this time, especially those of Gustav Adolf and Mike Stearns. And one thing had stuck out even though it hadn't involved Stearns or any of the other major military figures. Just a bunch of Germans, leavened by a few up-timers, at a place called Forchheim. They hadn't so much besieged Forchheim as they had bypassed it. Built a road that went around the place and otherwise just ignored it. Ivan had pointed out that the Forchheim bypass was about as close to the strategic offense/tactical defense doctrine they were trying for as anything they were likely to see.

The important thing here was that Tsaritsyn got most of its power and about all of its wealth through the fact that it controlled the portage from the Don River to the Volga River. Without control of the portage and the fees that went with it, Tsaritsyn didn't matter at all.

Having looked at the map of Tsaritsyn for long enough to be sure that it would be idiotic to attack it, Tim covered that map with the map of the portage route from the Don River to the Volga.

There were tributaries that were nominally passable for light boats that went a good part of the distance, but the consensus of the road builders was that the simplest thing would be a good solid road with a rail down the center that went from the Volga to the Don. That was the best way to go. By now there were crews, Russian and Kazakh, that could put in a solid macadam road or even a tarmac road at a rate of something close to a mile a day. With good mapping and multiple teams working, they could build the forty-three-mile road they'd mapped out in not much more than a month.

Well, maybe two months, and with winter coming on there was a good chance that it wouldn't be finished until after the spring thaw.

That was all right. He didn't need it finished. He didn't need it much more than started. The merchants and porters of Tsaritsyn would realize what it meant as soon as they started work on it.

About then Colonel Denisov and Major Platov came over to the table and looked at the map he was examining.

"That's not Tsaritsyn?" Colonel Denisov asked, the question in his tone.

"No. Attempting to take Tsaritsyn would be a stupid way to get an army killed," General Boris Timofeyevich Lebedev said, then apparently realizing how impolite he was being, looked up, blushing. He didn't, however, retract the statement. Instead he expanded on it. "With the improvements in weapons that the up-timers introduced, defense has become much stronger. That pendulum will swing back in a few years as armored steam trains and other mobile fortifications come into play. But even then it's going to be a different and much more distant sort of warfare, which will be much more dependent on strategy than tactics. Every battle is a gamble. The trick is knowing when to bet and when to change the game.

"Against a well-fortified city with modern weapons, it's a bad gamble. So we change the game."

"How exactly?" asked Major Platov.

Tim explained, starting with the background. "The whole reason that Colonel Greshnev thought he could pull this off, was that he thought he could force Astrakhan to support him.

Astrakhan needs the Volga trade. With it, Astrakhan is the doorway between the new industries in Russia and the Safavid Empire. But with Tsaritsyn cutting that off, they become just one more village on the Caspian Sea.

"Tsaritsyn also controls the portage between the Don and the Volga rivers. So if they control Astrakhan, they control the Don to Volga trade, through which most of the goods from western Europe reach the Safavid Empire. But without Astrakhan the caravan route from the Don to the Volga isn't actually worth anything. Both upriver and down are controlled by the Sovereign States. So when Astrakhan joined the Sovereign States, Tsaritsyn lost all the trade that would flow along the portage route.

"With the Sovereign States controlling the Volga below and above Tsaritsyn, there isn't anywhere for the goods portaged between the Don and the Volga to go. That means that simply by controlling the Volga River, we've won the war. All he can do is irritate us."

"A little more than that," Natasha disagreed. "The Don River provides us with access to goods from the Black Sea and points west. As well as goods shipped down the Don from central Russia."

"Of course, Princess," Tim agreed. "But without Astrakhan, we can hurt him a great deal more than he can hurt us."

"Not without hurting the Don Cossacks almost as badly as you hurt Tsaritsyn," Colonel Denisov said bitterly. "The portage fees charged by Tsaritsyn are why I have an AK2, not an AK4.7. If you cut off the trade *entirely*, well, we're Cossacks. We'd survive. But it would not be easy. And a lot of my people would die."

"This is going to avoid that problem," Tim said, pointing at the map. "In 1633 the city of Forchheim in Germany decided that they were not going to allow voting rights. They also were sitting on a transport route. A road not a portage route but..." Tim shrugged the difference away. "Rather than storm the walls, the State of Thuringia-Franconia simply built a new road that bypassed the fort at Forchheim. We're going to do the same thing, but we're going to do them one better. How long do you think Colonel Greshnev is going to survive once his people realize that we are building a tarmac road with a rail down the middle three miles upriver? One that will be able to send riverboats from the Volga to the Don and back in hours instead of weeks."

"Hours?"

"Hours. Using a steam train, a small riverboat will travel at ten to fifteen miles per hour. It's less than fifty miles if the road guys are right. They will be loading trains from the Volga in the morning and putting them in the water of the Don before the sun sets. And the same is true of cargo."

Then Czar Mikhail arrived. "Is everyone up to speed?" he asked, and Colonel Denisov and Major Platov looked confused.

"It's an up-timer-ism," Bernie explained. "It means 'has everyone caught up' or 'is everyone aware of what's going on.'"

"If so, let's go talk to the people of Tsaritsyn."

Any radio more sophisticated than a spark gap radio has the ability to transmit sound as well as data. Granted, the radio network wasn't used that way most of the time, but it could be, and there were crystal sets available. Homemade ones and factory-made ones. So if you had a radio transmitter and knew the standard broadcast frequencies, you could switch your radio to analog voice instead of digital data and just talk to anyone who had a crystal set. And most radio operators did for an hour or so a day, playing music or sharing the latest gossip from Ufa or Moscow, often enough announcing that so-and-so had a radio telegram waiting. It varied with the radio operator. Tsaritsyn's station had been sending out promises of wealth and power ever since Colonel Greshnev had declared for "Czar Ivan Romanov."

Czar Mikhail's steamboat had an excellent high-powered radio system. He was, after all, the czar.

A few minutes later, seated comfortably in his chair, Czar Mikhail began to speak into a microphone. "To the people of Tsaritsyn, this is Czar Mikhail Romanov of the United Sovereign States of Russia. Colonel Greshnev has seized equipment belonging to the federal government. I don't really care all that much about that, but he's also taken captive and ordered the execution of citizens of the Sovereign States. That is a much more serious crime and something I care deeply about. Through the wisdom of some of his subordinates, his orders to execute my people weren't carried out. And, by the way, to the people who chose to disobey that order, you are forgiven for the theft of Russian property because you didn't kill anyone, even though you were ordered to do so."

Colonel Denisov listened to Czar Mikhail's calm, almost mellow, voice and wondered how long Colonel Greshnev would let those men live if they were in Tsaritsyn. They probably weren't, but it didn't really matter. *They* didn't really matter. Czar Mikhail had just made it clear that he wasn't going to be looking for anyone's blood unless they killed someone. And giving them a reason not to obey Colonel Greshnev's orders to commit atrocities.

"I don't know the condition of the radio men in Tsaritsyn," Czar Mikhail continued, "but you need to be aware that your future well-being is very much dependent on their continued well-being.

"As to Colonel Greshnev's declaring my Uncle Ivan czar, that is a piece of foolishness that even my Uncle Ivan has more sense than to claim. But it also moves Colonel Greshnev's actions firmly into the category of treason.

"If the government of Tsaritsyn had declined to join the United Sovereign States of Russia, I probably would have let it stand as long as they didn't attempt to impede trade along the Volga. But, thanks to Colonel Greshnev, that option is no longer available. Tsaritsyn must now either become fully part of the Sovereign States, or it must die.

"I am sure that Colonel Greshnev has been bragging to you all about the strength of Tsaritsyn and the range of the rifles the men guarding your walls carry. And he's quite correct in that. General Lebedev has examined the defenses and confirms that any sort of frontal assault would do nothing but get our men killed and I accept his judgment. After their own recent experiences, so do General Birkin and anyone else with any sense.

"So here is what we're going to do instead." And now Czar Mikhail's voice seemed happy as well as calm. "Three miles upriver from here, we are going to construct a fort, a port, and a railhead. And from that railhead, we are going to build a road with a rail line down its center, and that road is going to go from the Volga to the Don River. The cargos and boats that were once portaged from Tsaritsyn will now take that road. While the Sovereign States will undertake the entire cost of building that road, the part of it within the lands of the Don Cossacks will belong to them. And the fees received for transport of boats and other goods on the rail line will be divided between the Sovereign States and the Don Cossacks in a ratio still to be worked out.

"What is not in question is who owns the Don River. The Don Cossacks own it from the headwaters to the mouth."

Which meant that Czar Mikhail had just given them a bunch of Russian territory currently controlled by Muscovy. Which wasn't going to make Ivan Romanov happy, but was going to make the Don Cossacks very happy.

"In exchange for that"—the czar's voice became grim—"Colonel Denisov, based in the new city, will continue the siege of Tsaritsyn until the city surrenders or *starves*."

Czar Mikhail waved at the radio man and he flipped a couple of switches and the little light went off and music, the Russian national anthem, started playing over the radio.

The czar rotated around in his chair until he was looking at Colonel Denisov. "I know I may have overstated what you agreed to at dinner a little, but the details can be worked out over time. And I suspect that your army's time in the siege lines will be brief. To get the support of the porters, Colonel Greshnev had to have promised them exclusive rights to handle the portaging of boats and supplies between the rivers. Now that they know he can't deliver on that, they will be trying to find a way out and the most straightforward way out is to deliver him to my justice, or perhaps just to deliver his head."

The czar stood up, and led them to a small but comfortable room on the steamboat. "You fellows think about it and decide what you want to do." Then he left them there.

Major Simeon Platov looked around the small room with its plush leather chairs and polished tables. Then he looked at the man who had been his friend and leader since they were boys. "Ivan, make whatever deal you can. Join the Sovereign States or don't. I don't care. But never, ever put us at odds with General Lebedev or Czar Mikhail. Because I don't want to wake up one morning and find out that we've already lost the war because Lebedev changed the game. And I'll probably be the one who has to shoot you in the back of the head when Czar Mikhail lays down the law."

Colonel Ivan Denisov looked over at his friend and nodded. Simeon was smarter than he was, but didn't have the makings of a commander. They'd both known that since they were kids. But Simeon was a Cossack for all of that. He'd blow Ivan's brains out if that was what it took to save the clan. Crying while he did it, but he'd do it. Better to make sure he didn't think it was necessary.

CHAPTER 16

𝔘𝔣𝔞 𝔅𝔬𝔬𝔪

Ufa Dacha cafeteria
November 4, 1637

Alla Lyapunov thought the speech was exciting and clever. And amazingly cold-blooded. Much more cold-blooded than anything Sheremetev had ever done, and Sheremetev was her ideal of cold-blooded evil since he'd killed her parents. This wasn't evil, but it was cold-blooded.

The speech Czar Mikhail had given to the people of Tsaritsyn had been recorded on magnetic paper tape. That was a special paper that had large amounts of finely ground iron oxide in the mix so that it came out brown. It had a smooth finish and it could record an oscillating magnetic field. It was three quarters of an inch wide and the tape player that it used weighed something like fifty pounds, but it produced excellent recordings. All of which she knew because she'd spent the whole afternoon a week ago being lectured about the stuff in the Dacha school.

Much to Alla's dismay, it turned out that the Lyapunov heir in this new world *had* to be an overeducated nerd. It wasn't an option. It was a job requirement. She really wished she could be back in the kitchen in Captain Petrov's house. At least she wouldn't have these headaches.

She bit a chunk out of her egg salad on black bread sandwich and wished she'd had one of Elina's hot buttered croissants instead. The Dacha cafeteria had good, solid food, but it wasn't great food.

Cook had been a master chef even before he'd gotten the translated up time French cookbook, and by the time Anna had become Alla again, he was really great. Even the servants in Captain Petrov's house were well fed. Especially the kitchen servants.

She finished her lunch, such as it was, and went back to school.

Dominika's and Zia Chernoff's townhouse, Ufa
November 4, 1637

Zia Chernoff was also listening to the speech. The baby was crawling now and was often a guest at the palace, played with by Princess Anna. And Zia's brother wasn't happy about the situation. It was increasingly plain that even if Muscovite Russia managed to survive, with Sweden to its north, Poland to its west, Cossacks and Ottomans to its south, and the Sovereign States to its west and southwest, and Shein's little pocket principality to its northwest, taking on the ever-increasing power of the Sovereign States was something it was unlikely to manage.

Larisa Karolevna Chernoff was going to be *the* Chernoff, whatever Karol Ivanovich thought about it. And apparently Czar Mikhail, or perhaps that boy general of his, had figured out a way to make war in this new world.

Meanwhile, Dominika's man of business was explaining, again, that they had too much money. Vasilii Lyapunov had put them in touch with a Dacha-trained "Financial Manager," who had taken a large chunk of the money that they had in the National Bank of the United Sovereign States of Russia, the NBUSSR—which even Russians couldn't pronounce—and invested it in businesses in consultation with Dominika and, surprisingly, with Zia. They now owned parts of companies that made glass, furniture, concrete, fabric, sewing machines, and a host of other products, which were sold from Moscow and Lithuania to the southern coast of the Caspian Sea. And the money poured in.

"The boom economy of western Russia can reasonably be expected to continue for at least another five years without even much of a slowdown. Market saturation is decades away. As fast as we can build it, they are going to buy it."

"So what sort of investment do you have in mind for us?"

Lukyan Grinin sighed. "I am still looking into the various start-up options, ma'am. You can still lose, even in this environment, so I actually recommend we wait for a few weeks, until I have more information on several of the startups."

Royal Palace, Ufa
November 7, 1637

Czar Mikhail and Czarina Evdokia were back from Tsaritsyn, and the family and friends were gathered for a dinner with the czar's family. Among the guests were Alla Lyapunov, representing her "parents," who were on the far side of the state of Kazakh, Zia Chernoff and Dominika, as well as half a dozen others.

The dessert was a French-style apple tart with whipped cream topping. They used honey rather than beet sugar in the cream, but that wasn't the problem. The cook didn't know how to make the pastry. It wasn't flaky, like a French pastry was supposed to be. And the gold electroplated fork wasn't able to cut the crust. Alla had to use the knife. It wasn't horrible. In fact, before she'd spent a year learning to cook and reading French cookbook recipes to Captain Petrov's cook, she would have thought it quite good. But when you compared it to an actual French pastry, it was *utterly* unacceptable.

Alla took one bite and left the rest on the plate. Zia Chernoff did the same. Dominika ate the whole thing, but didn't get a lot of joy out of it. No one complained, not about the czar's table. Czar Mikhail was an easygoing sort, the czarina less so. And considering what easygoing Czar Mikhail had done to a whole city that displeased him, no one was going to make a scene about a flat pastry.

After dinner the children were shuffled off to the playrooms. Dominika went with them and the wet nurse to watch over the baby. The playrooms were two connected rooms brightly painted using the dyes from the Ufa Dacha. They had paintings of dirigibles and flowers, dragons and cartoon dogs on the walls, and there was even a Barbie in a glass case on a shelf out of the children's reach. There was an open chest with games, blocks, and wooden Legos. And the whole place was lit with Coleman lanterns, also out of the reach of the children.

Tsarevna Anna, seven, and Tsarevna Martha, six, were playing with the baby under the supervision of the wet nurse, while ten-year-old Tsarevna Irina and nine-year-old Alexi were trying to interest Alla and Dominika in a new board game related to Monopoly, but different. It was called Ufa Investment and the object of the game was to be the richest person in Ufa. Aside, of course, from the czar and czarina.

It used paper play money and cards, which could be placed on the spaces around the board. The cards represented businesses like foundries and clothing factories. Finally, Alla was convinced to join and promised to help Dominika, who was still very weak when it came to reading.

Of course, the subject of the meal came up and Irina was explaining about the French pastries and how they weren't really all that good since they came from France, where Richelieu had ruined everything.

"It wasn't Richelieu. It was the cook," Alla muttered to Dominika, not taking into account the acute hearing of youth.

"I suppose you could do better," Alexi demanded.

Alla knew better, she really did. But in spite of that, she answered just as belligerently. "Yes, I could!" She'd watched Elina do it every day for months, after all, and even helped when she was assigned to. She knew the recipe and the tricks, like making sure the butter was cold, and keeping the whole thing cold when you rolled it out. Which she explained.

Irina pulled a sheet of heavy rag paper and, using a pencil, laboriously wrote out "Restaurant." She set it on a square and proclaimed, "I'm starting a restaurant on Irina Way."

"It will be a failure," Alexi insisted. "You don't know a thing about making restaurants and you don't have a cook."

"I'll hire Alla."

"You can't hire Alla. She's the Lyapunov. And, besides, she can't cook."

"She's not the Lyapunov yet, and she can too cook."

"She can hire a cook and explain to him how to make croissants and other French pastries," Dominika said with some authority. In her normal environment, Dominika was well named. She wasn't the shy and retiring sort. This wasn't her normal environment. But she was starting to get used to it and she was an adult. "On the other hand, she is the heir to what is now the senior Lyapunov line, so I don't think you can hire her for your restaurant. But if you can persuade her to open a restaurant, you can invest in it."

The rules as Alla had read them to her did allow for people to invest in other people's businesses, even to take them over if they bought enough stock. It was based on the business community in Ufa, which was boisterous and chaotic, as well as amazingly complex. The game was much simplified, but it was still more complex than the up-time Monopoly had been. And whoever had come up with the design was making a fortune because the fact that the royal children played it on a semi-regular basis was known.

Then a thought occurred to Dominika. "Actually if Alla wants to start a real restaurant on the real Irina Way, *I'll* invest in it."

"It was my idea!" Irina protested, then stopped as the "reals" in Dominika's comment registered. "Are you serious? Irina Way is some of the most expensive property in Ufa."

"I know it," Dominika agreed. "Our townhouse is on Irina Way, and we're constantly getting offers from people who want to buy the land. But a restaurant on Irina Way would be within a few minutes of anywhere in Ufa and less than a mile from the Kremlin and the Dacha. Besides, Irina Way has plumbing, water in and waste out. And electrical lines from the Dacha power plant."

The Dacha power plant was an oil-fed power plant that produced a fair amount of electricity. Not on the scale of the power plant in Grantville, but a lot.

Alla considered the offer. Her parents were in Almaty and it seemed unlikely that they would let her do it, but she'd spent a year as a scullery maid and recipe reader in Moscow. She knew how to run a kitchen. A restaurant might actually be something she could do. With the radio network, she could ask.

Almaty
November 9, 1637

The siege of Almaty was far from over, but the besieging troops had been pushed back a bit. They'd been moved far enough that the Heroes could land outside of Almaty proper and unload, then take off in relative safety, protected by riflemen with AK4.7s. And even better in a way, was the fact that they now had a radio station in Almaty, a full station with the aqualator and the tube radio, so the radio telegraph network stretched all the way to Ufa. Thus it was that the evening's incoming radio dump included not only the position of Ivan's war train, but also a radio telegram from Alla Lyapunov, asking permission to start a restaurant.

The notion that such messages arrived from Russia less than a full day after they were sent was enough to leave the residents of Almaty in something close to shock. The contents of the message were quite useful in bringing that shock down to manageable levels. What was it? A teenaged daughter asking her adoptive parents for permission to do something.

The question was raised "why a restaurant?" That led to a retelling by Vasilii of Alla's adventures as a kitchen maid in Moscow while she was hiding from the Sheremetev regime. All of which made it a romantic adventure to the men and women besieged in Almaty.

The citizens of Almaty had already been heartened by the courage of their khan. Salqam-Jangir Khan had flown to the city to join them in their struggle.

Then Brandy Bates and Vladimir Gorchakov were dropping supplies out of the sky.

And now the town was abuzz with discussion of Alla's restaurant. All in all, it amounted to an excellent distraction from the army that was still camped no more than a mile and a half from their walls.

It was an army that was growing as Erdeni Batur moved more and more of his forces to reinforce the siege of Almaty. He'd *had* to. The planes flying in and out of Almaty were a tremendous psychological blow to his forces. Like the Kazakhs, the Zunghar hunted with eagles. The size, speed, and prowess of their eagles were points of great pride for both peoples. And here came Salqam-Jangir Khan with mechanical eagles so large you could ride in them, flying over their siege lines and delivering supplies and taking passengers over the mountains to who knew where.

It wasn't that the Zunghar thought that it was magic. They knew perfectly well that they were made things, crafted by the same people who crafted rifles that could kill you from half a mile away and fire five times a minute or more.

But how were you to terrorize such people?

What difference did it make how strong your arm, how fleet your horses, or even how large your eagle, when your enemy could shoot your horse, then shoot you before you ever got near bow range, much less close enough to use your sword.

The bastards in Almaty were cheating, and it wasn't fair at all.

And now, as the spies in Almaty reported, they weren't even talking about the siege. They were talking about some girl opening an eatery and whether her parents should approve the project, as though the thousands of Zunghar outside their walls didn't even matter.

Almaty
November 11, 1637

Miroslava Holmes watched the postern gate open and close. Determining who the spies in Almaty were was taking effort, but it was her sort of effort. It was the careful observation and the correlation of facts. Something she did well.

Deciding whether to let Alla start a restaurant was much more difficult. Because, deep down, Miroslava didn't understand why it mattered. She knew that people cared because Vasilii told her so. But she did not know why they cared. If Alla wanted to open a restaurant it was fine with Miroslava, but as long as the food didn't make you sick, it was all the same to her.

Twenty minutes later, the postern gate opened again and a cousin of the sultan was briefly exposed to the light.

The steam train
November 12, 1637

Brigadier General Ivan Maslov climbed down from the train car to the frozen ground. The deaerator on the steam engine was malfunctioning, but that was not a serious problem. The boiler was robust, made of steel, but almost as solidly built as a cast iron boiler might be. A little rust wouldn't kill them, not in the next few months anyway.

Of greater importance was the frozen ground. The steam train didn't need a rail, not when the ground was this hard. He looked around, blowing out a puff of cloud with every breath. His hands were in insulated calfskin gloves. And his "general's cap" with its fur-lined ear protectors was keeping him sort of comfortable, but if he didn't get back inside his eyeballs were going to freeze. One more quick look, and he climbed the two steps up to the platform and went through the door into the map room. He had a new radio message from Almaty. They'd identified the Zunghar agent in Almaty, at least one of them, and wanted to know what to do about him.

Now they could move. They still couldn't move fast by up-timer standards, but they would be able to travel fifteen or even twenty miles an hour over flat ground and average ten miles an hour over the course of a ten-hour day.

That was a hundred miles a day. And that made Almaty no more than four days away.

He went to his desk and in a careful hand wrote out the radio message, each letter in its own little box.

> Find me a good place to get trapped by a clever Zunghar cavalry force.
>
> Make it clear that the train takes hours to convert from in motion to fort. If they catch us moving, they have us.

He handed the sheet to his aide.

"But it takes us less than five minutes to turn the train into a fort," his aide, a brand-new second lieutenant said. "We've been practicing it every time the ground froze since we started."

"I know that, Lieutenant Golovin," Ivan said. "And you know that. It is my hope that Erdeni Batur doesn't know that, or at least that he will choose not to believe it. The absolute best way to win a battle is to have your enemy do something *really* stupid.

"Erdeni Batur isn't stupid in the sense of having trouble lacing up his boots. He's not even stupid in the sense of never having read a book. What he is, is a hard-riding, courageous cavalry commander. Which is to say he's stupid in the way that George Armstrong Custer was stupid."

At the lieutenant's blank look, Ivan grinned. If his own aide Yevgeny Golovin didn't know about Little Bighorn, it was a safe bet that Erdeni Batur didn't.

So how could he know about a reverse Little Bighorn?

Almaty
November 14, 1637

It took Brandy two days to find the place. A lovely little box canyon, not all that steep, but with an exit that looked good until you got into it, then got rough. Worse, it was an exit that could be relatively easily blocked.

After that, there were several actual radio messages between

Brandy and Ivan, in which Brandy insisted he should avoid it, and Ivan told her to mind her knitting and let men handle the war.

They used Brandy because Vladimir could order Ivan to avoid the canyon. Brandy could only advise.

Those messages somehow fell into the hands of the sultan's cousin. Who, a bit of investigation showed, was deeply in debt and in desperate need of cash to cover the money he'd pilfered from the Almaty treasury. This was an actual room in the sultan's palace, full—less full now—of silver coins, including many from China.

Later that night, he again slipped out the postern gate, carrying the radio telegrams.

The next morning, three-quarters of the Zunghars rode out of the siege camp.

Box canyon
November 17, 1637

It was late afternoon as the steam train carrying General Ivan Maslov and just over a thousand riflemen, mostly from Kazak, but with a decent sprinkling of *streltzi* from Ufa, approached the "pass" that was actually a box canyon. It was an excellent hard point to control one of the passes into the mountains. Controlling it wouldn't make it impossible for the Zunghars to cross the Tian Shan Mountains to reach Issyk-Kul, but it would make it more difficult.

Of course, to do that, they would need to be there first, then use the train to hold the place while they built a permanent fort.

The cars on the steam train were thirty feet long and ten wide. They had double-thick wooden walls. The simple pulling of a cord would drop the outer wall to the ground, protecting those inside and exposing the firing slits for either the riflemen or the small cannon.

There were a total of twelve cars, including the engine. Four of them carried cannons, the rest *streltzi* riflemen. Ivan, the young and foolish boy that he was, had rushed ahead of his cavalry escort. They were at least a day behind.

As they approached the entrance to the "pass," Ivan was on the radio to Scout One. It was high, eleven thousand feet, a bit over two miles above the ground. It was also painted light blue on its underside. At that altitude, it was both invisible against the blue sky and silent to anyone on the ground. This was partly luck, but partly the prediction of the weather service, which used the weather data from the radio stations to produce a weather map of central Asia. That map suggested that today would be clear and cold, but tomorrow it would get cloudy, and so far it seemed to be on the mark.

Yury Arsenyev was in the front seat with a pair of binoculars, looking down at the Zunghars and reporting their movements. Of course, at this distance he couldn't distinguish all that much. An individual horseman would usually go unnoticed, but he could spot groups of cavalry readily enough.

The Zunghars knew about the planes, but their whole lives had been spent looking for scouts on the ground, expecting scouts on the ground seen on the horizon or by a flash of movement on a hillside. They knew about planes, but all their instincts and experience suggested that they could ignore an eagle overhead.

"We have a group of about three thousand to your left as you enter the canyon. There are perhaps that many to your right front, but farther away. I think they're going to let you in, then hit you from the side and rear. I figure two, maybe three, minutes for the group on the left to get to you from their hiding place. About twice that for the group on the right front," Yuri reported.

"Acknowledged," Ivan said. He looked at the map. It had been drawn by Yury and delivered by Brandy Bates Gorchakov yesterday in the Scout. Even the Scout could fly sixty miles from Almaty, land, give him a map, and fly back.

He took the map forward to the engine, and showed the engineer the route he wanted him to take once he was in the canyon.

The train was traveling over frozen ground, not railroad tracks. It had a steering wheel, and so did each and every one of the cars attached to it. What those other steering wheels could do was limited by the fact that they were being pulled by the engine, but it did give them a little control, so that the fort this train would turn into could look more like a box than a circle. Or even have an odd shape if that's what they wanted. But, in this case, Ivan wanted a circle fort with as little in the way of corners for the enemy to focus on as possible.

Ivan was still in the engine as they entered the box canyon. He knew where to look, but still couldn't see the Zunghars. They were good cavalry, quite capable of keeping out of sight until they were ready.

Ivan waited as long as he felt he could before he tapped the engineer on the shoulder and said, "Start the fort."

The engineer and Ivan both pulled on the wheel to put the train into the slow turn that would make the fort.

Erdeni Batur was nervous and deeply angry at what he saw as the steam train coming in through the pass. His goal had been as much to modernize the Zunghar into a Mongol horde for this century as it had been about his power. But the Russians had stolen the march on him. He'd heard the rumors of the town from the future, but hadn't believed them. Hadn't even believed them when he saw airplanes flying over Almaliq. He still didn't. The Germans had had centuries to develop better weapons while China stagnated and the Silk Road withered.

This wasn't an act of a god, not of Allah or the Christian god or even one of the supernatural figures that sometimes helped or hindered those attempting to reach enlightenment. It was just the workings of men.

It had to be.

Still, the train was impressive. And if he gave them time it would be decisive. He couldn't give them that time. As he watched the train move down the pass, start a right turn, then turn left, he knew that he was going to lose men in this attack. A lot of men. But if he waited, the Zunghar people would die, never having become a real people at all.

So as soon as he realized that the train was starting the process of turning into a fort, he gave the order and his army charged.

Yevgeny Golovin in the cannon car watched the hillside to their right erupt with Zunghar cavalry and was terrified. It was his first battle. Before this, all his military experience had been in drills and war games, reading books, listening to lectures, taking tests. No one had ever shot at him in anger. There had been that drill where they crouched behind a wall while riflemen shot above the wall into another wall behind them to give them the feel of being shot at. But they'd all known that the rifles were aimed over their heads, even if not that far over their heads.

It was nothing like this. Those men out there were coming to *kill* him. He was so frightened, and angry with himself for *being* frightened, that it took him a while to realize those men out there didn't have guns. They didn't have AKs. They didn't have the French Cardinals. They didn't even have matchlock blunderbusses.

If there was so much as a flintlock pistol out there, Yevgeny couldn't see it.

And the walls of the cars on the steam train were inch-thick planks of laminated wood. An arrow wasn't going through those, not all the way through. The tip might make it. Someone who was leaning against the wall might get scratched by an arrowhead, but...

Suddenly Yevgeny was laughing. He cut it off quickly, then turned to the gun crews who were manning the cannon. "Men, don't lean against the outer wall to rest. You might get scratched by one of those arrows the Zunghar are going to be shooting."

They looked at him blankly for a moment, then they laughed too.

"Granted, it's not very likely," Yevgeny continued, "but better safe than sorry."

The gun captain, a *streltzi* who'd been using cannon for his whole career and loved those cannons like they were his children, roared, "You heard the lieutenant, men! Anyone who lets one of those Zunghar arrows scratch them is going on report."

"But, Sergeant, I was going to take a nap between rounds," complained the powderman from the second gun, grinning all the while.

"Shut up, Gorbachev!" The sergeant sighed.

The closer oncoming attackers were still at least two minutes away from bow range. Meanwhile, the long arch the train was making as it curled into a round fort had brought Cannon Car One out of line of the right-hand group of Zunghars, and Yevgeny peered out of a shooting slit to see the second group. They were even farther away, and they were trotting their horses, which was wise. If they galloped that far, they were going to be exhausted by the time they reached the train. Shaking his head at his decision, Yevgeny said, "I'm going to climb up on the roof for a better look."

The war train was designed by Brigadier Ivan Maslov in consultation with the Dacha. It wasn't thrown together. It was planned. Perhaps not perfectly, but still planned. The walls extended two feet above the roof with drainage holes in case of rain, and the roof was a bit slanted so the rain would wash off.

There were also ladders that could be detached or attached to the walls, making them easy to climb on the inside of the fort. With the train still in motion, Yevgeny stepped out on the train car's platform and clamped the ladder in place on what would be the interior wall of the fort once the train stopped. He climbed to the roof of Cannon Car One and watched the battle develop.

The train was curving into a circle fort that was going to leave them facing the way they'd come into the canyon. There were two main groups of Zunghars approaching, one from the east and the other from the southwest. The one to the east was the closest, about another minute to bow-shot range. The farther group was still three or four minutes out. They would come in, fire arrows to keep the train troops heads-down, then try to go over the walls or through the cracks to get inside the fort.

The distance from ground to the bottom of the train car was three feet. The train car from bottom to roof was ten feet with another two feet of wall above the roof. That made the top of the wall fifteen feet above the ground. Even standing on horseback, that was a stretch. Not impossible, but not easy either. The real weakness was between the cars. At least that would be what it seemed like until the train stopped, and they closed the doors.

Even as he was doing that, Yevgeny realized there were flaws in the steam train's design. There ought to be spikes or knives embedded in the tops of the walls to make them harder to climb over. And there should be hatches in the roof of the cars so that you could climb up onto the roof from inside the car.

Having seen what he could see, Yevgeny climbed back down the ladder and went back into the car. The circle was made, the engine in line behind the last car. The train, which hadn't been traveling more than five miles per hour, came to a stop.

Yevgeny shouted, "Drop the skirt!"

The skirt was a four-foot-tall laminated wood-shield wall that was located just inside the outer wall. Dropping it meant it fell three feet, making the wall solid from ground to top. You could pry it up. It wasn't held down, but it was heavy. It took six men pulling on ropes inside the car to lift it back into place.

The gaps between the train cars were tougher to manage. The gaps were covered with more laminated wood panels, but they were heavy pieces that had to be attached by hand. The panels came in three segments, each five feet tall, that were stacked and lashed together. And even after that, the gaps would be the weakest point in the train's defenses.

Yevgeny and the half squad of *streltzi* were still lashing them in place when the Zunghar arrived.

Inside the car, the cannon was loaded with canister, a lot of lead balls in a sack designed to come apart after it left the barrel. It was basically a big shotgun loaded with elephant shot.

Horses aren't elephants.

"Fire!" shouted the gun captain. The lanyard was pulled, the hammer hit the cap, and the cap sent a spear of flame into the powder. The powder went *boom*, and the canister of shot spewed into a mass of horsemen riding hell-for-leather toward the gap between the cannon car and the fuel car. The shot went into and through the attackers, leaving hamburgered horse meat and human flesh in their wake, as well as spraying a geyser of blood and viscera.

In a way it was easiest for the men and horses who got the worst of the blast. For them, it was just over. There was no time for horror or pain.

For the ones farther back or off to the side, it was hell. Friends were spread over them, and even if they weren't wounded, they were shocked and horrified in a way that even seasoned killers had not imagined before.

There were four cannon cars, four rifle cars, the mess car, the surgeon's car, the fuel car, and the engine in that train.

The four cannon cars broke the charge.

The riflemen actually killed more Zunghars. They could fire accurately out to two and even three hundred yards.

The five-minute fort dominated the entire pass from side to side.

But it was the cannon that killed the Zunghars' spirit.

It didn't happen all at once. It took time for them to realize that they'd tried to have carnal knowledge of a hornet's nest. They lost hundreds of men, including Erdeni Batur. When they finally retreated, almost an hour after the first shot was fired, there were hundreds of Zunghars dead on the ground surrounding the train fort.

There were fewer than a dozen casualties from the train force. Most of them happened when the Zunghars had tried to go over the wall. They could do it by standing on their horse's backs and leaping up, but the casualties involved in getting even a single man in a position to make that leap were atrocious. And once he got there, he was still facing Russian and Kazakh soldiers armed with AK rifles and six-shot revolvers. But it was those few leapers who produced the only casualties that the train force suffered from combat. Most of the injuries were caused by accidents.

Not a single golden arrow had killed anyone, even though there were thousands of arrows sticking out of the walls of Fort Train.

"Golden arrows, sir?" Lieutenant Yevgeny Golovin asked.

"Another up-timer-ism," Ivan Maslov said. "A 'golden bb' is the single amazing, impossible shot that hits in spite of the odds. Like your chance of hitting a plane flying over at a hundred miles an hour and eight hundred feet altitude. They do happen now and then, though not nearly so often as people seem to think. The Zunghars were armed with swords and bows, and just demonstrated why you don't bring a knife to a gunfight. Their arrows couldn't reach us through the plywood walls and their swords only came into play once, and even then the swordsman standing on top of the fuel car was shot three times with a pistol and never got within striking distance of any of our forces."

He looked out over the carpet of dead horses and men that surrounded Fort Train. "What killed those men was ignorance. They didn't know, and couldn't guess, the amount of firepower we have in here. And we can do this at any siege. Even the best defenses do need armed men manning the walls, and the Zunghars with their bows and arrows might as well be unarmed."

"And this was what happened to Colonel Custer?"

"Nope. What happened to Custer was what they were expecting to happen to us. We fell into their trap just like Custer did at Little Bighorn. They had us outnumbered ten to one. They, to their way of thinking, should have done to us exactly what Sitting Bull did to Custer. What is not well remembered is that the men under Custer fought well and killed a lot of the enemy before they died. Even without cover. Sitting Bull and Crazy Horse were way too smart to attack a fortified position, so they lured Custer into a trap where his men would be caught in the open. It was still a costly victory."

"I would think it was more like the walking walls at Rzhev," Lieutenant Golovin said.

"No, not really. At Rzhev, *our idiots* were going up against pike squares. Not as obviously idiotic as going up against a walled fort. So we had to put Erdeni Batur in a position where he was convinced he'd mousetrapped us. Where his reputation would be destroyed, or at least badly damaged, by changing his mind at the last minute and skulking off with his tail between his legs.

"All right, Lieutenant. Let's start getting this mess cleaned up. Someone get us a white truce flag and let's see about saving as many of those men out there as we can."

Jochi Qong Tayiji rode up to the small group of men standing on the wall of the magic fort. Jochi didn't believe in magic, not magic that could do this, anyway. He just lacked a word for such a thing as stood before him. These people, whatever they were, could fly. They could make forts roll around the plains and then turn back into forts and they could kill in ways that left Jochi horrified and dismayed.

And Jochi hated them, from the first to the last. Yes, he hated them, and would until he died, and would still hate them in his next life and the one after that. But he didn't hate them enough to kill what was left of his people on the altar of his hate.

So he rode up to the fort and the men standing on its walls. "I am Jochi, Qong Tayiji of the Olot." He wasn't the only Qong Tayiji of the Olot, but he didn't need to go into that now. "What do you want?"

On the platform behind the outer wall stood a group of people. The one the others paid deference to was a redheaded youth with a neatly trimmed beard. He wore a billed cap with a star in front and some sort of gold inlay on the bill.

"Not all the men out there are dead," said the redhead. "We have medicines and techniques that may save some of them. We are willing to do that, but not if you're going to shoot arrows at us while we work on them. I want your word that from now until this time the day after tomorrow, your men won't come armed within two hundred yards of the walls of our train."

"And if I don't agree?" Jochi guessed the answer, but had to ask.

The redhead shrugged. "Then we just wait, shooting anyone who comes in range until they all die."

Jochi looked into those cold blue eyes and knew that this boy would do just that. There were glaciers in the mountains that would envy the coldness in those eyes.

"We will stay back," he bit out.

"Don't do that," the redhead said. "Just leave your swords and bows away, then you may come in and collect your dead and call us to the aid of your wounded."

"The ground is littered with bows and swords."

"The Zunghar who picks one of them up dies." The redhead waved at one of the men carrying one of the long guns. The man put it to his shoulder and pointed out at the field, said "*bang*," then brought it back down.

Two days of M*A*S*H surgery, and the area within Fort Train was full of Zunghars, most of whom would recover. Not all of them would have their full set of arms, legs, fingers, and toes, but most of them would live and heal.

In those same two days, most of the Zunghar army dissolved. Rode away in small- to medium-sized groups to report back to their tribes on what had happened here.

Fort Train
November 20, 1637

Two days after the trap, the Scout plane came down to a landing and taxied up to the train. Brandy got out and walked up the stairs to the open platform, then joined Ivan in the office. It had been a rifle car during the battle, but now it was back to its normal use.

"I did a flyover recon," Brandy said. "Most of the Zunghar have left. Salqam-Jangir Khan would like you to load up and proceed to Almaty to relieve the siege."

"There are a lot of wounded still in need of care," Ivan said. Then, "We can put some of the worst aboard the train and leave the best off with the Zunghars that are left. It's going to take tomorrow to get organized, then a day to get to Almaty. I'll see you the day after tomorrow. Good enough?"

"Good enough, but I won't be there. Vlad and I are heading back to Ufa. They have another Hero, the *Koshchey*, to take over the urgent material transfer. Czar Mikhail has something else in mind for Vlad and me, and he wants Miroslava back in Ufa."

"Who got murdered?"

"Got me. We got orders, not explanations."

CHAPTER 17

Ufa Spies

Ufa
November 20, 1637

Ufa was a boomtown. Being on the Belaya River, it had access to the Kama and Volga River systems. It was geographically on the eastern edge of the river system that connected western Russia. Czar Mikhail had moved the capital to Ufa in June of 1636. That move and the people who followed it had caused a great deal of growth. The fact that trade had been temporarily interrupted during the active siege of Kazan had slowed things a little, but not all that much. Russia was used to frozen rivers in winter and knew how to deal with trade interruptions. Warehouses filled over the winter and emptied into the Volga River system in the spring. And since the introduction of up-timer tech, those warehouses filled faster and fuller.

A great deal of Portland cement and aggregate made its way to Ufa as soon as the ice on the Volga melted, and that concrete was poured and shaped into buildings, roads, and sewers over the summer of 1637. This had the added advantage of making Ufa quite possibly the city with the lowest unemployment in Russia.

And as the *Nicky* made its way around Ufa coming in to land, Brandy Bates Gorchakov, who'd left the Scout in Almaty, saw again what the city was turning into.

The city was a huge sprawling mess, full of people, concrete, glass, and steel, with the Ufa Kremlin and the Ufa Dacha the twin hubs from which the city expanded. In Ufa there were indoor toilets, flush toilets. There was hot water, heat, and there were hotels with elevators.

"Ufa Control to *Nastas'ya Nikulichna.* We need you to make another circle. The *Lydia Litvyak* is about to take off."

The *Lydia* was the latest Hero-class airplane. They were alternating between male and female names. The *Lydia* was going to be on the Ufa–Shavgar run. This plane was named after a Russian female pilot of World War II in the other timeline.

Obedient to the tower, the *Nicky* took another wide loop around Ufa while the *Lydia* took off and headed south. Then they landed. Home sweet home.

Finally down, and with the *Nicky* in the hands of the maintenance crew, which was by now quite used to Hero-class airplanes, Vlad, Brandy, Vasilii, Miroslava, Yury and Ariq took a tram from the Ufa River to the Kremlin. The trams traveled on a single iron-capped wooden rail that went down the middle of a tarmac street and used a small steam engine to travel at about ten miles an hour. They were open to the air, but did have a roof in case of rain or snow.

As they went along, people climbed on, usually not waiting for them to stop, but instead running and grabbing a pole and jumping on, riding for a couple of blocks, then jumping off again.

When they got to the front of the Kremlin, the tram stopped, and Vlad, Brandy and crew dismounted at a more leisurely pace.

There were guards in the fur-lined baseball caps that had become part of the Sovereign States uniform. One of the guards asked for their ID, and they presented them, and got saluted.

Then they were escorted to the czar's office.

"So, do you want to go west or east?" Czar Mikhail asked, standing in front of his desk and not offering anyone a seat.

"Your Majesty?" Vladimir asked.

"I think I'll send Bernie and Natasha west. If I send you two back to Grantville, you'll take little Mikhail with you and not come back."

"What are you talking about?"

"It's the Heroes. We don't have enough of them, and by the time we do, they will no doubt be outmoded by something new. But we have a few now, and we can use them to move vital supplies to Shavgar and even eastern Kazakh. But we can also use them, with the cooperation of the Don Cossacks, to fly south of Muscovite Russia and Poland and link up with Baby Albrecht's

Army of the Sunrise." Albrecht Wallenstein, the king of Bohemia, had recently died, leaving his infant son the crown. There was a regency council and the death hadn't slowed the Army of the Sunrise in their advance east. "And from there, all the way to Grantville with a planeload of gold to clear your debts to Ron Stone.

"But we can also use one to go east and map out a steam train route to the Pacific."

"We'll run out of gas," Vasilii said. "They use more fuel than we expected, and even if they didn't, there aren't any fuel depots, unless you count the ones that are set up along the route in Kazakh."

"Vadim has come up with a new firebox."

"What sort of a new firebox?" Vasilii asked cautiously.

"Do I look like an engineer?" Mikhail asked. "It will let you use wood or coal, if you find any coal."

"You've got to be kidding," Brandy blurted.

"Do I?" Mikhail asked with a grin. "I thought I was quite serious. But you can keep thinking I'm joking if you want to. You'll find out soon enough."

"Yes, Your Majesty. I'm sure you're serious," said Vasilii. "But you are going to need a new engineer. Because I'm going to kill Vadim!"

"Now you see the difference, Princess Brandy. Vasilii *does* have to be kidding. Not that I don't sympathize, but Vadim was working at my order. Did you think I wasn't reading your reports on the fuel efficiency and supply chain problems?" Czar Mikhail shook his head and finally waved them all to seats and took his own.

"We need a route to the sea. Some sea. Preferably a seaport that isn't frozen solid for half a year or more. We need a way of getting our goods to markets in the west, even if it takes us through the South China Sea and around the Cape of Good Hope.

"Airplanes will help. Especially cargo and passenger planes like the Heroes, but we still need a port. A port that can support steamships, or at least ships that have a steam engine to get them through the doldrums. And the only place we're going to get that without going to war with Sweden or the Ottoman Empire is on the Pacific.

"So I need someone to fly over Siberia and map out a route

to the Pacific. And that team also needs to be able to make deals with the native tribes and with China and the Qing dynasty, which isn't in charge yet, but according to the histories is expected to be soon. The Ming dynasty seems to be cracking up ahead of schedule. I need you to go to China and buy me a port."

"I don't speak Chinese," Vladimir protested.

"You think Natasha does, or Bernie?" Mikhail asked. "Yury and Ariq both speak Chinese."

"We speak it well enough to argue about the price of silk or beer, Your Majesty," Yury said, "but if you expect us to negotiate a trade deal, China's going to end up owning Moscow."

"I hope we can avoid that," Mikhail said, "but in any case, over the next couple of weeks, you're going to need to plan your campaign, and I want you on your way by mid-December at the latest."

He looked over at Miroslava. "Meanwhile, Ivan Borisovich Petrov would like to have a few words with you, Miroslava. Please have a chat with him on your way out."

It was a clear dismissal.

Embassy Bureau, Ufa Kremlin
November 20, 1637

Simeon Budanov looked over at Ivan Borisovich Petrov with resentment flavored with just a touch of satisfaction. Simeon was the head of the Embassy Bureau of the United Sovereign States of Russia. But he was fully aware that Czar Mikhail didn't trust him and often went around him to Ivan Borisovich. He assumed that the young sprout was after his job. "Well, Petrov, have you found the spy?"

"No, General," Ivan said politely. As the head of the Embassy Bureau, Budanov's rank was the equivalent of a lieutenant general. And Ivan knew better than to be casual about such things with Budanov. The man was looking for an excuse to fire him. That was why he'd gotten this job, which had nothing at all to do with the Grantville desk.

"Why not? You've had a week."

A week ago, an ad in the *Pravdivyye Fakty* contained what everyone in the Embassy Bureau was sure was a code group. The *Pravdivyye Fakty* was a "newspaper" that reported on scandals and rumors, and had little regard for the truth or factuality of its reporting. *Well, at least it isn't claiming that the Czarina had a baby with space aliens, yet,* Ivan thought. The rest of the paper was filled with personal ads, and a week ago one of those ads contained the following:

> AR VE CH D
> BE GS DW F

With five more such groups. Everyone knew that it was a key group for a book code and the *Pravdivyye Fakty* was full of such things, but the day after they saw that one, one of their agents in Birkin's army was executed. While printed in Ufa, the *Pravdivyye Fakty* was shipped to Kazan and arrived there the same day. It had taken them three days to confirm that this was the message that was involved in the death. And they still didn't know it for sure. It was just the process of elimination.

There was a knock on the door.

"Yes!" Simeon Budanov shouted, though it was Ivan's door.

The door opened and Miroslava Holmes came in, followed by Vasilii Lyapunov.

"What are you doing here?" Simeon Budanov snarled.

It was Vasilii who answered. "We're just back from Almaty."

"This is a secure area. You can visit with Ivan when he's not at work."

Vasilii looked at Budanov, and Budanov looked back, while Ivan prayed that Vasilii, and especially Miroslava, would hold their tongues.

After a long moment, Vasilii looked at Ivan and said, "In that case, please drop by the Dacha this evening, Ivan."

They left and Ivan was left with Simeon Budanov. Simeon spent the next fifteen minutes saying very little, just as offensively as he could.

Ufa Dacha
November 20, 1637

Alla welcomed her "parents" home with cautious friendliness. She was happy enough for them to be back and she wanted their approval for the restaurant she was planning. But she still didn't completely trust them. And she was fully aware that her real parents never would have agreed to her being involved in an inn of any sort.

Vasilii was polite, but uncertain. Miroslava was indifferent in a positive way. That is, she didn't actually care that much about food as long as it wasn't objectionable, spoiled or otherwise dangerous to eat, and felt that if Alla wanted to open a restaurant, it was no more silly than anything else she might want to do.

Alla was still trying to convince Vasilii of the viability of the project when Ivan Borisovich arrived.

Ivan Borisovich looked like a younger version of his father, whom Alla had met in Moscow. He was short, a bit overweight, sturdy, a no-one of a man. He was just like his dad, but his dad was the one who had arranged for her to escape from Moscow and he was the one who'd been here to meet her when she'd arrived. That whole branch of the Petrov family was living proof of the notion that looks could be deceiving.

"Should I go to my room?" Alla asked. She didn't want to blow the restaurant by looking like she was too nosy and making Vasilii angry.

Ivan Borisovich looked at her and considered. "No, I don't think so. You've shown that you have discretion when you need it. And if you're sitting here with us, we can't be discussing anything secret, can we?" He smiled and suddenly he looked a lot less bovine than he had before.

So Alla got to listen as Ivan laid out the case of the spy in the Embassy Bureau for Miroslava.

"Are you really sure it's this message?" Alla asked after Ivan was finished. "After all, there were more messages the day before and it might have taken them a while to decode them and decide what to do. Or it might have been something else that tipped them off about your spy."

Ivan nodded. "It's a good question. We're about eighty-percent sure that it's this message. Several of the other encrypted messages, we've been able to decrypt. And not everyone has access to an aqualator."

"But you don't actually need an aqualator," Alla said.

Miroslava nodded. "I wouldn't need one."

"You're a special case, Miroslava. Most people who don't use an aqualator to do the encrypting end up going with early code groups. The aqualators do a lot of the work of encrypting, and without them people get lazy. We spent a lot of time back in the Moscow Dacha looking at spy novels and stories about the advances in encryption and how they failed in history, and we have experts in the field here. We also have aqualators. Aqualators that are more powerful than the Colossus Mark 2 used in World War II in that other timeline. That lets us crack a lot of the commercial encryption that comes across our desk. But we still need to know the code book. Fortunately, a lot of people use a group of books and always use the same book for their messages. It's easier that way, less work for the person encoding the message and for the person decoding it. The problem here is this isn't one of the books we know about."

"That doesn't explain why you think they are using an aqualator," Vasilii said.

"It's the high numbers. The natural thing to do when you're encoding something is to start at the beginning of the code book and look for the code phrase you're after. That means that your string is usually going to be somewhere early in the book. But an aqualator will automatically start at a random point in the code book and search from there. So the pages won't be low numbers.

"The groups represent page number, line number, letter number, and length. And they make patterns that an aqualator can find because people get lazy, and do things habitually. If, for instance, they happen to know where in a book a word or phrase is, they will use the same location several times because it's easier than looking for a different location in the code book that had the same phrase. A properly programmed aqualator won't do that.

"So we know that all of the other messages in that copy of the *Pravdivyye Fakty* were encrypted by people who didn't have an aqualator, but just knew the technique. And aqualators are expensive. We have them. Birkin has them, but most people don't."

"We have them at the Dacha," Vasilii said. "We use them in design work. It wouldn't be hard for someone at the Dacha to use one without anyone knowing."

"And that's the problem. A few years ago there would have been just one at the Dacha and one in the Kremlin. But now there is one with every new radio station. They are being mass produced, here and in Moscow."

"Yes, but not that mass produced," Vasilii said. Vasilii kept up with technical innovation. There were several technical journals being published. Now they were published in English, Amideutsch, and two were published in Russian, one in Moscow and another in Ufa. Vasilii read each and every one intently.

Alla knew that because she'd been the one to make sure that the packages of technical journals were loaded onto the planes making the trip from Ufa to Almaty. She knew that Miroslava read them too, though she didn't have Vasilii's technical background. In this sense, she was the opposite of her famous fictional cousin. Miroslava was convinced that there was no such thing as useless information. She read everything she could get her hands on.

While Alla had been thinking about all that, the conversation had moved on.

"What was that in your office today?" Vasilii asked. "You could, as Brandy is wont to say, 'cut the tension with a knife.'"

"Simeon Budanov is afraid that I want his job."

"Do you?" Miroslava asked.

As tactful as ever, Alla thought, though Ivan Borisovich didn't seem to mind.

"Perhaps eventually. I am not immune to ambition, but it's actually more that I wish someone competent had Simeon Budanov's job, or at least someone that would let me do my job."

"The Grantville desk?" Vasilii asked with a grin.

"Okay, I grant that this hardly falls within the proper scope of the Grantville desk. But when Czar Mikhail calls me in and asks me to look into something, what am I supposed to do?"

"You are supposed to direct him to the bureaucrat whose job it is," Vasilii said, still grinning. "So we are informed by the unwritten regulations of the bureaus."

"I know, but it's Mikhail. How did it happen that our nothing of an emperor has turned into a leader who invokes that sort of loyalty in a staid and solid bureaucrat like me?"

"Clearly, the up-timer witches Brandy Bates and Tami Simmons cast a spell on him," Alla said. "At least that's what they were saying in the servants' quarters all over Moscow."

"That must be it then," Ivan Borisovich agreed. Then he sat back and rubbed his temples. "Meanwhile, for the sake of my job, please try to avoid dropping in on me in my office."

"Czar Mikhail's orders," Vasilii said.

"What you need is a place to meet that isn't either of your

jobs," Alla said. "Say a restaurant that you both frequent. With a discreet staff who can pass messages without anyone the wiser."

And suddenly everyone was looking at her. Ivan Borisovich with consideration and Vasilii with something close to anger. It was clear he knew what she was doing, and didn't approve of her doing it to him.

Miroslava, on the other hand, seemed to know what she was doing, but did not care.

"Alla, I know you want to start a restaurant and we will consider allowing it, but . . ." He trailed off, as if he wasn't sure what to say.

"Diogenes!" Miroslava not quite shouted.

"What?" Ivan asked. "You mean the Diogenes Club from the Holmes stories? That's not a restaurant."

"No, but it does have the Stranger's Room," Miroslava said. Then, looking at Alla, "and I guess that they could serve food in the Stranger's Room, even serve food to people who aren't members."

That was the beginning of the Diogenes Club of Ufa. In the meantime, there was still a mystery to solve, and Miroslava agreed to look into the matter.

Ivan filled them in on the chain of events, and the next day Miroslava and Vasilii were on their way to Kazan.

Dominika's and Zia Chernoff's townhouse, Ufa
November 21, 1637

"Vasilii said I could start looking for places," Alla told Dominika and Zia Chernoff. "But the name, if it happens, is set. It's going to be the Diogenes Club and the restaurant is only going to be a part of it."

"Diogenes the Cynic, the Greek philosopher?" Zia Chernoff asked.

"I guess," Alla agreed uncertainly. "But it's based on this club in the Sherlock Holmes stories. You know Miroslava thinks of that storybook character as some sort of a cousin or something."

"There are worse peculiarities in families," Zia said, and Dominika nodded.

Alla, by now, knew that both Zia and Dominika had issues with their families. Alla's only issue with hers was that they'd all been murdered by Sheremetev's dog boys back in Moscow, except for her and Crazy Cousin Vasilii in Ufa. Her new family was weird, but important in a way that her parents had only thought they were. So maybe they were right and Cousin Sherlock should be considered a part of her family.

"Find me a copy of the Sherlock Holmes stories, please," Zia asked.

"That's no problem. We have the whole set translated into Russian. In fact, Cousin Vasilii, who was a mystery buff before he met Miroslava, translated 'The Sign of the Four.'"

Zia shook her head and repeated, "Bring us copies so we can read them."

Then the discussion went back to what they needed. Money wasn't going to be much of an issue if they got permission. Both the Lyapunov and the Chernoff families were rich. They'd been rich back in Moscow and were even richer here in Ufa. Besides, Princess Irina had a proprietary interest in the place. The trick was going to be to get approval.

Zia Chernoff was in touch with her brother back in Muscovy and had managed to convince him not to have his granddaughter killed. At least, she thought she'd convinced him. They weren't taking any chances. The baby had multiple bodyguards. But real or not, part of that agreement was the fact that Zia had agreed to cooperate with Kirill in regard to family businesses. This gave Kirill insider information on what was going on in Ufa. And that brought to mind the issue of codes and cyphers and the difference between them. Alla didn't mention the case that Miroslava was now working on for Ivan Borisovich. Alla had a reputation for being able to keep private things private, and she intended to keep it.

But she did take note of how Zia contacted her brother and made a mental note to tell Miroslava about it.

Kazan Kremlin
November 21, 1637

Miroslava and Vasilii were brought directly to General Tim and in moments they were alone together.

"What's going on?" Tim asked as soon as they were alone.

"What do you know about Colonel Popov?" Vasilii asked.

"He's on General Birkin's staff, or he was. According to my sources, he died in a tavern brawl a few days ago."

"He was an asset of the Embassy Bureau," Vasilii said. "The tavern brawl, if it happened at all, was arranged."

"You're saying they found out?"

"Yes."

"Well, it can't have been my people. We didn't even know he was on our side."

"No, the leak was apparently from the Embassy Bureau," Vasilii agreed.

"We're here to try and see what we can learn from the way the information was transmitted," Miroslava added.

"What?"

"How Colonel Popov sent information from Birkingrad to Kazan. There were only a limited number of people who knew who the agent was. Of necessity, those few included the person who transmitted the information from Colonel Popov to Kazan, where it was sent on to the Embassy Bureau in Ufa."

Tim looked at them. "Budanov doesn't want you investigating."

"Budanov doesn't know we're investigating." Vasilii clarified. "He's assigned discovering the mole in the Embassy Bureau to Ivan Borisovich Petrov. On the basis of the fact that Petrov, whose job is the Grantville desk, wasn't in the need-to-know group who knew that the spy in General Birkin's camp was Colonel Popov, which has the added benefit of making Ivan Borisovich a pariah among the Embassy Bureau."

"No one likes to be the target of an investigation." Tim nodded. "So what do you need from me?"

"Access to your records and an overview of how the information travels between Kazan and Birkingrad."

Four hours later, Miroslava and Vasilii were lying on the battlements of Kazan, watching with a pair of binoculars as soldiers and civilians slipped across the no-man's-land between Kazan and Birkingrad, mostly carrying large backpacks.

It turned out that both command staffs knew about the trade in goods between the two cities, and both found it useful. Things made in Moscow or Novgorod were shipped to Birkingrad, where they made their way to Kazan and were from there shipped to Ufa or Perm. Things like magnetometers from the Moscow

Dacha made their way to Perm, where they were used to help find deposits of copper, silver, chromium, and iron.

And that was just one example. At the same time, the aqualators made in Ufa were better than those made in Muscovite Russia and they were making their way in the other direction. So was Caspian Sea caviar and freeze-dried sturgeon steaks, which made their way to Moscow to be reconstituted and cooked for the tables of the great and the grand.

Trade went on, and both generals allowed it because the benefits were greater than the damage. Besides, both generals knew that the other side was too strong to attack with the forces they had, so there was very little actual benefit in making the life of the Russian soldiers on the other side more difficult.

It was a phony war in practice.

So Miroslava watched as every few minutes a person or small group would make their way from a gate in Kazan to one in Birkingrad, and a few minutes later back to Kazan.

They took careful note of who was making the trip and how often, because they were trying to find out if the agent who took the messages from Birkingrad to Kazan was compromised. This was made more difficult because the source of at least some of those messages was dead. Still, the mailman made his trip right on schedule, which at least suggested that he didn't know that Colonel Popov was no longer among his customers.

CHAPTER 18

Club Diogenes

2200 Block, Irina Way, Ufa
November 25, 1637

The 2200 block wasn't all the way to the dirigible base, but it was close and the investor had planned the building based on the assumption that the dirigible base at Ufa would continue to be a going concern, on the assumption, in fact, that there would be, over the years, more and more dirigibles. Based on that belief, the investors had built a large complex, including two stories of hotel rooms and a very large restaurant.

After the loss of the *Czarina Evdokia* and the *Czar Alexis*, Czar Mikhail had not completely abandoned dirigibles, but had deprioritized them. The Muscovite Russian government was still working on the replacement for the *Czar Alexis* in Bor. But that dirigible was unlikely to stop at Ufa even after it was finished sometime in 1638.

All of which meant that the investors who had spent several millions of rubles building the hotel, dining and entertainment complex were finally having to face up to the fact that though there was probably some market, their business there wasn't going to be nearly as much as they'd hoped. And a majority of them were looking for a way out, some of them fairly desperately.

It wasn't that they were going to lose money. In fact, they were probably going to make a decent amount as Ufa continued to grow. But they weren't going to make the piles and piles of money they'd been counting on.

That was what the Lyapunov financial advisor had explained

to Alla, Miroslava, and Vasilii, as well as Dominika, Zia Chernoff, and ten-year-old Princess Irina. They were all here now to look over the mostly finished complex that they could get for only a few million rubles.

There were, aside from the restaurant which would be named the Stranger's Room, also offices and meeting rooms, as well as guest rooms.

"I want that one," Irina said of a suite near the back of the complex whose glass windows looked out at the empty field that was going to be the dirigible base. It had three bed chambers and a sitting room and wasn't that different from three other similar suites.

"I like living in the Dacha," Vasilii complained, rather half-heartedly. They'd had a talk with Czar Mikhail that morning about the project. Mikhail couldn't fire Budanov for some very good political reasons, and the Embassy Bureau had several perfectly legitimate functions that included the instituting and staffing of embassies in the rest of Europe and Asia, which part of the job Budanov seemed at least fairly competent at.

As he preferred to do when he could, Mikhail had decided to go around the problem. The crown's investment in the Diogenes Club would officially be about the whim of a spoiled princess. In fact, at least some of the intelligence function of the Embassy Bureau was to be quietly transferred here, under the control of Ivan Borisovich Petrov, who would henceforth have the code name Mycroft, initial M.

Meanwhile, Alla was going to get her restaurant.

Three days later, they signed the contracts and Alla went to work with the help of the financial advisor, hiring staff for the restaurant. And on the first day of interviews, Elina showed up.

"Anna, what are you doing here?"

"Elina?" Alla said in something close to shock. She hadn't seen Elina since she'd been a servant in the kitchen of Captain Petrov.

"I ran off a couple of weeks after you did. I thought you'd be shacked up with Master Gregory. The captain was furious after you two ran off."

"Not as furious as he wanted people to think," Alla muttered. In fact, Gregory had "run off" with "Anna" on his father's orders, as a way of getting the dangerous-to-have-around Alla Lyapunov out of his house and to Ufa where she was needed. "Anyway," she said louder, "I know you can make croissants and other French pastries, so if you want the job, you're hired."

Elina was just standing there with her mouth open, and there were other potential employees in line. Not a long line. Work was available in Ufa. In fact, most of the people who were applying already had jobs. They were just looking for better ones. So Alla turned Elina over to their business manager who would be running the negotiations with potential employees, with one final command. "Don't mention where you know me from."

Several hours later, one of the new servants who was, in fact, a spy recently fired from the Embassy Bureau brought Elina to Alla's room in Club Diogenes. It was part of a three-room suite that Alla would share with Miroslava and Vasilii. Her suite was two doors down from Princess Irina's suite, which was unoccupied at the moment, and was the Royal Suite that was reserved for the use of the royal family when and if they decided to visit. The fact that the royal family had a suite here was a major draw, making it *the* club.

All of that made sense to Elina. The notion that Anna, the incompetent kitchen girl, was actually Alla Lyapunov...that was much harder to get her head around.

"Come in and have a seat, Elina," Alla said. "It's kind of a long story."

And over the next couple of hours, Alla told it. She explained that she'd seen her parents' bodies in the street and, not having anyplace else to go, had ended up on Irina Petrov's doorstep because she knew the girl from church, and rather than turn her over to Sheremetev, Captain Gregory Petrov had taken her in and hidden her as a servant. "It wasn't easy," Alla admitted. "If I hadn't been terrified half out of my mind I never would have been able to become Anna the servant girl." She explained how for months she'd lived in the servants' quarters, been a servant, and at first a not very good servant.

"That part I remember." Elina grinned. "For the first couple of months, Cook was constantly complaining that if they were going to bring someone in from the country, why couldn't they bring someone who had a brain."

"Yes. Every day, every hour, it seemed I did something wrong,"

Alla admitted. "I was dreadfully afraid that the cook would complain to the captain and I would be turned over to Sheremetev's hounds after all." Alla shivered in memory.

Elina looked at the young woman before her and realized for the first time that being born the daughter of a noble house didn't mean everything was always perfect. She'd worked in the same house, but the worst she'd ever feared had been the possibility of a slap, and the greater possibility that the cook might yell at her. The possibility that she might be killed for a poorly prepared goose had never entered her mind.

"You can't tell anyone that Alla Lyapunov and Anna, the kitchen girl in the household of Captain Gregory Petrov, are the same person. It might well get the captain, Mistress Petrov and Nadia killed. Sheremetev, or whoever is in charge back in Moscow now, can't get at me here or at Cousin Vasilii, but they can still punish the Petrov family for taking in Alla Lyapunov if they find out."

Elina wasn't a great fan of the Petrov family. She didn't hate them. They'd treated their servants fairly well. But they were still Russian lower nobility who, to Elina's mind, made them only slightly better than the upper nobility.

"The Flying Squirrel—" she started to say, but Alla interrupted.

"Would you like to meet him?"

"Meet who?"

"The Flying Squirrel. The man who writes the Flying Squirrel pamphlets."

"You know who he is?"

"He's a friend of Vasilii's," Alla said. Then added, "Do you want to see Nadia dead on the street? Is that what you want?"

"No, I guess not."

Royal Palace, Ufa
November 26, 1637

Eight-year-old Alexi Romanov was convinced that Irina got all the good stuff. This was most unfair, since he was the one who was going to have to be czar when he grew up. Even though his papa had explained that the royal suite at the Diogenes Club was the family's, not Irina's, everyone was saying it was Irina's suite. It wasn't fair. Besides, she was bossy and stuck up. But after some loud complaints, he'd gone off to play with his Hero-class model airplane.

While Alexi was making strafing runs on the evil Zunghar cavalry, Mikhail and Evdokia were having a chat with Vasilii.

"What do you think of the Diogenes Club?" Mikhail asked.

"I think you're being too clever by half, Your Majesty," Vasilii said. "The Embassy Bureau is where we've done intelligence work since Ivan the Terrible's time."

"I know, but we need a network in Muscovite Russia and Budanov isn't the man to do it, even if I could trust him."

"And you think Ivan Borisovich is?"

"I know he looks simple and straightforward, and in many ways he is. But he's a top flight analyst, and he's loyal." Mikhail raised a hand. "Anyway, that's not why you're here. I am trying to decide whether to send you east with Vlad and Brandy, or leave you here with Miroslava to help oversee the Diogenes Club."

"How about you leave me here and let me design steam engines?"

"Now that would be a waste," Mikhail said. "Besides, you're going to design steam engines no matter what other work I assign you. You can't help yourself."

"Not if I'm out in the back of beyond, loading wood into the new firebox."

"Okay. That decides it. You'll be staying. You will be moving out of the Dacha to the Diogenes Club, to look after your wife and daughter. But don't feel bad. We're going to have a nice little lab in the basement. I think we'll nickname you Q."

Vasilii looked over at the czarina and asked, "What's the penalty for regicide, Majesty? Taking into account the provocation. Q!"

"Even granting the provocation, it's quite severe," Czarina Evdokia said. "On the other hand, just thinking about it is perfectly legal." She smiled sweetly at her husband.

CHAPTER 19

Go East

Airfield, Ufa
December 10, 1637

Yulia watched Prince Vladimir making his inspection of the *Nicky*, part of the pilot's job, not hers. Yulia was a doctor. She'd been a midwife and had learned about infection and disease transmission at the Dachas. First the Gorchakov Dacha near Moscow, then the Ufa Dacha.

As Prince Vladimir continued his inspection of the plane, Yulia walked up the steps to the lower wing of the *Nicky*. Yulia would be going along as the expedition's medical expert, in an attempt to avoid killing all the locals with diseases from western and central Europe. She'd spent much of the last four years studying medicine from up-timer medical books and the last several months studying with Tami Simmons. So now she was going out to the back of beyond to inoculate the natives against smallpox.

Brandy hugged Anya Tupikova, who was now married to Filip Pavlovich Tupikov, and ran the Dacha. Anya was one of the czarina's kitchen cabinet, a small group of women who, despite their backgrounds, exerted considerable influence on the government of the Sovereign States.

She was going to miss them all, but Anya the most. She felt a kinship with the former slave that, as much as she liked Evdokia, she didn't really feel with her.

"Keep track of things, Anya, and don't let Evdokia screw up too badly."

"I'll do my best. You keep your eyes out for wild bears and Mongols out there in the wilderness."

Brandy passed out a few more hugs, then climbed up to the plane. She was going to be the copilot. Vlad had more hours. Yury Arsenyev and Ariq Ogedei were going to be splitting the duties of flight engineer and mapmaker.

Once in her seat, she did the internal flight check while Vlad did the walkaround. Once the walkaround was complete, Vlad climbed aboard and joined Brandy in the cockpit.

Yulia belted herself into the seat.

"Steam coming up," Yury informed them. He had gauges that told him the heat and pressure in the entire system. "Diverting steam to the condenser," he added, turning a knob.

The Jupiter Five, on which the new Hero-class aircraft were based, had an improved airframe with less parasitic drag. It carried sixteen passengers and a crew of three for a total of nineteen. Its cruising speed was right at a hundred miles an hour. The Hero had essentially the same airframe, so the same cruising speed. However, it used external combustion, that is steam, so it spent more of its weight on the engines, boiler, and condenser than the Jupiter, so it only carried eleven passengers and four crew; pilot, copilot, flight engineer and navigator. This plane, redesigned to use wood or coal as well as liquid fuel, could carry only eight passengers plus the four crew. The extra six hundred pounds of weight had to be used for fuel.

The rest of the weight was cargo for Tobolsk and wood sacks. They were heavy canvas sacks with collapsible frames of light wood which they would use to store the wood for the firebox.

When using fuel oil, the Hero didn't use much more fuel than the Jupiter, but it did carry less usable load. When using wood? Well, they really didn't know yet.

They needed the condensers warm because they wanted the feedwater hot when it went into the boiler. Brandy listened to Yury's reports as she checked her own gauges and control systems, adjusting the flaps and rudder to make sure the steering system was operating well. Then Vlad came, followed by Ariq.

"Tanks topped up," Ariq announced as Vlad was sitting down.

"Steam to the fans," Brandy said, and diverted steam to the fans that would fill the air cushion.

"Bringing up inboard engines," Vlad said as he pushed the two center levers forward. They'd all learned the importance of announcing their actions as they operated the plane. It was important for everyone to know what was going on and what everyone else was up to. Unlike the planes of the late twentieth century, these planes had almost no automatic systems. Everything was controlled by someone, so everyone needed to know what everyone else was doing.

The plane was moving now, down onto the icy river, floating on a cushion of air and throwing up an icy mist.

"Bringing up outer engines," Vlad said and pushed the two outer levers, and the plane slewed a little as Vlad adjusted the output. Then they straightened out and picked up speed rapidly. It was only seconds later that Vlad rotated and they lifted off. They were on flare effect for another few seconds, then they were in full flight mode.

"Retracting ACLG," Brandy said as she reversed the fans that filled the air cushion and ran the small motor that pulled the straps tight, compressing the skirt.

"Pulling steam from generators," Yury said. "On batteries for now. Reducing fuel flow to the boiler."

"Ariq, get us some bearings as soon as you can," Vlad said. Then he flipped on the radio and talked to the controllers, giving them compass heading and rate of climb.

After that, things settled down. It took them about fifteen minutes to get to their cruising altitude of six thousand feet. By that time Ariq had bearings from three radio stations, Ufa, Hidden Valley, and Kazak Station 1, and could place them exactly and provide direction and speed. This matched quite well with the other indicators. They had a fifteen-mile-an-hour crosswind and were cruising at ninety-seven mph indicated airspeed.

"Okay," Yuri said, "who wants tea?"

Three hours later, Vladimir saw a lake and they came in for a landing, taking careful note of the compass heading and terrain features. This would be a good refueling station. There was a thin layer of ice on the lake. As spread out as the weight of the aircraft was, they still left a trail of shattered ice in their wake as they skimmed over the lake surface to the shore.

"Okay, guys," Vlad said. "I know we still have fuel in the

tank, but I want to see how this contraption is going to work. Everyone, grab an ax and let's go gather some fuel."

"That's everyone but me," Brandy said. "We are now officially in Injun territory. I will be keeping watch."

"You just want to stay comfortable in the cabin," Yuri complained.

"Right you are," Brandy acknowledged happily. And he was. The inside of the aircraft was toasty warm. No matter how efficient they tried to make it, waste heat leaked into the cabin, which was just fine and dandy on a day like today.

They'd pulled up on the shore to the north of the lake and the whole lake was surrounded by woods, mostly pine. There was a lot of wood on the ground, but most of it was wet. It had snowed here recently, and the sun this morning had melted the snow into slush.

While Yulia and the boys were out gathering, Brandy put a packet of freeze-dried vegetables and pasta in a pot, added water and a beef bouillon cube to the mix, and put it on to boil.

"Steam is up and we're ready," Yuri said.

"But we seem to be going through the wood pretty fast," Ariq added.

"Steam to the fans," Brandy said, turning them on. The air cushion filled and the friction decreased. The fans inflated the air cushions and leaked air out around the bottom of the plane, eliminating friction, but it wasn't an on/off situation. You could, by the amount of power you fed the fans, control how slippery the air cushion was.

Reporting his actions, Vlad got them in the air and they were now flying completely on wood. They slowly rose to four thousand feet, and headed north for Tobolsk.

Tobolsk
December 10, 1637

General Mikhail Borisovich Shein watched the airplane make its slow, lazy circle around the town of Tobolsk and wondered if he had indeed lived too long. He'd lived longer than in that other history by more than three years so far. And every day seemed to bring more proof that he wasn't ready for this new age.

Mikhail Romanov was *winning!* It was impossible, but Mikhail was still in power in Ufa, had added the Kazakh Khanate to his territory while Sheremetev was missing—and, if Shein was any judge—the "guest" of some Lithuanian magnate. Or it could be that Sheremetev was filling a shallow grave somewhere between Moscow and Smolensk.

Shein had known about the plane, of course. He'd even been starting to get a little worried when the radio message from the plane arrived a quarter of an hour ago. He could take the plane. It held only five people, two of them women.

It would be the stupidest thing he'd ever done in either life. But he could do it. He wasn't going to, of course. It was a passing thought. So he watched as the *Nicky* landed on the river and pulled up on shore. Then he ordered a squad of *streltzi* to guard the plane as long as it was here, and went out to meet Vladimir Gorchakov and his barmaid wife.

Shein's wife wasn't going to like that. Maria Godunova was of the highest nobility in Russia, related to Czar Godunov. She set great store by bloodlines and propriety. She, as much as anyone, had argued against the alliance with Mikhail, seeing him as another Fyodor Ivanovich, who had died in 1598. Fyodor was both physically and mentally frail, and his only surviving son, Dimitry, was illegitimate and killed by Czar Godunov's agents. It was based on him that the three False Dimitris made their claims of royalty.

Arguably, the whole Time of Troubles was the fault of Fyodor's weakness.

But Mikhail wasn't Fyodor. Given the chance, he'd grown into the position and remade Russia. Not by brutality, as Ivan the Terrible, but by...

General Shien wasn't at all sure how he'd done it. He watched from the wooden walls of Tobolsk as the *Nicky* circled and landed, then went out to meet Prince Vladimir and the barmaid, in peace.

Brandy Bates Gorchakov wasn't looking forward to this any more than Shein was. She'd met Maria Godunova on her way south. Godunova was a bitter old woman who didn't approve of peasants getting above themselves. "Are you sure we can't just shoot them?" she muttered to Vlad.

"I'm sure. Now smile, dear, and pretend you have station."

"Welcome to Tobolsk," General Mikhail Borisovich Shein said, not offering a title.

"Thank you. You've been working." And it was true. When they'd sailed down the frozen river last winter, Tobolsk, while large for the east side of the Ural Mountains, was still basically a frontier fort. Now it was a city, a small one, but a city nonetheless.

"The summer sailing season was short, but knowing that Mangazeya was open again made a difference. Quite a lot of Russian fur went to England and the Netherlands and quite a bit of machinery arrived here. Your *Catherine the Great* made two trips before the ice closed in again.

"Besides, we've had a lot of people who ran from the boyars in Moscow come here. And we've gotten goods that way, as well."

It was true. Shein wasn't, in Vladimir's opinion, the great general people thought of him as. He was excellent at building, training, and equipping an army, but not nearly so good at using it, which was probably a good thing. He'd built an army here in the frontier, even something of a manufacturing center, if the weapons his soldiers carried were any indication. But, from all reports, he hadn't done much with it.

Hands were shaken and they got in out of the cold. They spent the night in the Tobolsk Kremlin and learned that while a mule train of fuel oil was reportedly on its way from Solikamsk, it would be at least a week before it arrived.

"And I'm afraid our attempts to find oil have so far failed to produce useful results, in spite of the fact that according to your books there is oil in the area."

"Well, keep looking. The demand is only going to increase for at least the next fifty years or so," Brandy said.

"It would help if we had someone who knew more about geology and how to find oil."

"All I know is some vague references to salt domes," Brandy said, which wasn't exactly true. She had looked into the records of the oil industry in Grantville in the 1920s, but that didn't make her a geologist or a wildcatter.

Dinner was stiff and formal.

Tobolsk
December 11, 1637

The next morning, stocked up with charcoal briquettes, they flew out, heading due east. They made it about two hundred and fifty miles before they started to run low on briquettes.

Oil was certainly the best available fuel. After that came charcoal briquettes. Wood is less energy dense than oil, but it's also less dense, period. It doesn't weigh as much per square foot as oil. Which meant that they could fly a good distance on the wood they could carry, but the firebox that used wood had to be bigger than the firebox that used oil. And that someone had to spend almost all their time in flight feeding wood or charcoal into the firebox, and the whole thing got dirty, and ash got everywhere.

They were looking for a place to land as the weather started to close in, and there was no place to land. The whole area was one huge forest. Then they found a gap in the trees and made it down. They were just in time. The weather closed in and they spent the next three days living in the *Nicky*, as the sky dropped snow, sleet, and rain on them.

CHAPTER 20

Stay Home

Ufa Kremlin
December 14, 1637

Ivan Borisovich Petrov looked over the new aqualator design. Russia's aqualator industry was growing. The up-timers were focused on digital computers. You could build digital aqualators. In fact, almost all the aqualators were at least partly digital. But you could also build analog aqualators, and aqualators that were both digital and analog. Both slide rules and calculators would solve problems, but the slide rule was simpler to make. The new radio station aqualators used a "slide rule" structure to get the best frequency and a digital system to count the errors in the checksum.

Ivan understood about a third of the technology. He had a solid overview and knew enough to know when the boffins at the Dacha were blowing smoke. Here, he was pretty sure, they weren't. But the radio system aqualators had a great deal of what in electrical computers would be called ROM. And the ROM wasn't programmable at all. You plugged in a ROM component, and it solves a particular sort of problem, and only that sort of problem.

It was something that they could quite possibly sell to the USE, or if the USE wasn't interested, to the Ottomans.

There was no knock on his door. It opened and Director Budanov came in. "I hope that's a report on who leaked the information to Birkin's staff."

"No, sir. It's a report on the new aqualators."

210   *Flint, Huff & Goodlett*
"Who cares?"

"Most of the radio techs."

Budanov just looked at him.

"I have people correlating who had access to the information. But until they finish, there isn't much I can do."

"So I'll report to the czar that you have made no progress." Budanov slammed the door on his way out.

Ivan sighed. According to Miroslava, this was likely a two-murder problem. That is, in Vasilii's books, it often took more than one murder for the detective to gather enough information to determine who the murderer was. That if the murderer stopped at one, they never would have been caught. And, in the real world, a disheartening number of murders were never solved. And all too often, when a murder was "solved," it wasn't. Instead, some handy scapegoat was caught and condemned for a murder he had nothing to do with.

Sighing again, Ivan got up, put on his heavy woolen greatcoat, and left. He caught a tram and rode it down Irina Way to the Diogenes Club.

There were two workmen hanging a sign over one of the doors. It said STRANGER'S ROOM, and, careful to avoid getting the sign dropped on his head, he slipped in the door. There was a guard in the foyer, and Ivan pulled out a laminated card. It had his picture on one side, and he showed it to the guard. After looking at it and looking at him, the guard let him through. A waiter showed him to a table, and a few minutes later Alla came out.

"Hello, Ivan," the girl said. "We're still working on the building, but the kitchen is open. The chef has a new recipe, beef Bourguignon over mashed turnips. Or you can have it over scalloped potatoes."

Potatoes were brought to Russia shortly after Bernie Zeppi got to Russia and had taken the country like the Polish hussars couldn't manage. The peasants loved them because of how much food you could get compared to wheat or rye. The Volga had spread them and there were potatoes being harvested from Moscow to the Caspian Sea and the Ural Mountains, but turnips had been here longer and were still more prevalent.

"What do you recommend?"

"Try the turnips. They work well and give a solid meal."

Ivan made his order, and Alla was right. The turnips worked well enough, and the beef stew was good. After eating, he went to an office down the hall from the Stranger's Room, where Vasilii was fiddling with an aqualator.

"Does Miroslava have any new ideas about who our mole might be?"

"Not exactly," Vasilii said. "Alla has an idea if you want to try it."

"What is it?" Ivan asked cautiously. In his opinion, Alla Lyapunov was a kid. And his personal belief was that if the Diogenes Club wasn't being quietly supported by the czar, it would already be a failure. But Ivan had been keeping his personal beliefs personal for most of his life.

"Arrange another murder," Vasilii said with a grin and waited for Ivan to react. Ivan looked at him and he continued. "Introduce a juicy piece of intelligence that your mole is going to want to get to Birkin as quickly as possible."

"What sort of information?" Ivan asked. "It took the Muscovy desk months to turn Colonel Popov. Birkin, it turns out, is a popular commander and most of his people are personally loyal to him, even when they aren't all that enamored of the chaos that has taken over in Moscow."

"The Muscovy desk?"

"It's not official. That would entail recognizing Muscovite Russia as a separate state. And the official position of Czar Mikhail is that Moscow and, well, that part of Russia that is northwest of Kazan is in rebellion. And after the rebellion is over and the miscreants are hanged, the people of Moscow will be allowed the option of becoming a state in the United Sovereign States of Russia, or becoming the personal fief of Czar Mikhail. He expects them to become states."

"I know he does. That's why I asked about the Muscovy desk. Look, I want to get Miroslava and Alla into this. Then let's adjourn to one of the meeting rooms."

A very few minutes later they were seated in a small wood-paneled room with a button to call the serving staff if they were wanted. They were in plush chairs and joined by Miroslava Holmes and Alla Lyapunov, who had brought a tray of cookies in the shape of little trees with green icing.

"You were telling me about the Muscovy desk?" Vasilii said.

Ivan looked at Miroslava and Alla. "As I said, it's *unofficial*. But we need something. We have to deal with them while this stationary war is going on. And I'm not saying General Lebedev is wrong in his approach." Ivan also felt that General Lebedev was too young for his rank, and believed that calling him General Tim only heightened the effect. And, yes, Ivan Borisovich Petrov felt he was too young for his rank too. And Vasilii knew it, and liked to tease him about it.

"So the unofficial Muscovy desk of the Embassy Bureau spends months getting an agent into Birkin's..."

Alla trailed off as Ivan shook his head.

"Spent months *turning* one of Birkin's top subordinates."

"How did you do that?" Alla asked.

"A woman named Valeria. She was a former serf who escaped after Mikhail's Emancipation Proclamation. She showed up on our doorstep only a few weeks after I got here. I never met the woman, but she knew what the Embassy Bureau was and what it did and volunteered.

"She was given a bit of training and late last winter she was sent to Birkingrad as the daughter of a merchant with a load of caps for caplocks. Birkin bought the caps and she set up a tailor shop in Birkingrad. She met and romanced Colonel Popov, and persuaded him slowly to support Czar Mikhail.

"They were just starting to get good information when, suddenly, Colonel Popov was killed in a brawl. But Colonel Popov wasn't a brawler and didn't like that tavern. And General Birkin hasn't investigated the death.

"Our conclusion is that Birkin or, more likely, one of his top subordinates, ordered the murder because they realized he was the leak. The thing is, we can't figure out any way for them to have figured it out, except that someone told him. Because in a separate incident, Valeria's shop was robbed and the robber killed her and the two tailors she had working for her. Again, there was no investigation, and Birkin doesn't like crime in Birkingrad.

"On the other hand, our courier is fine. Still going back and forth from Kazak to Birkingrad every few nights."

"So someone here told Birkin about Colonel Popov and the woman, but not about your courier?"

"Either that, or they were told about the courier and were told to leave him alone."

"It has to be something that Birkin will need to know soon," Miroslava said.

"What has to be something Birkin needs to know?"

"The information you leak," Alla said.

"I'm not going to leak any information," Ivan said indignantly.

"He's right," Vasilii said. "By now everyone in the Embassy Bureau knows that Ivan is in charge of finding the leak. If he suddenly leaks some vital information, someone is going to smell a rat."

"Yeah," Alla agreed. "And, besides, he probably couldn't carry it off."

Ivan looked at her for a long moment, and then said, "You're probably right."

"What you need to do is find someone else, someone that you can trust and who can't be the spy, and get them to leak it."

"Leak what?"

"The fact that General Tim has figured out a way to take out Birkingrad."

"There is no way to take out Birkingrad," Ivan said.

"Of course there is," Alla insisted. "General Tim came up with it. He's a military genius. Everyone knows that."

"Actually, it's General Maslov who is the military genius. General Lebedev is simply a decisive and effective commander," Ivan said. "And everyone knows that they've been working on the problem of fortifications for the last year and are no closer to finding an answer now than they were when they were both lieutenants."

"Yes, I know that," Alla said. "But General Tim has had a eureka moment, and he's fairly confident that he's figured out a way to take Birkingrad. He's not sure if it's applicable to other fortified positions, and he wants to talk it over with General Maslov before discussing it with the czar, or the general staff, or anyone, really. All that anyone really knows is he wants permission to either go visit General Maslov or bring General Maslov back to Ufa to work out the details."

"You know, after what Ivan did to the Zunghars," Vasilii said, "people might just believe that."

"Yes, but to what purpose? Even if they do believe it, which

I am not all that confident of, there's nothing for them to do about it."

"That's true."

"Kill General Tim," Miroslava said calmly. "That would be their only option. If they leave him alive, he's a threat to Birkingrad, and even to the rest of Muscovite Russia."

Vasilii laughed. "Tim's been a threat to Muscovite Russia since he took out the Nizhny Novgorod garrison at Bor. They haven't killed him yet."

"Lack of opportunity," Miroslava said.

"It's not done," Alla said. "Shooting the other side's general when it's not even a *battle*. It's not done." Then she sat back. "That's what the idea of the new trick to take Birkingrad will do for us. Give Birkin enough reason to put aside custom and decency and order General Tim's execution."

"It's still not enough," Ivan said, interested in spite of himself. "Even if Birkin was desperate enough to order it, he still couldn't do it."

"Then we leak that Tim is going to do something dangerous," Vasilii said. "Well, something that would expose him to an enemy attack."

"Let me get this straight," Ivan said. "You want me to paint a great big target on General Lebedev's back, then parade him in front of Birkin's sharpshooters?"

"They don't need to actually find him where we say. They just have to go look there," Alla said, then added enthusiastically, "We offer different locations to different suspects and see where Birkin's men go looking."

"It might well work," Vasilii said, "and even if it doesn't, listening to the rumor over the next few days might tell you who's careless with secret information."

"You're going to have to find multiple people in the Puzzle Palace to leak information for you."

"That's not going to be easy. Most of the people in the Puzzle Pup Tent are not actually very good liars."

The Embassy Bureau fulfilled the roles of the state department, the CIA, and the NSA for Russia. But seventeenth-century Russia wasn't late twentieth-century America. It had a lot fewer people and a whole lot less of an intelligence apparatus. In fact, while Vladimir Gorchakov and Brandy Bates had been in Grantville, they'd generated more actual intelligence than the whole rest of the Embassy Bureau, because Grantville was spy central for most of Europe, having agents from all of western Europe. There were even Spanish agents operating in Grantville, though they mostly reported to individual Spanish noblemen, not the king. And Murad had a whole group of agents, most of them French, working for him. So the analytical section of the Embassy Bureau was way smaller than a Puzzle Palace. It was more pup-tent size, even though it did have a couple of aqualators.

That was the thing Ivan Borisovich had going for him. It was a much smaller pool of suspects than there would have been in up-time America.

They spent the next couple of hours working out the details of how it might be done. But Ivan flatly refused to do it on his own. "We have to tell Czar Mikhail what's going on and, for that matter, we need to tell General Lebedev, to make sure that he's not actually in any of the places that the Muscovites expect him to be.

"And I can't go visiting Czar Mikhail right now. There are too many eyes on me."

"Alla can," Vasilii said. "She visits the palace fairly regularly to play with Princess Irina."

Alla grimaced. It was true. Her year as a kitchen servant was all very romantic and heroic to the ten-year-old princess, as well as the eight-year-old heir apparent, and Alla was smart enough to know that such a connection was going to be vital as Alexi and Irina grew up. So she acted as a trusted elder friend, and was kind to the children. And she actually liked them, though she was coming to leave the interests of childhood behind and sometimes found their focus on games and toys a bit boring.

Royal Palace
December 15, 1637

"I need to talk to your father," Alla told Alexi while they were playing a war game based on the war between the USE and Poland.

Alexi was insisting that Alla play the Poles, which Alla felt was more than a bit unfair.

"Papa's busy," Alexi said as though it was an automatic answer. Czar Mikhail was busy. So was Czarina Evdokia. But they did make time for the children in the evening. The other side of that deal was that the kids knew that they weren't supposed to interrupt their parents during the day.

"It's important," Alla said, then leaned in. "And secret. It's *Club Diogenes* business."

"What's it about?" Alexi demanded.

"It's need to know."

"I'm the heir apparent. I need to know everything."

Which was exactly what Alla should have expected him to say.

"And I'm an imperial princess and an investor in the Diogenes Club," Irina said. Which was legally true. The government's investment in the Diogenes Club was substantial, and done through Irina. She wasn't a majority shareholder, but she was on the board of directors.

Alla cudgeled her brain, then said, "It's not up to me. Ask your father after we talk."

That didn't satisfy them, and she was pretty sure that Czar Mikhail wasn't going to be happy with her solution either. But after complaining a bit more, they all trooped over to the czar's office. The secretary, a middle-aged man with a short graying beard and a not quite double chin, made them wait till the commoner president left. The constitution of the Sovereign States was a set of compromises, including the use of two co-presidents, one who had to be a commoner and one who had to be a noble. As long as they agreed, decisions on policy usually didn't come to Mikhail, but if they didn't agree Czar Mikhail was the deciding vote.

Then the secretary buzzed the czar to tell him they were there.

"Send them in."

When they went in, they found Czar Mikhail holding a hunk of gold as big as his fist. He held it up. "It's from the Kazakh field."

Alla looked at it. "Wow."

"Cool!" Alexi said. He'd picked the word up from Bernie Zeppi and used it more than Alla thought entirely necessary.

"Yes, very cool. The gold and silver from the mines is going a long way toward keeping the confidence in Sovereign States money high, at least locally. However, according to Iosif Borisovich Petrov in Grantville, the Sovereign States money has dropped a lot on the Grantville and Magdeburg exchanges, and isn't even traded on the Amsterdam exchange."

"So send the gold to Amsterdam and buy up all the rubles," Irina said.

"That's an excellent plan, Irina. I think we'll do it."

"You should send them to Grantville," Alexi insisted. "Grantville's more important than the Netherlands. Well, the USE is more important than the Netherlands."

"Also a good point. Now, how do we get the gold there without giving half of it to General Shein?"

"Put it on a plane," Alla offered. "If you can send planes all the way to the other end of Kazakh, you can send them west to the USE."

"Not through Muscovy, I can't." Mikhail grimaced.

"Go south," Alexi said. Alexi had a three-foot globe in his room and a large atlas. "I can find a route."

"Can you really?" the czar of the United Sovereign States of Russia asked with a bemused expression on his face.

"I think so." Alexi's enthusiasm was waning a bit as the prospect became closer to real.

"Very well. You map out a route from here to Grantville where they can get fuel. Irina, you help him. After all, you helped him interrupt my work."

"That's really my fault, Your Majesty," Alla said. "Well, Ivan Borisovich's fault, and Vasilii and Miroslava's, as well." She was wearing a vest over her blouse, and from the vest, she pulled some folded sheets of paper.

He took the sheets and read through them carefully, while Alla and the children waited. Then he looked up. "This is burn-before-reading stuff." Then he looked at the two children. "You two did well in bringing Alla to me for this. So no punishment. And order whatever you want for dessert tonight. If Alla brings you something like this again, you have my permission to interrupt. But we can't tell anyone that you're allowed. That too has to be a secret."

"What's it about?" Alexi asked, pointing at the sheets of paper.

Czar Mikhail—and it was Czar Mikhail, not Papa—looked at them. "It's going to be vitally important at times for you to know things and then act like you don't have the least idea of them. For both of you." He handed the sheets to Alexi. "Share with your sister."

Irina didn't wait. She came over and read over Alexi's shoulder. She was two years older and three inches taller than her little brother.

Alla looked on in shock. What was he doing, giving them this sort of information?

He looked at her and winked. After the two royal children had read the sheets, Czar Mikhail took the sheets and put them in the fire in the fireplace, so that they burned to ash in a few moments.

"All right. Alla, tell Ivan Borisovich Petrov that the plan is approved, but I want *you* to let Tim know what's going on." Then he looked at the children. "Now tell me how you're going to keep this a secret. It's important not just that you don't tell anyone, but that no one even knows you know a secret. At least not *this* secret."

"We know a *different* secret," Irina said. "What secret, Papa?"

"The secret airplane route to Grantville!" Alexi crowed.

"You don't keep a secret by shouting it out," Alla said, and Alexi blushed.

"Good. You two run along and work on the secret route to Grantville. Alla, stay a moment."

After the children were gone, Mikhail looked at her. "You're wondering why I told them about your plan, aren't you?"

"Yes, Your Majesty."

"I grew up in a snake pit. Alexi and Irina won't have that advantage. If you want to call it that. But they are going to have to learn to keep secrets, and to do that, you need practice. The same goes for you. You've had your share of living in secret, and I know you can keep your mouth shut when you need to, but you do need to know how to misdirect attention from the secret that no one can know to the secret that people can find out without any great damage being caused by it.

"In this particular case, it's a fairly safe secret. Neither Alexi nor Irina have much contact with anyone in the Embassy Bureau, especially the Muscovy desk. So they know the secret, but who are they going to tell? And even if they let it slip, even if one of their nursemaids is a spy—possible but unlikely—by the time the information makes its way to Birkin or the Muscovy desk, it will be too late. But I will get to see how well my two eldest keep secrets and how trustworthy their maids and tutors are.

"You are now the official supersecret conduit from the Diogenes Club to me. Which will make things easier. As you go out, send my secretary in. I need to let him know that the children were summoned so that I could give them a project and didn't interrupt my day."

Which Alla did, and then followed the children back to their quarters in the palace.

As his secretary came in Mikhail smiled at the man. "Matvey, I have a few things for you not to know."

Matvey rolled his eyes. "I take it this has to do with the children, Your Majesty?"

"Yes, officially I summoned them and they brought Alla along to tell me something about some service that the Diogenes Club is offering. I'm afraid I didn't think of that till just now. Oh, and the children will be deciding on dessert for tonight's dinner. Please let the czarina know."

"And why did you summon them?" Matvey asked. "Just so I can disapprove of the right thing."

"They are going to be mapping out a route for a Hero-class airplane to take to get from here to Grantville without going through Muscovy-controlled Russia, Poland, or the Ottoman Empire."

"You have already decided to send Bernie and Natasha to Grantville by the southern route, and why would that be secret?"

"So the children will have a secret project and so we can determine how well their maids keep quiet." Mikhail gave Matvey a look then continued. "The real secret part is what is going to be in the plane."

"Which is?"

"A bit over a ton of gold."

"Do we *have* that much gold?"

"Barely. It's going to pretty much clean out our reserves."

"Then why?"

"Because we have to restore confidence in the Sovereign States ruble. Most especially, we have to do it in such a way that Ron Stone and Her Serene Highness Millicent Anne Barnes are paid back."

"A ton of gold won't do that."

Mikhail nodded. A ton of gold was only a bit over twelve million USE dollars. As the economies of Europe had boomed over the last four years the price of gold had increased, but not as much as the value of an American dollar.

"We know that, but it will help—and restoring faith in the

Sovereign States ruble doesn't require that we ship enough gold to buy back every ruble in Grantville. Just that they know we mean to make sure that those people who have rubles can spend them at a decent rate of exchange."

Matvey, who was basically conservative, wasn't sure he agreed. But the czar was the czar, and by now Matvey was convinced that Czar Mikhail was a proper czar, hard enough and strong enough to rule Russia. He saw his job as facilitating that, so as he left the room, he was thinking of a good excuse for the children to have brought that young woman from the Diogenes Club with them. He remembered the upset over the pastries. That had, in a way, been the origin of the Club.

So, once he got to his desk, he wrote out an order, sealed it with his seal, and had a messenger take it to the children's room.

Back in the children's room, Alla and Irina watched as Alexi opened the sealed official order Matvey had sent. He read it and laughed. "We're ordering dessert from the Diogenes Club."

"What?" Irina asked, and about that time their younger sister Anna came up, followed by the youngest, Martha.

"Let me see," Anna demanded.

Alexi looked again at the note.

> In regard to the new delivery service of the Diogenes Club, your father confirms that you may order dessert from the Diogenes restaurant.

Alexi realized that even if Anna read it, it wouldn't give anything away. Anna was seven and Martha six, so both were just starting to learn to read. Alexi showed them the letter. And both of Alexi's younger sisters started insisting on their favorite desserts.

The noise brought the nannies and the children's tutor over. And they learned that the Diogenes Club was now offering delivery.

"Only to the royal family!" Alla said quickly, then added, "At least for now."

It took a few minutes and some questioning from Alla about what the czar and czarina liked for dessert before the orders were complete, then Alla made her excuses and took a carriage back to the Diogenes Club.

✧   ✧   ✧

In the Diogenes Club, the knowledge that they would be providing dessert for the royal family hit the restaurant staff like a hurricane. Czar Mikhail was incredibly popular in Ufa and so were the children. They were also all aware of how people would react. The knowledge that the royal children considered ordering dessert from the Diogenes Club as a special treat would be really good for business.

"Elina," Alla announced, "you will be making orange marmalade stuffed vol-au-vents. We will also be providing chocolate ice cream. And, not for dessert, but I want a dozen of your flakiest croissants to serve with whatever they are having for dinner."

Having thrown the kitchen into turmoil, she sent a reservation confirmation to Ivan Borisovich Petrov at the Embassy Bureau in the Ufa Kremlin.

CHAPTER 21

Go West

Royal Palace, Ufa
December 15, 1637

Bernie picked up the croissant and took a bite, then sighed in contentment. Then he had a spoonful of the excellent borscht. By now Bernie knew borscht. "This is marvelous, but why are we here?"

Alexi giggled. Bernie and Natasha had arrived on the *Koshchey*, Hero 4, less than an hour ago. Earlier that day they'd been in Tsaritsyn, accepting the surrender of the city by the new city government. It had taken a month and a half and the fighting in the city near the end had been brutal. None of that fighting had involved Russian or Cossack forces. After they started the bypass route, they'd simply let the city stew in their own juices while Bernie and Natasha negotiated with the Don Cossacks about whether they were going to join the Sovereign States. And even now that wasn't solid. Colonel Denisov of the Don Cossacks wanted to join, but he was only the leader of one clan of Don Cossacks. They needed consensus, or at least a large majority of the tribes, to approve. It was a delicate and time-consuming negotiation, and one that Bernie wasn't all that thrilled to be called away from.

Bernie gave the giggling Alexi a curious look before turning back to Czar Mikhail.

"Just another job I have for you and Natasha. We'll talk about it after dinner."

❖   ❖   ❖

Artemi Fedorovich Polibin tasted the croissant, sighed and took another to the czar's pastry chef. That person had been insisting that there was nothing wrong with his croissants for the last month and a half. "Eat."

The pastry chef ate. Not happily, but he ate. The croissant was light, airy, flaky and buttery tasting. It melted in the mouth. "How?!" he blurted.

"I don't know, but we are going to find out," Artemi told him.

Back at the main table, Natasha and Bernie were talking over politics while the children talked over dolls and airplanes and other toys. Dessert arrived and almost reconciled Bernie to being called away from the negotiations with the Don Cossacks.

Later, after dinner, in the czar's private office, Bernie and Natasha got to watch as Alexi and Irina showed them their route from Ufa to Grantville.

"I'm not a pilot, and neither is Natasha," Bernie said.

"We have pilots, Bernie. We've been using and overusing the Heroes for months now. We have pilots, flight engineers, and complete crews. You and Natasha are going to be diplomats. You'll be arranging things with Cossacks and others along the route to provide wood, charcoal, or, better yet, oil of some sort to run the boiler. And, of course, once you get to Grantville, you will be negotiating with Mr. Ron Stone and Princess Millicent Anne Barnes."

"Little Milly Barnes is a princess? How the heck did that happen?"

"You know perfectly well how that happened," Czarina Evdokia said tartly.

They both followed the doings of Grantville and Grantvillers in what Bernie called the "gossip rags." Bernie had known Ron Stone slightly in high school. They hadn't run in the same circles, but Bernie had given one of the Stone boys a swirly and had fallen afoul of one of the Stone kid's pranks. Bernie honestly didn't remember which had come first. But all that had been before the Ring of Fire. The truth was that Bernie was in Russia before any of the Grantville wealthy had become wealthy, so as much as he knew that things had changed, he didn't feel it.

He remembered nothing about the Barbie Consortium themselves. The only thing he remembered from Grantville about HSMC was a drunken comment that it would never work, probably after they'd gotten one working. And as for the Stone Family's prominence in medicine and chemistry, all he remembered was that he'd been pissed that the pot was reserved for sick people. The whole time from the Battle of the Crapper to his leaving for Russia was sort of a drunken haze.

"Vlad would be a better choice, Your Majesty," Bernie said. "I don't actually remember Millicent Anne Barnes at all, and I think that the Stoner boys are all going to hate my guts. I wasn't a very nice teenager."

"We're going," Natasha said. "I want to see the fabled walls of the Ring of Fire. And you're not a teenager anymore. Besides, Ron Stone and the Barbies—in the person of Millicent Anne Barnes—have supported the Sovereign States from the beginning. We need that support to continue."

"I want to see home again too, Natasha. The reason I said Vlad and Brandy would be the better choice is because they have relationships with the grown-up Ron Stone and the grown-up Barbies."

"You're just going to have to do your best," Mikhail said. "In the meantime, this meeting is about how we are going to get you there. So pay attention."

And Alexi and Irina continued the discussion of possible landing places.

"We need Colonel Denisov. He's well known and respected."

"You said you have planes and pilots?"

"We have five planes and eight pilots," Czar Mikhail said. "That is, we have five Hero-class steam planes and eight pilots qualified to fly them. What do you have in mind?"

"I want to make a couple of quick trips with Colonel Denisov," Bernie said. "To get permission and maybe ship extra fuel. It's not like we're short of oil here. Establish a base, maybe two or three bases, where we can land, refuel, and take off again."

Alexi was nodding vigorously and they spent the next few minutes talking about where to put those bases.

Tsaritsyn docks
December 16, 1637

The plane had Bernie, Captain Irina Novikov and her flight engineer Gregory Petrov, and fuel. That was pretty much it. And, at the moment, not all that much fuel. Tsaritsyn was again a city involved in trade. They landed on the river with Bernie watching and trying not to get in the way, even though he was in the copilot's seat. As they pulled up onto the shore, he saw that Colonel Denisov was there to meet them. So was Major Kalashnikov of the Sovereign States Marine Corps. Radios were wonderful things. Behind the major was a squad of Marines, their carbines neatly stacked, each of them carrying two jerry cans of fuel oil.

"Come aboard, Colonel," Bernie said. "We'll be more comfortable on the plane."

Gregori Denisov looked around the plane then sat in the wicker chair that Bernie indicated. "You think this will convince my fellow Cossacks to join the Sovereign States?" Gregori asked, thinking that it well might.

"Maybe a little bit," Bernie said. "But all I'm after for right now are landing and refueling stations."

"It uses fuel oil. Your Major Kalashnikov told me."

"Yes, but it's actually more flexible than that. It can use charcoal or even, in a pinch, wood."

"And you would pay for the charcoal?"

"Of course. In ruble notes or in silver."

They talked on while the plane was filled with fuel. First the tanks, then jerry cans were tied down against the walls of the plane.

Then they took off. They flew west-northwest for two hours and forty-five minutes and were over mostly open, lightly hilled prairie that at this time of year was coated in snow. They spotted a village, landed, and asked for directions.

The farmers, Cossacks, told them where some other villages were, but the truth was the farmers and herders of the area knew how to get to places like Port Azov. But they didn't know the direction of Port Azov in more than a vague "it's south of here, around a week's travel" way.

They found a slightly larger village that had a stock pond that was plenty big enough for the Heroes to land on, even in summer. They established, as best they could, its location relative to Tsaritsyn.

They made arrangements and unloaded all the jerry cans of fuel oil, and got an agreement from the villagers to make and store charcoal for the planes. Then they flew back to Tsaritsyn.

They landed as the sun was setting and the next morning they took another load of fuel to the village of Syromakha. Landed, unloaded, and flew back, then loaded up on fuel and went back to Syromakha, by which time it was too late to get back to Tsaritsyn, so they spent the night.

Syromakha air station
December 19, 1637

It was snowing the next morning and Captain Irina Novikov wasn't going to take off until it cleared. So they spent better than half the day in Syromakha, which meant "orphan." Bernie and Gregori Denisov spent the time with the village blacksmith, talking about charcoal and charcoal briquettes.

Finally, about two in the afternoon, it cleared enough for Captain Novikov to agree to take them back to Tsaritsyn. That established Air Station Syromakha, the first air station on the southern route to Grantville.

It took until Christmas to establish Air Station Two and it was after New Year's before Bernie was satisfied that both air stations had adequate fuel reserves.

Diogenes Club
December 19, 1637

General Tim had been informed by Princess Irina that he just had to have the dessert pastries at the Diogenes Club. That, he could have ignored, but the suggestion was endorsed by the czar. So here he was. Duck à l'Orange, using oranges from the Ottoman Empire, was the dinner, and it was really quite good. It also cost a week's wages for one of the privates in the army. Okay, that was an exaggeration, but the prices in the Strangers Room were ridiculous. It was getting to be time for dessert when the hostess, Alla Lyapunov, came over to him and quietly suggested that he have dessert in one of the private rooms. "It's quieter there."

He got up and followed her into a hall and down it to a room that was equipped with a table. And at that table sat Ivan Borisovich Petrov.

Tim spent the rest of the evening listening to the plans. Then he had a thought. "You need me to be in the target zone, at least close enough to it so that the failure will be seen as chance, not a leak or false intelligence."

"I don't think Czar Mikhail will approve of you being risked," Ivan Borisovich said.

"Well then, it's fortunate that this is a purely military decision," Tim said.

"Ah, General..." Ivan started.

"If you feel you need to report this conversation to the czar, go ahead," Tim said. "In the meantime, we will plan this with me in theater and in such a way that General Birkin and his staff have every reason to believe that they can catch me. And when they fail, it will look like bad luck." Tim grinned. "It won't be that hard or all that risky. Birkin knows as well as I do that luck plays a major role in the outcome of any battle."

They got down to cases and Alla listened as General Tim and Ivan Borisovich planned how they would put the general in a place to be ambushed. Kazan was on the northeast side of the Volga as it bent from flowing east to south. Kruglaya Mountain was on the southwest, a few miles upriver from Kazan. Birkingrad was located just west of Kazan, but on the same side of the Volga as Kazan.

"What we'll do," Tim said, drawing on Alla's table with his finger, which was wet from condensation from a cold beer, "is send me up the west side of the Volga on one of the Scouts to scout the northwest of Birkingrad. As though I was considering a counter-encirclement, using Kruglaya Mountain as one end of a half circle of defensive works that would extend on the north side of the Volga across from Kruglaya to Kazan."

"Would that work?" Alla asked.

"No, not really. The problem is it would take too long..." Tim trailed off. "I'd forgotten about Ivan's war train. It just might. And as soon as you leak what I'm doing, Birkin will remember Ivan's war train. He'll..." Tim stopped talking and leaned back and just stared at the lines of condensate between the plates on the table. Then he slowly whistled. "No, it still won't work, but it's a credible threat, not just me being stupid and arrogant."

Alla looked at the lines and plates and could almost see them matching the maps of the area that she was familiar with, but had no clue at all about what General Lebedev was talking about. She looked at Ivan, and at first he seemed as confused as she was, then he started to stare intently at the table. "Will someone tell me what you two are staring at?"

"Well, Ivan," General Lebedev asked, "do you want to explain it to her?"

"I would, General, but as I look at this, it should work," Ivan said. "I don't see why it wouldn't."

"The friction of war that Clausewitz was so concerned about," General Tim said.

"Clausewitz? I remember his famous quote. 'Everything in war is very simple, but the simplest thing is difficult,' and I can see that this will be difficult even with the war train. But—"

"You didn't finish the quote," said General Lebedev, and he didn't look or sound like a boy general as he spoke. He sounded like an old and hard man, the sort you didn't want to meet in a dark alley or, especially, on a battlefield. "The rest of the quote goes, 'The difficulties accumulate and end by producing a kind of friction that is inconceivable unless one has experienced war.' It's not one difficulty, Ivan. It's the accumulation of difficulties. Way too many nails that might fall from way too many horse-shoes. And while it was happening, Ivan would be exposed and so would my army." General Tim sighed and shook his head, and he was the boy general again, open faced and friendly, regretting that a move on a chessboard wasn't as clever as it first looked. "It's tempting. If everything broke just right." Then he actually grinned. "Tempting enough so that when Birkin misses me, it will push him. Maybe even push him into a mistake. In the meantime, Ivan, include in your report that in my view, it is important that Birkin knows that I have seen the ground. Meanwhile, I need to call Ivan Maslov home, because that's what I'd do if this were real."

He stood, bowed to Alla, and left.

Outside Almaliq
December 20, 1637

The war train had a busted axle on the third car back from the engine. Almaliq, before the sack, had been a larger city than Almaty. After the defeat the Zunghars had faced at the pass, the coalition that was the Zunghars had started to fragment, but a group mostly consisting of Derbet tribesmen had decided to hold Almaliq.

When they got the news of the defeat, they figured the coalition was over. But they also figured they were in a defensible position, and as long as they forted up rather than fight the Russians in the open, they would be able to make it too expensive for the Kazaks or even the Russians to take Almaliq back. That way they would get something out of the mess that Erdeni Batur had led them into. Their chieftain was a descendant of Genghis Khan and figured that it was the mongrel's bad blood that was the real problem.

And, so far, that was proving true. Not because the leader was all that good, but just because the luck seemed to have turned against them for the moment. Ivan wasn't one to raise on a busted flush, not if he had any choice, and he did.

All he had to do was wait for the axle to be repaired and move the train into position to knock down Almaliq's walls with his cannon. They weren't heavy guns, but they were plenty heavy enough for this.

It was while he was ruminating over this that the Hero-class *Yuri Gagarin* radioed the train that they had a message from Ufa and were landing.

Leonid Volodin jumped down from the *Yuri*'s lower wing. The ground was rocky and frozen, and his pilot's uniform was fur lined. He saluted. "General, there are orders here," he said, holding out a folded and wax-sealed sheet. The orders had been sent by radio telegraph as far as the telegraphs went, then flown the rest of the way so the seal was just the military message seal. Ivan opened it to see code groups, rather than a message. The key in the upper right corner of the page told him which code module to use.

"Okay, Captain. Have the cook fix you something. You're going to have to wait for me to decode this." Ivan looked over at the *Yuri*. "You might spend the time replacing that panel." He pointed to where one of the panels of the air cushion skirt had been ripped by a rock on landing.

It took only about five minutes to key in the message and attach the right decoder module.

COME HOME. WE HAVE A NEW GAME.
HIGH STAKES LIKE THAT ONE AGAINST
ANDY POVOLOV.

Andrei Petrovich Povolov was the younger son of a mainline branch of a boyar-ranked family who was killed at Rzhev in the cavalry charge. Before that, he'd been in the academy with Tim and Ivan and had bet fifty rubles on one of the war games Ivan had managed to convince him that Tim was screwing up by the numbers. Made it seem that Tim was gambling on his doing one thing when it didn't actually matter. So this had to be a ruse of some sort, but one thing was clear: Tim wanted him back in Ufa ASAP.

That was going to be a little complicated. This was an allied army. There were more Kazakh cavalry than there were Russian troops by a factor of ten, but the Russian troops actually had more striking capability than the Kazakh cavalry did. Or at least, they would once the axle was fixed.

"I'm going to need to speak to Salqam-Jangir Khan. In the meantime," Ivan got up, "call Colonel Vershinin and Sultan Togym."

Salqam-Jangir Khan had left Togym in charge of the Kazakh contingent when he'd been called back to Shavgar. Togym was learning about the modern army. He was also an older man whom the Kazakhs would be more comfortable with than they were with Ivan. Ivan's only concern about the man was that he might rush in to prove his bravery.

Colonel Lavrenty Vershinin and Sultan Togym arrived at the same time. They had both been overseeing the work on the axle.

Lavrenty knew the train. Togym knew the local craftsmen and their abilities. This was also not an altogether new issue among the Kazakhs. They used huge wheeled yurts when following their herds. The two men were arguing amiably about the best way to fix the wheel as they came in. Lavrenty Vershinin had ten years on Ivan. Togym had three times that.

"If you could put that aside for a moment, gentlemen, I need to consult with Salqam-Jangir Khan, then report back to Ufa."

The amiability of a moment before was absent as the two men looked at each other. "Sultan Togym will be the expedition commander until I get back, Salqam-Jangir Khan arrives, or you get new orders. It will probably be Salqam-Jangir Khan."

"What's going on, sir?" Lavrenty demanded.

Ivan considered for a moment, then handed him the dispatch.

He read it quickly and looked up. "What the hell does this mean?"

"If I recall the game in question," Ivan said, "Birkin is about to have a really bad year."

Togym cleared his throat and looked pointedly at the strip of paper tape. At Ivan's nod, Lavrenty passed it over.

"How is this going to work?" Togym demanded, then he smiled. "And I thought you were the clever one!"

"We take turns, Togym. Now, Lavrenty, if you don't mind, I have a few things to talk over with Sultan Togym before I leave."

Lavrenty left rather stiffly.

"Have a seat, Sultan. You know the politics involved here, I'm sure."

"Rather better than you do, General Maslov," Togym said, taking the offered chair. "Your czar can't allow federal forces to be seen as under the command of state forces."

"He's your czar too, Togym," Ivan said. "But aside from that, you're correct."

"Is he? Then why doesn't he trust me in command of his forces? It's not like Colonel Vershinin attended your famous war college."

That was, Ivan realized, a very good point. And a solution to about half of Ivan's problem if he could get Salqam-Jangir Khan and Czar Mikhail to agree. But only half the problem. "Sultan, there is another problem. It's not a political problem. It's..." Ivan wasn't sure how to put it. The truth was, he didn't want Togym to do anything. As long as he just sat here and fixed the damn wheel, they were in grand shape. They'd won the war. It was just going to take the other side a while to realize it. But that didn't mean that if Togym did something stupid he might not lose.

"Just say it, General," Togym said.

"All right. The thing that concerns me is that you will decide you need to prove to the world, to Salqam-Jangir Khan, or even to yourself, that you can command a modern army as well or better than some jumped-up child, and do something unnecessary to prove you can. If that happens you could waste this army, these men, and leave a mess for me to clean up. And if you do the smart thing, sit out here, fix the wheel, people are going to think you're afraid to command a modern army.

"But that is the smart move, Togym. It's what I was planning to do."

Togym looked at him for a long moment, then he slowly grinned and then laughed. "Do mention your concerns to Salqam-Jangir

Khan. He will no doubt reassure you that I'm a timid old man."
There was humor, but also bitterness, in that last.

"I know, and that's half the reason I'm concerned," Ivan said.
"I've examined the battle of Ufa and that first day's charge. And
given what you knew, your reaction was perfectly correct." That
was about half true. On Irina Way, in those first few minutes.
A charge probably would have carried the day. But there was no
way for Togym to have known that.

"Really, you don't think a forceful attack would—"

"I said 'given what you knew,'" Ivan said. "You were faced
with unknown numbers and unknown weapons. What concerns
me most is that you will, if faced with another situation of such
unknowns, remember that day and say to yourself, 'If I'd just
attacked, I could have won the battle and the Kazakh people
would own Ufa rather than being part of the Sovereign States.'"

Togym looked at Ivan, and after a moment he said, "You
know the most irritating thing about you, General Ivan Maslov?"

"No. What's that?"

"It's that I am starting to think you might actually be as
good as people say you are."

"Nobody's that good," Ivan said with a half-smile of his
own. "On my own authority, I am giving you the acting rank
of brigadier general in the army of the United Sovereign States
of Russia. I will be asking Salqam-Jangir Khan's approval and
Czar Mikhail to confirm it."

"You're only a brigadier yourself. Do you have the authority
to do that?"

"I rather doubt it," Ivan agreed. Then he stood, and so did
Togym. He shook the older man's hand and went to catch the plane.

Almaty
December 20, 1637

The sun was setting as they landed in Almaty. Ivan used the
radio in the plane to send radio telegrams to Salqam-Jangir Khan
and Czar Mikhail telling them what he'd done, and asking them
to confirm it.

He got back messages the next morning confirming the promotion of Togym to brigadier and making him *okol'nichii*. Then
he got on the *Yuri* and started the trip back to Ufa.

CHAPTER 22

War and Baseball

Just across the Volga from Kruglaya Mountain
December 28, 1637

"You know, Tim," Ivan Maslov said as he diverted power from the fans that powered the air cushion. "This is a really stupid idea." Tim had told Ivan the plan once he got back to Ufa. They'd had Christmas dinner at the palace, even at the same table as the czar and czarina. While they were dining, they'd been photographed. The photographs would be converted to print versions and spread all over Russia, especially Muscovite Russia. It was all done with malice aforethought. It had been a glittering affair full of fine fabrics and electric lights, demonstrating that Czar Mikhail was not hiding in a cave somewhere out in the back of beyond, which was the way Muscovite Russia was trying to paint the situation.

The thing about air cushion landing gear was that it would let you travel on the land, water, or on a frozen river. And the "reason" they were here was so that Ivan, who was familiar with the steam train, could check out the terrain from ground level. They were going to ride horses since the Volga was frozen anyway, but at the last minute a Scout had become available, and they'd decided to use it for comfort.

It was comfortable compared to horseback in December in Russia in the Little Ice Age. It had an enclosed and heated cabin. And by traveling on the air cushion they would be seeing the ground from ground level. The leak had said they'd be on horseback, which was the "proper" way to do it. But the Scout would let them fly away before the enemy got close enough to attack them.

✧　　✧　　✧

General Birkin shook his head. "It doesn't matter."

"But, sir, they—"

"I said no, Captain. I know what Maslov's here for. And I know Lebedev's plan. But I also know that that damn steam train of theirs is stuck on the far side of Kazakh with a busted wheel. By the time they get the wheel fixed and get it back here, it will be spring."

"And if they find the prepared road?"

"That's why we're moving now," Birkin said. Then he looked at the captain. The captain was a political appointee. An ally of Assistant General Secretary Romanov. "Captain, I am not going to become known as a sender of assassins. If you're smart, you won't want that reputation either.

"We move *now*. I want the lead element out of the fort by nightfall, and I want them at the first waypoint by dawn."

That first waypoint was roughly twenty miles north-northwest of the fort that everyone but Birkin called Birkingrad. It had stocks of food and equipment hidden under trees. There was another one just like it twenty-three miles further northeast. Then another eighteen miles further. They were pre-stocked and made ready to allow Birkin's army to make much better time than would be possible otherwise.

The waypoints didn't go all the way to Perm, but they went far enough so that Birkin would have a lead on the forces at Kazan, or Ufa for that matter. That way they could take Perm and force Lebedev to divide his forces. Almost more importantly, they would provide a much needed morale boost, and at the same time threaten Shein, preventing him from joining Mikhail.

Lebedev would have to attack him. And Birkin was confident that if he was defending, Lebedev would lose.

In the air, over Birkingrad
December 28, 1637

The second Scout was flying at three thousand feet. Its undercarriage, even its air cushion skirt, was painted blue gray to make it hard to see from the ground. At this height, even its noisy engines wouldn't be heard from the ground. Its whole purpose was to warn the generals so that they could take off and get away from the assassin teams that they expected Birkin to send.

What it saw instead was troops of cavalry leaving Birkingrad and heading northwest, away from the Scout that held the generals.

Ivan was handling the radio when the report came in. "They're where?"

The report was repeated. "Leaving Birkingrad and riding quickly north-northwest."

"Stay up and give us the best track you can," Ivan Maslov said. Then he looked over at Tim and said, "Boss, I don't think Birkin cares about us or the steam train."

"Where's he going, Ivan?"

"It can't be close. He's going to want time to fortify. And that's not easy in winter."

The Scout was moving along on the air cushion, with just enough prop to pull them forward. Tim looked around them, looking for a longish straightaway with no trees in front of it. Then he gave up and turned around using flaps and rudder. They went back to the Volga and Tim took off. Then he headed east for twenty miles, then north for ten. By then they had a track on the cavalry contingent and flew back west on an interception course. Not for the cavalry themselves, but for their route. That is, Tim flew the little Scout to where they would be around midnight if they kept going that way. That took about an hour, and then he headed back for Birkin's army. Tim was looking for campsites hidden under the trees.

Kazan
December 28, 1637

"All they're leaving is a token force," Tim told Abdul Azim, the effective mayor of Kazan, that evening. "That's all you'll be facing by next week. A force small enough so that they wouldn't have any chance of taking Kazan, even if we left nothing but the town guard here. Most of his army, almost all of it, is headed toward Perm."

"That will take months."

"A month, depending on how many of those camps they've hidden away in the woods. And how strung out he's willing to let his army get."

"He'll take a small force ahead," Ivan said. "Maybe a thousand men, all cavalry, all with good mounts and with spare mounts for those whose horses go lame on the trip. Use that to take Perm, then hold it while the rest of his force makes its way there. It's a clever move. We should have seen it."

"It's not that clever, Ivan. It doesn't pay enough attention to either radios or aircraft."

While the Sovereign States were busy switching over to heavier-than-air aircraft, the Muscovite Russians were sticking with dirigibles, and large dirigibles at that. They were close to completing their second large dirigible at Bor. It would carry eight tons of cargo and as many as forty troops. On the other hand, after working on the thing for the better part of a year, and starting with a lot of extra parts that they had from the construction of the *Czar Alexis*, they would only have the one.

That meant that in the meantime Birkin didn't have much in the way of aircraft, and while he knew about the Scouts and the Heroes, he didn't have actual experience with them. And when you looked at them flying a thousand feet in the air, they just didn't look all that impressive, not compared to something the size of the *Czarina Evdokia*.

"Okay, Ivan. He sends an advance contingent, all cavalry, all equipped with AK4.7s. When do they get to Perm?"

"A week. Ten days at most," Ivan said. "And remember, Perm hasn't declared either way. Not for us, not for Moscow."

"Which means if we land a force there, they might just tell us to go away."

"Which is why Birkin is taking a thousand men ahead," Abdul Azim said. "He's not going to take no for an answer."

"Unfortunately, I don't see any way for us to prove that until his army reaches the walls of Perm, and that will be too late," Tim agreed.

Ufa
December 30, 1637

"That's the situation as I see it, Your Majesty," Tim finished his report.

"I may have a solution. At least part of one," Czar Mikhail said.

He pushed a button on his desk and a few moments later, his secretary opened the door. "Matvey, find Vera Sergeevna Ruzukov.

And quickly. Also that fellow who got stuck in the boiler with Stefan Ruzukov. I don't remember his name."

"Efrem Stroganov, sire," Matvey said without hesitation. "The Stroganov family aren't fond of your actions in regard to serfs, and they are also concerned about your 'coddling' the native tribes."

The heirs of the Mongols still lived in Siberia. They were divided into clans and tribes. And, as Bernie and Brandy had pointed out, lived and fought like the Native Americans—or, as Bernie put it, "wild injuns." The Stroganov family had been paying Cossacks to advance eastward, setting up outposts, and suppressing the native tribes. In return for paying the Cossacks, the Stroganov family got first crack at the tribute that the Cossacks extorted from the native tribes. That was the big difference that Vladimir had pointed out between the Mongol tribes and the Native Americans. In America, the immigrants from Europe had produced massive population growth, so when they went west they were after land. Farm land, range land. As the Cossacks went east, they were mostly after tribute: furs, wood, all the natural products of Siberia.

That, however, was changing. The Emancipation Proclamation was having an effect. Serfdom, which had mostly died out in the Germanies, was still common in Russia and Poland before the Ring of Fire. The USE had been getting runaway serfs from Poland, and since the Emancipation Proclamation, so was the Sovereign States. The constitution had simply added to and focused the effect, encouraging immigration to the free states. Those people wanted land. Czar Mikhail was of a mind to buy the land and turn it into free states. The Stroganov family wanted to use the Cossacks to take it and turn it into slave states.

They hadn't been thrilled when they learned of Vladimir and Brandy's trip into the back of beyond. If the czar already had agreements with the Mongol tribes, it would make it a great deal more difficult to abuse them.

"I know, but they aren't going to like the idea of giving Perm to Uncle Ivan."

Vera Sergeevna Ruzukov arrived first. She was in the house chamber in the Kremlin. Vera was about five foot five with dark hair and a stocky body.

It was over an hour later that Efrem Stroganov arrived. Plenty of time for Tim, Ivan, and Vera to be fully briefed on the situation. Vera already knew most of it. Efrem Stroganov had been a guest in their house several times since the day he and Stefan had taken shelter in the boiler.

"Come in, Efrem," Czar Mikhail said. "Have you met Generals Lebedev and Maslov?"

"Ah, no, Your Majesty?" Efrem said. The question was in his tone, and it was *"What the hell am I doing here?"*

"We have some fairly bad news for your relatives in Perm," Mikhail said. "But we suspect that they aren't going to want to believe us. In fact, won't believe us until it's too late."

"What bad news, Your Majesty?"

Mikhail waved to Tim, and Tim proceeded to brief Efrem. "Two days ago, a force of Muscovite Russians consisting of most of the army investing Kazan left. We, mostly by luck, had a Scout above and tracked them. General Birkin has been setting up bases to allow his forces to move quickly by marching from one already prepared base to the next."

Tim looked at Efrem Stroganov to see if he understood the technique. It had several advantages in moving an army quickly, and one massive disadvantage that meant it was almost never used. It telegraphed your move, told the enemy where you were going, and how you were going to get there, assuming they found the bases.

Efrem nodded.

"General Birkin is very good," Tim continued. "He focused on keeping the supply points hidden, rather than defensible. And we haven't found them all. From the ones we have found, we're fairly sure that he's going after Perm."

"That's stupid. He could just head for the convergence of the Kama and the Belaya."

"Not in the open," Tim said. "Any works that they could put up quickly, we would pound with rockets and cannon. But that's not the only reason to take Perm. It also cuts off Solikamsk, and so Shein. Preventing him from joining or even allowing trade across the Urals. And your family has done an excellent job of fortifying the place."

"So my family will stop them."

"No, you won't," Tim said bluntly. "First, while you have a small force of Cossacks backing you, most of your miners are serfs or outright slaves, who you can't count on, or even trust, with guns. Almost as bad, both the miners and the Cossacks are mostly not in Perm. They are in copper mines as much as fifty miles from

Perm. It's going to take you time to call the Cossacks back to Perm from the mines, and what are you going to do about the serfs and slaves who are working those mines? You know that as soon as your Cossacks leave them, they are going to run south to Ufa. At least, a lot of them will."

Efrem Stroganov looked at Tim, then at the czar, then at Vera. "I believe you," he said. "But my family won't. They trust my word, but not necessarily my judgment. They will convince themselves that you are lying to me. They will insist that I am influenced by my friendship with Stefan and Vera. And they may be right. I don't think they are, but I don't know how to prove it."

"How do you feel about flying?" Czar Mikhail asked.

"Your Majesty, I've never been in any sort of aircraft in my life."

"Then this is a good time to start," Mikhail said. "In fact, as I think about it, I think now is a good time to repeat the Kazan maneuver." He grinned.

"What?" Efrem asked, just as Ivan Maslov said, "That's not necessary, Your Majesty."

It was a beat later when Tim said, "No, he's right. It's a risk, but not an unreasonable one."

Mikhail looked at Ivan. "General Maslov, you will stay here and organize the relief force, assuming we reach an agreement with Efrem's relatives in Perm. The mission will consist of Tim, Vera, me, and two of my personal guards." He looked at the clock on the wall. It read 10:32. "We will be leaving at noon. See to it, Tim."

It was a dismissal, so Tim and Ivan left to perform their appointed tasks.

In the air, between Kazan and Perm
December 30, 1637

The *Koshchey* was loaded with fuel oil, and flying at four thousand feet. And Efrem Stroganov couldn't see anything but forest and plains covered in snow. Earlier, he'd seen the track of horses leaving Birkingrad and going to the first waypoint, then to the next. He even saw the follow-on force on the march, but now they were well ahead of Birkin's advance force. And the truth was, at this point, it was still perfectly possible that Birkin's army would turn south rather than north and make for the confluence of the Kama and the Belaya.

Czar Mikhail was standing in the door to the cockpit. He looked at the pilot. "Take us down."

"Your Majesty—" the pilot started.

"Take us down, Captain. We, all of us, need to see the camp."

And down they went.

As she thought about the orders, the pilot considered what she knew and was learning about Czar Mikhail Romanov. She realized that if they didn't get a good clear view, he'd make her do it again, even lower, and every trip increased the risk.

The *Koshchey* went by the depot at fifty feet above the ground and at a speed of a hundred and twenty miles per hour. There were twenty people in the camp, mostly cooks. One guard got his AK4.7 up in time to fire three shots. None came close to the airplane.

But Efrem got an excellent look at the camp. He even saw the guard shooting at them.

Perm
December 30, 1637

The sun was setting as they landed outside Perm. The settlement was located on the southeast bank of the Kama River. The land was hilly, but the river was flat, so the *Koshchey* landed on the Kama, then pulled up onto the shore near the north gate. It was a well-built settlement set atop a hill, and the Stroganov family had used fresno scrapers and labor to build up the bastions. They were the piled-earth sort that would shrug off cannon fire, and they were twenty feet high with shoulder-high stone walls topping them. This place would be hell to take if it was defended.

But they'd gotten ambitious and overbuilt the town. They didn't have enough men to guard the amount of wall they had. A thousand men could hold off an army. A hundred men couldn't man the walls, not if the attackers struck in several places at once.

It wasn't a surprise. Tim had full reports and an excellent map of the place in Kazan. Still, it was impressive.

The first man out of the plane was Efrem Stroganov. After him came the two guards, then Czar Mikhail and, finally, Tim. The pilot and engineer were staying on the plane.

By the time they walked to the gates they were met by Anatoly Stroganov, the patriarch of the Stroganov family.

"You didn't tell us you were coming." Perm had a radio telegraph station. In fact, it had one with the tubes for the radio and an aqualator for encrypting and decrypting messages. Which only made sense, since it was on the route from Shein's territory to Ufa.

"It came up suddenly, Uncle Anatoly. May I present His Imperial Majesty Mikhail Romanov, Czar of all Russia."

"Your Majesty." Anatoly Stroganov bowed, looking daggers at his nephew.

"It's not really his fault," Czar Mikhail said. "General Birkin is planning to take Perm. And we drafted your nephew so that we would have a witness you would believe."

"Birkin?" Anatoly Stroganov looked around. Quite a crowd had gathered. Airplanes landing on the Kama River and coming to rest next to the gates of Perm wasn't an everyday occurrence. "Such *accusations* shouldn't be made in public." Now he was looking daggers at Mikhail. Mikhail looked back calmly and lifted an eyebrow. After a moment, Anatoly added, "Your Majesty."

"It's not an accusation. It's a fact, and everyone in Perm is going to know in about five days." Mikhail shrugged away the notion that he should have been discreet.

"It's true, Uncle Anatoly. I saw Birkin's army, and I saw the supply depots that he hid along their route."

"We can discuss this inside," Anatoly gritted out.

Anatoly Stroganov wasn't happy that the czar had announced the attack in public. He didn't want to be in the United Sovereign States of Russia. He wanted to be in Russia, the real Russia, his Russia. His slave brought them small beer. He had no intention of manumitting his slaves or serfs and Mikhail's Emancipation Proclamation had already cost him a fortune. At the same time, both the Sheremetev clan and Ivan Romanov were thieves. His copper mines would rapidly become *their* copper mines if Birkin were to take Perm. "If." Anatoly didn't want to believe that if.

Efrem showed him the places on the map where he'd seen with his own eyes Birkin's army and Birkin's camps. But Anatoly wasn't convinced, because he didn't want to be convinced. Maybe Efrem had been fooled somehow. Perhaps he'd been corrupted by Czar Mikhail and all those freed serfs and slaves.

After the better part of an hour of back and forth, Efrem shouted, "Then come see for yourself if you don't believe me!"

And immediately Anatoly started wondering if it was some

sort of trap. Anatoly wasn't actually a stupid man in spite of the fact that just now he was acting the proper fool.

It was just that he knew how to operate in the world before the up-timers came and he didn't know how to live in this one. So he looked for ways to pretend that this world was still the world where Mikhail was a weak, ineffectual monarch controlled by his family. The tangled web of self-deceptions kept requiring more and more outrageous self-deceptions. Those self-deceptions built up until now he was afraid that his nephew was trying to kidnap him to Ufa so that Czar Mikhail could steal Perm from him.

And that was a bridge too far even for *his* paranoia. He *trusted* his nephew, and had for years. Nervous and upset, he went with his nephew and boarded the *Koshchey*.

Camp between Kazan and Perm
December 30, 1637

They saw the Hero fly by. They shot at it and missed, not that it mattered. Whether they hit it or not, the fact that it had flown so close to the camp meant that the camp was known.

General Tim knew they were here. And General Birkin was about to get screwed with his pants on again, and them with him. The cooks and guards in the camp didn't have a clue how it was going to happen. They weren't generals. Heck, most of them couldn't read.

On the other hand, they didn't need to know how. This was a secret base and General Tim knew about it. That was enough. Before the plane was out of sight, one of the guards was on his horse riding hell-for-leather to the next camp along the route.

In the air, between Kazan and Perm
December 30, 1637

The *Koshchey* did a second flyby and this time they were ready. They spotted the Hero a good thirty seconds out and watched it as it dove. A Hero, in spite of its name, wasn't a fighter plane. It wasn't designed for aerial combat. It would be dead meat if it ever faced a Gustav in the air. So its dive was actually pretty shallow. The Hero-class aircraft had a cruising speed of ninety-seven miles per hour, eighty-four knots. But cruising speed is just that: drop your nose 5 degrees and you're going faster. Drop your nose 15 degrees and you're going to pick up speed even with feathered engines. With throttles full on and a down-angle of 20 degrees, the *Koshchey* reached a hundred and fifty miles per hour. Then, as the nose came up as they got closer to the ground, they started to slow. They made their pass over the camp at eighty feet above the ground and traveling at a hundred and eighteen miles per hour, one hundred and two knots. This time thirty rounds were fired at them by good marksmen. No bullet came within a hundred yards of the airplane.

As they slowly climbed after their pass, trading forward momentum for altitude, Anatoly was convinced. There is an old rhyme that applies. "A man convinced against his will is of the same opinion still."

Anatoly knew that Birkin was coming. He knew that he didn't have the troops to stop him. But he was still convinced that he could play the two sides against each other and keep his independence.

And he was right. He was right, because Czar Mikhail decided to let him be right, at least for now. It was the best way to stop Birkin.

The agreement they finally reached was that Perm would let a unit of militia from Ufa visit it, and help in the defense of the walls, but Perm wouldn't become a member of the Sovereign States, at least not now. Czar Mikhail promised that the troops would leave once Birkin was stopped.

Ufa
December 31, 1637

The iceboats were sail powered. Balanced on three skates, they had streamlined compartments that would hold cargo or people, and these were carrying twenty men, each with full kit, in brand-new uniforms produced in Kazan over the summer. Twenty men per iceboat and ten iceboats set out for Perm. For the first two days, they made excellent time with a decent breeze from the southeast. On the third day, the wind died and the men put on their ice skates and pushed the boats on. It was a lot more work, but they still made pretty good time.

On the evening of the thirty-first of December, Tim was talking with Bernie, trying to describe the maneuvers that General Birkin and he were engaged in.

"Not football, Tim. Baseball. Birkin tried to steal second base, and you have him in a hotbox."

"What's a hotbox?" Tim asked.

"That is, Birkin tried to get to Perm before you could respond, taking the better part of his army with him. But you got there first, and he's going to have to turn around and come back. But now you're putting another force in his way, to prevent him from getting back to first base. Which is Birkingrad." Bernie spent a few minutes telling Tim about baseball, and Tim agreed that this was a better metaphor than any football play he could think of.

"What do you think he'll do?" Bernie asked. "Go on for second base?" Bernie pointed at Perm. "Or try to get back to first?" He pointed at Birkingrad.

"He won't do either. He'll turn west and head for Bor and Nizhny Novgorod."

"That's even farther."

Tim smiled. "Yes, it is."

Bernie looked at the map. Birkin's army, the thousand-strong lead element, and the thirty thousand following, were going to be out in the open with no supply base within reach. No supplies, no way to reinforce. Facing much smaller forces, yes. But forces that were entrenched, and in better positions to receive supplies and reinforcements.

"What about your mission?" Tim interrupted his musing.

"We fly to Saratov tomorrow with a refueling stop at Samra. On the second, we go to Casanski, which is on the Don. We'll refuel there from fuel oil we've flown in, and then Kamyanka, where Colonel Gregori Denisov has arranged things with Ivan Sulyma. We have fuel oil stocks there as well. Vinnytsia is more of a question mark. Gregori and I visited it and, well, they're pretty hunkered down, but they have promised us landing rights."

"After that?"

"After that is Cluj, and according to latest reports, Gretchen Richter is headquartered there and has an airport complete with aviation fuel. And we can go on to Prague and Grantville, using known airports."

"Good luck." Tim took Bernie's hand and shook it firmly.

"Thanks, Tim. I wonder how Vlad and Brandy are doing out in the eastern wilds."

CHAPTER 23

𝔖𝔫𝔬𝔴 𝔞𝔫𝔡 𝔍𝔠𝔢

Landing 1,258 miles east-southeast of Tobolsk
December 15, 1637

The day dawned clear and bright. That was the good news. The bad news was that the day was covered in snow. And so was the plane. The inside of the plane smelled of unwashed bodies. Also, they were running low on wood, and that meant that they were going to have to spend at least another day chopping wood into chunks small enough to fit into the firebox.

They got to it. Vlad, Yury, and Ariq put on snowshoes and went out to gather wood and if they were lucky, hunt. Women's lib was fine, but Brandy decided to let the guys do this. She stayed in the plane with Yulia.

Once the first load of wood was brought in, they collected up snow and melted it into water to refill the water tanks and then more water to melt the snow and ice that covered the wings and the skirt. Brandy was right. It took a day and more to get a load of rather damp wood. The dampness made the wood heavier and meant that part of the heat of the fire was used in drying the wood before it caught. The exhaust from the firebox was blown by a small fan into the spreading chamber of the ACLG. In flight, it was pushed out the back of the spreading chamber, so the evaporated water and smoke meant that the *Nicky* left a trail of smoke and condensing steam as it flew, a line across the sky from where it had been to where it was going.

Right now it meant that the chimney was below the house, and if the wind was wrong—which it was at the moment—smoke surrounded the plane and flew in their faces.

Brandy inflated the ACLG and using the props rotated the plane until it faced into the wind. That was the advantage of the Hero-class aircraft. Once the boiler was working, steam could be set to a variety of functions, charging the batteries, inflating the ACLG, running the engines, even cooking.

For another day they collected wood and hunted, getting a couple of rabbits, but Brandy was starting to get a bit worried. They were spending a lot of time collecting wood and people had to eat. So their food, mostly freeze-dried, was being used up rather more quickly than they had expected.

"Vlad, let's keep low when we can."

"Why?"

"I want to look for game."

"I am not going out on the wing and trying to sharp-shoot a deer." Vladimir grinned at her.

"I'll give it a try," Ariq offered.

"No one is going to shoot from the wing while we're in flight!" Brandy said. "But if we spot a herd of something from eight hundred feet, we can land and go shoot a deer, or whatever we find."

They were, if their readings were right, two hundred and fifty-eight miles east-southeast of Tobolsk and near the Irtysh River, which was starting to turn south on its way to China. While it wasn't the most direct route to the east, after some thought they decided to follow it south. It was a natural highway from the eastern edge of Kazak to Tobolsk, so if locks could be placed on the river, it might provide a trade route. They flew for two hours at a height of between eight hundred and a thousand feet, keeping the river in sight.

By now they were out of range of any radios, so radio location was out. They had their inertial compass and the magnetic compass, and they took regular sightings to determine their ground speed. But errors were going to creep in. As it was, Brandy figured that they were from one to ten miles away from their estimated location.

They were getting a little low on wood before they spotted a group of *Altai wapiti*. Keeping well away, they landed and everyone but Yulia went hunting.

Landing 2,480 miles southeast of Tobolsk
December 16, 1637

Brandy wasn't great on skis, but they were better than snowshoes, so she made her way along with Vlad, Ariq, and Yuri to stalk the herd. They found a small group of bachelors, nibbling on the bark and leaves from a grove of trees. Brandy took off her skis, uncased her AK and, shuddering, got down into a prone position in the snow two hundred yards from the group of small animals. She adjusted her scope and found one of the young bucks. She took careful aim and squeezed the trigger. The *Altai wapiti* jumped and started to run, but it didn't get far. The bullet had hit it in the chest, and if it hadn't hit the heart, it had punctured both lungs.

Brandy and the men went to collect the buck and the other bachelors left the area.

It was while they were butchering that the guests arrived.

Gan had seen the flying thing because of the trail it left in the sky. It was moving fast but he set his men to following it. He was the leader of his clan, who were partly herders, but mostly hunters. He had a steel helmet and a steel breastplate, but that wasn't why they called him Gan. Gan was his people's name for steel, and he had the name because he was hard as steel.

The hunting party heard the bang and slowed, then a couple of *Altai wapiti* bucks appeared around a clump of trees. Trotting nervously, almost as though they were being herded to Gan and the hunting party.

Khasar, who was a very good archer, drew his bow and fired. It was a snap shot from almost thirty yards, so the arrow caught the buck in the rump. It would slow it, but probably not kill it.

"Curse you, Khasar," Gan said. "You should have waited. Take Enkh and track that buck. The rest of you, come with me."

They rode around the clump of trees to see a group of hunters on skis. They were strangely, if warmly, dressed. And Gan, who had never seen a Chinese gun but had heard of them, guessed that the long stick that the... That was a woman!... that the *woman* was holding, was a gun, and the men who were even now butchering the animal had similar guns strapped to their backs.

Gan was considered hard among his people because he had

an iron sense of right and wrong. These people hadn't hurt him or his. They'd stopped to hunt, but that was no great crime, and their hunt had led him to game. So, so far as Gan was concerned, that was even. Gan wasn't a thief and he wasn't a fool. It was a safe bet that these people had come from the flying thing, and if they had, he didn't want a fight with people who could fly, even if just now it looked like he had the upper hand.

He rode forward with his men following. Examining the track of the skis, he followed them back, and back, and back some more, to where, from the tracks, the woman had stopped to shoot. He looked at the strange weapon in her arms and was no longer sure if his people had the upper hand.

By now, the strangers were all looking at him. He pulled up and said, "You are on our lands."

At first it looked like no one understood him.

Then one spoke. "We are just passing through and stopped to hunt and gather firewood." The speaker had a truly horrible accent. "I am Ariq, and this is our leader, Prince Vladimir Gorchakov."

"That's a lot of name," Gan said, guessing that most of it was titles intended to impress. But Gan wasn't impressed. Not by the name. The weapons and the flying thing, those impressed him. "Where are you from?"

"The United Sovereign States of Russia," said Ariq.

Again with the long names, but he recognized Russia. The Cossacks that demanded tribute sometimes said they were from Russia. "We don't pay tribute to your chief. This is part of the Kazakh Khanate."

"Excellent. Salqam-Jangir Khan joined the Kazakh Khanate with the Sovereign States. We are countrymen. But don't worry. We aren't here for tribute."

That wasn't good news, in spite of the last bit. While his clan's lands were technically in the Kazakh Khanate, they were on the northeastern edge and extended out of the Khanate. For the most part, they simply ignored the Kazakhs and were ignored by them.

The strangers talked among themselves, and then Ariq spoke again. "Vladimir wonders if you would like part of the buck since we took it on your lands, and also wonders if you would like to come with us back to our"—he said a strange word, then continued—"flying canoe."

"Yes, I saw your flying thing and the trail of cloud that it left behind. I would like to see it."

They finished butchering the elk and packed it on their horse then went to the "flying canoe."

Vladimir was nervous about the encounter. There were ten men in the hunting party, all armed with bows and arrows compared to his four. Three of them had breast plates, none of which would stop a bullet, but bullets or not, those odds sucked. Especially out in the open. The local leader of the hunting party was called Gan, which meant steel or iron. At least according to Ariq, who was the only one who spoke these people's language. It wasn't Kazakh, which Vladimir could speak, though it was a related language.

When they got back to the plane, Vlad invited Gan into the plane, but asked that the rest of the hunting party wait outside since it was crowded inside. And it was, with all the firewood containers. But he did bring Gan in and showed him their maps.

Gan knew about Tobolsk, but had never been there. He knew of Shavgar and Almaliq but had never been to either. His people lived in and hunted in a range of a few hundred miles, and there were no cities, just moving camps, with herds of horses and cattle. They moved their horses and cattle from summer to winter grazing and back again, very much like the more rural Kazakh clans.

They spent two days with Gan and his tribe, traded most of the elk they'd killed for dried meat and dried cheese, then flew on, still mostly following the Irtysh River.

Landing 3,670 miles southeast of Tobolsk
December 17, 1637

They took off from Landing Two, carrying mostly charcoal. By now they'd learned that the kind of wood they burned and the condition of the wood affected the range. With charcoal, the Hero had a range of better than two hundred fifty miles, with a tail wind as much as three hundred. Fuel oil gave a range of better than three hundred fifty miles.

It didn't matter in this case. They found a lake near the river that had an island on it. It was only three miles south of the Irtysh River, and at the moment it was covered in ice. But it would make an excellent refueling station. They landed and spent some time mapping and taking sightings. The stop was without incident.

"I've been thinking about this since we left Tobolsk," Brandy said that evening. "We need to go on south until we connect up with the Kazakh air route."

"Why?" Vlad asked. "I'm not disagreeing, I just want to know your reasoning."

"Honestly, it's a little vague. Things have been going well and we have gathered a lot of data. I want that data in the hands of the Ufa nerd brigade. And I want to have an actual fuel dump here on the island. Once we get to Almaliq, we can send all the maps back to Ufa, and while we're going on east, they can set up fuel depots back the way we came."

"When we left Tobolsk, Almaliq was still in enemy hands."

"Even so, it's under siege." Brandy waved that away. "It doesn't matter whether we've captured it or not. The train will be there and they will have oil."

"Probably," Vladimir agreed.

They gathered more wood and flew south the next morning.

Almaliq
January 1, 1638

The plane was out of wood, but not yet of steam, when Vlad brought it down next to the steam train outside of Almaliq.

Vlad climbed out of the plane and immediately saw Togym. The Kazakh sultan was wearing a Sovereign States uniform, complete with the baseball cap with scrambled eggs on the brim and a star on the pate.

"General," Vlad asked more than said.

"Yes, and once this mess is done"—Togym hooked a thumb at the city of Almaliq about half a mile away—"I'm going to be a senator from Kazakh."

"Well, congratulations," Vladimir said. "Where's Ivan?"

"Recalled to Ufa. That's why I got the promotion."

"Not the only reason, I'm sure," Brandy said.

"I like to think that the khan has some confidence in me," Togym acknowledged. "But what are you doing here?"

"It's a long story involving maps, wood, and a need for fuel oil."

"We're starting to get a little low on fuel oil," Togym said. "The air support has been using it at a phenomenal rate and the steamboats don't bring it much farther than Shavgar. We've been the fuel depot on this end of the airlift. But let's go inside out of the weather while we talk."

In the command car of the war train, they sat down to an excellent meal prepared by Togym's personal chef, and talked about their adventures. They showed Togym the maps and, using the radio links, sent a report to the capital. Since it was going to be going through twenty intermediary radio stations to get to Ufa, they would get the news sometime tomorrow.

"We're using up the tubes too fast," Togym complained. The down-time-made tubes did have vacuums, but those vacuums weren't as consistently good as the mass-produced tubes they had had up-time, which meant they wore out faster. And they needed a lot of them as the radio telegraph system expanded.

"I know. All we can do is the best we can do," Brandy said. "So, tell us what's been going on?"

Togym told them about Ivan being called back to Ufa, the rumor that Tim had some magical way of taking Birkingrad, that they'd gone to Perm for some reason, that Bernie was shuttling back and forth setting up air stations to the east, and about the Derbet, who had forted up Almaliq, and were prepared for a siege.

"You know we might be able to help with that," Vladimir said cautiously. "Are they talking to you at all?"

"Yes," Togym said, "promising to kill us all if we attack them and insisting that we can't run the Silk Road without them."

That wasn't true, but there were large groves of apple trees surrounding the town. This could be a really valuable agricultural center, and apparently had been until fairly recently. The Derbet, one of the tribes that had made up the Zunghars, hadn't trashed the surrounding groves of apple trees. They, or at least the Zunghars, had looted the town, which probably had a population of six or seven thousand. They'd killed almost all the men and taken the women. These weren't nice people by up-timer standards and honestly Vladimir's first impulse was to kill them off to the last man.

But Vladimir was a diplomat. That was why he'd been sent to Grantville in the first place. And that job required a level of cold-blooded pragmatism that sometimes left Vladimir disgusted with himself. This was one of those times. He spent the next three days convincing the murdering bastards to switch sides and join the state of Kazakh and thereby the Sovereign States.

By that time they had at least a basic idea of what was going on north of Ufa.

CHAPTER 24

Hotbox

Birkin's army, 80 miles west of Perm
January 8, 1638

The only good news was that it was the middle of winter. General Ivan Vasilevich Birkin looked out at the snow-covered frozen ground. The sort of thick earthen walls that could be built in spring, summer, or fall using the fresno scrapers and steam tractors were virtually impossible to build in winter. The ground was frozen into rock and basically immoveable.

Unfortunately, that was the only good news. For a few days, General Ivan Vasilevich Birkin had thought the fact that the one and only steam train was stuck out in Kazakh—and not just Kazakh, but the far eastern edge of Kazakh might save them. But he'd known better even then. The walking wall had been being used for just this purpose for a hundred years before the Ring of Fire.

The Ring of Fire had added wheels and thin metal sheeting to them. It took a bit longer than the train, but by now the army at Kazan had set up a ring of walking walls that went from the walls of Kazan all the way around Birkingrad to the river. Retreat back to Birkingrad, as humiliating as that would have been, was no longer an option. And his cousin, Iakov Petrovich Birkin, was in command of a force that could defend Birkingrad, but not have any hope of breaking out and opening a road for Ivan Vasilevich.

Ivan Vasilevich Birkin still had one hope. He kept the men moving east. His hope was the new dirigible. It was ready ahead of schedule and now named *Patriarch Filaret* in honor of Ivan's brother and Mikhail's father. It was proclaimed to be a defender of the true eastern Orthodox faith. And it carried bombs. Lots and lots of bombs. Birkin couldn't storm the walls of Perm but he could drop enough bombs to kill enough people in the city so that they could no longer defend those walls.

It was an ugly sort of war but no uglier than a sack. At least that was Birkin's guess. He'd never seen a bombed-out city. Of course, the *Patriarch Filaret* was going to have to stay pretty high so as to avoid rockets like the ones that had killed the *Czar Alexis*, but it could do that if it just had to drop bombs on a target that wasn't moving.

Perm
January 11, 1638

General Tim and Anatoly Gregorovitch Stroganov stood atop the walls of Perm while General Birkin's aide rode up and demanded the surrender of the city and, for that matter, Tim, for treason against Russia.

Tim shouted, "Tell Ivan Vasilevich that it would have been a good plan if he'd been able to get here before we reinforced the town. But now he's in a hotbox."

"A what?"

"Never mind," Tim said. "We aren't surrendering and you can't take the city." Tim wasn't quite as confident as he made himself sound. What worried him was what was Ivan Vasilevich Birkin doing here? He had to know that this was hopeless as well as Tim did.

Fifteen miles away and two miles above, Colonel Alexi Petrov readied the *Patriarch Filaret* for its first combat mission. The enemy rockets could reach two miles in height. What they were hoping for was that at two miles, especially going up, those rockets were inaccurate. A rocket fired at the *Patriarch* was as likely to land on Perm as it was to hit the dirigible.

The dirigible was five miles out when it was spotted. Tim, on hearing, called Ufa. It went through channels and then it was noted that there were no Hero-class aircraft available. Two were in Kazakh providing air support and air transport for the siege of Almaliq. Another was by now headed to points east. And a fourth was taking Bernie and Natasha and a ton of gold to Grantville. A fifth was shipping fuel oil to air stations along the southeastern route. The brand-new sixth Hero-class airplane was going through its flight trials and there was a problem with its radio control system.

"Well, turn off its radio and get it here," Tim demanded. "We have a dirigible approaching, and I'm pretty sure we are about to get bombed."

Ufa airport
January 11, 1638

The Ufa airport was a real airport with a tower and everything. Yes, the airplanes landed on the frozen Ufa River, but that wasn't a problem for the Heroes or the Scouts. At the moment, there were three Dacha-trained technicians lying on their backs in the cockpit of the *Ivan Susanin*, cursing the aqualators and the whole concept of aqualators and the idiot who introduced them into the world.

Vasilii was one of the angry techs and Miroslava was watching with amusement. She'd spent her life in a brothel, at least most of it, and she was familiar with men cursing when stuff didn't work quite as it should. At least in this case, no one was going to hit her because they couldn't get their equipment working. Besides, she thought she knew what the problem was and it wasn't actually in the aqualator. It was in one of the connections between the aqualator and the aircraft electronics. The switch wasn't switching because the aqualator was out of position.

She would have told them, but one of the techs was Vadim Ivanovich and Vadim had told her not to bother them. Vadim had never been comfortable with her. He was uncomfortable not because she'd been a whore, but because to Vadim she seemed weird.

So she kept her mouth shut, and then the runner arrived telling them to get the *Ivan Susanin* ready to fly.

"What's going on?" Vasilii asked.

The note was passed over, and a moment later Vasilii said, "Vadim, go to the stores and collect up the dirigible bombs. Have them sent to the plane. Petrov, you're going to be bombardier."

"And have them send all the jerry cans of fuel that they have," Miroslava added. Full tanks would take a Hero-class airplane about four hundred miles. Meaning that a full tank would get the *Ivan Susanin* to Perm and let it fight for about half an hour, but not let it get back. If they wanted to get back, they were going to have to carry extra cans of fuel. The cans the Sovereign States used were a copy of twenty-liter cans introduced by the Germans in World War II. Each can weighed a bit over forty pounds and carried a little more than five gallons. Each jerry can would up their flight time by about a quarter of an hour, or around twenty-five miles.

Vadim left and Petrov went to the passenger compartment of the plane to see about the racks. The Hero-class airplane had no bomb bay. To drop a bomb, someone had to step out onto the wing and walk to the back of the lower wing, then drop the bomb from there. Even at close to stall speed, that meant winds of sixty miles per hour or so, so aside from the bombs there were harnesses and lines that were locked into the side of the plane so that the wing walker wouldn't be blown away. But they'd practiced this.

The timing was a surprise. The fact that they would be facing dirigibles wasn't. And the way the first dirigible was brought down in that other timeline was well known. Someone had dropped a bomb onto it.

As soon as the cockpit was clear, Miroslava lay down on the floor of the cockpit, took a screwdriver, and started adjusting the position of the aqualator. It took five minutes before the ready signal pinged.

It was over an hour later before the *Ivan Susanin* took off to protect Russia from invaders from the west one more time.

In the air, over Perm
January 11, 1638

The *Patriarch* was in position and ready to instruct the ungodly. No wing walking was necessary. The *Patriarch* had a bomb bay and it dropped its first bomb fifteen minutes after it had been spotted. It was holding position over Perm. The bomb dropped and the wind moved it as it fell. It landed twenty-five feet outside the walls of Perm. The bomb had a contact fuse that set it off when it hit the ground. It was a mix of a black-powder charge and fuel oil to produce an incendiary effect. It worked quite well, and a stretch of ice-covered ground just outside the walls of Perm burned merrily for a few minutes.

People along the walls of Perm laughed, but Tim wasn't laughing. The aim would get better. He looked around. Aside from the walls, Perm was a city of wood. So much kindling, as soon as the bombs started falling inside the walls.

The next bomb fell and it landed inside the wall. Fortunately, it landed on a street and not on a roof, but some of the burning oil hit two buildings and people were way too busy with buckets to be laughing anymore.

Now that they had what they thought was the range, they dropped ten five-hundred-pound bombs, about half of which landed inside the town of Perm and half outside it. They did have the range. It was just that a bomb dropping through two miles of air isn't a precision instrument. It goes where the wind takes it, even if it is heavy.

But Perm was a really big bonfire before the *Ivan Susanin* arrived.

Ivan Susanin *over Perm*
January 11, 1638

Petrov clipped his line to the side of the door and clipped the other end of the line to the back of his harness. Then he opened the door and, fighting the wind, stepped out onto the wing. The bomb he was carrying was considerably lighter than the five-hundred-pound bombs that the *Filaret* dropped on Perm. It weighed thirty-five pounds and it was pointed. In fact, its front end was specifically designed to cut through the doped fabric covering of a dirigible, then to rip open the goldbeater skin bags that held the hydrogen, and then to go off after it had done all that. It didn't have a contact fuse. It had a thirty-second clockwork timer. Pull the cord, drop the bomb, thirty seconds later, boom.

It was a marvel of wartime engineering, which made it no easier to carry through a sixty-mile-per-hour gale. Carefully, Petrov let out the line until he was at the trailing edge of the wing and waited. He was wearing goggles and a flight suit, but it was still freezing cold with a wind chill that was frankly unbelievable.

With his back to the wind, he watched the sky behind and below the *Ivan Susanin*.

Meanwhile, in the cockpit Vasilii watched as the *Filaret* turned northwest and made for Bor, rising just as fast as it could.

The *Ivan Susanin* was faster than the *Filaret*, which had a top speed of seventy miles per hour. In level flight, the *Ivan Susanin* cruised at ninety-seven miles per hour. But that didn't include the fact that they were climbing to keep up with the rising *Filaret* and that they had a man out on the wing with a bomb in his hands. Of course, the *Filaret* was climbing too, and that was costing it a considerable amount of speed.

Vasilii pushed the engine levers to their stops and the *Ivan Susanin* picked up speed and rose higher.

On the wing, the shift caused Petrov to stumble and in catching himself, he dropped the bomb which fell to the ground and shattered without ever going off. Meanwhile, Petrov climbed back to the door, and went back into the cabin. Part of that was because he was climbing uphill against an eighty-mile-per-hour gale, but part of it was because they were now passing thirteen thousand feet and at that height, the atmosphere doesn't have quite enough air to keep one going. You don't suffocate. It's more like being a third of the way up the side of Mount Everest. Energetic activity is not recommended.

He breathed deeply for a few minutes trying to get enough oxygen into his system so that the spots would leave his eyes. Then, he got another bomb.

On the *Patriarch Filaret* things weren't any better. That damned airplane was gaining on them. By now an internal combustion engine would be stuttering and getting ready to fail, but steam was different. It was getting hard to breathe and the hydrogen bags were full and venting. That was potentially dangerous. But the captain had no choice. They too knew the history of how the first dirigible was taken down. Their only safety was getting high enough so that the airplane couldn't get above them.

It worked. They hit fifteen thousand feet and the damned airplane turned away, but they were venting hydrogen. Venting hydrogen at need was something that these dirigibles were designed to do, especially after what had happened to the *Czarina Evdokia* over Germany. But the *Patriarch Filaret* had been rushed into service before its trials and one of the vents was stuck. Some worker had put the parts together without waiting long enough for the lacquer to dry, so what should have opened and closed, as the pressure in hydrogen sack one changed, just stayed closed. The pressure wasn't relieved. Worse, the thin cord that was supposed to open the vent instead put extra stress on a particular point on the goldbeater's skin bladder. The pressure built up. Hydrogen sack one ripped open, venting the hydrogen into the body of the *Patriarch Filaret*. The *Patriarch Filaret* had little chimneys on the top of the outer skin, so that even if ice coated the skin, the hydrogen could still vent out the top. This didn't eliminate, but did diminish, the risk of fire.

It worked quite well.

However, in about five minutes, hydrogen sack one went from full and providing lift to empty, and just adding to the weight of the dirigible. By that time, they'd hit seventeen thousand feet, well above their safe sealing, and the crew were more than a little woozy from lack of oxygen. Their reactions were slow, and worse, the other hydrogen sacks were working just fine, venting hydrogen until the pressure was released and leaving the *Patriarch Filaret* with not quite enough hydrogen to stay aloft. Not at ten thousand feet or lower.

The thing about a balloon, whether it holds hydrogen or air, is the higher it goes, the less gas it requires to stay inflated. And the lower it goes, the more gas it needs, because the outside pressure is greater at lower altitude.

They had enough hydrogen in the three remaining hydrogen sacks to maintain altitude at seventeen thousand feet, even at fifteen thousand feet, but by the time they noticed the problem and put together what it was, they were at seven thousand feet and pointing nose down at about 20 degrees.

They used the engines to try and get their nose up, while at the same time venting even more hydrogen from the rearmost hydrogen sack to balance the lift.

None of this happened fast, and it all happened while they were running toward Bor. Bor is four hundred and sixty-four miles west-northwest of Perm, as the crow flies, give or take. And from the moment that the *Ivan Susanin* had appeared on the scene, they'd been running for Bor and the hangar that was their home. The wind, which at seventeen thousand feet was strong and from the northeast, had been pushing them southwest. Just a little south of the direction they wanted to go. In the confusion, no one had noticed the southerly drift to their course. So the report they sent to Bor and Birkin just before they "landed" was about thirty miles off, showing them both farther east and farther north than they actually were.

The *Patriarch Filaret* came down in a large stretch of forest. The trees poked holes in the bottom of the dirigible, but not in the remaining hydrogen bags. Those were half deflated at ground level anyway. The sudden stop cracked spars, ripped loose wires and threw crew to the floor. Three members of the crew had broken bones and one unfortunate, working on a nacelle, was thrown loose and fell thirty feet to break his neck on a tree trunk. Electronics were screwed and the radio lost its triode tube, making it unusable until the tube was replaced. Steam pipes came loose, releasing steam and causing even more damage. They would be days fixing all the problems, and cutting away tree limbs so they could get out of the forest.

Patriarch Filaret had crashed, but not crash-*landed*. It was still in the trees, held up partly by the trees and partly by the hydrogen in its three remaining hydrogen sacks, which did more damage. It was going to take time to fix.

But the idea of abandoning it never even crossed the crew's mind. Dirigibles are *expensive*. They aren't *airplane* expensive, they are *space shuttle* expensive. They are huge for the amount of useful load they carry. The materials they are made from have to be light and strong, so they involve huge amounts of very expensive materials plus the labor of hundreds of highly skilled laborers working for months. Sheremetev, then Ivan Romanov, had spent a considerable portion of the military budget of Muscovite Russia on the *Patriarch Filaret*.

Now there was a fortune in the form of an almost but not quite fully functional airship sitting in the forest around halfway between Kazan and Perm.

Vasilii, seeing spots in front of his eyes, turned the nose down and then did a slow bank left to go back to Perm and see how things were going. By the time they got back to Perm, they were down around eight thousand feet, and if the air was still a little thin for real comfort, it was thick enough to breathe. Also, Vasilii had gotten enough oxygen back in his brain so that he realized that there wasn't anything that he could do for Perm. The town was still burning, though it looked like they were getting the fires under control. He put in a call to the city. Birkin had made an attack on the north wall while the city was burning, but it was repulsed and it was unlikely he would try again, not without the *Filaret* to support them.

So General Tim's orders were to track the *Filaret* and destroy it.

"I can't, Tim. Don't have enough fuel to get back to Ufa. I'll be on residual steam by the time I land at Letyaga."

"Do what you can."

Vasilii landed at Letyaga, a small village just upriver of the convergence of the Belaya and the Kama Rivers. It was part of the radio grid and it had a fuel depot. They landed, refilled their tanks and the jerry cans, then took off again, which took them the better part of an hour. Then they had to find the *Filaret*. That was the big advantage of airships over airplanes. Range. The *Filaret* could go for a thousand miles without refueling. On the other hand, from what Vasilii had seen, the only place it wanted to go was back to Bor.

By the time they got the *Filaret* in sight again the situation was more complicated. The dirigible was way too low. It was at less than a thousand feet and losing altitude slowly.

Petrov wanted to go out on the wing and drop a bomb on the sucker, but Vasilii refused. He kept the *Filaret* in sight but didn't approach it. It continued to lose altitude and continued to travel east-southeast getting closer and closer to Kazan and farther and farther from Birkin's army outside Perm. Since that was exactly what Vasilii wanted, he let it keep going. Vasilii knew approximately how much the *Filaret* was worth and he knew how much its parts were worth too. The hydrogen sacks, the electrical hydrogen separator, the steam engines, the boiler, the condensers... there was a fortune in salvage and Vasilii wanted that fortune as close to Kazan as he could get it.

By the time they watched the *Filaret* crash, they were getting low on fuel again, but they were also closer to Kazan than to Letyaga, so they went there.

The Volga south of Kazan was Sovereign States territory. They landed on the Volga and taxied to Kazan.

Headquarters, Kazan
January 11, 1638

They reported to Ivan Maslov, who was running this end of the hotbox.

"Yes, General, I know your game plan," Vasilii said, "but a new player entered the game and you may not know how much it's worth."

"What do you mean?"

"The *Filaret* is down in the woods and basically intact. And we need to take it intact."

"Why?" Ivan asked. "I think de-emphasizing the dirigibles was an excellent move on the part of Czar Mikhail, however much the czarina loved the things."

"I agree, but do you know why that decision was made?"

"Cost and time. It doesn't take nearly as long to build an airplane as it does to build a dirigible."

"It costs as much to make one Czarina-class dirigible as it does to make fifty Hero-class airplanes," Vasilii clarified. "But in the case of the *Filaret* that money has already been spent, and by Moscow, not us. If we can seize it, repair it, send it to Hidden Valley or use it to deliver fuel to air stations out east or any number of noncombat roles, that's a lot of money added to the Czar's treasury."

"Birkin has to know that," Ivan said consideringly. "But is he going to think about it when he has an army stuck in the open?"

"If he doesn't, Ivan Romanov will," Miroslava said. The greed of the Czar's uncle was famous throughout Russia.

"And Ivan Romanov is going to want them to fix it and fly it back to Bor," Ivan Maslov agreed.

"We need to get to it and seize it before that happens," Vasilii said.

"Well you've got a plane," Ivan said "I can—"

"No place to land. Not within ten miles of the crash site."

"Valeriya Zakharovna," Ivan said.

"Where is she?" Vasilii asked. They all knew about her. She was the first Russian to make a parachute jump and had trained the rest of the Russian paratroopers.

"Hidden Valley. She's on the crew of the *Princess Anna*," Ivan said. The *Princess Anna* was the small mail carrier dirigible that had been made out of parts of the *Czar Alexis* after it had crashed. Before Czar Mikhail had been forced to de-emphasize airships as a cost-saving measure. It was still in operation and spent most of its time either in mapmaking or in carrying small loads of this or that between secure bases. It was kept far away from anything approaching combat. And it wasn't flown unless the weather was good and expected to remain that way. Even the smallest of Russia's airships was too expensive to risk. That was the reason that it hadn't been sent east. Yes, it could make the trip, but bad weather was expected. In bad weather a Hero could land and be fairly safe. The *Princess Anna* wasn't safe unless it was in a hangar at Hidden Valley.

"Well, considering she knows a lot about dirigibles she's probably who we need."

"She isn't trained in combat but some of the other paratroopers are," Ivan agreed. Then he asked, "By the way, what happened with that business with the spy in the Embassy bureau?"

"That's need to know, General, and I'm afraid you don't," Vasilii said.

"You shouldn't have been told why you and General Lebedev were making that scouting mission yourselves," Miroslava added.

Miroslava by now knew precisely who the spies were. One of them was one of Simeon Budanov's top aides, and another was a member of the Streltzi Bureau. They were working together. And, for now, Ivan Borisovich Petrov and Czar Mikhail had decided to leave them right where they were and feed them bad information. But there would be a reckoning sooner or later.

Hidden Valley
January 12, 1638

Valeriya Zakharovna, in the uniform of a chief petty officer, saluted as they exited the Hero-class airplane in Hidden Valley. They'd landed on a small pond that was produced by a dam on the creek that ran through Hidden Valley.

Beside it was a dirigible hangar suitable for a much larger dirigible than the *Princess Anna*. It was also only about half finished. The dirigible part of the air force had been left to muddle on with a very limited budget. They had also based their uniforms and ranks on the navy, whereas the heavier-than-air air force had gone with army-style ranks. It was a confusing mess and one that Czar Mikhail wasn't going near, since his wife was still very much an airship fan.

"Can your people jump out of an airplane?" Vasilii asked without preamble. He wasn't wearing any uniform. He was dressed in civilian clothes in the fashion of Ufa, which was a blend of pre–Ring of Fire Russian dress and civilian dress of late twentieth-century America. It was winter so he was wearing a greatcoat and one of the fur-lined baseball caps with earflaps.

"We can, but the *Princess Anna* is better."

"It might be at that, but we need to drop as large a force as we can," Vasilii said. "And let's go somewhere warmer."

There was very little wind. That was the main reason for the location of Hidden Valley. It was surrounded by hills and once you got below the height of the hills, you might get snowed on or rained on, but high winds were unlikely. Still, it was about 5 degrees below freezing and Vasilii wanted to be comfortable as they planned this out.

In an office located next to the main hangar, Vasilii pulled out his maps and described the location of the dirigible and the area around it. "Forest, with a few clearings. There's a stream to the east about a mile, but it's not big enough to land a Scout, much less a Hero. And we need to have people in there before they make repairs and fly away home."

"What's the crew?" Dimitry Ivanov asked.

"You should know better than I," Vasilii said. Miroslava was being quiet and Vasilii realized it was because Valeriya Zakharovna was nervous about her. Many of the more common attributes of Miroslava's condition had been beaten out of her, but that wasn't all that made people uncomfortable around her. She was also beautiful, and that in itself made some women uncomfortable around her. Valeriya Zakharovna was a large, rawboned woman. It wasn't the first time either of them had seen the phenomenon, and Miroslava preferred to have him do the talking anyway.

After Vasilii had described the location, Valeriya and Dimitry described what they had.

"Five of our paratroop scouts are out right now," Valeriya said. "We only have twenty-five paratroops and the five pilots that know the basics."

"We can carry eight on the Hero," Vasilii said.

"And the *Princess Anna* can carry ten, at need."

"That's eighteen in two drops. If we coordinate our timing, they can both land within hours of each other."

"Paratroopers aren't..." Valeriya hesitated. "...normal soldiers. They don't march around with guns on their shoulders or do volley fire."

"What are they?" Miroslava asked. Curiosity, as it usually did, overrode her reticence.

"Scouts and trackers. Their job is usually to land, hook up with someone trying to escape to the Sovereign States, and lead them out of Muscovy, or sometimes Lithuania. They can fight and are as brave as anyone in the czar's army, but their training and skills are different."

"I understand, but until Ivan can get some cavalry there, they are going to be all we've got. Besides, they are going to be facing an airship crew," Vasilii said. And, seeing the expression on Dimitry Ivanov and Valeriya Zakharovna's faces, added, "Again, brave people without doubt, but not stand in line and shoot soldiers. What we need your paratroopers to do is to make sure that the *Filaret* doesn't fly home to Bor. If they can bring it back to Hidden Valley, great. But if not that, at least hold it there until the cavalry arrives.

"Understand this. I have my orders from the czar. If it looks like the *Filaret* is going to escape back to Bor, I will drop a bomb on it."

In the air, over crash site
January 12, 1638

Valeriya Zakharovna stood on the bottom wing of the Hero-class airplane as the sixty-mile-an-hour wind whipped by her. They were at ten thousand feet. She wanted plenty of time to stabilize before she pulled her rip cord. She was wearing goggles and she looked at the window where Miroslava Holmes was seated. There was a sheet of red-painted board against the window. Then it was removed and a green-painted piece of wood was held up.

Valeriya let go of the handhold, took a step, and was falling. She did a couple of flips caused by the turbulence off the back of the wing, then she was in smooth air. She put her arms and legs out, not exactly straight but out, and stabilized her fall until she was falling facing down. She pulled her rip cord and the drag chute came loose. The wind caught it and pulled the main. It started to open, but was slowed by the drag canopy, just as it was supposed to be. The drag canopy was a small cloth device that was attached to the risers to keep the main parafoil from opening too fast and jerking the paratrooper too hard. Going from terminal velocity to close to a dead stop in one jerk could be terminal for the trooper or rip the chute because of the sudden stress. So the drag canopy slowed the opening of the main just a little so that it only felt like you were stopped in a sudden jerk.

Then she was flying under a parawing. She looked around. The rest of the team were out with chutes opened. And they were dropping. She could see the *Filaret* to the west and the creek below her. She headed toward where the clearing ought to be and then saw it and started circling in. The parawings were blue gray to blend with the sky, so that the troopers would be harder to spot. She wouldn't know if that worked until they got to the airship.

As she reached the ground, Valeriya jerked both controls down and the wing tilted into a stall just as she landed, but she still did her roll just as she was supposed to. Then she started gathering up her chute, while the rest of the team landed and did the same. It was five minutes later, while they were still collecting their chutes, that the second team arrived, jumping from the *Princess Anna*.

An hour later, the sun was down and they approached the dirigible in the dark, while the paratroopers complained about the noise she was making. Valeriya was skilled at jumping out of aircraft. She was also an excellent rigger and knew perfectly well how to repair all sorts of things in a dirigible. She wasn't a wood-wise scout, and it seemed like a stick or a piece of ice broke with every step she took.

No one in the dirigible seemed to notice, though.

It was hard to tell in the dark, but it seemed like the bottom of the dirigible was suspended about ten feet off the ground by four trees. Those same trees had poked holes in the bottom of the dirigible body. One of those trees had pulled the port-side engine nacelle loose, and it was hanging by one of its struts.

How much damage that had done, they couldn't see, in spite of the fact that the dirigible had its lights on.

The *Filaret* had a crew of twelve: captain, first officer, chief engineer, electrician, two nacelle engineers, and the rest riggers. The captain and first officer shared responsibility for navigation, and the electrician doubled as the radio and weatherman.

One of the scouts motioned Valeriya to stillness and started climbing a tree to reach the starboard nacelle.

It was unoccupied and the steam engine was cold. He dropped a rope ladder and the rest of the team climbed into the nacelle. From the nacelle, it was a walk along the catwalk to the main body of the *Filaret* and they were inside. The *Filaret* creaked as they moved. They reached the crew quarters and found everyone asleep, including the guard.

By the time the first of the crew woke, they each had a scout with a loaded revolver next to them.

Valeriya learned that the radio was busted. The tubes used had been shattered by the crash. And she learned that they were at least three days away from being able to lift the ship. Then she spent the next two hours consulting with the captured captain of the *Filaret*, who was cooperative. She made a list of what they needed to get the *Filaret* flight ready and then she sent one of the scouts off to the rendezvous, the closest place to the crash site that the Hero could land.

Birkin's army, outside Perm
January 13, 1638

The radio operator brought General Ivan Vasilevich Birkin the message.

> The *Filaret* down in forest near Kazan.
> Must be secured with all haste.

"And how exactly am I supposed to do that?" Ivan Vasilevich muttered under his breath. He looked across at the walls of Perm. They'd gotten here too late thanks to the airplanes that Tim had and he didn't. Russia had created five airships. The *Testbed*, the *Czarina Evdokia*, the *Czar Alexis*, the *Princess Anna*, and the *Patriarch Filaret*. Of the five, only the *Princess Anna* was still in operation. And it was only in operation because it was small and used with extreme caution. There were six Hero-class airplanes and three Scout-class airplanes in operation now. There had been one crash of a Scout plane and one crash of a Hero. The Hero had been put back in operation. Granted, it wasn't a large sample, but the evidence seemed overwhelming. Heavier-than-air craft was the way of the future. And he really needed an excuse to get out of the trap that Tim had put him in by getting here first with enough troops to hold the walls.

He went to his writing desk and wrote out his return message. The desk was a foldable table in his command tent, made of lightweight, thin pine with leather fastenings. The tent was double-walled with a camp stove and chimney.

He wrote:

> Urgent. *The switch from airships to airplanes cannot be delayed any longer.*
>
> Sending a large enough force to secure the Filaret *would mean abandoning the attack on Perm.*
> Instructions?

Birkin sent the message off to Moscow with a twinge of guilt, but only a twinge. The Perm mission was a disaster. And he desperately needed a way out that wouldn't be blamed on him. The *Filaret* might well be that way out.

He started giving preparation orders to abandon the siege of Perm and head west.

It wasn't until the next day that he got orders from the capital. Part of that was the time it took for the radio chain to transmit the messages across the two dozen or so radios between here and Moscow, but only part of it. Clearly Moscow had spent some time debating the question.

> *Abandon siege of Perm.*
> *Defend the* Filaret.

Birkin put his army in motion.

Filaret
January 14, 1638

Chief Petty Officer Valeriya Zakharovna was overseeing two men with saws as they cut branches off the limbs that were keeping the *Filaret* stable. More soldiers had arrived by airplane, ferried to the river about sixteen miles away, and from there they skied with packs on their backs carrying spare tubes, parts, and equipment, as well as their AK4.7s and ammunition. There were now some eighty men at arms surrounding the dirigible and those of the crew that hadn't switched sides were under guard, marching back to the river.

Among those walking in was the *Filaret*'s new captain, Dimitry Ivanov. He was exhausted. A sixteen-mile cross-country ski trip will do that to you, even if you're trained, and Dimitry Ivanov wasn't.

"Ignat Berezin says he has the radio working and has sent an encrypted message to Ufa by way of Kazan detailing the damage and ongoing repairs," Kirill Veselov shouted.

Kirill had been the engineer before they'd arrived, and had switched sides with every show of enthusiasm. Ignat had marched in last night because the radio man was in a position to tell Moscow precisely where they were. And in these circumstances, defectors were less trusted than those who came in on their own. So the *Filaret*'s previous radio man was skiing back to the frozen river, where he would be picked up and taken to Kazan. From there he would be able to decide whether to switch sides or be interned long enough for the *Filaret* to get airborne, which was looking like it was going to take another two, perhaps three, days.

Valeriya waved acknowledgment and got back to work.

CHAPTER 25

𝔓olitics

Ufa Kremlin
January 14, 1638

"You need to fire Ivan Borisovich Petrov," Simeon Budanov insisted. "He's completely failed to catch the leak. And at this late date, it's unlikely that we will ever find out who it was."

That was half true. Ivan Borisovich had, at Czar Mikhail's instruction, failed to *apprehend* the leak, but Czar Mikhail knew exactly who the leak was. After a fair amount of discussion, it had been decided to leave the leak in place and simply control the information flowing through it.

"Don't be so harsh, Simeon. We don't want to piss off his father. You know we get a lot of tech through Boris," Mikhail said. He didn't mention that Boris was also providing his son, and therefore Mikhail, with a great deal of intelligence about the goings-on in Moscow and Muscovite Russia. That was information that was above Simeon's pay grade. Also above his pay grade was the story of how the spy was identified.

"Your Majesty, he's useless. He spends most of his time at the Diogenes Club, ordering expensive lunches and dinners that he bills to my department."

"Calm yourself, Simeon. I'll have a talk with him and perhaps I can get him to retire and manage his affairs in the private sector. You know that his family has several freeze-drying facilities here and in Muscovite Russia."

It took a few more minutes, but Simeon Budanov was ushered out. Then another door opened and Ivan Borisovich Petrov

270

came in. "So I resign without prejudice, which will calm Simeon Budanov's paranoia. You need to put Kirill in charge of the Grantville desk."

"I need Kirill on the China desk." Mikhail shook his head. "The destruction of the Zunghars has scared the crap out of Güshi Khan, and the imperial governor of China's western province."

"The Grantville desk is important. You know Budanov is going to give it to one of his cronies, quite possibly the spy." Even here Ivan Borisovich didn't say the name of the agent that Ivan Romanov had placed in the Embassy Bureau.

"No, the Grantville desk isn't important," Mikhail corrected. "It *was* important and contact with Grantville continues to be important, which is why Bernie and Natasha are on their way to Grantville even now. But the Grantville desk is no longer our only source of information; we have the Ufa Dacha and your father gathering up everything Muscovy gets from the USE and sending it on to his son."

"I thought the Diogenes Club was to focus on internal security?"

"Don't be too wedded to twentieth-century American practice. You won't be heading the CIA or the FBI. Your agents will operate in the Sovereign States, in Muscovite Russia and, when necessary, in other countries. Your job is to provide me with intelligence on what's going on in the world so that I will have more than one source." Mikhail considered, then added, "Where I want you to restrict yourself is in the scope of your actions. Your people will observe and report, not instigate or act. Spies, not saboteurs."

Ivan bowed, then commented, "I wonder how Bernie's doing."

Cluj
January 14, 1638

The Hero circled the city twice and the radio did a frequency search to find the radio frequency. They found it and transmitted by voice, in clear, who they were and that they wanted to land. Clearance to land came quickly enough. But once they landed, they were met by armed men.

This had been a war zone in the last few months and the people were antsy.

It took a few minutes until they found someone who could

confirm it was Bernie. The somebody was Jeff Higgins, who'd been in high school the last time he'd seen Bernie. Bernie had seen him at the Battle of the Crapper, but Bernie had been behind the logs with a deer rifle, not on a dirt bike facing down mercenaries with a shotgun. When Jeff and Gretchen got married, Bernie had been drunk in the Gardens or perhaps the 250 Club.

They got clearance, radio frequencies, and by the use of gold and silver coins they arranged gasoline—aviation fuel, that is—for the rest of the trip to Prague and hence to Grantville. They also got charts to the various airfields along the way.

Jeff, a nerd even in high school, wanted to look at the Hero. He was familiar with the Jupiter Five, the airframe of which was clear to see in the Hero's shape.

"The condenser is in the expansion chamber."

"Expansion chamber?"

"We ended up having to invent some of the terms since the designs that came through the Ring of Fire were less than complete," Bernie explained. "The main hovercraft fans blow air into a wide flat chamber. That's what we call the expansion chamber, because the air from the fans expands from a stream of air to a high-pressure zone. The expansion chamber is opened around the sides at the top. That lets the air out evenly all around the bag or skirt. It goes into the skirt, which is designed to leak air, but to leak more air inward. This, all put together, gives you areas of pressure. The highest pressure is in the expansion chamber, then the skirt, then the area under the skirt. So the skirt flexes over rough ground, leaking air all around but not so hard that it can't get out of the way of a rock or fill hole. What we found was that by putting the condenser in the expansion chamber where there is a constant flow of air over them, we get more efficient condensing of the steam and heat the air going into the skirt, which is especially helpful in snow and ice conditions."

"Royal Dutch had problems with the skirts and has mostly abandoned them," Jeff pointed out.

"We have problems with them too, but by making the skirts in removable and replaceable sections, those problems are kept manageable. Besides, we don't have enough airfields to use a wheeled, or even a skied, aircraft."

What struck Jeff about this was how much self-centered jock Bernie Zeppi had changed. The Bernie from high school wouldn't give credit to someone else with a gun to his head. And Jeff had been privately convinced that Bernie couldn't count to eleven without taking off his shoes. But then again, the Jeff from high school didn't go armed or lead an army. So clearly Bernie wasn't the only one who'd changed.

The mission spent the night in Cluj, then, using the maps and weather information provided, headed for Prague. There were several refueling stops, but they made it by the end of the day.

In Prague, they met with the regency council and recognized Wallenstein's heir as the king of Bohemia, left a draft of a trade agreement with the regency council for them to consider, got fuel oil that had come up the Elbe from the oil fields in Germany, and took off again on January 18. They landed at Grantville Airport shortly before noon.

Grantville
January 18, 1638

After they taxied to their designated parking spot and tied down the Hero, Bernie went to the tower and asked to use the phone. "And do you know how I can reach Her Serene Highness Millicent Anne Barnes?"

The air traffic controller told him and he called the Higgins Hotel.

The phone, a down-time-made rotary dial phone that would have been right at home in the Forties, was located on a counter on the bottom floor of the tower. Besides, he'd had to go through an operator at the Higgins, who might still be listening in. So, with the ton of gold hidden under the floorboards at the center of lift of the Hero making him paranoid, Bernie said, "Hi, Your Serene Highness. Brandy Bates sent me to return your lipstick."

There was a pause. "The whole lipstick?" Millicent asked.

"No, but a good part of it. Bring friends. Big, strong friends, and well-armed," Bernie said quietly. He wasn't sure why, but he'd managed to make the whole trip here hardly thinking of the gold under the floorboards. But now that they were getting ready to deliver it, he was seeing bandits in every shadow. And not just bandits. Muscovite Russia had its own embassy in Magdeburg, and a consulate right here in Grantville.

"I don't recall. What color was that lipstick? Was it silver?"

Bernie cupped a hand over the receiver. "Gold."

"Wait there," Millicent Anne Barnes said. "I'll call some friends."

Astrid Schäubin answered the phone at NESS. "Neustatter Security Services. How can we help you?"

"This is Millicent Anne Barnes. I have something of a rush job for you, transporting something from the airport to the bank."

"Transporting what?"

"Honestly, I'm not sure. The form it's in might be coins or bars, but it's a fairly large amount of gold. At least, if I'm reading Bernie Zeppi right."

Astrid kept track of the powers in the world, and the Emancipation Proclamation and the constitution of the United Sovereign States of Russia had both been fairly big news. It was well known that Bernie Zeppi was, at last report, one of Czar Mikhail's top advisors.

She checked her books to see who was available. There were wagons and horses to draw them. She put together four teams of five men each, armed, and two wagons, just in case, gave Her Serene Highness Millicent Anne Barnes a price, and started getting the job organized.

An hour later, Bernie and Natasha were having a hamburger and fries with real ketchup. They were in the Hero, eating with the crew, when Millicent Anne Barnes arrived in a steam car. She was invited in, and they pulled up the floorboards, displaying canvas sacks full of gold coins minted in Ufa from gold from Kazan and the Urals. The weight was two thousand pounds. Each coin was one ounce, so there were thirty-two thousand coins in sixty-four sacks. Each sack weighed a bit over thirty pounds.

Millicent was, by this time, used to doing business at very high levels and bank drafts in the millions of thalers didn't bother her at all. This was just a little different.

"The guys from NESS will be here in another hour or so."

They were, and everything went quite smoothly. The wagons were loaded with half the bags each, and they, with an escort of NESS guards, made the eight-mile trip to the bank.

In the year 1638, the Grantville bank had a very professional assaying service attached. It could weigh and test for purity gold and silver coinage quickly and accurately.

These coins were twenty-four-karat gold, freshly minted, with reeding. Several random coins were tested, then they were just weighed.

The coins were put in the accounts of the Barbie Consortium and the Stone family accounts, based on the amount that Ron Stone and Millicent Anne Barnes, acting for the Barbies, had loaned the Sovereign States over the last year since Brandy Bates Gorchakov had said it wasn't like she was asking for Millicent's last up-time lipstick.

Before the gold was counted, the news was all over the business community. There were two instant effects. First, the price of a Sovereign States ruble, which had never fallen to that of waste paper, but was moving in that direction, rebounded. Drastically! The second was the effect on the Austro-Hungarian thaler, otherwise known as a "Judy," which had also been losing value since the Ottomans took Vienna, but bounced back somewhat. Because, while the gold didn't pay either Ron or the Barbies back in full—not even close—it said two things very loudly. Russia, at least the Sovereign States of Russia, paid its debts, and the Barbies still had the knack for picking a good investment, which had the follow-on effect of improving confidence in the Austro-Hungarian Empire and its chances against the Ottomans.

After all, what was riskier than loaning money to a czar in exile, and that had apparently paid off.

For the next several days, Bernie and Natasha made visits to Magdeburg, Brussels, and several other places.

Then, with a load that mostly consisted of tubes, but included other high-end stuff, they went back to Ufa, following the same route. There would be more trips now that the air route was opened. Though some of the people who had air stations along the way were going to be pissed when they learned what had been on that first plane. And future planes were likely to be examined fairly thoroughly. But that was a negotiation for later.

At least on this route, they weren't going to have to chop wood for the boiler.

Siberia
January 18, 1638

Brandy and Vlad watched the ground ahead, looking for a likely spot.

When they'd left Almaliq they'd flown east but as soon as they had reached ten thousand feet they'd seen a large lake. It was over a mountain but only about thirty-three miles northeast of Almaliq.

They scouted the alpine lake, then flew back in the afternoon.

It turned out that the locals of Almaliq knew of the place, though it was difficult to get to without aircraft. They called it Sayram Lake. So instead of going east immediately, they took a crew to set up an air station at Sayram Lake.

That had taken four days and ten trips back and forth before they had a small village of about twenty people, aside from the fuel oil that the other Hero would be bringing. The locals would spend the rest of the winter chopping down pine trees and charcoaling the wood, and hunting and fishing so that there would be stocks of charcoal and food for the trip back.

After the Lake Sayram Air Station was established, Brandy, Vlad and crew went on.

Ninety-four miles just north of due east of Lake Sayram was a salt lake. Salty enough that nothing lived in the water, though fish did live in the rivers that fed it. They named it Sal Lake and spent a few days first collecting wood and brush, then a few more searching for a place they could reach in the desert to the east of it.

Finally they found a lake that was the center of an oasis. They called it Air Station Green, because it was the only green spot they could find, and frankly, they were getting tired of naming things.

Again it was load up on wood and prepare for days, then spend more days looking for a good spot for the next station. Ulungur Lake was one hundred nineteen miles north-northeast of Sal Lake. It was also occupied by one of the tribes that had made up the Zunghars. That produced a rather delicate negotiation which took more time, then took even more time, because once they learned what had happened to Erdeni Batur, they had a proposal. They very much didn't want to be absorbed by Salqam-Jangir Khan and the Kazakh state. They also realized that they didn't have a chance on their own, with the Kazakhs to their southwest and China to their southeast. They wanted to become a state in their own right.

Vladimir thought that was an excellent idea. Kazakh was already by far the largest state in the Sovereign States, and if it kept growing... Well, temptation arises in the noblest heart. Salqam-Jangir Khan was smart enough to restrain his ambition, but that didn't mean that he and his nobles didn't have it. And that put the whole bloody exploratory mission on hold while they picked up a representative of the Zunghars who was empowered to negotiate and make binding agreements, and flew him back to Ufa.

Shavgar
January 20, 1638

Salqam-Jangir Khan had gotten the radio message, so he was right there when Vladimir and Brandy landed. He looked at Vladimir as they deplaned and shook his head. "I thought better of you, Vladimir. I thought of you as a friend."

"We were outside of your lands and Qong Tayiji Jochi here made it clear that he and his tribe didn't want to become part of your state," Vladimir said.

Qong Tayiji was a basically Chinese term that meant prince or crown prince and Jochi's people used it about the way the Kazakhs used the word "khan."

They spent the night in Shavgar and the next morning they had Salqam-Jangir Khan on the plane with them. They landed in Ufa, dropped off their passengers, picked up a few things that they'd learned they needed in the wilderness, and then took the southern route back.

They had letters in Chinese script from Qong Tayiji Jochi and, using that and a bit of gold, set up an air station at Ulungur Lake. Two hundred twelve miles east of Ulungur Lake was Khar-Us Lake, but from there they were moving into the Gobi Desert, where there were neither trees nor water. So they went north a hundred forty-three miles to Uvs Lake, a salt lake that wasn't so salty that it didn't have fish and birds living in and around it. From there they went further north over mountains to a place of trees, even if it was a place covered in snow this time of year. They found a frozen lake surrounded by snow-covered pine trees and spent several days chopping wood and loading the wood sacks to take them farther.

Ufa
January 30, 1638

Mikey was having a ball. He was stacking wooden blocks then knocking over the towers he made and laughing as they fell. He, along with Larisa Chernoff, were Anna and Martha's favorite toys slash playmates, with nannies to oversee.

Irina and Alexi were too big for babies. Irina getting close to eleven and Alexi almost ten. Both of them were in school, or, rather, both of them were being tutored by scholars from the Ufa Dacha. It was a very different life than their early childhood. Among the bits of knowledge that the up-timers had brought was the notion that child abuse wasn't a necessity in child rearing. That sparing the rod often produced perfectly nice kids. That notion wasn't universally accepted, but Czarina Evdokia had accepted it and the kids had benefited.

Both children spoke, read, and wrote in Russian and English. They both also studied Latin and Greek, as well as Polish, Spanish, and French. So they were busy kids. Not that their world was perfect. Irina was, at the moment, suffering under the glare of Rodion Anosov, who was discussing her latest paper on supply chains.

"And where do they get the laminated wood?" Rodion Anosov asked.

"They buy it," Irina insisted. "*Plywood*"—she used the up-timer English word—"is made right here in Ufa from the pine forest just to the east. And it's used for everything from desks to walls and shipped up the Volga to Moscow and down to the Caspian. It's one of Ufa's more profitable exports, so there is plenty available for making wing struts and all the other plywood parts."

"Good enough, but why isn't that in your paper?" Rodion Anosov asked.

"Because it's not specific to the airplanes!" Irina didn't shout, but she really wanted to.

"But they are—"

"No, they aren't!"

"Let me finish, please," Rodion Anosov said. "The ready availability of plywood was one of the factors that led the design section to go with an internal wooden strut and doped canvas wing and body design rather than the fiberglass monocoque construction used in the Jupiters. So you see the supply chain works both ways. It's not just 'can you get one product,' but 'is another available.'

"Now. Tell me about the wing factory."

"It's on Anna Street," Irina said. "Out near the Ufa River. It's steam powered and uses drill presses and band saws to cut the wing spars and other parts." Irina had visited the plant as part of her lessons. It employed about three hundred former peasants and was owned by the Chernoffs. At least the Ufa branch of the Chernoff family. As well as the factory was partly owned by the Chernoffs, the factory was also owned by the government of the Sovereign States and a chunk by the Romanov family.

Dominika and Zia Chernoff had invested heavily in wood products. Larisa, who was in the crib next to Mikey, was going to be incredibly rich when she grew up. And the plant used a steam engine to run dozens of machines to make the various parts that were put together into the Hero-class airplanes. It was tens of thousands of man-hours for each plane, but with about three hundred workers in the plant, it was working out to a new airframe every month or so. They weren't turning them out like sewing machines or pliers, but it wasn't like it was one guy in a shack either.

Czar Mikhail, on the other hand, wasn't having a great time. He was in a room three doors down, having Salqam-Jangir Khan and the Zunghar representative, Qong Tayiji Jochi, lobby him to override the congress. And he wasn't going to do it.

"First off, I can't. The setting of the borders between states is the business of the congress."

"But, Your Majesty, we didn't have any say in the setting of those borders," the Zunghar complained.

Actually, Czar Mikhail thought the man had an excellent point, but not so good as to have Mikhail override congress when he was trying to establish the precedent that congress, not the czar, made the laws and set borders.

"But the congress has given the Zunghars lands that we could readily take," Salqam-Jangir Khan complained.

"That the Sovereign States could take, you mean," insisted Qong Tayiji Jochi. "Without Ivan the wizard and his war train, even Erdeni Batur would have won."

"That's rather beside the point," Czar Mikhail said. "The constitutional convention determined the borders of the state of Kazakh, and in a majority vote of the congress, they confirmed those borders. Neither of the consuls have seen fit to veto the measure, and neither will I. Not to give Kazakh territory to the Zunghars, nor to give Zunghar territory to the Kazakh."

"Your Ivan is busy," Qong Tayiji Jochi said belligerently. "If I don't get . . ."

He trailed off at Salqam-Jangir Khan's expression. It wasn't hostile or threatening, not exactly. Salqam-Jangir Khan was smiling. A very confident smile. Not worried in the least. "Qong Tayiji Jochi, even if Ivan and Tim were going to stay busy, which they aren't, the Zunghar alliance isn't there anymore. And none of the four clans that made up the Zunghars can individually stand against Kazakh. The only thing keeping me from taking all of your people's territory is the Sovereign States congress and my respect for their laws."

And that was when Mikhail realized that Salqam-Jangir Khan was on his side. The whole thing, the impassioned speech before congress, the insistence that the Zunghars should lose territory in recompense for their attack on Kazakh. He'd never expected any of it to do anything but keep the Zunghars from getting some of the territory that he'd claimed in the constitutional congress back.

"And considering he's setting up steam plants and aircraft factories in Shavgar, that's only going to become more true over time."

Qong Tayiji Jochi looked at them, and sighed. "Then I formally request admittance into the United Sovereign States of Russia with the borders as specified by the congress."

Czar Mikhail reached over and took Qong Tayiji Jochi's hand. "Done. Can you sell it back home?"

"I could have sold even worse terms back home. We had rather a lot of troops in the battle of the train. And the whole town saw the Hero land," Qong Tayiji Jochi said. "I'm to get the best deal I can. But, at *all* costs, make a deal."

"Maybe we should renegotiate—" Salqam-Jangir Khan started.

"And maybe we shouldn't," said Czar Mikhail repressively.

CHAPTER 26

𝕾urrender

Northeast of the **Filaret** *crash site*
January 30, 1638

The Rekaloban River was a creek and frozen besides. And there was forest on either side of it. Heavy forest with no cleared spaces for the range of the AKs to come into play. Ivan was looking at what might be the last cavalry battle in Russian history, and it was going to happen because everyone was out of position and ill-prepared.

And all because a damned snowstorm had blown through starting on the sixteenth and not letting up until the twenty-seventh. There were drifts three yards high and about two percent of his forces had suffered frostbite on hands or feet. And that was with excellent gear, fur lined boots, heavy coats, and gloves.

His force was mostly Kalmyks. The Kalmyks were steppe people like the Kazakhs. They lived on either side of the southern Volga and ranged widely. They'd had several representatives at the congress and were spread out among the city states along the Volga. They were also excellent cavalry who'd adopted the AK4.7 carbines and the six-shot revolvers being made in Ufa and Kazan with glee. They were disciplined in their way, as long as they respected their commander.

Ivan had been afraid that they wouldn't respect him, but after the battle of the train that wasn't a problem. This was a different situation, though. The tactics of the battle of the train wouldn't work. Instead, what he was forced to use were the tactics of the American colonials against the British. Guerilla war. Hide and snipe. Ambush foraging parties, then run away before the enemy could respond. This was exactly the sort of fighting that the Kalmyks excelled at and the armies of western Europe sucked at.

There was shooting in the distance. It started fast and furious, then built, and then cut off amidst angry shouting. By now Ivan could make a good guess at the course of the skirmish just from the sound. The Kalmyks were in hiding. They'd shot up one of Birkin's lead elements, then crawled back out of sight and ran for their horses. Meanwhile, Birkin's troops had emptied their rifles into the woods, hitting very damned little, until an officer managed to get them under control.

Ivan smiled. He had an excellent supply situation. Wagonloads of powder, shot, food, and drink coming up every day from Kazan. But Birkin's situation was different. Every bullet fired was one less they would have at the next battle. If it weren't for that damned airship, he'd just fall back to the walls of Kazan and let Birkin starve.

But he couldn't do that. Just like Kazan, Czar Mikhail had insisted that it was up to Tim. He remembered the radio telegram.

> To: General Lebedev
> From: Czar Mikhail
>
> *The dirigible named after my father would be of great value to our nation, both logistically and politically. However, I don't want the army risked. I leave it to your judgment whether we can afford to guard it until it's ready to fly.*
>
> *If in your judgment it is too expensive to protect, your orders are to destroy it.*

And Tim, the bastard, had left it up to Ivan.

> To: General Maslov
> From: General Lebedev
>
> *He's done it to us again, Ivan.*
>
> *Look, I know there probably won't be time, but do your best to keep Birkin's army away from it as long*

as you can. Every day he's trying to get to that darned airship, he's not running for Nizhny Novgorod, which is what he should have done the minute he got word that we were here. All we have to do is keep him busy out here until his food and shot run out, and he won't have an army.

Luck, Tim.

The snowstorm had helped, and pinprick raids using the Kalmyks had helped more, but the airship was less than twelve miles behind him, easy raiding distance. He still wasn't sure if he could save it.

Filaret *crash site*
January 30, 1638

Chief Petty Officer Valeriya Zakharovna was pushing a broom. The snowstorm had covered the top of the *Filaret* in snow and the airship was big enough that that amount of snow represented its entire useful load. So Valeriya and the rest of her crew were walking along the top of the dirigible, pushing snow far enough away from the top so that it would slide off. Other than that and the repairs the storm had made necessary, the *Filaret* was ready to fly.

Her foot slipped on the wet doped fabric surface of the dirigible, and she slid down fifteen feet until the safety line caught her. Her broom went flying and followed a small avalanche of snow down off the side of the *Filaret*. They were using brooms, not shovels, because they weren't going to risk ripping holes in the shell. Pulling hand over hand, Valeriya pulled herself back up to the railed top of the dirigible and went to collect another broom and get back to it.

In the captain's cabin, Captain Dimitry Ivanov sipped sweet hot tea from China and read a report. The captain's quarters on an airship were luxurious. And overall, he was quite pleased. They'd spent the last eight hours doing steam and function tests on the four engine nacelles. The *Filaret* had a modified design with two boilers, one fore and one aft. Each boiler ran two nacelles, which would provide directional thrust. The branches had been cut away in the first days, then they'd had to build a framework to keep the airship stable as the storm came through, blowing high winds and dumping snow on them. If they hadn't done that, the storm would have dragged them through the forest canopy and ripped the airship to shreds.

Dimitry Ivanov was a smart and well-educated man. He'd studied at the Dacha since mid-1632 and much of that time had been spent in the study of aircraft. He knew that airplanes, not airships, were the future of aviation. He knew it from that other history and knew it from grim experience in this history. But he didn't like it, for he loved the huge, spacious airships.

He finished his tea and the report, then got up and put on his uniform coat with the four rings of an airship captain, put on his cap, and went to the bridge.

"All right," he said as he got there. "Bring the boilers up to full steam and get Chief Petty Officer Valeriya Zakharovna and her crew back inside. We'll finish repairs in Hidden Valley."

Birkin's camp, fifteen miles east of crash site
January 30, 1638

General Ivan Vasilevich Birkin sat on a camp chair and sipped hot broth. He held the clay cup with both hands to warm them, and looked out at an increasingly ragged army. They were low on ammunition, and lower on food. The Heroes—villains from Birkin's point of view—had first identified, then bombed his depots. That had been less than fully successful. They missed more than they hit, but it had done enough to decrease his supplies from barely enough to not nearly enough.

But the real killer had been the storm. That had slowed everything down, and by now his army lacked food, shot, and fodder for the horses.

His scouts reported that Birkingrad was surrounded by a screen of *golay golrod*. They were set just outside artillery range so the forces in Birkingrad couldn't get to him, and he couldn't get to them. Birkingrad was kept quite well supplied by the iceboats on the Volga. So were Kazan, Ufa, and Perm. But not him. He considered surrendering just as he had considered it every day since the *Filaret* had crashed, but his wife and younger three children were in Moscow. His oldest boy was in Birkingrad with his cousin Iakov Petrovich. But Iakov Petrovich's wife and children were also in Moscow. So he wouldn't have a lot of choice if he got ordered to send Ivan Vasilevich's son back to Moscow for trial.

There was a shout, and he saw men pointing up. In the evening sky the *Patriarch Filaret* flew east over his camp at three thousand feet or more.

He looked around at the men in his camp, and realized that he might face a mutiny. His army was better than half Cossack at this point. Mercenaries hired by the government as more and more of the regular Russian troops had defected.

Mutiny. Suddenly Ivan Birkin smiled. It was a bitter and sardonic smile, but he smiled nonetheless.

That was his way out. He called over his staff, his few truly trusted staff, and two of the Cossack commanders.

Ivan Perebiinis, commander of Cossacks, was nervous about the summons. He knew what the dirigible meant as well as the Russian general. He was a registered Cossack out of southern Lithuania. And he was seriously thinking about taking his men and going back to Lithuania.

"Ivan." General Birkin waved him closer and he and the other officers leaned in. "I need you to do me a favor."

"What favor is that?" Ivan Perebiinis asked cautiously.

"I need you to mutiny, take me and these other officers prisoner, and turn us over to the Sovereign States army."

"What?" said another Russian officer.

"Think it through, Petrov. Think it through."

That was good advice, so Ivan Perebiinis took it. He thought about what it would mean. It would protect General Birkin because he didn't surrender his army to the Sovereign States. It would get the army fed, including Ivan Perebiinis' Cossacks. It would probably get Ivan Perebiinis a nice reward from the Sovereign States.

"And after I turn you over?"

General Birkin shrugged. "Take your men home. It's not like Ivan Romanov has your family hostage."

Ivan Perebiinis looked around the command council. Right now they were all shocked and considering it. They weren't ready to act, but give them time, and at least one of them would decide that their honor required them to refuse.

He pulled his pistol and pointed it at Birkin. "You're under arrest, General Birkin. The rest of you too." Then he looked around the little group. "He's right, gentlemen, and even if he's not, I'm committed now. So put your guns on the table or die."

It was two hours after dark that the party with white flags flying approached Ivan Maslov's camp. Ivan was busy getting his army ready to retreat back to Kazan. Not because he was afraid of Birkin, but because Birkin didn't matter anymore, not since the *Filaret* flew off east.

This, however, mattered. He sent a radio message to Ufa and to Tim in Perm, letting them know that he had some twenty thousand prisoners.

Perm
February 2, 1638

"I don't believe it," General Boris Timofeyevich Lebedev said as he passed the radio telegraph printout over to Anatoly Gregoro- vitch Stroganov.

"Why not? You've been singing the praises of your friend Ivan Maslov since you arrived here," Anatoly said. "I'm the one who shouldn't believe it." He looked back at the telegraph, then he looked at the maps in the half-rebuilt war room. "And, oddly enough, I *do* believe it."

"It's not that. I didn't think Birkin had the guts to surrender. Or the brains for that matter."

"Huh?"

"Moral courage. Not physical."

"He didn't. That Cossack, Ivan Perebiinis, captured him and surrendered the army."

"Without the army fragmenting?" Tim asked. "I don't buy it."

"Buy it?"

"It's an up-timer phrase translated," Tim said. "I don't believe the story that telegraph tells. Birkin's internal security is quite good. We wouldn't have known about the supply dumps if we hadn't been incredibly lucky."

"Yes. How was it that you and Maslov were scouting just in time to catch Birkin making his run? What were you looking for?"

"Why, a way to capture Birkingrad," Tim laughed. The secret

of the spy was still tightly held. So tightly held that he didn't know the details, aside from what Birkin was doing and the fact of the supply depots Miroslava Holmes had figured out. That and the fact that for political reasons Czar Mikhail had determined that no further action should be taken.

"What was that magical plan of yours to take Birkingrad?"

Tim grinned. "But, *tovarich* Stroganov, if I told you that, it wouldn't be magic." Then he laughed.

"You're not going to tell me?"

"Not for your weight in gold, sir," Tim said. Anatoly Gregorovitch Stroganov was a big man in his late fifties, going somewhat to fat. It would be a lot of gold. "Having a secret way to capture a walled and defended city is worth several cities. And once you tell someone, it's not a secret anymore. And the enemy can start figuring out ways of defeating it.

"In the meantime, we need to gather up every iceboat in the city and get them on the ice and on the way to Kazan."

"Why?"

"Because with Birkin out of the way, we can invest Nizhny Novgorod before the spring thaws."

"That's the war!" Anatoly Gregorovitch Stroganov said. He didn't sound happy.

"Not necessarily. Moscow is now thoroughly in the hands of the most conservative boyars, the sort who would rather see Russia burn than change. What it will do is deny Moscow access to the Volga." Moscow accessed the Volga by way of the Oka River. "And that we will be in a position to push northwest along the Volga, bypassing Moscow, and getting to the Swedish-held Baltic Sea. At that point, it won't matter much if Moscow surrenders or not. Not militarily, anyway."

"It will still matter politically," Stroganov said, but Tim could tell that wasn't what he was thinking about. Perm still wasn't a state in the United Sovereign States of Russia. It had let the Sovereign States come to their aid and defend their walls, but it had still refused to join, maintained its independence in an attempt to wrest a better deal from Ufa and Czar Mikhail. Mostly because the Stroganov family wanted Siberia as their tax farm. They wanted the wood, animal pelts, and ores from Siberia and they wanted, later when they had the drilling equipment, the Siberian oil fields that had been Russia's major source of income in the late twentieth century.

And Anatoly Gregorovitch Stroganov was looking at the map and considering the mission that Vladimir and Brandy were on. The Sovereign States of Russia were going to completely surround Perm for hundreds or thousands of miles in every direction, except through Tobolsk and Shein. And who knew how long Shein could hold out.

He looked at Tim and saw Tim looking at him.

"How long would it take you to take Perm, General, if you were outside the walls?"

"I wouldn't take it. I would just block it off from your mines. That's the source of your income. You would wither in a year. Probably less. You, personally, would probably be deposed by your family within a month or two."

"Moral courage, you said?" Anatoly asked. "What is my best move here, General, for my family."

Tim remembered that the Stroganov family had a branch in Moscow, very much under the thumb of Ivan Romanov and the boyar council. That part of the family included two of Anatoly's sons.

"The best thing you can do for this town, all the people living in it and all the miners and farmers surrounding it in smaller villages built around farms or mines, is to bring Perm into the Sovereign States. As for your family, those in Ufa are perfectly safe. None of them are hostages for your good behavior. If you order me and my troops out of the city, we'll leave. But you mentioned moral courage. Best for your people, even your family in the long run, is to join the Sovereign States. That, sir, is my honest opinion."

"I'll see about sending the iceboats to Kazan. Would you radio Ufa and ask them to send a plane to take me there?"

"Yes, sir," Tim said, and gave the order.

Ufa
February 2, 1638

Czar Mikhail read the radio telegraph and wondered where he was going to get another airplane. The ones he had were all busy. The Scouts were busy in Kazakh, scouting the eastern border. Three of the Heroes were also in Kazakh, shipping urgent supplies in both directions. Russia still had two seasons: winter and construction. The trains could travel on the ice, but the riverboats couldn't, and the iceboats carried a great deal less. So the Heroes were called into service. And he had two Heroes off in the back of beyond, exploring Siberia and in western Europe, trying to restore Russia's credit rating. And while they had two airframes ready to go, the holdup now was the steam engines. The boilers and condensers too, but mostly it was tooling the steam engines. "He wants me to send him a plane," Czar Mikhail complained to Evdokia. "And just where am I going to get a plane?"

"Use the *Princess Anna*," Evdokia said, "or, if it's ready, the *Filaret*."

"That's an excellent idea, my dear."

She looked up from the book she was reading. It was a romantic comedy set in an airship in the year 1658 and the airship was traveling from Ufa to the new Russian colony in America, located where San Francisco was in that other history. They had televisions in the lobby showing plays broadcast from Grantville and retransmitted all the way to eastern Siberia, where the dirigible was at this point in the story. "Yes, definitely the *Filaret*. And if the weather is going to be clear, we should take the children. Fly to Perm, pick up this Stroganov fellow, and then fly to Moscow." At Mikhail's look she added, "Staying well above cannon and rocket range. Ten thousand feet ought to be high enough. Then come home, which will have given us time to explain the situation to Stroganov. And by the time we land, Perm joining the Sovereign States will be a done deal."

The weather reports, by this time, were based on a solid network of radio telegraph stations which had weather stations attached. They went east into the Ural Mountains and farther in Kazakh, and west all the way to the Polish border. Both sides in the Russian civil war shared meteorological information with the other, because whatever the governments wanted, the farmers who lived around the individual radio stations wanted the information shared. Both Dachas, the one outside Moscow and the one in Ufa, issued daily weather reports that were about eighty-percent accurate out to two days. In other words, about up to World War II standards.

Mikhail picked up a phone. The royal residence had phones, and those phones went to the Ufa Dacha. They used an operator. "Please connect me to the weather department."

This was winter so the sun had set and everyone important

had gone home for the night. The clerk in the weather station wasn't expecting a call from the czar.

"Bureau of Politics. We tell you where the windbags are."

Mikhail laughed. "That's excellent. But for right now, I need to know what the latest report on the weather is for tomorrow."

"Ah, who is this?"

"The head windbag. Czar Mikhail."

"Ha!" came from Evdokia. "You haven't heard Senator Borgof pontificate."

It took Mikhail a few moments to get the clerk to calm down and a few more for the latest reports to be fed into the aqualator bank and a weather map to be printed on the dot matrix printer. Evdokia was back in her book by the time the clerk told Czar Mikhail that the weather tomorrow would be mostly clear with a light breeze from the southeast. "Excellent. Please forward copies of that report to Hidden Valley, General Tim in Perm and General Maslov in Kazan. Have a nice evening." He hung up and called the radio telegraph room, asking that a message be sent to Hidden Valley, asking about the readiness of the *Patriarch Filaret*. And if it was ready, seeing to it that it was sent to Ufa first thing in the morning.

Ufa
February 3, 1638

The dirigible hangar at Ufa was unfinished, but it had a mooring pole and stairs for loading and unloading. So it was bright and early on the morning of February 3 that Czar Mikhail, Czarina Evdokia, Princess Irina, Prince Alexi, Princess Anna, and Princess Martha were all waiting to board. The children were arguing about what the *Patriarch Filaret* should be renamed. Alexi and Irina because they'd been cheated out of theirs, and Martha insisting that since the last dirigible was named after Anna, it was her turn.

Their parents were mostly ignoring the argument since Mikhail didn't have any intention of changing the name. It was, after all, named after his father, whom he loved, even if he hadn't liked the man all that much.

The *Filaret* was docked and the ramp from the gantry to the passenger section of the *Filaret* was in place. They boarded as the children argued. It was a pleasant three-hour trip to Perm and a fairly tedious few minutes as they winched up Anatoly

Gregorovitch Stroganov. A chair attached by a hemp cable was lowered to the ground and Anatoly sat in it and belted himself in. Then the electric winch was engaged, lifting the chair to the height of the dirigible, where it was brought inboard and tied into place. At this point, a moderately frightened Anatoly Stroganov unbuckled and stood up, swaying a little. Mikhail, Evdokia, and the children were there to greet him.

They escorted Anatoly to the galley, a large dining area with many tables and angled windows so you could look out and down at the terrain. "I know that the airplanes are more efficient," Evdokia said with a sigh. "But I honestly much prefer the dirigibles. There is something glorious about sitting at a table having tea and little cakes as the world floats by beneath you. Don't you think so?"

Anatoly Stroganov had flown once before and he'd boarded the airplane that time while it was on the ground. Then he'd been in the plane the whole time, looking out a small window. This time he'd been sitting in the chair as it was winched up from the ground. In the open, just sitting there in the chair. And yet he was inside again, looking out large angled windows at the ground thousands of feet below them, in a quiet, comfortable room. It was terrifying, but not in any immediate way. It was the *idea* that was terrifying.

The czarina loved flying. She was as comfortable in the sky as on the ground. Seven hundred miles and a bit more travelling west-southwest with a trailing wind. But it was still after dark before they got to Moscow. They could see Moscow quite clearly. Seven years after the Ring of Fire, Moscow had electrical generators and strategically placed arc lights. If any people looked up, they might see the *Filaret*, but that was unlikely. This trip wasn't about being seen in Moscow. It was about letting Anatoly Stroganov see Moscow from the sky, so that he would understand the way the war was going. No, more than that, to make him feel it, feel it in his bones.

They had spent the day with Mikhail trying to convince Anatoly Stroganov that Perm should join the Sovereign States and be a free state. But in spite of the persuasive effect of the *Filaret*, Anatoly wasn't budging on that. Perm would enter the Sovereign States as a slave state.

Mikhail didn't like that, but he was now a constitutional monarch, not a dictator. It would be up to the congress and the congress had enough slave states so that it would accept Perm's preference. They'd be back to square one.

CHAPTER 27

𝕹𝖎𝖟𝖍𝖓𝖞 𝕹𝖔𝖛𝖌𝖔𝖗𝖔𝖉

Nizhny Novgorod
February 8, 1638

Nizhny Novgorod was of two minds. It had been of two minds since Czar Mikhail had sailed on a riverboat waving to the populace way back in July of 1636. But it wasn't thoughtful. It wasn't like Boris was of two minds or Ivan was unsure. No, Boris and Ivan were both quite confident in their opinions. Boris was terrified and Ivan was out for blood. Even before Czar Mikhail had escaped from the place he'd been held incommunicado and gone to Ufa, Nizhny Novgorod had been less than harmonious. It had had tensions before the Ring of Fire. At their base, those tensions were between the have-a-littles and the have-even-lesses. In a backwater like Russia in the seventeenth century, the number of actual haves was quite low.

The introduction of the Dacha had started to change that and there started to be actual haves in places like Nizhny Novgorod and the have-nots were getting enough so that they were actually able to look up from the plow and see the more that was coming into the world. That increased the tensions a lot. Especially when not all of the new wealth stuck to the hands of the already less impoverished.

So by the time Czar Mikhail steamed by waving, there were serious tensions between the new industrial wealthy and the old landed wealthy. When Birkin put a garrison in Nizhny Novgorod to make it the main supply base for the advance on Ufa, that garrison came down on the side of the old rich. Not the uppity new rich.

And the old rich had used accusations of witchcraft and

"treason," accusing the new rich of supporting the czar, not the Duma, then killed a bunch of them and stole most of their property.

But they couldn't kill all of them. First, there were too many, and second, a lot of them were skilled with the new machines and so too valuable to kill. Instead, they brutalized them, threatened their families, and made regular public examples. By the time Kazakh had become a state in the United Sovereign States of Russia, the hatred between Boris and Ivan made the Hatfields and McCoys seem the best of buddies.

It was still like that. A walled city with excellent walls, but with a population where about seventy percent hated the thirty percent who were running things. Then came the news of the mutiny in Birkin's ranks and the surrender of his army. It was at that point that the smartest of the haves of Nizhny Novgorod got out of town. They found excuses to go visit Moscow or just to visit the villages they owned outside town.

What were left were the dumb and the desperate, those with no place to go, and those who had convinced themselves that they'd been right in everything they'd done and justice would prevail.

Ivan Belochkin swept out the halls in the radio towers. His father had owned a factory that made leather goods before he'd been attainted for treason for supporting the czar. The family's property was seized, and his father executed by a drumhead court martial, while his mother was forced to take holy orders. He lived in a basement room and the girl he had been planning to marry was now the mistress of Boris Agapov.

The education his family had provided meant that he could read, and he did. He read every message he could that came in over the radio telegraph, when the soldiers weren't looking. Nizhny Novgorod's telegraph station had been taken over by Birkin's forces and was in the control of the army.

Boris Agapov was among the desperate. His family had been *deti boyars* before the Ring of Fire, and while they'd adopted some of the practical things, like the new plows and horse collars, they'd worked very hard to keep the peasants from getting out of control. The new industrialists introduced by the Dacha had been a threat to the stability of the nation. And when Birkin had arrived, his family cooperated with the authorities in cutting out the rot. In the process, factories and shops had come into the Agapov family's hands, making them quite a lot of money. Especially since those factories worked quite well by using serf labor, which was much cheaper than paying employees. Production might have gone down a bit, but profits were up.

What Boris was afraid of was what would happen if General Tim came to Nizhny Novgorod. By now it was acknowledged even among Birkin's forces that Boris Timofeyevich Lebedev was a military genius. If you thought about it, it wasn't even that much of a surprise. He was a member of an excellent family that had included boyars in it. Yes, it was Lebedev who was the genius, not the baker's son, Maslov.

All of which didn't protect them from the insanity of Czar Mikhail. Letting peasants vote? Crazy.

Boris wished every day that someone had shot Czar Mikhail when he'd steamed by on that riverboat. He shouted, "Bring me a vodka," and his mistress, Marta Vasin, did.

Marta Vasin was also from one of the new industrialist families that had fallen on hard times when Birkin arrived. Her family hadn't been executed. They had just lost a lot of their wealth. The wealth that would have made her a good marriage. Instead, she'd traded her virginity to save her family and lived in this small apartment that Boris kept. She put up with Boris. Most of the time he was a decent enough guy, and he liked to give her presents, new shawls and dresses, the occasional piece of jewelry.

He was better than that bastard, Ivan Belochkin, who she would have married if Birkin hadn't arrived. He'd called her a whore and threatened to cut off her nose and worse if he ever got the chance, after she'd thrown in with Boris.

The problem was if the news about Birkin's army was true, he was liable to get that chance. She still had most of the gifts that Boris gave her. He liked to look at them. She was well dressed when she went shopping or went to church, but her wealth wasn't all that portable. After Boris had his vodka and her, he went home to his wife, and Marta tried to remember what it had been like before Birkin came, when she thought she'd loved Ivan Belochkin.

When she'd loved herself.

Then she crawled into her bed and cried, then slept, while the world prepared to throw another monkey wrench into her life.

Outside Kazan
February 8, 1638

The army of Kazan was well trained, well equipped and had excellent morale. It had chaplains, both Russian Orthodox and Muslim. It had heavy winter cloaks and boots, AK4.7s with at least ten spare chambers for every man, and most had twenty or more. And by now it had a large cavalry contingent made up of Kalmyks. It also had a large infantry contingent who were marching up the Volga toward Nizhny Novgorod along the banks of the Volga. The iceboats scooted ahead and prepared camps for the marchers at noon and in the evening, setting up double-walled tents to keep the cold out. That speeded up the march. It didn't make marching through Russia in hard winter any fun, though.

And though the prepared camps made things faster, it still took the army of Kazan eleven long dreary days to reach Bor and cross the frozen river to invest Nizhny Novgorod.

That wasn't an altogether bad thing. It was plenty of time to recall the three Heroes and a Scout from Kazakh.

Outside Nizhny Novgorod
February 19, 1638

General Ivan Maslov saluted as General Boris Timofeyevich Lebedev stepped out of the Hero. "Welcome to igloo central, General," Ivan said, though in fact it was a tent city, not an igloo in sight.

Tim stepped down from the bottom wing of the Hero and shook Ivan's hand. "What are you seeing of Muscovy troops?" he asked quietly.

"You'd know better than I, sir," Ivan said even more quietly with a jerk of his chin at the Hero that Tim had flown in on.

"I didn't see any large masses of troops," Tim admitted. Then added with frustration, "Where the hell are they?"

There was no possible way to keep secret the movement of large masses of troops. Not with the radio networks in place. Moscow had to have known that they were marching up the Volga before they got out of sight of Kazan, and yet nothing. Where the hell was the Russian bear?

"Boss, I'm starting to think that M is right. I think every

trooper that Uncle Ivan can get his hands on is busy keeping
Moscow from going up in flames."

Moscow Kremlin
February 19, 1638

Assistant Secretary General Ivan Romanov thanked the gods that
he hadn't yielded to the very real temptation to take the crown
and become Czar Ivan Romanov. It meant that there was still a
chance of a rapprochement between him and Mikhail. Ivan knew
for a fact that the reason the boyars had selected Mikhail rather
than him was because he was too competent. They and the bureaus
hadn't wanted another Ivan the Terrible. They'd wanted a weak
czar that they could manipulate and that's what they'd gotten.

Until the Ring of Fire.

Mikhail had been manipulated first by his mother and her
family, then by Ivan's brother, Feodor Nikitich. Now he was being
manipulated by Bernie Zeppi, the Gorchakovs, and the knowledge
in the up-timer libraries. In Ivan's opinion, Mikhail was still a
weather vane, pointing in the direction of the most recent wind.

But the wind was blowing from Ufa now, straight at Moscow.
And it was looking to be one of those Russian storms that leaves
mountains of snow and anyone unprepared as a block of ice buried under the snow. Ivan had no intention of ending his life as an
icicle. He was going to have to make arrangements, but the rest of
the Boyar Duma could see the writing on the wall as well as he
could. And Ivan had one great advantage. He was Mikhail's uncle.
He had a better chance than anyone else in the Boyar Duma of
keeping them all alive. Even what was left of the Sheremetev family. Director-General Fedor Ivanovich Sheremetev was still missing,
and by now Ivan's sources were sure that he was either dead or the
unwilling guest of one of three Polish or Lithuanian magnates.

Ivan started making arrangements. He would need allies in
the Boyar Duma and especially in the army.

Outside Bor
February 20, 1638

Tim sat his horse easily, dressed in his fancy uniform with an
aide just at his left, holding up a large white silk flag with gold

trim. By now Bor had a population of about four thousand, almost two thousand of whom worked in the dirigible works. Many of those workers were women who were converting the intestines of thousands of cattle into goldbeater skin gasbags to fill with hydrogen and provide lift to dirigibles. It was good, steady, well-paying work. At least for the floor supervisors. A lot of the women actually doing the work were serfs or increasingly slaves from Nizhny Novgorod and points west. In spite of which, it was a surprisingly loyal and dedicated workforce. They saw the mighty airships they made, and they took pride in what they were creating, even though they held no official ownership in it.

On the other hand, Bor wasn't well fortified. It was fortified, but most of the fortifications were focused on Nizhny Novgorod across the river. Actually, most of what was expected to "defend" Bor was the fort just upriver from Kazan. The place known as Birkingrad. Bor was two hundred miles of hard riding from the front, after all.

It had been when the planning and fortifications had been put in place. Now, of course, they were looking at Mikhail's demon, General Tim, at the front of an army of ten thousand and more troops arriving every day.

The dirigible hangar was visible above the walls, a huge building that, like the dirigibles it housed, was mostly empty space. Still, it was an impressive sight.

The gates opened and a colonel came out, along with his aide, riding very good horses and carrying their own white flag. They were dressed in their best. And as they got closer, Tim recognized his cousin, Colonel Ivan Borisovich Lebedev.

"What are you doing here, Ivan Borisovich?"

"They needed someone familiar with technology to command the garrison here. And after what you did to me in Murom, I couldn't stay there."

His older cousin sounded bitter. He also sounded sober, which was surprising. "Ivan, I didn't do anything to you in Murom, except act in loyalty to Czar Mikhail."

Ivan Borisovich looked at him for a long moment, then nodded. And Tim was shocked. Ivan blustered. Ivan blathered. Ivan didn't bother to learn and never, ever, studied. Tim didn't know who this was, but it wasn't the Ivan Borisovich Lebedev he'd known all his life.

Finally, Ivan spoke. "Yes, I know. I knew it at the time. I just didn't know what to do."

"Do you know what to do now, cousin?"

"I have instructions from our grandfather, as it happens," Ivan Borisovich Lebedev said. "Those instructions don't match the instructions I received from the boyar council when I got this posting six months ago."

Tim grinned at that. Their grandfather wasn't a very nice man, but at eighty he still had all his faculties and lots of experience in living in a very tough neighborhood.

"Faced with overwhelming force, and unwilling to sacrifice the lives of innocent civilians for no purpose, I hereby surrender the city of Bor to the forces of Czar Mikhail." Ivan shook his head then. "You know, Boris Timofeyevich, I was shocked when Grandfather gave me my instructions on what to do in case you or the baker's boy showed up."

Well, maybe Ivan Borisovich hadn't changed *that* much. He still refused to call Tim Tim, and he still called General Ivan Maslov the baker's boy. Still, considering he was getting Bor without a shot being fired, Tim could put up with Ivan Borisovich being an ass when it came to his name.

After that it was straightforward. The garrison of Bor, about four hundred and fifty men, surrendered their weapons and were put on iceboats to go down the Volga to Kazan, where those who swore loyalty to Czar Mikhail would be given new jobs well away from Muscovite Russia.

Outside Nizhny Novgorod
February 21, 1638

Ivan Belochkin crunched across the ice on the Oka River. He reached the Czarist lines and was captured by two alert sentries. "I have a message for General Tim."

"That's General Lebedev to you," one of the guards growled, shoving Ivan with the butt of his AK. Ivan struggled not to fall, and yet he knew that if the butt of the rifle had been used with more force or less control he could well have broken ribs or a ruptured gut. They were being gentle with him. "General Lebedev then. But he's going to want to hear what I have to say."

It took an hour to get to see the general and by then the sun was up. There was no way for Ivan to sneak back into Nizhny Novgorod. So he spent the day in the general's tent, having everything he knew about the city brought out and added to a detailed map. He wasn't the only person being questioned. Dozens had slipped out, either by bribing guards as he had, or by knowing the guard schedule and making a run for it when they weren't looking. And that wasn't all. Until a couple of days ago, there'd been regular commerce between Bor and Nizhny Novgorod, and all those people were answering questions too.

There was, however, one piece of information that Ivan had and none of the rest did. Day after tomorrow, if the general agreed, the guards at the west gate would open that gate and let his forces into the city.

The general agreed.

Outside Nizhny Novgorod
February 23, 1638

The boots were wrapped in cloth to muffle the sound of men walking on icy ground as the thousand men of the Second Kazan Infantry battalion made their way to the gate. Their commander had volunteered them.

Faris Shamil was born in Kazan and his family had been forcibly converted to the Russian Orthodox faith in Ivan the Terrible's time. The conversion hadn't taken, and for all of his childhood and young adulthood, he'd been a secret Muslim, forced to drink wine and eat pork. When Czar Mikhail had allowed freedom of religion in Kazan, Faris had been thrilled. He'd started going openly to the mosque and discovered several things about himself. He liked wine and beer. He liked pork. He didn't like praying five times a day. And finally, and most disturbing, he wasn't convinced that the Koran had all of knowledge in it. He wasn't the only one.

In the year since General Tim took Kazan without firing a shot, the religion of Islam had fractured, and fractured again. Faris had found himself among the least orthodox of the Muslims in the Sovereign States. His father and brother were among the most. Faris preferred the army life. His battalion was mostly Muslim, but had over three hundred Russian Orthodox and five Ringers, the new religion based on the Ring of Fire.

It was a solid and cohesive unit that had spent most of last year defending the walls of Kazan and Faris knew better than to be wool-gathering in the moments leading up to a battle. But the truth was, Faris didn't think there was going to be a battle, at least not much of one. He believed Ivan Belochkin.

Ivan Belochkin walked up to Peter Ivanovich, the commander of the west gate. He'd talked to Peter Ivanovich before, and knew how frightened he was. The man could count, after all. He knew that with the Sovereigns holding Bor and having camps on the Oka, Nizhny Novgorod was cut off. And by now General Tim's reputation was downright scary.

"Peter Ivanovich, listen to me. You and your men need to put down your weapons and let us open the gates."

"I have my duty, Ivan."

"Duty to traitors. What about your duty to him?" Ivan pulled a banknote from his pouch. The face on the banknote showed Czar Mikhail Romanov in profile. The note was black, red, and gold ink on white paper, and in the corner it said 25 RUBLES. That was a lot of money. Ivan had received a backpack full of them when he'd convinced General Tim that he really was on their side. The money changed hands and so did the rifles. Then Ivan Belochkin and his friends, as well as some of the guards, cranked open the gates.

The first of Colonel Faris Shamil's soldiers passed through the gates, climbed the stairs, and found about twenty soldiers seated comfortably against a wall, their weapons stacked against the far wall. They held the west gate. Colonel Shamil's signalman used a battery-powered directional lamp to flash out a signal. "Gate ours." And the rest of the army, at least a good portion of it, repeated the Second Kazan Infantry battalion's march, also trying to be quiet about it. Meanwhile, most of Colonel Faris Shamil's men marched toward the Nizhny Novgorod Kremlin.

The Nizhny Novgorod Kremlin was built on a hill and had stone curtain walls, not the sort of walls that would protect you once the artillery was brought to bear, but perfectly adequate to prevent an infantry battalion from taking the place. Colonel Faris Shamil's job wasn't to take the place. It was simply to cut it off from the rest of the city. He did this by assigning platoon-sized units to the streets approaching the Kremlin.

It was while he was placing these units that everything went to hell.

✧   ✧   ✧

The guard on the walls of the Kremlin thought it was a mugging at first. Someone shooting at this time of night in the city not more than a couple of hundred yards away from his post had to be a mugging gone wrong. Then there were more shots, and he called his sergeant. There was more shooting from all around the Kremlin. Not everywhere, but in a number of places.

It took five minutes for the commander to be awakened and runners to be sent to the city's walls. The runners didn't come back. Then there were shots that grew into a firefight on the wall between the second and third outer bastion and all of it inside the outer walls. The fight didn't last long. But it lasted long enough and made enough light that the duty officer in the Kremlin could tell what had happened. Someone had opened the gates, at least one, and it was probably the west gate. There was no fighting there. From there the Sovereign States forces went north and south, taking the fortifications from the flank and rear, and with only scattered resistance. The guards on the walls were flanked and knew it. There were a few holdouts, and they died.

It woke the sleeping city.

Tim's troops never got out of control, but Tim's troops weren't the only people in the city. Nizhny Novgorod had been a powder keg for over a year, and it had only gotten worse. As soon as the populace realized that Tim's forces were in the walls, they decided that the best time to get their revenge was in the middle of a sack.

The populace of Nizhny Novgorod got out of control. They knew who'd managed the trials for treason and witchcraft, and while those people lived in the richest parts of the city, they didn't live in the Kremlin. The Molotov cocktail had been introduced to seventeenth-century Russia by the up-timers. And fuel oil had been traveling up the Volga all summer.

The richer parts of Nizhny Novgorod went up in flames and if the "innocent" got caught in the fire? Well, if they'd *really* been innocent, they wouldn't have been there.

Tim was caught completely unprepared. Townhouses and some warehouses burned in the weeks following the day-long riot. It was estimated that half a million rubles worth of damage was done.

Marta Vasin was lucky. Her apartment wasn't in the best part of Nizhny Novgorod. It was near it, but not in it. She heard the riot and could see the burning buildings out her window when she opened the shutters. And she was bright. She gathered what she could, dressed in her worst and least revealing clothing, and crept out of her apartment, down the stairs, and out onto the icy streets. By now the fires just to the southwest of the Kremlin were producing a lot of light, enough to reflect off the low clouds above the city.

She couldn't run with what she was carrying, but she walked as fast as she could, keeping to the shadows, and heading for the west wall. Her present protector was gone, or would be by nightfall, and her former lover was probably going to try to kill her if he ever found her. She needed a new protector, and it wasn't going to be anyone from the Muscovite side.

She'd gone several blocks when she had the bad luck to encounter a small group of men who were apparently taking the opportunity to loot the shops on the street she was traveling. She ducked back, but not in time. One of them shouted, and they were on her. Her hands were full with everything she owned wrapped in a bed sheet, and for just that vital moment she couldn't give it up. She'd earned those dresses and those jewels. So, for just too long, she tried to carry the sheet and they caught her. She threw the sheet at the first to reach her and started hollering for the watch.

There was no watch tonight. She hollered anyway, and they laughed and jeered.

Corporal Roman Ivanovich Kazakn heard the noise and alerted the sergeant. "Take your team, Roman, and check it out."

He led his team in the direction of the shouting at a trot, AKs at port arms. There was a man in the street looking into an alley, and as Roman and his men approached, the man shouted and ran off. There was shouting in the alley and Roman turned the corner to see five or six men running off, and a pretty, young woman with her blouse ripped open and a cut on her face leaning against the wall.

Roman had gotten chapter and verse from General Ivan Maslov, and his colonel, and his captain, and his sergeant on the penalties that he would receive if he went about looting and raping. And Roman's attitude was, if he wasn't allowed, no damned civilian was. He didn't think it out like that, not in the moment. He just brought the AK up and fired into the back of the one in the rear. That was the one who had stopped to pick up the sheet full of clothing and jewels. The bullet hit the man in the left shoulder, a crippling but not necessarily fatal wound.

It didn't matter. All five of his team followed suit. Three of them hit. The man was dead before he hit the ground. Roman fired again, and thought he winged another, but they were going around the corner and the squad didn't pursue. There was a half-dressed woman leaning against the wall, trying unsuccessfully to hold her blouse closed with her bloodied fists.

He kicked the body off the sheet bundle and the bundle came open, displaying dresses of good fabric in the new paisley pattern that had become so popular in the last two years or so.

He didn't figure this was the property of the rapist. He looked over at the woman and asked, "This stuff yours?"

She'd been looking at his team with fear. Now she looked at him, and something like comprehension came back into her face. "Yes, it's all I own."

Roman wasn't sure if he believed her. After all, the clothing in the bundle was a lot better than what she was wearing. "What were you doing out on a night like this?" It would be just his luck if he rescued a thief from the town watch.

"I was trying to get to General Tim's army."

"Well, you've done that," Roman said. "Luka, pick up this bundle. No souvenirs, mind, or I'll have your guts for garters. We'll let the officers sort this mess." He turned back to the woman. "Come along, ma'am. You're with the Second Kazan now."

They went back to his squad. The rest of that morning she spent with the squad, then around noon they all went to chow, and she was passed up the line. Confirming that she was most likely the owner of her property, it was returned to her, and she was sent along with several hundred other civilians across the frozen river to Bor. By the time she was having a plain meal of cabbage stew in Bor, news of the conquest of Nizhny Novgorod in just three days by General Tim was all over Russia and into Swedish and Polish territory. And, in Ufa, the celebrations had begun.

CHAPTER 28

Consequences

Ufa
February 27, 1638

The fireworks started before the sun had fully set. Czar Mikhail sat bundled up on a veranda located on the third floor of the still under construction royal palace and watched the fireworks with his wife and children. Filip Pavlovich Tupikov—who Czar Mikhail now knew wrote the Flying Squirrel pamphlets—his wife, Anya and a few others were also there. There was a starburst and the children oohed.

Mikhail looked over at his wife and said, "I think I am going to keep the capitol here in Ufa." His tone invited her opinion.

"We haven't won the war yet," Evdokia cautioned.

"Uncle Ivan isn't an idiot. He is quite capable of reading a map. The Muscovy River to the Oka, the Oka to the Volga at Nizhny Novgorod. We own Nizhny Novgorod. As soon as the ice melts, we'll own the Volga all the way to Rzhev. For that matter, we're going to own the Oka probably all the way to the Muscovy River. That means we own most of the Muscovy tax base, and most of the lands. And I'll tell you something else, my dear. Neither Bor nor Nizhny Novgorod switched sides willingly, so they and the territory they control will come into the Sovereign States as free states, whatever the owners of that property might want. And that will let the boyars and the *deti boyars* that follow them know that there is a cost to continuing to hold out against us."

It was a cold-blooded calculation, and every adult on the

304

veranda knew it. Not an explicit promise to let the boyars of western Russia keep their serfs and slaves if they switched sides willingly, but an implicit promise to leave the serfs chained to the land in order to end the war.

Filip Pavlovich Tupikov looked at the czar of all the Russias and said, "Your Majesty, I suspect that the Flying Squirrel is somewhere in the trees, listening to us speak."

"I'm sure of it, Filip," Czar Mikhail said.

"I don't think you're going to like the pamphlet he's likely to write. He will approve of making the states of Nizhny Novgorod and Bor to be free states. But the promise to leave Muscovite Russian serfdom in place? He's not going to like that one little bit."

"I don't like it either, Filip, but unlike that winged rat, I have a country to rule, and that means I have to make compromises sometimes." He shrugged. "Still, I doubt I'll assign Miroslava Holmes to ferret out the squirrel over this."

"She wouldn't anyway," Anya said. "She's quite fond of the squirrel, you know."

"As for me," Evdokia said. "I'll believe it when I see your Uncle Ivan bowing to you in the palace right here in Ufa."

It took rather longer for the news to get to the USE. Radios took it to the Don River and with Nizhny Novgorod again in friendly hands, one of the Heroes from Novgorod took the news the rest of the way by the southern route.

Grantville
March 3, 1638

Hans Josephson looked up as the computer beeped, afraid he was going to have to call in an up-timer to reboot the thing again.

The control tower at Grantville was by 1638 a modern place. It had its own tube radio complete with a computer. It was, however, an old computer. A Compaq Presario and it had occasional glitches. It did frequency-scanning across the approved aircraft radio frequency range. Also by 1638, the eight-bit-byte from up-time was standard. So were the basic handshake codes that computers use to talk to each other over the phone or radio. In other words, the Grantville control tower could recognize a "squawk," not that it got many. Most airplanes didn't have radios and the ones that did couldn't afford the weight or the price of an aqualator, much less an actual up-time computer.

So Hans' first thought was that Betsy was being fussy again and something had gone wrong. Not so. On the screen was a squawk notice.

Aircraft type: Hero
Aircraft number: 3
Aircraft Name: Valentina Vladimirovna Tereshkova
Aircraft location:
   N 50 33 37
   E 12 07 33
Direction: 289 Magnetic
Indicated airspeed: 103 mph

Right. Hans Josephson had been notified when they'd taken off from Prague a bit over an hour ago. They must have caught a tail wind. He tapped a key and the computer showed today's weather. There was indeed a high just east of Prague and moving west.

And now he remembered the Hero that Princess Natasha of the Sovereign States had arrived in, with her up-timer consort Bernie Zeppi. The Hero had aqualators like the Jupiters. They could and did "squawk," sending out digital signatures, including the name of the aircraft, the country of origin, the owner and the last input location. There were no satellites, so the locations were estimates punched in by the pilots.

The aqualators hadn't taken the role of a personal computer. One, they were too weak in terms of processing power, and two, they were much more difficult to program. Instead, they'd taken on more specialized roles. They could be "hardwired" with the liquid equivalent of ROM read-only memory, and as long as the individual aqualator was used for only a few standardized functions, they worked just fine.

Wanting to know how far out they actually were, Hans Josephson got on the radio.

Captain Irina Novikov had her headphones on as they approached Grantville Airport. Her flight engineer was busy with the fuel consumption readings and a slow steam leak that appeared to be in engine four, which was the left-side outboard engine.

So she heard, "Grantville ground control to Hero 3. Give your position and heading, over."

"This is the *Tina*," Irina said. "Heading 288 magnetic. Give us a minute on the position. I don't have landmarks. Will try a radio fix."

She turned to her copilot slash navigator, Gregory Petrov. "Get us a read from a couple of the repeater stations and plug them into Baby." Baby was the aqualator and it already had the locations of all the repeaters between Prague and Grantville. She'd picked them up in Prague. It took Gregory and Baby about forty-five seconds to get the two directions. They were approximate. The equipment worked, but wasn't as precise as Irina would have preferred.

Gregory Petrov plugged them into the computer and Baby updated their position. Gregory pushed a button and the *Tina* squawked her position again.

"Thanks, *Tina*," ground control said. "Did your General Tim really take Nizhny Novgorod in three days?"

"Well, it took his army eleven days to march there, but after that, *da*. Three days." She was speaking Amideutsch. It was the international language of aviation, because just about every text on how to fly or build an airplane was in up-timer American. And once they'd hit the radio network that centered on Grantville and Magdeburg the news had raced ahead of them.

The air traffic controller kept her occupied with stories of Nizhny Novgorod's conquest until they landed.

Prince Petr Ivanovich Odoevskii's father was, right now, sitting in the Boyar Duma in Moscow. His grandfather had been the exchequer when Filaret was running things from behind Mikhail's throne. He was about as noble as it got, barring being the czar. At least as Russians counted such things. His father had instructed him to defect to Czar Mikhail in 1636, and he'd been placed in the Embassy Bureau and on February 27, two hours after the news that Nizhny Novgorod had fallen, he'd been assigned as the new ambassador to the USE.

From Petr's point of view, it had been horrible timing. Petr had a girlfriend and she would be staying in Ufa. Still, duty was duty. And he was a Russian noble. What made it worse was he had a handler. Czar Mikhail had informed him that should he feel it necessary, Lavrenty Belikov could relieve him of duty. Lavrenty Belikov was one of those old Embassy Bureau types, the sort of bureaucrat that knew where all the bodies were buried, mostly because he'd buried them himself. He, like Prince Petr Ivanovich, was in the Embassy Bureau. And, like Petr, had been sent to the plane with very little notice on the twenty-seventh.

"What do you think?" Prince Petr Ivanovich asked the balding little man with the gray beard.

"I think we should check in with Princess Natasha and the up-timer," Lavrenty Belikov said.

Petr knew from experience that Lavrenty never referred to Bernie Zeppi or Brandy Bates by their names. They were "the up-timer" and "the up-timer woman."

They were down now, so Petr called the cockpit and asked about Bernie Zeppi and Princess Natasha.

"Let me check with the tower."

There was a shortish pause, then the captain came back on. "They're in Denmark. In the capital, that apparently King Christian IV has named after himself. And the rumor among the radio operators is that he wants to buy the Hero they arrived in. Or at least he wants to buy a Hero. Bernie and Natasha were using the Hero to make a grand tour of the capitals of Europe or some of them."

Petr and Lavrenty's mission wasn't nearly as well stocked with gold and silver as the first one, but it was well funded. So, after getting in touch with Natasha and Bernie, they took over Vladimir's home outside of the Ring of Fire to use as their headquarters. Then they got on the radio telegraph system and contacted Magdeburg and King Gustav's government, asking that the Muscovite Russian ambassador to the USE have his accreditation removed.

They got the runaround. The news that the Sovereign States had taken Nizhny Novgorod was met with surprise and a fair amount of consternation. The crowned heads of Europe had found a Russia torn by internal strife to be convenient. And they weren't willing to give that up.

They'd been too busy with their own wars to take any real advantage of the situation, but the possibility of gaining territory or even just trade concessions from one side or the other had appealed to them. And, in fact, the USE had been getting excellent prices for mica capacitors from Muscovite Russia, while the Ottomans had been buying copper and steel from the Sovereign States at excellent prices. Sweden was holding on to the Baltic coast of Russia with a death grip. That meant that the government of the USE wasn't in any hurry for the revolution in Russia to be over.

Petr and Lavrenty spent their days being shuttled from one bureaucrat to another, while Bernie and Natasha visited the crown heads of Europe.

Kristiania
March 3, 1638

King Christian IV of Denmark looked at the airplane firebox with great interest. Bernie and Natasha didn't object. For a variety of reasons, the decision had been taken at a very high level in the Sovereign States that the design wasn't to be kept secret. So after the king had looked at the firebox and the boiler, they removed a panel from under the skirt so that His Majesty could see the condenser. Bernie explained that part of the reason that the condenser worked was because of all the space that the ACLG provided for it. And the fans forced generally cold air over the coils of the condenser also helping the condenser work, while, at the same time, warming the air that flowed into the skirt of the ACLG.

King Christian crawled out and took a beer skin from a handy porter. He took a healthy swig, wiped his mouth, and asked about the flight controls. Bernie was again impressed by the mindset of the seventeenth century. In this world, people—at least rich, well-educated people—were convinced that they could learn everything there was to know. Christian had designed cities and ships even before the Ring of Fire. He didn't see any reason he couldn't design airplanes too. Nor did he accept the idea that there was anything too complex for him to understand.

To a surprising extent, that belief let him do just that. He did seem to follow the many interconnected systems that made up the airplane, while at the same time trying to figure a way to get around Gustav so that he could open up direct trade with Russia.

Handing the beer skin back to the servant, he asked, "Now that you have Nizhny Novgorod, how close can you get to the Baltic Sea? I may not own any coastal land, but I own ships. And this baby"—he patted the Hero affectionately—"doesn't need land to land on. A ship in the Baltic could refuel it. Avoiding Gustav's territory by flying over it."

It isn't a bad plan, Bernie thought, *whether it will work in practice is another matter.* For that matter, Gustav might argue that flying over his territory didn't relieve the airplane of the duties owed to Sweden. But all of that was going to have to wait for summer to discover, because simply due to the weather, it was unlikely that any more territorial gains would be made before the spring flooding had passed. And even if it worked, and *was* legal, it was still going to annoy Gustav Adolphus, and Denmark was still part of the Union of Kalmar.

On the other hand, Bernie suspected that that was half the reason King Christian IV liked the idea. He still resented the fact that Denmark had been forced to the junior role in the League of Kalmar. In spite of the fact that his younger son was engaged to Christina and would be effectively the next emperor after Gustav, since Christina was unlikely to be interested in the nuts and bolts of rulership. But King Christian had an ego to match his intellect. He was quite sure that he could run just about everything better than the people who were running it now. Which made him a great deal like King Gustav, and quite different from Czar Mikhail. In Bernie's considered opinion, a worse monarch. Mikhail listened, while, all too often, people like Christian, Gustav, and even Mike Stearns, didn't.

Bernie explained again that Russia wasn't selling any of the Hero-class airplanes to anyone. Not because they were unwilling, but because they didn't have enough for their own use yet. "We're making them just as fast as we can, Your Majesty. But Russia has a great deal of ground to cover. And it's going to be decades before we have enough steel for even a single rail line to the Pacific. Even if we make a deal with the Qing to build part of it. Which is problematic because the Ming and Qing are fighting for control of China, Czar Mikhail has no desire to get into the middle of that mess."

"But Russia still intends to rule all of greater Siberia to the Pacific coast?" King Christian sounded doubtful.

"Not exactly," Bernie said. "Czar Mikhail meant it when he gave most of the governing power of the United Sovereign States of Russia over to the people of those states. The idea is to include the people of Siberia, not conquer them."

King Christian snorted in disbelief, which Bernie understood. But while he understood Christian's snort, he didn't agree with it. Bernie had known Czar Mikhail for years now and he'd been in the constitutional convention and the private meetings leading up to Brandy and Vladimir's exploration trip to the east. If Mikhail had anything to say about it, the lands between the Ural's and the Pacific were going to become *states*, not *conquered territories*. And to Bernie's mind that made all the difference.

A messenger arrived with a radio telegram. Bernie read it and said, "I'm sorry, Your Majesty, but I have been called back to Magdeburg and will probably be going back to Moscow from there."

Bernie passed over the telegram.

"Well, since you have another plane you can sell me this one," Christian said happily.

Bernie sighed, looked the king of Denmark in the eye, and said, "No."

"That isn't a word that is used with kings, Bernie." King Christian overdid the menace enough so that Bernie was pretty sure it was a joke. But not *entirely* sure.

"I use it all the time with Czar Mikhail," Bernie said with a smile. "He doesn't seem to mind."

Magdeburg airport
March 3, 1638

As the *Lydia* skimmed along the runway and pulled up beside the *Viki*, Natasha saw Captain Irina Novikov showing Princess Christina around the *Viki*. Not surprisingly, she'd shown the princess around the *Lydia* when they'd visited Magdeburg before. King Christian was unlikely to get a Hero anytime soon, but if Gustav was willing to provide a Russian port on the Baltic, Princess Christina might well get one. Natasha had spent enough time lobbying the princess and the future prince consort on that issue the last time they were here.

Christina was in favor because she wanted her own airplane. Ulrich was considering the issue as a way of avoiding a war between Sweden and Russia, which *would* happen if Sweden continued to restrict Russia's access to the Baltic and therefore trade with the rest of Europe, especially the USE.

The fans stopped and the *Lydia* settled to the ground. Natasha unbuckled her seatbelt, and she and Bernie exited the plane to be met by Prince Petr Ivanovich Odoevskii.

"Princess Natasha." He bowed. "Bernie." He nodded.

"Pete." Bernie nodded back.

Natasha sighed.

The sun was setting in the west and there would be no more flying today.

Petr leaned in to Natasha and whispered, "We've been getting the runaround on the matter of the Muscovite Russian ambassador since we got to Magdeburg. Don't they realize what the taking of Nizhny Novgorod means?"

"Drop the matter," Bernie said, not whispering but quietly. "Of course they know what it means. At this point, they are just using him as a bargaining chip. And Czar Mikhail isn't spending political capital on that. We need all the capital we can get to get a trade corridor through Swedish-controlled Russia."

"Have you offered them freedom of religion?"

"Of course," Natasha said. "The Swedes don't want freedom of religion. The peasants are all Russian Orthodox. They've been converting by the sword since they took over and freedom of religion means they won't be able to do that anymore."

"Well, that's a *casus belli* right there," Petr said.

"Sure, but a war with Sweden means a war with Gustav, who is the captain general of the SoTF and the emperor of the USE. And we don't want a war with the USE. The politics of central Europe are the same sort of interlocking alliances that led to World War I."

"You don't speak for the czar, Bernie," Petr said. "I'm the new ambassador to the USE."

"Not for long," Bernie said. "Not if you start a war with Gustav."

"Settle down, gentlemen," Natasha said. "However, I'm afraid Bernie is quite correct on the czar's intent with regard toward Sweden and King Gustav. Aside from the fact that the civil war has cost Russia a great deal of wealth and military strength, Czar Mikhail is something of a fan of Gustav. There may be a war if Gustav remains intransigent on the matter of Baltic ports, but not for the next ten years anyway. Russia needs to recover her strength."

The conversation ended as Princess Christina and Irina Novikov came over. After that, they talked about the two Hero-class airplanes, how they differed and how they were the same.

The next morning, Gustav accepted Prince Petr Ivanovich Odoevskii's credentials as ambassador to the USE, the Union of Kalmar, and Sweden.

Three hours later, the *Lydia* was in the air again, heading for Grantville on her way home to Russia. As they took off from Grantville the next morning, Bernie wondered how Vladimir and Brandy were doing in the wilds of Siberia.

CHAPTER 29

𝕾𝖎𝖇𝖊𝖗𝖎𝖆

Yakutsk
March 4, 1638

Brandy saw the *ostrog* from the air. Vlad was piloting and she was navigating. The *ostrog* was a small fort made of logs. It was a bit like Ufa had been when they'd arrived, but even smaller. They were flying at about seven thousand feet. She saw the river first. The Yana River was frozen, a shiny strip through the forest.

When the Hero landed, they were met by a Cossack named Pyotr Beketov. They knew who he was, though. He'd been sent east in 1631 before the Ring of Fire had happened. Vladimir had actually met him once in 1626. He was sent out here to collect taxes from the Buryats, a Mongolian people of eastern Siberia. He had a working relationship with the locals, speaking their language. At the same time, he was out here as a tax collector, and those taxes were furs, as well as copper and whatever gold or silver the locals had or could get hold of. Tax collectors are never the most popular of fellows.

He showed them the warehouse in the *ostrog* that would grow into the city of Yakutsk, or would have in that other timeline. He wasn't all that thrilled about their mission. He was out here to collect tribute from the local tribes, not to invite them to join the Sovereign States. Which hadn't even existed when he'd established the fort in 1632. In fact, he'd never even heard of the Sovereign States. The last he knew, Filaret was still managing the empire for his slow-witted but kindly son.

In spite of which, he gathered together the local chiefs and

314

they held a little state convention, and sent off a delegation to see about joining the Sovereign States. The tribal leaders decided to join after a couple of airplane rides. But it still took time to work out the details of their proposal. Brandy and Vladimir weren't waiting for the chiefs' deliberations. They were going to see the Pacific.

Ostrog Yakutsk had plenty of charcoal. The Aldan River was just under two hundred miles southeast of Yakutsk. A refueling station there, manned by a couple of Beketov's Cossacks and a couple of natives, was established, then they spent two more days taking extra sacks of charcoal to the refueling station. Basically it was a tent and a lean-to filled with charcoal next to a river. A marked place for them to land, take on charcoal, and fly out again. With just enough people there to make sure that there was always plenty of charcoal in the lean-to.

One more refueling station after that, and they had a workable plane route from Yakutsk to the Pacific coast. They hit the Pacific coast where the Ulya River did.

This turned out to be very useful, in that the three fueling stations between Yakutsk and the Sea of Okhotsk allowed them to fly from Yakutsk to the Pacific in just under one day. That impressed the heck out of the native tribes.

Back among the tribal leaders at Yakutsk, they discussed the airplanes and their effects. Brandy was telling Pyotr Beketov, "There will be more planes coming over time. And sooner or later—probably sooner—we're going to put a port somewhere around here," and Pyotr translated. "So there will be goods from the Pacific and from Ufa, and even eventually Moscow, flowing through Yakutsk, and markets for your goods."

Yakutsk
March 14, 1638

When they took off they had Pyotr Beketov with them as the delegate from Yakutsk. The natives didn't love Pyotr. A lot of them hated him. But they did, in a strange way, trust him to do what he said he would, and he'd agreed to get them the best deal he could.

They still didn't take much. Fuel, especially wood, took up room and lifting capacity in a way that fuel oil didn't. But they had completed their mission for Czar Mikhail. They had mapped a route from Ufa to the Pacific Ocean. Actual settlements would wait for later missions and a rail line would wait for a much larger and stronger industrial base than Russia had. Until then, it was going to be airplanes and that was an incredibly small pipeline to ship the goods of a nation through.

Vlad and Brandy talked it out. The Siberian expansion wasn't a failure. Twenty or thirty years from now, it would be invaluable to Russia. Little Mikey might well take a train to the Pacific coast, if not on his honeymoon, certainly by his twenty-fifth anniversary.

But for right now, even for the foreseeable future, the Sovereign States' access to the West was going to have to be through the Baltic. They would just have to tell Czar Mikhail that when they got back.

CHAPTER 30

𝕽esolutions

Ufa
March 14, 1638

The iceboat docked at Ufa and Nikita Ivanovich Romanov stepped down onto the docks. He checked his USE-made pocket watch and looked around. Nikita was clean shaven and dressed in a combination of German and up-timer clothing. His coat was down-filled; it wasn't polyester; actual up-time-made polyester was impossible to get. So Nikita had had to make do with silk. But it was a very tight weave, and almost as "wind breaking" as polyester would be. At least, the experts in the Dacha insisted that it was. He meant the *real* Dacha, the one located outside Moscow. So his coat did an excellent job of keeping his body warm, even though the temperature was 5 degrees below freezing. His boots were brown leather lined with fox fur, as were his gloves. And his shaved face was protected by an angora scarf.

The place was busy. Nikita had to give it that. Also the docks were well-made hardwood and mostly ice free. Whether that was because of salting or the constant heavy traffic, he couldn't tell. Instead of pondering the matter, he set off down the docks looking for a cab. He found one pulled by two Russian ponies. Fifteen minutes later he was dropped off outside the palace. There were guards. He walked up to one and said, "I'm here to see Cousin Mikhail."

"Cousin?" the guard asked.

"Czar Mikhail Romanov, my cousin." In point of fact, Nikita looked rather a lot like his older cousin Mikhail. Both were dark-haired stocky men, though Cousin Mikhail was eleven years older and his face showed more lines.

And finally, Nikita liked his cousin. He hadn't been fond of

Filaret. A more hidebound old curmudgeon than Filaret, Nikita never wanted to meet. But Mikhail had always been nice to him. Ineffective, but nice. Always under the thumb of one of his more forceful relatives and now, to hear Father tell it, under the influence of the Gorchakovs and the up-timers.

Nikita was coming to believe that that influence was a good influence. His father didn't share that opinion. He didn't in fact know that it was Nikita's opinion.

The door guard called his sergeant and in due time, Nikita was allowed entrance and escorted to an office. The door opened and Mikhail waved him in. "Come in, Nikita. What brings you out of your imitation Western Europe?"

Not only was Nikita clean shaven, he insisted that his servants and retainers were clean shaven and dressed in Western styles. He had paintings and knickknacks in the style of the West and since the Dacha had been established, he'd been collecting equipment and knickknacks from the Ring of Fire. He had three Barbies, a Spock doll and one of the only three in the world 16-inch Michael Jordan dolls. He also had over ten thousand serfs on his lands. Or, at least, he had had that many serfs before Mikhail's Emancipation Proclamation.

It was those serfs and the land they farmed and forested that allowed him to buy the various toys he enjoyed and to turn his private estates into an imitation of the West and, since the Ring of Fire, an almost imitation of Grantville. He didn't have a microwave, but he did have a generator, record players, electric heaters and other such devices.

"Father sent me to insinuate myself into your councils and try to persuade you back to the path of reason," Nikita said.

Mikhail laughed aloud.

"Officially, I have defected."

"In that case, were you supposed to tell me that first part?"

"Probably not, cousin. But the truth is, I'm not as convinced as Father is, that you've been led astray by the up-timers."

"You know why kings are so resistant to giving up power?" Mikhail asked.

"Yes, Your Majesty. It's what happened, or would have happened to Czar Nicholas II, in that other timeline."

"And what's happened to any number of other kings throughout history who just seemed weak," Czar Mikhail agreed. "And what your father's buddy, Sheremetev, had in mind for me. But a constitutional monarch might get fired without getting executed."

"I don't think that's it," Nikita said.

Mikhail looked surprised, then waved at him to go on.

"Lebedev didn't take Kazan. *You* did. And you did it by flying there in the *Czarina Evdokia* and then walking into Kazan with very few guards to convince them to join your side.

"Then you got back in the dirigible and visited cities from the Caspian Sea to the Ural Mountains to convince people to trade with you and send delegates to the constitutional convention. When Birkin went after Perm, you got in one of the Heroes and *flew* to Perm. There you persuaded Stroganov to go with you, then you did the next best thing to landing at Birkin's supply dump, getting out and counting the canned pork."

"Hardly that, Nikita," Mikhail laughed. "You have apparently learned to flatter. Father never thought you would."

Nikita felt his face go stiff at the mention of Patriarch Filaret. "I never saw anything in your father worthy of flattery."

Mikhail just looked at him, and after a few tense moments, Nikita went back to his earlier point. "You're not a coward, Mikhail. A coward would have assigned someone to go to Perm and Kazan. There's another reason. There must be."

There was another reason, though Mikhail wasn't sure that he knew how to express it. At sixteen he honestly hadn't felt that he'd had the right or ability to rule a nation. At this point in his life, he doubted that *anyone* had that right *or* that ability. And he *knew* from the experience of the last year that the more ideas in the room the more likely you were to find one that would work. Often those ideas were ones that he hadn't liked when they'd first been proposed.

He changed the subject. "What does your father want?"

"The best deal he can get," Nikita said. "He can read a map, Mikhail. So can the other members of the Boyar Duma. At least those that aren't blinded by their anger."

"How many of those are there, Nikita?" Mikhail asked.

"Too many. I'd guess about half will keep fighting until they are killed or captured. That includes the Sheremetev family, by the way." Nikita shook his head. "Down to the last baby born, the best I can tell. And it's not just the boyars. At least a third of the service nobility will die before they will give up their serfs. Even if you offer to pay them."

In Muscovite Russia, the system of paying service nobility in land and the peasants to farm it was still in full swing. In the Sovereign States, bureaucrats and soldiers were paid in cash. Paper money issued by the national bank. Though most of them had owned land back in Muscovite Russia and got land deposits in the bank based on their rank, they didn't get the serfs to farm it. So they ended up having to either make a deal with former serfs to farm it, or take the land in cash and invest or live on the cash. At this point, a good number of them were living "paycheck to paycheck," as Bernie put it. Others had gotten filthy rich. "What about you, Nikita? Your family owns a lot of land and a lot of serfs."

Nikita grimaced. "We've had a lot of runaways. The new tools, the new plows and seeding machines have helped but not enough. A lot of fields went fallow last spring and more will go fallow this spring. Also, a lot of wild pigs running around are causing mischief, and ending their lives in a peasant's stewpot rather than as salted pork on a ship to Sweden." Russia had been a major exporter of wheat and other foodstuffs to Sweden even while Russian peasants starved.

Sheremetev's government had continued that tribute, which was a large part of the reason that Sweden was accepting the Muscovite Russian ambassador as legitimate, in spite of the recent military gains of the Sovereign States. That meant that there had been food riots in Moscow and even more serfs running away east, meaning more fallow fields and less grain available.

There was a knock at the door, and Mikhail said, "Come."

The door opened and Natasha Gorchakov came in, followed by Bernie Zeppi. "Hello, Nikita. Why aren't you under arrest?"

"Why, I'm coming over to your side. To keep my lands," Nikita said. He smiled a smile that looked a lot like Mikhail's.

Natasha snorted in disbelief. Natasha and Nikita were age-mates, closer to age-mates than Natasha and Mikhail, anyway. Still, most of what she knew about Nikita was from Evdokia, who called him a horsefly. "Always buzzing around looking for a place to bite or a plate of food to ruin."

"Do you believe him, Your Majesty?"

"Yes, actually, I do. Come in, Natasha. We were mostly catching up on family matters. I hadn't started the debriefing yet."

"Debriefing?" Nikita asked.

"Over the next few days, you're going to tell me and certain members of the Embassy Bureau everything you know and everything you think about what's going on in Muscovite Russia," Mikhail said. "As well as anything you know about my uncle's military location, morale, supply, everything. It will then be correlated with other sources, which will tell us how valid it is."

"I don't actually know that much. Father gave me a briefing before he told me to defect, but I don't know most of it from personal knowledge."

"Your father—" Natasha started.

"Yes, Natasha. Try to keep up," Mikhail said, smiling. "Uncle Ivan is looking for a way out and Nikita here is his emissary."

"I have a couple of questions of my own. We heard through the radio network that you've opened up an air route to the USE? Is that true?"

Natasha looked at Mikhail and he nodded, so she said, "Yes. We just got back a few days ago. As more planes are built, there is going to be a regular flight schedule, and airports no more than a hundred and fifty miles apart. Probably less, because we want to tie in the weather stations we have with those in the west. And that means we are going to need radios within contact range."

"What is contact range?" Nikita asked.

"It depends on the radio," Bernie said, "the position of the antenna, and the shape of the antenna. If you get a good directional antenna so that your signal loss is less, you can have them reach over a hundred miles even with the crappy tubes made down-time. But a system like that needs a crew to operate it. You need generators, batteries, aqualators with tuning modules. The installations that have any real reach aren't cheap.

"The good news is even though you want your radio on the top of a hill or a mountain, you can often put your airport near it. Which aids navigation and makes supplying the radio telegraph station easier. That was part of what we were doing on the way home. What we are going to be doing over the next few months is transporting equipment to the airports and radio telegraph stations along the route between Ufa and Prague."

"Prague? What about Grantville?"

"We've made a deal with Royal Dutch Airlines. They are going to set up regular flights from Grantville to Prague. Actually, Magdeburg to Grantville to Prague, and back. We'll be carrying passengers along our route from Ufa to Prague. With a stop in Kolozsvár, where Gretchen Richter has been made Lady Protector of Transylvania."

"Gustav ate Transylvania. Is he trying to conquer the world?"

Bernie grimaced. "I think he might well want to. We don't want a war with the USE, but I'm not at all sure that His Imperial Majesty is going to give us any choice."

"That's why Vlad and Brandy are out east," Mikhail said. "If we are going to expand, that's the direction open to us."

Ufa
March 29, 1638

The Ufa River was still frozen when Vladimir landed on it and taxied to the hangar next to the tower. The plane was looking a bit ragged, but it was still flying well. It had been a rough couple of months, but they were back. And, with them, they brought Pyotr Beketov, who was acting as the representative of the eastern tribes. Pyotr wasn't a great flier. He'd spent the first couple of days with his hands clamped to the chair arms from takeoff to landing, only removing them to empty his gut into the airsick bag.

He was less frightened by it now, but he still got airsick. On the upside, he had rare furs, some gold, and quite a few jewels either collected by the natives or bartered for with the Chinese to the south. It wasn't the full tax train that would be coming by pack mule, and would take most of the summer to get here, but it was a sample. More importantly, he brought a proposal.

Ufa Kremlin
March 30, 1638

Pyotr Beketov was making a fairly good showing of himself as he sat in front of the States Committee. "The confederated tribes are concerned about the Qing, and want to join the Sovereign States as a state, 'Eastern Siberia.' It will stretch from the Sea of Okhotsk to the Arctic Ocean, and west to the Vilyuy River."

The capitol building was located in the Ufa Kremlin. It was a domed building and the paint was dry, but there was no doubt that it was new. For one thing, it used a lot of concrete in its construction. But it had paintings on the walls and statues in the mezzanine. This room was one of the offices located in the south wing. It had a high ceiling with an electric fan hanging from it. The fan was off at the moment, but it was still as impressive as heck to a man whose only experience with electricity had been in the last couple of weeks. Still, Pyotr was doing well. He was presenting the case of the tribes clearly and as favorably as he could.

Brandy watched as he presented the case of a united people condescending to join out of a reasonable concern. What was really out there were a bunch of tribes that disliked each other rather a lot, and were terrified that the Qing might turn north instead of south, as they did in that other timeline. There were good reasons for the Qing to do that. The other reason that most, but not all, of the tribes in Eastern Siberia wanted to join the Sovereign States of Russia was that they wanted to grab as much land for themselves as they could and were afraid that if they didn't join, other tribes could and would claim their territory.

Unfortunately for Pyotr Beketov, the States Committee, which was the initial point that a prospective state presented its case, was made up of representatives of states that already existed. And many of those states had pulled exactly the same shit that Eastern Siberia was trying to pull.

The questioning started gently enough about how many tribes were in the confederation and how many tribes occupying the territory weren't. Then they got into how much of the land in the proposed state of Eastern Siberia was going to be owned by the state of Eastern Siberia and how much by the federal government. Also, how much was owned by individuals.

Turned out that not a lot was owned by individuals. It was mostly owned by tribes, and if that was the case, the federal government of the Sovereign States should, in the committee's opinion, own quite a bit of it.

About an hour in, Vlad and Brandy left the meeting. They knew that Pyotr Beketov's instructions from the tribal leaders was to make the best deal he could, but make a deal. They really were terrified of gunpowder-armed Qing armies eradicating them on their way to the north. Vlad and Brandy had done all in their power to instill that fear in them.

Fifteen minutes later, they were in the czar's living room in the palace. The czar and czarina were there, and there was coffee from Turkey and tea from China, as well as French pastries with orange marmalade from North Africa. Brandy warmed her hands on the fire, then picked up Mikey and sat him on her lap. Little Mikey immediately wanted down. He was still angry at them for leaving him for months.

"So, how's it going in the committee?" Evdokia asked.

"Well enough. Unless the committee gets really stupid, we'll have a new state of Eastern Siberia in the next six months or so. After that, I suspect we'll get a petition from Western Siberia and then General Shein."

"General Shein has already applied for statehood," Czar Mikhail said. "We got the news two days after Tim took Nizhny Novgorod. It will be going before the full congress in a couple of weeks and is expected to pass with no more than a few rude comments. Mangazeya is also applying for statehood, mostly so that Shein won't annex them."

"That gives us a port on the arctic ocean at lease for a couple of months a year. And from what you've been saying, we're going to have a port in the Pacific?" Evdokia asked.

"Technically, yes," Vladimir said.

"But *practically*, no," Brandy added.

"Explain?" Evdokia demanded.

"It's going to take fifteen or twenty years to build a rail line from here to the Pacific," Vladimir said. "And even after it's built, it's going to be a bitch to maintain. It's a very expensive way to put a port in Russia, and we aren't going to get it anytime soon."

"What about the Heroes?" Mikhail asked.

"They are great, Your Majesty, but they have limited cargo capacity," Brandy explained. "Very limited. Yes, we can move people a few at a time from here to the coast in a week or two, and as we get more planes that will improve a bit. Even a lot. Fuel dumps with lots of charcoal or oil available will make it easier, and faster, but you're still talking a lot of planes to fill a single ship. We *still* need a port on the Baltic."

"The problem is that Sweden gains rather a lot by controlling our access to the Baltic," Czar Mikhail said. "He has been getting a wheat subsidy from us every year for over a decade, and Sheremetev paid it, and Uncle Ivan is doing the same. Also, anything we sell to Europe has to go through him, and the port is only open for a few months every year. That goes for both Arkhangelsk and Mangazenya."

"What about Arkhangelsk?" Brandy asked.

"It freezes up for six months out of the year, which makes it better than Mangazenya, but not good," Mikhail said.

"Even so, I would focus on putting a railway to Arkhangelsk rather than the Pacific," Vlad said. "We can do that in a couple of years, not a couple of decades."

"You suggest that we abandon Siberia?"

"No. Keep the air route, and start on a land route. A rail line, but don't expect anything from it soon," Brandy said.

"What we will get from Siberia is a frontier to absorb the people escaping from Poland," Evdokia said.

"Poland?" Brandy asked.

"Even with Muscovite Russia in the way, we've been getting serfs escaping from the Polish–Lithuanian Commonwealth," Evdokia explained, "and with the expected collapse of Muscovite Russia, that trickle is going to turn into a flood. Peasants are running from the huge estates in Poland and Lithuania looking for a better life in Russia. They know about the czar's Emancipation Proclamation. 'Get past Smolensk and you're in Russia, and your master can't get you back. Then you go west to Ufa and Czar Mikhail will give you land.' That's not what it said, but it's what Polish peasants showing up here over the winter thought it said."

"What did you do with them?"

"My idiot husband gave them land in the land bank, just like the Russian peasants running from Muscovite Russia. Some of them took it in land. A lot of them got jobs in the factories. But there are Polish villages just east of here."

"How many?" Vladimir asked.

"Not all that many, so far. Most of them get grabbed up by the serf hunters in Muscovy and get planted on some boyar's estate in Muscovy. Darn few are being returned to Poland or Lithuania, though."

"How are the Poles reacting to that?" Vladimir asked.

"The Polish government isn't doing much of anything. It's

almost paralyzed by the Sejm. Besides, they have Gustav sitting in what they consider to be Polish territory, and what amounts to a revolution in southern Poland. But the Lithuanian magnates... at least some of them are sending serf-catching raids into Russia to bring back serfs, and they don't much care if those serfs are Polish or Russian."

At that point, Little Mikey decided to throw a temper tantrum. The conference was delayed until the child was consoled.

A couple of hours later, Mikey was down for his nap and they were discussing the political and economic situation in the Sovereign States and Muscovite Russia.

"Not all of the boyars are going to accept Uncle Ivan giving us Moscow and the rest of Muscovy in exchange for his head," Czar Mikhail said.

"And most of his property," Evdokia clarified with a bit of rancor. She wasn't as forgiving of Mikhail's uncle as he was, and would have left Ivan Romanov a great deal less wealthy if it had been up to her.

"Anyway," Mikhail said, "the issue is going to be Gustav. I really don't want a war with Sweden, especially if there is even a small chance that the USE will come in on his side. But we need access to the Baltic. In a smaller way, it's the same problem we have in the East. The planes work, but ships carry a great deal more. So between Sweden and Poland, our access to the West is badly restricted. We're not going to fall back into the Time of Troubles, and we're not going to turn into the sort of dictatorship that caused the Communist Revolution in 1917 in that other history. At least not this year."

"I know," Vlad agreed. "But you still sound worried."

"Russia can't remain cut off from the West with the advances it's making in science and engineering. We have to have trade."

"We will have," Brandy reassured him. "The situation in Poland is profoundly unstable and whatever happens there, it's going to mean that Gustav is going to need us. If for no other reason than to keep them from focusing all their forces against him." She looked around the room. "We're not quite out of the woods yet. But I can see the edge of the forest from here."

Cast of Characters

Anya	Runaway slave, manages the Ufa Dacha, married to Filip Pavlovich Tupikov
Arsenyev, Yury	Scout with Vlad and Brandy
Polibin, Artemi Fedorovich	Head of Czar Mikhail's kitchen
Batur, Erdeni	Zunghar leader
Beketov, Pyotr	Russian tax collector and explorer in Siberia
Birkin, Iakov Petrovich	Brigadier general
Birkin, Ivan Vasilevich	Lieutenant general in command of the "siege" of Kazan
Budanov, Simeon	Head of the Embassy Bureau in Ufa
Chernoff, Zia	Sister to the patriarch of the Chernoff family
Chernoff, Larisa Karolevna	The Chernoff. See *A Holmes for the Czar*
Denisov, Gregori	Registered Cossack commander of Cossack forces at Tsaritsyn
Dominika	Guardian of Larisa Chernoff. See *A Holmes for the Czar*
Elina	Pastry chef at Diogenes Club

Gorchakov, Brandy Bates	Princess and advisor to the Czar and Czarina
Gorchakov, Natalia (Natasha) Petrovna	A princess of Russia, advisor to the Czar
Gorchakov, Vladimir Petrovich	Married to Brandy Bates. Advisor to the Czar
Petrov, Gregory	Flight engineer for Irina Novikov, cousin to Ivan Borisovich
Holmes, Miroslava	Licensed private detective and investigator
Ignat Berezin	Radioman on *Filaret*
Ivanovich, Vadim	Steam head in Ufa
Ivanov, Dimitry	Captain of the *Filaret*
Kalashnikov, Ivan	Major in RRMC (Royal Russian Marine Corps)
Khan, Salqam-Jangir	Tatar ruler, attacks Ufa
Kirill Blinov	Embassy Bureau China desk
Kirill Veselov	Engineer on *Filaret*
Lavrenty Belikov	Aide to ambassador from Ufa
Lavrenty Vershinin	War train commander
Lebedev, Boris Timofeyevich	General Tim, commanding the army of the USSR
Leonid Volodin	Pilot
Lyapunov, Alla	Heir to the Lyapunov family, owner of the Diogenes club
Lyapunov, Vasilii	The Lyapunov, engineer and husband of Miroslava
Maslov, Ivan	Brigadier general, army of the Sovereign States of Russia
Maslov, Ivan	General of the Czar's army
Matvey	Czar Mikhail's secretary

Novikov, Irina	Captain, female pilot of a Hero-class airplane *Tina*
Odoevskii, Ivan Ivanovich	Prince, with Sheremetev
Odoevskii, Petr Ivanovich	Prince, and ambassador from Ufa to USE
Ogedei, Ariq	Scout, with Vlad and Brandy
Petrov, Boris Ivanovich	A bureaucrat of Moscow
Petrov, Iosif Borisovich	Boris' son, in Grantville
Petrov, Ivan Borisovich	Boris' son, in Ufa
Petrov, Pavel Borisovich	Boris' son
Platov, Simeon	Major, second-in-command of the Cossacks at Tsaritsyn
Polzin, Olga Petrovichna	Effective mayor of Ufa city, Stanislav's wife
Polzin, Stanislav Ivanovich	Commander of the "garrison" at Ufa
Romanov, Alexi	Heir apparent to Czar Mikhail
Romanov, Alexis	Son of Czar Mikhail
Romanov, Anna	Tsarevna Anna, daughter of the Czar, born 14 July 1630, seven in Jan 1638
Romanov, Evdokia "Doshinka"	Czarina of Russia
Romanov, Irina	Tsarevna Irina, daughter of the Czar
Romanov, Ivan Nikitich	Czar Mikhail's uncle, at present running Muscovite Russia
Romanov, Martha	Tsarevna Martha; Daughter of the Czar 19 August 1631, six in Jan 1638
Romanov, Mikhail Fedorovich	Czar of Russia
Ruzukov, Stefan Andreevich	Part owner, shop foreman at New Ruzuka Foundry

Ruzukov, Vera Sergeevna	Congressperson District Two, Ufa
Shein, Mikhail Borisovich	General of Russia, forms Siberian State
Sheremetev, Fedor Ivanovich	Russian boyar, cousin to Czar Mikhail, takes over as director-general
Simmons, Tami	Up-time nurse hired by Czar
Stroganov, Anatoly Gregorovitch	Head of the wealthy Stroganov family
Stroganov, Efrem Ivanovich	Member of the wealthy Stroganov family
Sulyma, Ivan	A PLC Szlachta and later leader of the Zaporozhian Cossacks
Togym	Sultan, General, Kazakh leader
Trotsky, Fedor Ivanovich	A Russian spy
Tupikov, Filip Pavlovich	Artisan and natural philosopher, Flying Squirrel
Utkin, Ivan Nikolayevich	Colonel of Russia
Utkin, Izabella Ivanovna	Part owner and manager of New Ruzuka Foundry
Utkin, Nikita Ivanovich	Son of Ivan, soldier of Russia
Yulia	midwife and medical expert on the mission east
Yurisovich, Ivan	Minor and Dacha-trained geologist
Zakharovna, Valeriya	Crewwoman on *Czarina Evdokia*
Zeppi, Bernard "Bernie"	Up-timer hired by Vladimir, counselor to the czar